THE WATER-BABIES

broadview editions
series editor: L.W. Conolly

"But Tom was very happy in the water."

THE WATER-BABIES

Charles Kingsley

edited by Richard Kelly

broadview editions

Library and Archives Canada Cataloguing in Publication

Kingsley, Charles, 1819-1875
    The water-babies / Charles Kingsley ; edited by Richard Kelly.

(Broadview editions)
Includes bibliographical references.
ISBN 978-1-55111-773-7

    I. Kelly, Richard, 1937-   II. Title.   III. Series.

PZ8.K619Wa 2008   823'.8   C2008-900967-3

Broadview Editions

The Broadview Editions series represents the ever-changing canon of literature in English by bringing together texts long regarded as classics with valuable lesser-known works.

Advisory editor for this volume: Marie Davis Zimmerman

Broadview Press is an independent, international publishing house, incorporated in 1985. Broadview believes in shared ownership, both with its employees and with the general public; since the year 2000 Broadview shares have traded publicly on the Toronto Venture Exchange under the symbol BDP.

We welcome comments and suggestions regarding any aspect of our publications—please feel free to contact us at the addresses below or at broadview@broadviewpress.com.

North America
Post Office Box 1243, Peterborough, Ontario, Canada K9J 7H5
2215 Kenmore Ave., Buffalo, NY, USA 14207
Tel: (705) 743-8990; Fax: (705) 743-8353;
email: customerservice@broadviewpress.com

UK, Ireland, and continental Europe
NBN International, Estover Road, Plymouth PL6 7PY UK
Tel: 44 (0) 1752 202300   Fax: 44 (0) 1752 202330
email: enquiries@nbninternational.com

Australia and New Zealand
UNIREPS, University of New South Wales
Sydney, NSW, 2052 Australia
Tel: 61 2 9664 0999; Fax: 61 2 9664 5420
email: info.press@unsw.edu.au

www.broadviewpress.com

The interior of this book is printed on 100% recycled paper.

Typesetting and assembly: True to Type Inc., Claremont, Canada.

PRINTED IN CANADA

Contents

Acknowledgements

In preparing this volume I am indebted to the work of many scholars and critics, especially Brian Alderson, Susan Chitty, Colin Manlove, Brendan Rapple, Margaret Thorp, and Larry Uffelman. I wish to thank the librarians at the University of Tennessee for helping me to track down some of Kingsley's obscure references and for acquiring books and articles difficult to access. I also wish to thank the Florida State University Libraries for granting me permission to quote from an unpublished letter from Edward Lear to Charles Kingsley. Finally, my thanks go to the wondrous editors at Broadview Press for their continuing support.

Introduction

The Paradoxical Curate

Charles Kingsley swept through the Victorian age like a comet, leaving a trail of brilliant particles of light, most of which have now faded into darkness. Compulsively restless and filled with extraordinary curiosity and physical energy, he sought to change the world around him, and in doing so assumed many roles and spoke from many different pulpits. This controversial curate, in his country parish of Eversley, Hampshire, set forth his Christian beliefs as a poet, novelist, naturalist, socialist, environmentalist, and author of books for children. For nine years he was Regius Professor of History at Cambridge and was appointed chaplain to Queen Victoria and tutor of the Prince of Wales. The major misstep in his career came in 1863 (the same year he published *The Water-Babies*) when he gratuitously attacked John Henry Newman, declaring that truth, for its own sake, had never been a virtue with the Roman clergy. Newman responded the following year with his *Apologia Pro Vita Sua*, which demolished Kingsley's assertions and went on to become recognized as one of the great spiritual autobiographies.

Now that the dust has settled upon all of Kingsley's sermons, lectures, poems, histories, novels, social reforms, and disputes, one work emerges from all the others for its lasting power to enchant readers and its innovative genius—*The Water-Babies*, a book written for his youngest son, Grenville Arthur, "and other good little boys." A narrative fantasy interspersed with numerous asides on all manner of subjects—architecture, fishing, evolution, natural scenery, geology, along with satiric comments on America, pedantry, education, and medicine—*The Water-Babies* is unique among children's books.

Eager to follow the compelling story of Tom, the sweeper turned water baby, many readers find Kingsley's frequent intrusions into the narrative annoying and unnecessary. To accommodate such readers, especially young ones, many subsequent editions were abridged to remove all the erudite and satiric diversions, which amount to nearly one quarter of the work.

And yet, this book is a perfect expression of the mind and character of its author, a complex man filled with contradictions, unbridled curiosity, passion, and strong prejudices. He celebrated the soul and indulged in an odd personal sexuality. He was a conservative who practiced a liberal theology. A clergyman in the Church of England, he possessed a firm faith in God and still was able to accept the evolutionary principles of Darwinism. He argued for a muscular Christianity and derided the Roman Catholic Church. As a Christian Socialist he argued that it was the duty of the Church of England to speak out against all social abuses, and at the same time he expressed his contempt towards the Irish and the black race. He possessed a creative imagination offset by a scientific intellect given to detailed empirical studies of nature. He prized marriage and manliness and despised celibacy and effeminacy. A brief look at key formative portions of his life, therefore, may well elucidate the authorial voice that drives all these diverse elements of his unusual book for "good little boys."

Kingsley was strongly attached to his mother during his formative years. His father, a curate, was a stern and remote man, who saw to it that his son learned his lessons, requiring him to recite memorized passages from Latin or Greek texts. One biographer believes that these gruelling sessions may have led to Kingsley's stammer and fear of corporal punishment.[1] During this period, educators insisted on students learning facts above all else. Kingsley's hatred for this painful ordeal is later presented in *The Water-Babies*, where Tom meets a boy whose head is so crammed with facts that it turns into a turnip, and where the author satirizes the American pedagogue Samuel Griswold Goodrich as "Cousin Cramchild."

When Kingsley was twelve years old he was sent to a preparatory school at Clifton, near Bristol. He stayed there only a year but his real education came not from the schoolroom so much as from his witnessing the violent Bristol riots of 1831, stirred by the refusal of the Lords to pass the second Reform Bill. The rioters burned down buildings in the night and Kingsley saw men burn to death as the brandy they had been drinking spilled along the streets and suddenly caught fire. All this death and destruction instilled in Kingsley a contempt for the lower class. It was only later, when he came under the influence of Frederick Maurice, that he came to realize that the poor and working class were the victims in this society. Nevertheless, the character of Grimes, Tom's cruel, uneducated, and hard-drinking master, may well have been shaped by Kingsley's memory of the violent Bristol

---

1 Susan Chitty, *The Beast and the Monk: A Life of Charles Kingsley* (New York: Mason/Charter, 1974), 31.

night. Grimes' behavior also reflects Kingsley's revulsion at corporal punishment practiced in schools. He explains that when Tom "did get up at four the next morning, he [Grimes] knocked Tom down again, in order to teach him (as young gentlemen used to be taught at public schools) that he must be an extra good boy that day."

By the time he was appointed curate at Eversley, Kingsley had acquired an excellent education at King's College, London, and Magdalene College, Cambridge. He was always concerned, however, to develop his body as well as his mind, and spent as much time as possible fishing, rowing, and swimming. He took special delight in rambling among the rocks and plants of the countryside taking detailed notes on his discoveries. Getting out into nature and marveling at its infinite variety became his lifelong passion. Influenced by the writings of Thomas Carlyle, who argued that all of nature can be viewed as supernatural, Kingsley came to see in the world about him the unmistakable signature of God. Thus, he began to shape a theology that would eventually accommodate many of the controversial discoveries of such geologists and naturalists as Sir Charles Lyell and Charles Darwin, both of whom later became his friends. As will be discussed later, the idea of "Natural Supernaturalism," as Carlyle called it, forms one of the underlying themes of *The Water-Babies*.

In addition to investigating the external landscape, Kingsley faced the more daunting task of exploring his own sexuality. As an undergraduate at Cambridge University, he lacked a religious faith, a moral authority and incentive for shaping his future. In 1839, however, he began to reevaluate his life after his meeting a young woman named Frances Grenfell (Fanny, as she was called), in whom he could confide all his youthful anxieties. About this same time it appears that he had his first sexual encounter with a woman, probably a prostitute at one of the brothels popular among the students. He felt so dirtied by the experience that three years later he wrote to Fanny: "You, my unspotted, bring a virgin body to my arms. I alas do not to yours. Before our lips met I had sinned and fallen. Oh, how low!"[1] He went so far as to form a bizarre project to enter a monastery and allow the monks to scourge his naked body. His sexual drive, however, was too powerful to allow him to endure a celibate life, especially now that Fanny's beauty possessed him. At age twenty two, he finally atoned for his sins, accepted Christ and the

---

[1] *Ibid.*, 57.

Church, and vowed to become a clergyman, albeit an unorthodox one. Fanny would serve as his mediator with God and his sexual fulfillment as a married man.

Marriage was still some way off. Fanny's family did not approve of her marrying Kingsley and the couple was separated for over a year. During this time, the young curate mortified his body by fasting on gruel, bread and water in the belief that his suffering would purify and make it fit one day for marital bliss. He even went so far as to go into the woods at night and lay naked upon thorns in order to curb his sexual desires. He began at this time to prepare a group of illustrations for his biography of the married Saint Elizabeth of Hungary. The drawings depict Elizabeth being tortured by a monk in horrific, sexually sadistic poses. Kingsley later admitted that the sensuously drawn Elizabeth was his Fanny, "not as she is but as she will be."[1] Having suffered an emotional breakdown during her year-long separation from her lover, Fanny sought comfort in Kingsley's erotic Christian counsel. In 1843 he wrote "Matter is holy, awful glorious matter. Let us never use those words *animal* and *brutal* in a degrading sense. Our animal enjoyments must be religious ceremonies. When you go to bed tonight, forget that you ever wore a garment, and open your lips for my kisses and spread out each limb that I may lie between your breasts all night (Canticles I, 13)."[2] Whereas Christian poets such as John Donne, Saint Theresa of Avila, and Saint John of the Cross drew heavily upon sexual metaphors to describe their relationship with God, Kingsley was writing about the actuality of physical sex with a woman, as he anticipated the sanctification of their orgasmic union in marriage. His experience with the prostitute left him with only shame and a sense of uncleanliness. Now that he had accepted God into his life, he could look forward to the pleasures of the holy flesh of his saintly Fanny.

The duality of pleasure and pain, spirit and flesh, recurs again and again in Kingsley's thinking. Still separated from Fanny, he wrote her a letter in which he describes how to make a hair shirt of the coarsest and roughest canvas she can find, and to wear it out of sight of other people. He goes on to describe how she will some morning come to him, kneel at his feet to receive his absolution for her sins. He included in this letter a drawing of Fanny wearing only a nightdress, kneeling before him as he lays his hand

---

1   *Ibid.*, 77.
2   *Ibid.*, 80.

on her head and prays for her forgiveness. So, like him, she will purify her body according to his counsel, in anticipation of the glorious marital moment.

In an odd twist on his revulsion at celibacy, Kingsley goes so far as to offer Fanny a temporary monastic marriage. He claims to love her body as an expression of her soul, and invites her to sleep with him as a virgin for the first month of their marriage: "Will not these thoughts give us more perfect delight when we lie naked in each other's arms, clasped together toying with each other's limbs, buried in each other's bodies, struggling, panting, dying for a moment. Shall we not feel then, even then, that there is more in store for us, that those thrilling writhings are but dim shadows of a union which shall be perfect."[1] Thus, their marital sex will foreshadow a perfect union of sexual and spiritual oneness in heaven, the unfulfilled dream of Dante Rossetti's erotic Blessed Damozel, leaning over the edge of heaven in hopes of being joined by her earthly lover.

Kingsley's fusion of sex and religion can also be seen in two of his drawings. In one he depicts himself and Fanny floating upon a cross in the sea. Each has one leg and one arm tied to the cross, their legs are entwined, and they caress each other with their free hands. In another drawing he and Fanny ascend to heaven together. He has huge, eagle-like wings and she has small diaphanous wings. Both are naked and he holds her limp body between his thighs and supports her buttocks with his hand. A scroll over their heads reads "She is not dead but sleepeth." Nathaniel Hawthorne remarked that "no pure man could have made or allowed himself to look at" these drawings.[2] But Kingsley believed that the body could be made holy and pleasurable at once, provided that he restrained his erotic impulses until he could enjoy his sexuality within the confines of marriage.

One of the themes in *The Water-Babies* is that a boy must resist temptation of all sorts and keep his body clean if he is to grow up pure and marry. Tom's desire for hidden sweets, however, sets him back in his path towards manhood and the company of the virginal Ellie. After stealing the sweets from a secret cabinet, Tom's entire body becomes covered with prickles. The implication here is that forbidden sex leads to hideous guilt and a repulsive presence. It is only after Ellie gives him lessons "clear and pure" that the prickles vanish "and his skin was smooth and clean

---

1   *Ibid.*, 81.
2   *Ibid.*, 17.

again." Like Fanny, who rescued Kingsley from his sinful past, Ellie is a mediator between Tom and the divine Mother Carey. Because he endured his tribulations, Mother Carey finally awards him the spotless lover of his dreams: "You may take him home with you now on Sundays, Ellie. He has won his spurs in the great battle, and become fit to go with you, and be a man; because he has done the thing he did not like." We are told that he also went home with her on weekdays, too, but when asked if they married, Kingsley coyly remarks that no one ever marries in a fairy tale.

Kingsley's obsession with cleanliness may be derived from his childhood, when he was a student at Helston Grammar School in Cornwall. He became ill with a severe case of English cholera, which he believed was the cause of his weakened left lung, that continued to trouble him later in life. When cholera later spread throughout England, Kingsley began his life-long crusade for sanitary reform, railing against the government's failure to rid its cities of the contaminated water and sulfurous air that were killing thousands. His sermons, essays, and novels, especially *Alton Locke* (1850), dramatized the horrific living conditions among the working poor. Like Dickens, he hoped that his writings would stir his readers' compassion and eventually lead to social reform. *The Water-Babies* was the most successful in this regard. Readers were so outraged by Kingsley's story of the little sweep that Parliament, under great public pressure, passed the Chimney Sweepers' Regulation Act the following year (1864), which outlawed the use of children under age sixteen for climbing chimneys.

Kingsley's obsession with his own personal hygiene is evident in a letter he wrote to a friend: "If I have a spot on my clothes, I am conscious of nothing else the whole day long, and just as conscious of it in the heart of Bramhill Common, as if I were going down Piccadilly."[1] He advocated a regime of cleanliness for schoolboys that would have them take cold showers upon awaking in the morning. This routine would not only keep their bodies clean but would instill in them an early toughness on their way to a manly, Christian adulthood. He had good reasons for these concerns. As a young curate he toured the London slum district of Bermondsey with the Christian Socialists and was horrified at the filth and sewerage that permeated the dwellings and

---

1 *Charles Kingsley: His Letters and Memories of His Life*, 2 Vols., ed. Frances Kingsley (London: Macmillan, 1891) 1, 272.

led to the outbreak of cholera. In the years that followed, he wrote tracts, gave sermons, thundered in the press and in other public forums denouncing landlords, public corporations, government, and members of his own class who refused to pay for clean drinking water and proper sewerage. He was equally concerned with agricultural workers living in putrid hovels hardly fit for animals. As a Christian clergyman, he saw an inextricable connection between the body and the soul and the need to reverse the adage "*mens sana, corpora sana.*" His belief that "matter is holy, awful glorious matter" accords with his outrage at the defilement of God's gift of pure air, water, and bodily health.

It is little wonder, then, that the central theme of *The Water-Babies* focuses upon Tom's physical and spiritual purification. When his blackened body dies at the water's edge, he is reborn as a water baby, released from the soot and filth of his cramped childhood and about to set forth on a purifying journey towards a Christian manhood that could satisfy both his physical and spiritual desires.

At the beginning of the story, the Irishwoman, speaking to Tom and Grimes, says "I have one more word for you both; for you will both see me again before all is over. Those that wish to be clean, clean they will be; and those that wish to be foul, foul they will be. Remember." (50) Tom shortly afterwards has a dream: "[he] felt so hot all over that he longed to get into the river and cool himself; and then he fell half asleep, and dreamt that he heard the little white lady [Ellie] crying to him, 'Oh, you're so dirty; go and be washed;' and then that he heard the Irishwoman saying, 'Those that wish to be clean, clean they will be.' And then he heard the church-bells ring so loud, close to him too, that he was sure it must be Sunday, in spite of what the old dame had said; and he would go to church, and see what a church was like inside, for he had never been in one, poor little fellow, in all his life. But the people would never let him come in, all over soot and dirt like that. He must go to the river and wash first. And he said out loud again and again, though being half asleep he did not know it, 'I must be clean, I must be clean.'" (69)

The word "clean" (and its variants) appears over forty times throughout the tale. Although Kingsley mainly employs images of cleanliness and filth to suggest the spiritual condition of his characters, on occasion he uses his fantasy narrative to further his cry for sanitary reform:

And this is the reason why the rock-pools are always so neat and clean; because the water-babies come inshore after every storm to sweep them out, and comb them down, and put them all to rights again.

Only where men are wasteful and dirty, and let sewers run into the sea instead of putting the stuff upon the fields like thrifty reasonable souls; or throw herrings' heads and dead dog-fish, or any other refuse, into the water; or in any way make a mess upon the clean shore—there the water-babies will not come, sometimes not for hundreds of years (for they cannot abide anything smelly or foul), but leave the sea-anemones and the crabs to clear away everything, till the good tidy sea has covered up all the dirt in soft mud and clean sand, where the water-babies can plant live cockles and whelks and razor-shells and sea-cucumbers and golden-combs, and make a pretty live garden again, after man's dirt is cleared away. And that, I suppose, is the reason why there are no water- babies at any watering-place which I have ever seen. (145-46)

In the opening description of Tom's life as a chimney sweep Kingsley demonstrates a remarkable understanding of the stoicism and circumscribed dreams of an oppressed young boy:

As for chimney-sweeping, and being hungry, and being beaten, he took all that for the way of the world, like the rain and snow and thunder, and stood manfully with his back to it till it was over, as his old donkey did to a hail-storm; and then shook his ears and was as jolly as ever; and thought of the fine times coming, when he would be a man, and a master sweep, and sit in the public-house with a quart of beer and a long pipe, and play cards for silver money, and wear velveteens and ankle-jacks, and keep a white bull-dog with one gray ear, and carry her puppies in his pocket, just like a man. And he would have apprentices, one, two, three, if he could. How he would bully them, and knock them about, just as his master did to him; and make them carry home the soot sacks, while he rode before them on his donkey, with a pipe in his mouth and a flower in his button-hole, like a king at the head of his army. Yes, there were good times coming; and, when his master let him have a pull at the leavings of his beer, Tom was the jolliest boy in the whole town. (44)

Unlike the stock fictional character of the orphan ingenue, a sentimentalized innocent trodden down by cruelty and poverty, Tom is portrayed as a tough-minded young man on the wrong end of the stick, who knows his day will come to yield that stick. He manfully endures the cruelty of his apprenticeship by dreaming of the good times coming when he will be a master sweep and ride like a king on his donkey leading an army of poor sweeps. In his small, enclosed world the future can only allow him to recycle the violence, power, and cruelty of his master.

Although Tom may have learned many lessons as a water baby, his moral character does not change much by the end of his adventures, even though he is served with several rewards and punishments from Mrs Doasyouwouldbedoneby and Mrs Bedonebyasyoudid. Ironically, the most significant change in his moral, psychological, and sexual development comes before he transforms into a water baby. When he is taken by Grimes to Harthover House to clean the chimneys of that great country estate, he experiences the most dramatic transformation of his life, one that soon after drives him into the water and ultimately towards his union with Ellie. This epiphany occurs when Tom gets lost among the inter-connecting chimneys and winds up in Ellie's bedroom: "Tom had never seen the like.... The room was all dressed in white,—white window-curtains, white bed-curtains, white furniture, and white walls, with just a few lines of pink here and there." He then notices "a large bath full of clean water" and, finally, looking towards the bed he discovers the sleeping beauty: "Under the snow-white coverlet, upon the snow-white pillow, lay the most beautiful little girl that Tom had ever seen. Her cheeks were almost as white as the pillow, and her hair was like threads of gold spread all about over the bed. She might have been as old as Tom, or maybe a year or two older; but Tom did not think of that. He thought only of her delicate skin and golden hair, and wondered whether she was a real live person, or one of the wax dolls he had seen in the shops. But when he saw her breathe, he made up his mind that she was alive, and stood staring at her, as if she had been an angel out of heaven."(55) Thrust into the role of a peeping Tom, he is overwhelmed by his remarkable discovery.

There is a quiet sexuality in this scene as Tom, staring at the sleeping girl in the intimacy of her bedroom, begins to study her delicate white skin and golden hair and to watch her breathe. This foretaste of forbidden sweets, however, is quickly cancelled when Tom suddenly sees his reflection in a mirror: "And looking round, he suddenly saw, standing close to him, a little ugly, black, ragged figure, with bleared eyes and grinning white teeth. He turned on it angrily. What did such a little black ape want in that sweet young lady's room? And behold, it was himself, reflected in a great mirror, the like of which Tom had never seen before. And Tom, for the first time in his life, found out that he was dirty; and burst into tears with shame and anger; and turned to sneak up the chimney again and hide." (56)

All of Tom's earlier dreams of becoming a master sweep, knocking his apprentices about, and riding proudly before them on his donkey have vanished in this terrifying moment of self-recognition. Now in a position to see himself for the first time, he is filled with anger and shame. A similar moment occurs in Dickens's *Great Expectations*, where the beautiful Estella makes Pip aware of his country speech, rough hands, and dirty nails. Like Tom, Pip sees himself in a new light, and his shame and anger drive him towards becoming a gentleman. When Tom runs to the water's edge and begins hearing church bells, he cries out that he must be clean, and enters the water to begin his new life as a water baby, one destined to return him to his "little white lady." The word "white" appears nearly fifty times throughout the story, usually associated with Ellie, his earthly angel. The black-and-white world of Tom and Ellie is clearly reminiscent of Kingsley's early relationship with Fanny, as when he wrote her: "You, my unspotted, bring a virgin body to my arms. I alas do not to yours. Before our lips met I had sinned and fallen. Oh, how low!" Like Kingsley, Tom undergoes a series of trials and hardships that finally prepare him for his rendezvous with Ellie at the end of the story. Kingsley finds sexual and religious fulfillment in his marriage to Fanny, and, despite his remark that "no one ever marries in a fairy tale," Tom is accorded much the same reward for his endurance on the path to the Other-end-of-Nowhere and St. Brandan's Isle. At this point, Tom has grown to be a tall man and Ellie a beautiful woman. The nurturing female figures—Mrs Bedonebyasyoudid, Mrs Doasyouwouldbedoneby, the Irish woman, and Mother Carey—coalesce into a single maternal image. As Tom and Ellie look into her blazing white, flashing eyes they are dazzled by the orgasmic moment and hide their faces, after which she blesses them with a final, lasting reunion.

Authorial Voices

Readers who expect *The Water-Babies* to be a conventional fairy tale may be disappointed to find the many digressions with their difficult allusions and lists. Some critics find the work too discursive and disorganized. Children certainly are incapable of understanding his scientific, philosophical, and historical discourses that weave in and out of the fairy tale narrative. Kingsley's story is to the traditional fairy tale what Laurence Sterne's *Tristram Shandy* (1759- 67) is to the traditional novel. Employing the style of François Rabelais, Sterne created a radically new kind of narrative, one that bears little resemblance to the orderly and structurally unified novels of his day. Sterne weaves together a number of different stories, as well as such disparate materials as essays, sermons, and legal documents that combine to disrupt the plot and its chronology. The work of both Sterne and Kingsley might arguably be viewed as precursors of postmodernism.

Despite his bawdy reputation, Rabelais was one of Kingsley's favorite authors, and Kingsley made a point of reading his work every year. Like Sterne, his follower, Rabelais delighted in digressions, satiric fantasy, long lists, and authorial intrusions that fracture the fictional narrative. *The Water-Babies* incorporates the spirit and stylistic innovations of these authors into the format of the traditional children's story, making the work truly unique and not well suited for most children. The cerebral critique in *The Anthropological Review* makes this quite clear.[1] The numerous abridgements of the book, however, that simply present the fantasy narrative, are perfectly designed for young readers.

Kingsley assumes several authorial voices throughout his story that contribute to its unique character as a work of children's literature. His dedication of the book to his son and other good little boys prepares the reader for his paternal tone and his interest in engaging the imaginations of a youthful audience. He frequently addresses his child readers directly, instructing them on various subjects with which they have a basic familiarity. He begins his story with the traditional opening of the fairy tale: "Once upon a time there was a little chimney-sweep, and his name was Tom." The next sentence addresses the young reader and takes into consideration his limited range of knowledge: "That is a short name, and you have heard it before, so you will not have much trouble in remembering it." (43) And so the narrative continues with no indication of the labyrinthine turns it will take over the course of its telling.

After Grimes and Tom arrive at Harthover House, Kingsley adopts the voice of a posturing, erudite tour guide, detailing the

---

1 See Appendix J1.

eclectic nature of the architecture of the building. Descriptive phrases and allusions come flying: from Cinque-cento, Doric, Bœotian, Tajmahal, and the caves of Elephanta to the Pavillion of Brighton. Then, in the next chapter, after Tom becomes a water baby, Kingsley assumes the voice of a polemicist as he sets forth his case for the existence of water babies and challenges the writers and scientists to reexamine their blindness to their reality. He spends nearly one third of the chapter presenting his curious case, leaving Tom, now only 3.87902 inches long, in suspended animation.

In Chapter 3 Kingsley presents a central idea in the story: "the doctrine of this wonderful fairy tale ... is that your soul makes your body, just as a snail makes his shell." He introduces this notion into his story by way of a Rabelaisian list of words that describe the doctrine as "orthodox, rational, philosophical, logical, irrefragable, nominalistic, realistic, inductive, deductive, productive, salutary, comfortable, and on-all-accounts-to-be-received." (87) As with his other lists, each word or phrase appears on a separate line, giving it a poetic emphasis and authority. At the same time, the list generates a playful, almost nonsensical tone that enlivens an argument that might otherwise become tedious and dull. The graphic analogy of the snail making his shell is replicated later when Tom's prickly appearance reflects his sinful soul after he eats the stolen sweets.

As Tom enters the salmon stream on his way to the sea, Kingsley suddenly stops the narrative to reflect on various waters ideal for salmon fishing in Wales, Scotland, and Ireland. He takes this opportunity to patronize "a poor Paddy" named Dennis, a stereotype of the blarney-filled fisherman so eager to please others that he cannot be trusted to tell the truth. It is because of such fellows that "poor ould Ireland does not prosper like England and Scotland ... where folk have taken up a ridiculous fancy that honesty is the best policy." (104) These several pages about fishing, however, arise out of Kingsley's great love of the sport, and in the following passage his voice changes to that of the enraptured poet, a sort of piscatorial Wordsworth, remembering and romanticizing his days on the water:

Ah, my little man, when you are a big man, and fish such a stream as that [described in a poem by Arthur Clough], you will hardly care, I think, whether she be roaring down in full spate, like coffee covered with scald cream, while the fish are swirling at your fly as an oar-blade swirls in a boat-race, or flashing up the cataract like silver arrows, out of the fiercest of the foam; or whether the fall be dwindled to a single thread and the shingle below be as white and dusty as a turnpike road, while the salmon huddle together in one dark cloud in the clear amber pool, sleeping away their time till the rain creeps back again off the sea. (105)

Kingsley's most extensive use of the Rabelaisian catalog appears in Chapter 4, where he lists all the medicines administered to Professor Ptthmllnsprts in an attempt to restore his sanity. Since this professorial epitome of nonsensical pedantry refused to believe in a water baby when he actually saw one, an old fairy makes him believe in all sorts of terrifying monsters that drive him out of his wits for three months. Doctors, as foolish as the professor, prescribe medicines ranging from those devised by the ancients to contemporary nostrums. The mind-boggling nonsense list runs for several pages and includes everything from the fat of a dormouse to pouring mercury down his throat. Tom's adventures, once again, are left hanging because Kingsley has some scientific fish to fry. The professor is, in part, a satiric portrait of the biologist Richard Owen, who argued that man is distinctly different from the ape because he possesses a unique section of the brain which he called the hippocampus minor. Kingsley's professor, however, argues before the British Association "that apes had hippopotamus majors in their brains just as men have." (123) Both Owen and the professor appear to have ignored, as Kingsley points out, that men can speak, make machines, know right from wrong "and other little matters of that kind," an observation that underscores the absurdity of the scientists' narrow focus on physiology. Kingsley especially mocks the professor for his inability to see beyond the material world. Tom the water baby is Tom's spirit—his blackened body was left at the water's edge. The rejection of the spirit world by empirical scientists and philosophers, such as Thomas Henry Huxley and Herbert Spencer, disturbed Kingsley, who confessed himself a Platonist who believed that God and the human spirit were beyond all intellectual notions.

Kingsley mounts a further attack upon foolish men of science and philosophy later on through a story Mother Carey tells to Tom. She recounts an instructive parable about two brothers, Prometheus and Epimetheus. Prometheus always looked before him and boasted that he was wise beforehand, while Epimetheus always looked behind him and preferred to prophesy after the event. When they meet Pandora with her mysterious box,

Prometheus would have nothing to do with her. Epimetheus, however, marries her and opens the box. Out pours all manner of ills: self-will, ignorance, fear, and dirt. Kingsley then provides a satiric list of specific ills, including popes, monks, measles, wars, quacks, unpaid bills, tight stays, and despots. Besides venting his anti-Catholic feelings, he manages to keep the list playful by juxtaposing such terrible ills as famines and scarlet fever with potatoes and bad wine. Despite the visitation of all these evils, Epimetheus turns out to be the hero of the story: "So Epimetheus got a great deal of trouble, as most men do in this world: but he got the three best things in the world into the bargain—a good wife, and experience, and hope [which lay at the bottom of the box]." (198-99) By working hard and carefully observing the world around him, and with his wife's assistance, Epimetheus prospers and becomes a practical scientist, creating looms, ships, and railroads.

Although Prometheus is usually viewed as a rebellious romantic hero, the Titan who stole fire from Olympus and gave it to humans, Kingsley depicts him as a fool, whose only invention was a box of lucifers with which he accidentally set the Thames on fire. Whereas Epimetheus' children are the men of science who get things done in the world, "the children of Prometheus are the fanatics, and the theorists, and the bigots, and the bores, and the noisy windy people, who go telling silly folk what will happen, instead of looking to see what has happened already." (199) And so, through Mother Carey's parable, Kingsley presents his case for the real men of his age, thinkers—not unlike himself—who have been educated not only by schools but by practical experience with the evils and hardships of the world, who have been strengthened by marriage, and who sustain the redeeming virtue of hope.

Finally, at the conclusion of *The Water-Babies*, Kingsley addresses his young audience in the voice of a concerned father to explain "what we should learn from this parable." (230) In one sense, his "Moral" is a conventional one in that it draws lessons from the story about how to behave in order to develop into a proper adult. It is a moral that in different guises has appeared in countless Victorian books for children. Kingsley's moral is a parable within a parable as it advises how to treat efts (immature newts): don't throw stones at them, don't catch them with pins or place them in vivariums with sticklebacks, who can prick their stomachs. These efts, he explains, "are nothing else but the water-babies who are stupid and dirty, and will not learn their lessons and keep themselves clean." Thus, they will devolve into small-brained, dirty creatures, doomed to live in dirty ponds lying in the mud and eating worms, never to enjoy clear rivers or get into the wide sea. But these poor efts, like Epimetheus, are not hopeless: "if they work very hard and wash very hard ... their brains may grow bigger, and their jaws grow smaller, and their ribs come back, and their tails wither off, and they will turn into water-babies again, and, perhaps, after that into land-babies, and after that, perhaps, into grown men." (231) And so, this mini-parable recapitulates the story of Tom, himself, and offers a cautionary tale for all "bad" little boys.

Tom's Nurtured Evolution

Tom's odyssey takes him from the river in which he turned into a water baby to the wide sea and then onto the fairy island of St. Brandan, where he meets the fairies Mrs. Bedonebyasyoudid and Mrs. Doasyouwouldbedoneby. From there he goes to the home of Mother Carey at Shiny Wall and is directed by her to descend beneath the floor of the sea to the Other-End-of-Nowhere, where he meets Grimes locked up in a reformatory's chimney. After successfully pleading for Grimes' release, Tom is shown the way up the fairies' secret back stairway to the idyllic St. Brandan's Isle once again, where he is reunited with Ellie.

There are clearly elements of Christian allegory at work here, suggestive of Bunyan's *Pilgrim's Progress*: Tom's entrance into the water (baptism), Mrs. Bedonebyasyoudid (rewards and punishments), Mrs. Doasyouwouldbedoneby ("do unto others as you would have them do unto you," namely, proper Christian conduct), Mother Carey (the life-force that drives evolution), and the Other-End-of-Nowhere (*utopia* in Greek means *nowhere*). One may thus attempt to follow the linear path of an allegorical narrative that moves from Tom's Christian rebirth in the water all the way to his dazzling vision of the coalesced female-fairies in the utopia of St. Brandan's Isle that marks his redemption from his earlier life as a dirty heathen sinner. These clear allegorical elements provide the general direction of the narrative which, in the light of the many authorial intrusions, help keep the reader on the path. Nevertheless, the tale is more complicated than a simple allegory allows. Kingsley's unusual perspective on science, theology, morality, and education designs a fantasy that evolves from the real world of Victorian controversy.

When Kingsley was a Cambridge undergraduate, Fanny sent him some books by Thomas Carlyle, an author who helped to formulate and articulate his view of the world. He wrote to Carlyle in 1849, explaining the powerful effect these writings had on his life: "At a time when I was drowned in sloth and wickedness, your works awoke in me the idea of Duty; the belief in a living righteous God, who is revealing Himself in the daily events of History; the knowledge that all strength and righteousness, under whatever creed it may appear, comes from Him alone; and last, but not least, the belief in the Perfect Harmony of the Physical with the Spiritual Universe."[1]

Carlyle's philosophy is an odd mixture of Calvinism, German romanticism, and Puritan mysticism. He possessed a powerful sense of a divine presence in all objects and events and in his most famous work, *Sartor Resartus*, sets forth the idea of Natural Supernaturalism: "We speak of the Volume of Nature: and truly a Volume it is,—whose Author and Writer is God. To read it! Dost thou, does man, so much as well know the Alphabet thereof? With its Words, Sentences, and grand descriptive Pages, poetical and philosophical.... It is a Volume written in celestial hieroglyphs, in the true Sacred-writing."[2]

The impact of Natural Supernaturalism upon Kingsley's thinking is clearly revealed in a letter he wrote to Fanny in 1843:

... this earth, I say, is the next greatest fact to that of God's existence, the fact by which *we know Him*. This is the path the Bible takes. It does not lay down any description of pure Deity. It is all about earth, and men, and women, and marriage, and birth and death, food and raiment, trees and animals; and God, not as He is in Himself, but as He has shown Himself in relation to the earth, and its history, and the laws of humanity.[3]

It is no surprise, then, that *The Water-Babies* (like *Glaucus* and *Madame How and Lady Why*) focuses so intensely upon the particulars of nature, physical science, and aquatic wonders as the hieroglyphs of a divine script. Kingsley wrote a letter to his friend and mentor, Frederick Maurice, in 1862 that explains this fundamental Christian theme:

---

1 Quoted in Margaret Thorp, *Charles Kingsley* (Princeton: Princeton UP, 1937), 22.

2 *Sartor Resartus*, ed. Charles Frederick Harrold (New York, Odyssey Press, 1932), 258.

3 *Charles Kingsley: His Letters and Memories of His Life*, 2 Vols., ed. Frances Kingsley (London: Macmillan, 1891) 1, 83-4.

When you read the book, I hope you will see that I have not been idling my time away. I have tried, in all sorts of queer ways, to make children and grown folks understand that there is a quite miraculous and divine element underlying all physical nature; and that nobody knows anything about anything, in the sense in which they may know God in Christ, and right and wrong. And if I have wrapped up my parable in seeming Tom-fooleries, it is because so only could I get the pill swallowed by a generation who are not believing with anything like their whole heart, in the Living God. Meanwhile, remember that the physical science in the book is *not* nonsense, but accurate earnest, as far as I dare speak.[1]

It is significant that the characters who direct Tom throughout his journey are all female: the Irishwoman, Mrs. Doasyouwouldbedoneby, Mrs. Bedonebyasyoudid, and Mother Carey. In Kingsley's view of Catholicism, however, he deplores the role of its most famous woman—the Virgin Mary: "'Go to the blessed Virgin,' said a Romish priest, to a lady I love well. 'She, you know, is a woman, and can understand all a woman's feelings.' Ah! thought I, if your head had once rested on a lover's bosom, and your heart known the mighty stay of a man's affection, you would have learnt to go now in your sore need, not to the mother but to the Son—not to the indulgent virgin, but to the strong *man*, Christ Jesus—stern because loving—who does not shrink from punishing, and yet does it as a man would do it, '*mighty* to save.'"[2] Ironically, the only male role model in *The Water-Babies* is the degenerate Grimes, a weak and selfish man. Unlike the Virgin Mary, whom Kingsley saw as weak, cold, and indulgent, his female fairies are strong, stern, sensuous, loving, and eager to save Tom from the depravity of his earlier life.

Kingsley's attitude towards sexuality, noted earlier, and his profound devotion to his mother and the other females who nurtured him as a child helped to shape the maternal matrix of *The Water-Babies*. According to Susan Chitty, when he was five years old "he suffered from frequent and dangerous attacks of the croup and it took all the skill of Betsy Knowles (an old servant of his father's family) and of the nursemaid Anne Simpson ... to keep him alive. Not only did these devoted women have to nurse

---

1 *Charles Kingsley: His Letters and Memories of His Life*, 2 Vols., ed. Frances Kingsley (London: Macmillan, 1891), 2, 127.
2 *Ibid.*, 1, 211.

him through various childish afflictions but through the effects of the medicines that were prescribed for them."[1] Since he was a delicate child, he enjoyed the privilege of sleeping in his mother's room. His father, a stern and remote man, offered the boy little emotional support. In fact, Kingsley later confessed to Fanny that "I have nothing to care for in reality but my mother and you."[2] The influence of these women upon Kingsley is reflected in several of the characters in *The Water-Babies*.

The Irishwoman is an earthy creature, poor, barefoot, "a very tall, handsome woman, with bright grey eyes, and heavy black hair hanging about her cheeks." (48) When Grimes begins beating Tom, she looks him "fierce in the face" and cowers him with her threatening presence. Mrs. Doasyouwouldbedoneby and Mrs. Bedonebyasyoudid combine the powers of love and punishment. Mrs. Doasyouwouldbedoneby is a sensual mother who succors thousands of water babies and allows Tom special attention: "she took Tom in her arms, and laid him in the softest place of all, and kissed him, and patted him, and talked to him, tenderly and low, such things as he had never heard before in his life, and Tom looked up into her eyes, and loved her, and loved, until he fell fast asleep from pure love." (158) This passage is reminiscent of Kingsley's letter to Fanny, in which he counsels her to "open your lips for my kisses and spread out each limb that I may lie between your breasts all night." Emotionally nurtured at the fairy's breast, Tom later desires to be cuddled again, but because he has stolen some sweets he is punished by having his body covered with prickles, keeping him from the sensual comfort of the maternal fairy.

Mother Carey is the ultimate maternal figure in the story. Formerly believed by sailors to be a sea spirit, she derives her name from the Latin *Mater Cara* or Italian *Madre Cara* ("dear mother"), an epithet of the Virgin Mary. Kingsley's Mother Carey, however, is more like a Nordic goddess sitting motionless in her Arctic Peacepool: "She sat quite still with her chin upon her hand, looking down into the sea with two great grand blue eyes, as blue as the sea itself. Her hair was as white as the snow— for she was very old—in fact, as old as any thing which you are likely to come across, except the difference between right and wrong." (195) Here is the land of stasis, the still point in a changing world. From this frozen, calm, and remote place she exercises

---

1 Chitty, 27.
2 Quoted in Chitty from an unpublished letter, 30.

her power as the élan vital,[1] the life force that makes things make themselves. While accepting the basic Darwinian principle of evolution, Kingsley, by positing a life force that drives the creation and continuity of species, sidesteps the issues of the Christian literalists, who disputed Darwin and his ideas of natural selection and insisted that God created and fixed all things that are. Unlike the other female fairies, Mother Carey is cold, aloof, ancient. She does not cuddle Tom; rather, she advises him to walk backwards and to follow his dog on his journey to the Other-End-of-Nowhere. Like her famous chickens, the stormy petrels, the dog works by instinct, the very force that drives the evolutionary flow of life.

Sometimes this flow can be reversed, at least according to the cautionary tale in Mrs. Bedonebyasyoudid's "wonderful waterproof book," entitled *The History of the great and famous nation of the Doasyoulikes, who came away from the country of Hardwork, because they wanted to play on the Jews'-harp all day long.*" Two thirds of these selfish, easy-going, happy-go-lucky inhabitants are one day killed when a volcano erupts. With their comfortable civilization obliterated, the survivors live on roots and nuts. Centuries later the strongest Doasyoulikes are living in trees to keep from being eaten by lions. As more centuries pass, they become fierce, stupid, hairy, speechless, as they finally devolve into apes and ultimately become extinct. Thus, at the end of Kingsley's "little parable," the fairies explain why Ellie may finally take Tom home with her: "He has won his spurs in the great battle, and become fit to go with you, and be a man; because he has done the thing he did not like." (229)

Extinction is not always self-inflicted, as the story of the Gairfowl attests. The Gairfowl is another name for the great auk, which became extinct during the nineteenth century. Large breeding colonies of this flightless, penguin-like sea bird were once common on rocky islands and coasts of the North Atlantic in Canada, Greenland, Iceland, the British Isles, and Scandinavia. They were slaughtered for food, bait, fat, and feathers until the last known living pair and one egg were collected in Iceland in 1844, and the great auk is now represented in collections only by bones, skins, and eggs. In Kingsley's story, the last living Gairfowl, standing up on the Allalonestone, recounts the tragic story

---

1   In this same vein, Henri Bergson (who coined the phrase *élan vital*) in his *Creative Evolution* (1907), later argued that the creative urge, not the Darwinian concept of natural selection, is at the heart of evolution.

of her breed. Despite the implicit criticism of unrestrained hunting in this tale, Kingsley suggests that the Gairfowls bear some responsibility for their extinction, since their flightless niche in the bird world made them vulnerable. He portrays the Gairfowl as a foolish aristocrat who looks down upon the "vulgar creatures" with wings. She is a member of the shabby genteel class who laments "we have quite gone down in the world ... and have nothing left but our honour." (182) When there was one remaining male auk, the Gairfowl, "being a lady, and with right and honourable feelings," drove him away and he was eaten by a shark. She refused to marry him because he was her deceased sister's husband. In 1835, a law was passed in England to make such marriages illegal, but a later bill, around the time of *The Water-Babies*, sought to legitimatize such marriages, a bill Kingsley approved of.

In the tales of the Doasyoulikes and the Gairfowl, Kingsley establishes a moral dimension to the process of evolution. Laziness and pride dislocate the Doasyoulikes and the Gairfowl from the natural process of evolution, leading both to extinction. Tom's water journey roughly recapitulates the evolutionary process in microcosm. He begins life in the stream as an amphibious creature less than four inches long with a set of external gills. By the end of his adventure he emerges from the sea as a man. In one sense his moral character does not radically change, since he displays the same youthful cruelty towards the sea beasts in St. Brandan's Isle as he did when he tormented them in the stream. Still, he accepts the fact that he must continue to move forward, following the guiding force of the fairies, or face the devolutionary fate of the Doasyoulikes and regress into an eft. And so he follows the current of the life-force that drives him towards the Other-end-of-Nowhere, where he appears fated to confront his old nemesis, Grimes. By getting this man he does not like released from his chimney, Tom wins final favor from the fairies, becomes a man and goes off with Ellie. For all his flaws, this stolid little English boy bravely faces the trials and tribulations he encounters and continues to be embraced by the evolutionary flow and guidance provided by the fairies. He has all the hallmarks of Kingsley's paradigm of a future manly man.

The sea fairies play an interesting role in the evolutionary scheme of things in this story. Mrs. Bedonebyasyoudid describes herself as a machine: "I cannot help punishing people when they do wrong. I like it no more than they do; I am often very, very sorry for them, poor things; but I cannot help it. If I tried not to do it, I should do it all the same. For I work by machinery, just like an engine; and am full of wheels and springs inside; and am wound up very carefully, so that I cannot help going." (153) The question, of course, is who wound her up. Kingsley hints at a mysterious and compelling force that drives not only the natural world but its moral dimension as well. This fairy, lacking free will, and apparently the agent of a greater power, adds the element of determinism to the story. Mother Carey, on the other hand, resides higher in the hierarchy: she appears to be beholden to no one. She is the detached creator, living in a remote tranquil frozen world: "I am not going to trouble myself to make things. I sit here and make them make themselves." (196) Unlike the gods of mythology or the Christian God, she does not intervene in the affairs of the world but simply allows her creations to carry out their evolutionary mandate. She has not abandoned the world of her making, like the God of Deism, but she is removed from the evolutionary forces she has set in motion. She observes the flow of life with a cold dispassion and allows it freely to run its course. Indeed, she does counsel Tom and advises him how to proceed to the Other-end-of-Nowhere, but with this caveat: "You must do without me, as most people have to do." (196) Tom is thus made to be on his own, walking backwards towards his destiny by following the finely tuned instincts of his dog.

An Educational Parable

Kingsley's letter to his friend Maurice explains that his purpose in writing *The Water-Babies* was to educate an entire generation: "If I have wrapped up my parable in seeming Tom-fooleries, it is because so only could I get the pill swallowed by a generation who are not believing with anything like their whole heart, in the Living God." And in the "Moral," which concludes the story, he asks "And now, my dear little man, what should we learn from this parable?" (230) Kingsley clearly views his work as an educational text enlivened and enriched by a compelling narrative fantasy. His initial motivation in writing the book was to offer it to his youngest child, mindful of the dangers that lie ahead of him. When his wife reminded him that his other children had their books, and that baby must have his, "He made no answer, but got up at once and went into his study, locking the door. In half an hour he returned with the first chapter of 'The Water-babies,' written off without a flaw. The whole book was more like an inspiration than a composition."[1]

Literary history has many examples of fathers, such as Lord Chesterfield and Benjamin Franklin, writing memoirs, autobiographies, or instructive letters to their children, while keeping their eyes on a much broader audience for their works. Kingsley may have begun his tale with only Grenville Arthur in mind, but as the work progressed it moved beyond a simple fantasy designed for a young boy to a complex, intellectual, and satiric parable meant for the general public. Here was Charles Kingsley, Regius Professor of History at Cambridge University, professing in a unique and imaginative style, one that was at odds with the educational system of his day.

A Royal Commission chaired by the Duke of Newcastle investigated the increase in public expenditure for education. Newcastle's report, published in 1861, recommended that public money for education be continued, but suggested that such support should be dependent upon a system of "payment by results." Robert Lowe accepted the main points of the Newcastle Commission and in1862 issued a Revised Code for Education. In future, schools could claim four shillings a year for each pupil with a satisfactory attendance record. An additional eight shillings were paid if the pupil passed examinations in reading, writing, and arithmetic. Every year, Her Majesty's Inspectors visited each school to test pupils in these subjects. Teachers, whose salaries normally depended on the size of the grant, were tempted to change their approach to education. In many schools, teachers concentrated exclusively on preparing the children for the yearly Inspectors' visit.

Kingsley found this new educational system to be a perversion of sound learning and one that was damaging to the minds and spirits of children. He dedicates several pages of the last chapter of *The Water-Babies* to satirizing this system. In the Isle of Tomtoddies, where the people are "all heads and no bodies," Tom hears them singing to their great idol Examination the only song they know—"I can't learn my lessons: the examiner's coming." The children, who are forbidden to have playthings, spend their time going over nonsensical questions, such as "Can you tell me the name of a place that nobody ever heard of, where nothing ever happened, in a country which has not been discovered yet?"

---

1 *Charles Kingsley: His Letters and Memories of His Life*, 2 Vols., ed. Frances Kingsley (London: Macmillan, 1891) 2, 127.

These children, who spend all their time preparing for the coming of the Examiner, grew large brains and smaller and smaller bodies until they turned into turnips, with heads filled with little but water inside. When the Examiner-of-all-Examiners arrives on the scene, the turnips crammed themselves so full of absurd facts to be ready for him that they burst open and died. As Tom leaves the Isle of Tomtoddies, he thanks his stars that "nought I know save those three royal r's: Reading and riting sure, with rithmetick." (217)

In a letter to A.J. Scott, Principal of Owens College, Manchester, in 1849 Kingsley inquired about taking on pupils to help pay expenses after an illness obliged him to resign from his professorship at Queens' College: "I am not going to talk about what I *can* teach. But what I should try to teach, would be principally physical science, history, English literature, and modern languages. In my eyes the question is not what to teach, but how to educate; how to train not scholars, but men; bold, energetic, methodic, liberal-minded, magnanimous. If I can succeed in doing that, I shall do what no salary can repay—and what is generally not done, or expected to be done, by private tutors."[1] And in 1866 Kingsley wrote to his wife about his eldest son, then an undergraduate at Trinity College, Cambridge: "Ah! What a blessing to see him developing under one's eyes, and to be able to help him at last by teaching him something about one's self. It is quite right that the school-masters should have the grounding and discipline, but the father who can *finish* his boy's education, and teach him something of life besides, ought to be very thankful."[2]

The Water-Babies is clearly an educational parable initially designed for the edification of his youngest son, but it grew into a more complex text that revealed the gravitational mind of its author, which pulled into the narrative all manner of subjects—from reflections on angling to Darwinian parody—presented in a variety of literary styles and authorial voices. The opening phrase of the book—"Once upon a time"—suggests the book will be a conventional fairy tale, but Kingsley subverts this expectation time and again with his various discourses and shifting manipulations of the genre. There is no other "children's" book quite like it. The ultimate subversion of the fairy tale comes in the last sentence: "But remember always, as I told you at first, that this is all

---

1 *Charles Kingsley: His Letters and Memories of His Life*, 2 Vols., ed. Frances Kingsley (London: Macmillan, 1891) 1, 159.
2 *Ibid.*, 2, 189.

a fairy tale, and only fun and pretence; and, therefore, you are not to believe a word of it, even if it is true." (232) The child-like master of nonsense, Edward Lear, perhaps the ideal reader of this book, wrote to Kingsley "I have often thought I should like to thank you for so much satisfaction given me by your many works —(perhaps above all—'Water Babies,' which I firmly believe to be all true)."[1]

---

1 Quoted from an unpublished letter from the John MacKay Shaw Collection in the Strozier Library at the Florida State University.

Charles Kingsley: A Brief Chronology

1819	Born 12 June at Holne, Devonshire, the son of Charles Kingsley (1781-1860), a curate, and his wife Mary Lucas Kingsley (1788-1874).
1831	Attends Clifton School, Bristol, where he witnesses the Bristol Riots, occasioned by the refusal of the Lords to pass the second Reform Bill.
1832-36	Attends Helston Grammar School, Cornwall, under the headship of Derwent Coleridge (1800-80), son of the poet Samuel Taylor Coleridge; another teacher, Charles Alexander Johns (1811-74), the author of popular books on natural history, leads Kingsley to develop an interest in botany and geology.
1836	Family moves to London when his father is appointed rector of St Luke's, Chelsea; attends King's College, London, until 1837.
1838	Matriculates at Magdalene College, Cambridge.
1839	Meets and falls in love with Frances Eliza Grenfell (1814-91); she and Frederick Denison Maurice (a clergyman, social reformer and professor of Literature at King's College, London, who was to become an influential friend), sway him to enter the Church.
1842	Ordained and becomes curate of Eversley church, Hampshire.
1844	Marries Frances Grenfell on 10 January and becomes rector of Eversley, where he serves for most of his life; a daughter, Rose Georgiana, born in November.
1847	Maurice, his first son, born in February.
1848	Publishes *The Saint's Tragedy*; becomes involved with the Chartist movement and begins association with Christian Socialists; under the pseudonym "Parson Lot" contributes to the new periodical *Politics for the People*; *Fraser's Magazine* serializes anonymously his first novel, *Yeast: A Problem*; as a result of Maurice's influence, he is appointed Professor of English Literature and Composition at the newly founded Queen's College, London.
1849	*Twenty-Five Village Sermons*; *Introductory Lectures*, delivered at Queen's College, London.

1850	*Alton Locke, Tailor and Poet,* a novel, published anonymously by Chapman and Hall; writes for *The Christian Socialist,* the successor to *Politics for the People;* assists in organizing the Society for Promotion of Working Men's Associations.
1852	*Hypatia,* a novel, serialized in *Fraser's Magazine* between January 1852 and April 1853; second daughter, Mary St Leger, born in June.
1853	*Hypatia; or, New Foes with an Old Face* reprinted from *Fraser's Magazine* in two-volumes.
1854	Publishes "The Wonders of the Shore" in the *North British Review,* an article later expanded as *Glaucus; or, The Wonders of the Shore* (1855).
1855	*Westward Ho!,* a novel, published by Macmillan.
1856	*The Heroes; or, Greek Fairy Tales for My Children,* illustrated by the author.
1857	*Two Years Ago* published by Macmillan; reviews Hughes's *Tom Brown's Schooldays* for the *Saturday Review.* Elected Fellow of the Linnean Society.
1858	Second son, Grenville Arthur, born; *Andromeda and Other Poems.*
1859	Appointed chaplain to Queen Victoria.
1860	Appointed Regius Professor of Modern History, Cambridge.
1861	Appointed tutor to the Prince of Wales at Cambridge.
1862	*The Water-Babies,* serialized in *Macmillan's Magazine* for eight months, from August 1862 to March 1863.
1863	*The Water-Babies* published as a book in May by Macmillan; elected fellow of the Geological Society.
1864	"*What, Then, Does Dr. Newman Mean?* A Reply to a Pamphlet lately published by Dr. Newman, which results in John Henry Newman's *Apologia pro Vita Sua.*
1865	*Hereward the Last of the English* serialized in *Good Words.*
1866	*Hereward the Wake,* a novel, published by Macmillan.
1869	Resigns chair at Cambridge and is appointed Canon of Chester; travels to the West Indies, accompanied by his daughter Rose; *Madam How and Lady Why* serialized in *Good Words for the Young.*
1870	*Madam How and Lady Why or First Lessons in Earth Lore for Children* published as a book by Bell & Daldy.

1871 *At Last; A Christmas in the West Indies* published by Macmillan.

1873 Appointed Canon of Westminster; *Plays and Puritans, and Other Historical Essays; Prose Idylls, New and Old.*

1874 Visits North America, travelling with his daughter Rose; comes down with pleurisy; *Health and Education; Westminster Sermons; David, Five Sermons.*

1875 Dies 23 January and is buried in Eversley churchyard.

A Note on the Text and Illustrations

The Water-Babies was first published in *Macmillan's Magazine* on a monthly basis from August 1862 to March 1863. Kingsley made several minor revisions and added substantial material for the story's appearance in book form in 1863. This text apparently has the authority of Kingsley's final approval, since subsequent editions show no significant revisions. The Broadview edition, therefore, follows the 1863 edition, published by Macmillan, and includes the "L'Envoi," which was removed during the press run ("lest it should be misunderstood and give needless offence," possibly to Thomas Henry Huxley and Bishop Wilberforce). Kingsley's unusual spellings have been retained from this edition.

The first edition featured two illustrations by the distinguished Scottish painter Joseph Noel Paton (1821-1901), now best remembered for his fairy paintings, such as the "Quarrel of Oberon and Titania." In 1886 Macmillan published a plush edition in blue cloth gilt with 100 wood engravings after drawings by Linley Sambourne. This illustrated edition became the standard for the various versions Macmillan produced thereafter.

Several artists began to illustrate the book after it came out of copyright in 1906. Perhaps the best known of these artists is Jessie Willcox Smith (1863-1935), an American illustrator who had studied under Howard Pyle. Her twelve lavish drawings appeared in Dodd and Mead's publication of *The Water-Babies* in 1916 and now reside in the Library of Congress. Her work is colorful, charming, sweet, romantic, sentimental, and a delight to view. Her drawings, however, are more suited to an abridgement of the story (and there were many such) that simply sets forth the narrative fantasy. But Kingsley laces his narrative with numerous discussions of all manner of topics, from contemporary theories of evolution to the ideas of ancient philosophers and scientists. Smith's illustrations fail to accommodate these breathless leaps into abstraction.

Sambourne, on the other hand, came well prepared to the task. Born and educated in London, he became a draughtsman in a firm of marine engineers in Greenwich. In 1871 he joined the staff of *Punch*, where he became its chief political cartoonist. His work there was characterized by surreal comedy, remarkable accuracy in detail, and consummate draftsmanship. He owned a library of 100,000 photographs that he used as the models for his series "Mr. Punch's Portraits." It is his meticulous care for detail and his decorative-grotesque imagery that make his style suited to Kingsley's story. Better than anyone, he was able to capture Kingsley's satire, as in his drawing of Richard Owen and Thomas Henry Huxley examining a bottled water-baby. Avoiding the sentimental, he creates a visual atmosphere of the grotesque: the skull of a ram picked clean by crows, a terrifying lobster rising out of the waves, a gorilla and otter snarling and viciously showing their teeth, Tom with his body covered in horrid prickles, and a nightmarish eft lying on its back. Sambourne thus creates a Darwinian world, where one's survival is always at risk and where this reality is rendered in exquisite, frightening detail.

Tom, who appears distressed, brooding at times, and somewhat ugly, is a far cry from the cherubic Tom drawn by most of the other illustrators.

It should be noted that Sambourne presents the initial letter of the opening sentence of each chapter within his illustration. Graphic initial letters have a long tradition that goes back to the days of illuminated medieval manuscripts. Sambourne's initial letters, however, are sometime difficult to discern, so closely are they woven into the fabric of the illustration. In Chapter 2, for example, the branches covering the roof of the house form the letter "A." In Chapter 3, the tail of the mermaid is in the shape of the letter "T." In Chapter 6 the letter "H" appears demurely on the drum. It is only in Chapter 4 that Sambourne's imagination fails him, and he simply places the "S" and "O" on each of the boat's sails.

The Broadview edition thus combines the Sambourne illustrations from Macmillan's 1886 edition with the first edition of the text published by Macmillan in 1863. The two decorative illustrations by Paton that appeared in the first edition may be seen in the Appendix I.

THE WATER-BABIES
A Fairy Tale for a Land-Baby

TO MY YOUNGEST SON,

GRENVILLE ARTHUR,
and to
ALL OTHER GOOD LITTLE BOYS.

Come read me my riddle, each good little man:
If you cannot read it, no grown-up folk can.

L'ENVOI.

Hence, unbelieving Sadducees,
And less-believing Pharisees,
With dull conventionalities;
And leave a country muse at ease
To play at leap-frog, if she please,
With children and realities.

CHAPTER I.

"I heard a thousand blended notes,
    While in a grove I sate reclined;
In that sweet mood when pleasant thoughts
    Bring sad thoughts to the mind.

To her fair works did Nature link
    The human soul that through me ran;
And much it grieved my heart to think,
    What man has made of man."[1]

                                            Wordsworth.

NCE upon a time there was a little chimney-sweep, and his name was Tom. That is a short name, and you have heard it before, so you will not have much trouble in remembering it. He lived in a great town in the North country, where there were plenty of chimneys to sweep, and plenty of money for Tom to earn and his master to spend. He could not read nor write, and did not care to do either; and he never washed himself, for there was no water up the court where he lived. He had never been taught to say his prayers. He never had heard of God, or of

---

1 From "Lines Written in Early Spring" (1798).

Christ, except in words which you never have heard, and which it would have been well if he had never heard. He cried half his time, and laughed the other half. He cried when he had to climb the dark flues, rubbing his poor knees and elbows raw; and when the soot got into his eyes, which it did every day in the week; and when his master beat him, which he did every day in the week; and when he had not enough to eat, which happened every day in the week likewise. And he laughed the other half of the day, when he was tossing half-pennies with the other boys, or playing leap-frog over the posts, or bowling stones at the horses' legs as they trotted by, which last was excellent fun, when there was a wall at hand behind which to hide. As for chimney-sweeping, and being hungry, and being beaten, he took all that for the way of the world, like the rain and snow and thunder, and stood manfully with his back to it till it was over, as his old donkey did to a hail-storm; and then shook his ears and was as jolly as ever; and thought of the fine times coming, when he would be a man, and a master sweep, and sit in the public-house with a quart of beer and a long pipe, and play cards for silver money, and wear vel-veteens[1] and ankle-jacks,[2] and keep a white bull-dog with one grey ear, and carry her puppies in his pocket, just like a man. And he would have apprentices, one, two, three, if he could. How he would bully them, and knock them about, just as his master did to him; and make them carry home the soot sacks, while he rode before them on his donkey, with a pipe in his mouth and a flower in his button-hole, like a king at the head of his army. Yes, there were good times coming; and, when his master let him have a pull at the leavings of his beer, Tom was the jolliest boy in the whole town.

One day a smart little groom rode into the court where Tom lived. Tom was just hiding behind a wall, to heave half a brick at his horse's legs, as is the custom of that country when they welcome strangers; but the groom saw him, and hallooed to him to know where Mr. Grimes, the chimney-sweep, lived. Now, Mr. Grimes was Tom's own master, and Tom was a good man of business, and always civil to customers, so he put the half-brick down quietly behind the wall, and proceeded to take orders.

Mr. Grimes was to come up next morning to Sir John Harthover's, at the Place, for his old chimney-sweep was gone to

---

1 Trousers made from cotton resembling velvet.
2 Boots that rise above the ankle.

prison, and the chimneys wanted sweeping. And so he rode away, not giving Tom time to ask what the sweep had gone to prison for, which was a matter of interest to Tom, as he had been in prison once or twice himself. Moreover, the groom looked so very neat and clean, with his drab gaiters, drab breeches, drab jacket, snow-white tie with a smart pin in it, and clean round ruddy face, that Tom was offended and disgusted at his appearance, and considered him a stuck-up fellow, who gave himself airs because he wore smart clothes, and other people paid for them; and went behind the wall to fetch the half-brick after all: but did not, remembering that he had come in the way of business, and was, as it were, under a flag of truce.

His master was so delighted at his new customer that he knocked Tom down out of hand, and drank more beer that night than he usually did in two, in order to be sure of getting up in time next morning; for the more a man's head aches when he wakes, the more glad he is to turn out, and have a breath of fresh air. And, when he did get up at four the next morning, he knocked Tom down again, in order to teach him (as young gentlemen used to be taught at public schools) that he must be an extra good boy that day, as they were going to a very great house, and might make a very good thing of it, if they could but give satisfaction.

And Tom thought so likewise, and, indeed, would have done and behaved his best, even without being knocked down. For, of all places upon earth, Harthover Place (which he had never seen) was the most wonderful; and, of all men on earth, Sir John (whom he had seen, having been sent to gaol by him twice) was the most awful.

Harthover Place was really a grand place, even for the rich North country; with a house so large that in the frame-breaking riots,[1] which Tom could just remember, the Duke of Wellington, with ten thousand soldiers and cannon to match, were easily housed therein; at least, so Tom believed; with a park full of deer, which Tom believed to be monsters who were in the habit of eating children; with miles of game-preserves, in which Mr. Grimes and the collier-lads poached at times, on which occasions Tom saw pheasants, and wondered what they tasted like;

---

1 Between 1811-1816 British workmen (known as "Luddites") rioted and destroyed laborsaving textile machinery which they believed generated unemployment.

with a noble salmon-river, in which Mr. Grimes and his friends would have liked to poach; but then they must have got into cold water, and that they did not like at all. In short, Harthover was a grand place, and Sir John a grand old man, whom even Mr. Grimes respected, for not only could he send Mr. Grimes to prison when he deserved it, as he did once or twice a week; not only did he own all the land about for miles; not only was he a jolly, honest, sensible squire as ever kept a pack of hounds, who would do what he thought right by his neighbours, as well as get what he thought right for himself, but, what was more, he weighed full fifteen stone, was nobody knew how many inches round the chest, and could have thrashed Mr. Grimes himself in fair fight, which very few folk round there could do, and which, my dear little boy, would not have been right for him to do, as a great many things are not which one both can do, and would like very much to do. So Mr. Grimes touched his hat to him when he rode through the town, and called him a "buirdly awd chap,"[1] and his young ladies "gradely[2] lasses," which are two high compliments in the North country; and thought that that made up for his poaching Sir John's pheasants; whereby you may perceive that Mr. Grimes had not been to a properly-inspected Government National School.[3]

Now, I dare say, you never got up at three o'clock on a midsummer morning. Some people get up then because they want to catch salmon; and some, because they want to climb Alps; and a great many more, because they must, like Tom. But, I assure you, that three o'clock on a midsummer morning is the pleasantest time of all the twenty-four hours, and all the three hundred and sixty-five days; and why every one does not get up then, I never could tell, save that they are all determined to spoil their nerves and their complexions, by doing all night, what they might just as well do all day. But Tom, instead of going out to dinner at half-past eight at night, and to a ball at ten, and finishing off somewhere between twelve and four, went to bed at seven, when his master went to the public-house, and slept like a dead pig: for which reason he was as piert[4] as a game-cock (who always gets

---

1 Husky, well-built.
2 Desirable, fine.
3 Schools set up to provide the poor with a rudimentary education and the principles of the Established Church. Kingsley protested their low standards and expectations.
4 Pert.

up early to wake the maids), and just ready to get up when the fine gentlemen and ladies were just ready to go to bed.

So he and his master set out; Grimes rode the donkey in front, and Tom and the brushes walked behind; out of the court, and up the street, past the closed window-shutters, and the winking weary policemen, and the roofs all shining grey in the grey dawn.

They passed through the pitmen's village, all shut up and silent now; and through the turnpike; and then they were out in the real country, and plodding along the black dusty road, between black slag walls, with no sound but the groaning and thumping of the pit-engine in the next field. But soon the road grew white, and the walls likewise; and at the wall's foot grew long grass and gay flowers, all drenched with dew; and instead of the groaning of the pit-engine, they heard the skylark saying his matins high up in the air, and the pit-bird[1] warbling in the sedges, as he had warbled all night long.

All else was silent. For old Mrs. Earth was still fast asleep; and, like many pretty people, she looked still prettier asleep than awake. The great elm-trees in the gold-green meadows were fast asleep above, and the cows fast asleep beneath them; nay, the few clouds which were about were fast asleep likewise, and so tired that they had lain down on the earth to rest, in long white flakes and bars, among the stems of the elm-trees, and along the tops of the alders by the stream, waiting for the sun to bid them rise and go about their day's business in the clear blue overhead.

On they went; and Tom looked, and looked, for he never had been so far into the country before; and longed to get over a gate, and pick buttercups, and look for birds' nests in the hedge; but Mr. Grimes was a man of business, and would not have heard of that.

Soon they came up with a poor Irishwoman, trudging along with a bundle at her back. She had a grey shawl over her head, and a crimson madder[2] petticoat; so you may be sure she came from Galway. She had neither shoes nor stockings, and limped

---

1 Reed warbler.

2 An Asian perennial, the root of which is used to make a strong red dye.

along as if she were tired and footsore: but she was a very tall handsome woman, with bright grey eyes, and heavy black hair hanging about her cheeks. And she took Mr. Grimes's fancy so much, that when he came along-side he called out to her:

"This is a hard road for a gradely foot like that. Will ye up, lass, and ride behind me?"

But, perhaps, she did not ad-mire Mr. Grimes's look and voice; for she answered quietly:

"No, thank you; I'd sooner walk with your little lad here."

"You may please yourself," growled Grimes, and went on smoking.

So she walked beside Tom, and talked to him, and asked him where he lived, and what he knew, and all about himself, till Tom thought he had never met such a pleasant spoken woman. And she asked him, at last, whether he said his prayers; and seemed sad when he told her that he knew no prayers to say.

Then he asked her where she lived; and she said far away by the sea. And Tom asked her about the sea; and she told him how it rolled and roared over the rocks in winter nights, and lay still in the bright summer days, for the children to bathe and play in it; and many a story more, till Tom longed to go and see the sea, and bathe in it likewise.

At last, at the bottom of a hill, they came to a spring: not such a spring as you see here, which soaks up out of a white gravel in the bog, among red flycatchers, and pink bottle-heath, and sweet white orchis; nor such a one as you may see, too, here, which bubbles up under the warm sand-bank in the hollow lane, by the great tuft of lady ferns, and makes the sand dance reels at the bottom, day and night, all the year round; not such a spring as either of those: but a real North country limestone fountain, like one of those in Sicily or Greece, where the old heathen fancied the nymphs sat cooling themselves the hot summer's day, while the shepherds peeped at them from behind the bushes. Out of a low cave of rock, at the foot of a limestone crag, the great foun-tain rose, quelling and bubbling, and gurgling, so clear that you could not tell where the water ended and the air began; and ran away under the road, a stream large enough to turn a mill; among blue geranium, and golden globe-flower, and wild raspberry, and the bird-cherry with its tassels of snow.

And there Grimes stopped, and looked; and Tom looked too. Tom was wondering whether anything lived in that dark cave, and came out at night to fly in the meadows. But Grimes was not wondering at all. Without a word, he got off his donkey, and clambered over the low road wall, and knelt down, and began dipping his ugly head into the spring—and very dirty he made it.

Tom was picking the flowers as fast as he could. The Irish-woman helped him, and showed him how to tie them up; and a very pretty nosegay they had made between them. But when he saw Grimes actually wash, he stopped, quite astonished; and when Grimes had finished, and began shaking his ears to dry them, he said:

"Why, master, I never saw you do that before."

"Nor will again, most likely. 'Twasn't for cleanliness I did it, but for coolness. I'd be ashamed to want washing every week or so, like any smutty collier-lad."

"I wish I might go and dip my head in," said poor little Tom. "It must be as good as putting it under the town-pump; and there is no beadle here to drive a chap away."

"Thou come along," said Grimes, "what dost want with washing thyself? Thou did not drink half a gallon of beer last night, like me."

"I don't care for you," said naughty Tom, and ran down to the stream, and began washing his face.

Grimes was very sulky, because the woman preferred Tom's company to his; so he dashed at him with horrid words, and tore him up from his knees, and began beating him. But Tom was accustomed to that, and got his head safe between Mr. Grimes's legs, and kicked his shins with all his might.

"Are you not ashamed of yourself, Thomas Grimes?" cried the Irishwoman over the wall.

Grimes looked up, startled at her knowing his name; but all he answered was, "No: nor never was yet;" and went on beating Tom.

"True for you. If you ever had been ashamed of yourself, you would have gone over into Vendale long ago."

"What do you know about Vendale?" shouted Grimes; but he left off beating Tom.

"I know about Vendale, and about you, too. I know, for instance, what happened in Aldermire Copse, by night, two years ago come Martinmas."

"You do?" shouted Grimes; and leaving Tom, climbed up over the wall, and faced the woman. Tom thought he was going to strike her; but she looked him too full and fierce in the face for that.

"Yes; I was there," said the Irishwoman, quietly.

"You are no Irishwoman, by your speech," said Grimes, after many bad words.

"Never mind who I am. I saw what I saw; and if you strike that boy again, I can tell what I know."

Grimes seemed quite cowed, and got on his donkey without another word.

"Stop!" said the Irishwoman. "I have one more word for you both; for you will both see me again, before all is over. Those that wish to be clean, clean they will be; and those that wish to be foul, foul they will be. Remember."

And she turned away, and through a gate into the meadow. Grimes stood still a moment, like a man who had been stunned. Then he rushed after her, shouting "You come back." But when he got into the meadow the woman was not there.

Had she hidden away? There was no place to hide in. But Grimes looked about, and Tom also, for he was as puzzled as Grimes himself, at her disappearing so suddenly; but look where they would, she was not there.

Grimes came back again, as silent as a post, for he was a little frightened; and getting on his donkey, filled a fresh pipe, and smoked away, leaving Tom in peace.

And now they had gone three miles and more, and came to Sir John's lodge-gates.

Very grand lodges they were, with very grand iron gates, and stone gate-posts, and on the top of each a most dreadful bogy, all teeth, horns, and tail, which was the crest which Sir John's ancestors wore in the Wars of the Roses; and very prudent men they were to wear it, for all their enemies must have run for their lives at the very first sight of them.

Grimes rang at the gate, and out came a keeper on the spot, and opened.

"I was told to expect thee," he said. "Now, thou'lt be so good as to keep to the main avenue, and not let me find a hare or a rabbit on thee when thou comest back. I shall look sharp for one, I tell thee."

"Not if it's in the bottom of the soot-bag," quoth Grimes, and at that he laughed; and the keeper laughed and said—

"If that's thy sort, I may as well walk up with thee to the hall."

"I think thou best had. It's thy business to see after thy game, man, and not mine."

So the keeper went with them; and to Tom's surprise, he and Grimes chatted together all the way quite pleasantly. He did not know that a keeper is only a poacher turned outside in, and a poacher a keeper turned inside out.

They walked up a great lime-avenue, a full mile long, and between their stems Tom peeped trembling at the horns of the sleeping deer, which stood up among the ferns. Tom had never seen such enormous trees, and as he looked up he fancied that the blue sky rested on their heads. But he was puzzled very much by a strange murmuring noise, which followed them all the way. So much puzzled, that at last he took courage to ask the keeper what it was.

He spoke very civilly, and called him Sir, for he was horribly afraid of him, which pleased the keeper, and he told him that they were the bees about the lime-flowers.

"What are bees?" asked Tom.

"What make honey."

"What is honey?" asked Tom.

"Thou hold thy noise," said Grimes.

"Let the boy be," said the keeper. "He's a civil young chap now, and that's more than he'll be long, if he bides with thee."

Grimes laughed, for he took that for a compliment.

"I wish I were a keeper," said Tom, "to live in such a beautiful place, and wear green velveteens, and have a real dog-whistle at my button, like you."

The keeper laughed; he was a kind-hearted fellow enough.

"Let well alone, lad, and ill too, at times. Thy life's safer than mine at all events, eh, Mr. Grimes?"

And Grimes laughed again, and then the two men began talking quite low. Tom could hear, though, that it was about some poaching fight—and at last Grimes said surlily—

"Hast thou anything against me?"

"Not now."

"Then don't ask me any questions till thou hast, for I am a man of honour."

And at that they both laughed again, and thought it a very good joke.

And by this time they were come up to the great iron gates in front of the house; and Tom stared through them at the rhododendrons and azaleas, which were all in flower; and then at the house itself, and wondered how many chimneys there were in it, and how long ago it was built, and what was the man's name that built it, and whether he got much money for his job?

These last were very difficult questions to answer. For Harthover had been built at ninety different times, and in nineteen different styles, and looked as if somebody had built a whole street of houses of every imaginable shape, and then stirred them together with a spoon.

For the attics were Anglo-Saxon.

The third-floor Norman.

The second Cinque-cento.

The first-floor Elizabethan.

The right wing Pure Doric.

The centre Early English, with a huge portico, copied from the Parthenon.

The left wing Pure Boetian, which the country folk admired most of all, because it was just like the new barracks in the town, only three times as big.

The grand staircase was copied from the Catacombs at Rome.

The back staircase from the Tajmahal at Agra. This was built by Sir John's great-great-great-uncle, who won, in Lord Clive's[1] Indian wars, plenty of money, plenty of wounds, and no more taste than his betters.

The cellars were copied from the caves of Elephanta.

The offices from the Pavilion at Brighton.

And the rest from nothing in heaven, or earth, or under the earth.

So that Harthover House was a great puzzle to antiquarians, and a thorough Naboth's vineyard[2] to critics, and architects, and all persons who like meddling with other men's business, and spending other men's money. So they all were setting upon poor

---

1 Robert Clive, a British soldier and statesman (1725-74), who furthered England's influence in India.

2 A highly desirous place. In 1 Kings 21, Ahab, the king of Samaria, desired the vineyard of his subject, Naboth, for a garden of herbs and proposed to buy it from Naboth or give him a better one in exchange. Naboth, however, refused to part with the vineyard on the ground that it was the inheritance of his fathers. Later, Ahab's wife has Naboth killed.

Sir John, year after year, and trying to talk him into spending a hundred thousand pounds or so, in building to please them and not himself. But he always put them off, like a canny North-countryman as he was. One wanted him to build a Gothic house, but he said he was no Goth; and another to build an Elizabethan, but he said he lived under good Queen Victoria, and not good Queen Bess; and another was bold enough to tell him that his house was ugly, but he said he lived inside it, and not outside; and another, that there was no unity in it; but he said that that was just why he liked the old place. For he liked to see how each Sir John, and Sir Hugh, and Sir Ralph, and Sir Randal, had left his mark upon the place, each after his own taste; and he had no more notion of disturbing his ancestors' work than of disturbing their graves. For now the house looked like a real live house, that had a history, and had grown and grown as the world grew; and that it was only an upstart fellow who did not know who his own grandfather was, who would change it for some spick and span new Gothic or Elizabethan thing, which looked as if it had been all spawned in a night, as mushrooms are. From which you may collect (if you have wit enough), that Sir John was a very sound-headed, sound-hearted squire, and just the man to keep the country side in order, and show good sport with his hounds.

But Tom and his master did not go in through the great iron gates, as if they had been Dukes or Bishops, but round the back way, and a very long way round it was; and into a little back-door, where the ash-boy let them in, yawning horribly; and then in a passage the housekeeper met them, in such a flowered chintz dressing-gown, that Tom mistook her for My Lady herself, and she gave Grimes solemn orders about "You will take care of this, and take care of that," as if he was going up the chimneys, and not Tom. And Grimes listened, and said every now and then, under his voice, "You'll mind that, you little beggar?" and Tom did mind, all at least that he could. And then the housekeeper turned them into a grand room, all covered up in sheets of brown paper, and bade them begin, in a lofty and tremendous voice; and so after a whimper or two, and a kick from his master, into the grate Tom went, and up the chimney, while a house-maid stayed in the room to watch the furniture; to whom Mr. Grimes paid many playful and chivalrous compliments, but met with very slight encouragement in return.

How many chimneys he swept I cannot say: but he swept so many that he got quite tired, and puzzled too, for they were not like the town flues to which he was accustomed, but such as you would find—if you would only get up them and look, which perhaps you would not like to do—in old country-houses, large and crooked chimneys, which had been altered again and again, till they ran one into another, anastomosing[1] (as Professor Owen[2] would say) considerably. So Tom fairly lost his way in them; not that he cared much for that, though he was in pitchy darkness, for he was as much at home in a chimney as a mole is under-ground; but at last, coming down as he thought the right chimney, he came down the wrong one, and found himself standing on the hearthrug in a room the like of which he had never seen before.

Tom had never seen the like. He had never been in gentlefolks' rooms but when the carpets were all up, and the curtains down, and the furniture huddled together under a cloth, and the pictures covered with aprons and dusters; and he had often enough wondered what the rooms were like when they were all ready for the quality to sit in. And now he saw, and he thought the sight very pretty.

The room was all dressed in white; white window curtains, white bed curtains, white furniture, and white walls, with just a few lines of pink here and there. The carpet was all over gay little flowers; and the walls were hung with pictures in gilt frames, which amused Tom very much. There were pictures of ladies and gentlemen, and pictures of horses and dogs. The horses he liked; but the dogs he did not care for much, for there were no bull-dogs among them, not even a terrier. But the two pictures which took his fancy most were, one a man in long garments, with little children and their mothers round him, who was laying his hand upon the children's heads. That was a very pretty picture, Tom thought, to hang in a lady's room. For he could see that it was a lady's room by the dresses which lay about.

The other picture was that of a man nailed to a cross, which surprised Tom much. He fancied that he had seen something like it in a shop window. But why was it there? "Poor man," thought Tom, "and he looks so kind and quiet. But why should the lady have such a sad picture as that in her room? Perhaps it was some kinsman of hers, who had been murdered by the savages in

---

1 Anastomosis: "Intercommunication between two vessels, channels, or distinct branches of any kind, by a connecting cross branch. Applied originally to the cross communications between the arteries and veins" (*OED*).

2 Richard Owen (1804-92), naturalist and England's foremost authority on animal anatomy.

foreign parts, and she kept it there for a remembrance." And Tom felt sad, and awed, and turned to look at something else.

The next thing he saw, and that too puzzled him, was a washing-stand, with ewers and basons, and soap and brushes, and towels; and a large bath, full of clean water—what a heap of things all for washing! "She must be a very dirty lady," thought Tom, "by my master's rule, to want as much scrubbing as all that. But she must be very cunning to put the dirt out of the way so well afterwards, for I don't see a speck about the room, not even on the very towels."

And then, looking toward the bed, he saw that dirty lady, and held his breath with astonishment.

Under the snow-white coverlet, upon the snow-white pillow, lay the most beautiful little girl that Tom had ever seen. Her cheeks were almost as white as the pillow, and her hair was like threads of gold spread all about over the bed. She might have been as old as Tom, or maybe a year or two older; but Tom did not think of that. He thought only of her delicate skin and golden hair, and wondered whether she were a real live person, or one of the wax dolls he had seen in the shops. But when he saw her breathe, he made up his mind that she was alive, and stood staring at her, as if she had been an angel out of heaven.

No. She cannot be dirty. She never could have been dirty, thought Tom to himself. And then he thought, "And are all people like that when they are washed?" And he looked at his own wrist, and tried to rub the soot off, and wondered whether it ever would come off. "Certainly I should look much prettier then, if I grew at all like her."

And looking round, he suddenly saw, standing close to him, a little ugly, black, ragged figure, with bleared eyes and grinning white teeth. He turned on it angrily. What did such a little black ape want in that sweet young lady's room? And behold, it was himself, reflected in a great mirror, the like of which Tom had never seen before.

And Tom, for the first time in his life, found out that he was dirty; and burst into tears with shame and anger; and turned to sneak up the chimney again and hide, and upset the fender, and threw the fire-irons down, with a noise as of ten thousand tin kettles tied to ten thousand mad dogs' tails.

Up jumped the little white lady in her bed, and, seeing Tom, screamed as shrill as any peacock. In rushed a stout old nurse from the next room, and seeing Tom likewise, made up her mind that he had come to rob, plunder, destroy, and burn; and dashed at him, as he lay over the fender, so fast that she caught him by the jacket.

But she did not hold him. Tom had been in a policeman's hands many a time, and out of them too, what is more; and he would have been ashamed to face his friends for ever if he had been stupid enough to be caught by an old woman: so he doubled under the good lady's arm, across the room, and out of the window in a moment.

He did not need to drop out, though he would have done so bravely enough. Nor even to let himself down a spout, which would have been an old game to him; for once he got up by a spout to the church roof, he said to take jackdaws' eggs, but the policemen said to steal lead; and when he was seen on high, sat there till the sun got too hot, and came down by another spout, leaving the policemen to go back to the station-house and eat their dinners.

But all under the window spread a tree, with great leaves, and sweet white flowers, almost as big as his head. It was a magnolia, I suppose; but Tom knew nothing about that, and cared less; for down the tree he went, like a cat, and across the garden lawn, and over the iron-railings, and up the park towards the wood, leaving the old nurse to scream murder and fire at the window.

The under gardener, mowing, saw Tom, and threw down his scythe; caught his leg in it, and cut his shin open, whereby he kept his bed for a week: but in his hurry he never knew it, and gave chase to poor Tom. The dairymaid heard the noise, got the churn between her knees, and tumbled over it, spilling all the cream; and yet she jumped up, and gave chase to Tom. A groom cleaning Sir John's hack at the stables let him go loose, whereby he kicked himself lame in five minutes; but he ran out, and gave chase to Tom. Grimes upset the soot-sack in the new-gravelled yard, and spoilt it all utterly; but, he ran out and gave chase to Tom. The old steward opened the park gate in such a hurry; that he hung up his pony's chin upon the spikes, and for aught I know it hangs there still; but he jumped off, and gave chase to Tom. The ploughman left his horses at the headland, and one jumped over the fence, and pulled the other into the ditch, plough and all; but he ran on, and gave chase to Tom. The keeper, who was taking a stoat out of a trap, let the stoat go, and caught his own finger; but he jumped up and ran after Tom, and considering what he said, and how he looked, I should have been sorry for Tom if he had caught him. Sir John looked out of his study window (for he was an early old gentleman), and up at the nurse, and a marten dropt mud in his eye, so that he had at last to send for the doctor; and yet he ran out and gave chase to Tom. The Irishwoman, too, was walking up to the house to beg—she must have got round by some byway: but she threw away her bundle, and gave chase to Tom likewise. Only my lady did not give chase; for when she had put her head out of the window, her night-wig fell into the garden, and she had to ring up her lady's-maid, and send her down for it privately; which quite put her out of the running, so that she came in nowhere, and is consequently not placed.

In a word, never was there heard at Hall Place, not even when the fox was killed in the conservatory, among acres of broken glass, and tons of smashed flower-pots, such a noise, row, hubbub, babel, shindy, hullabaloo, stramash, charivari,[1] and total contempt of dignity, repose, and order, as that day, when Grimes, gardener, the groom, the dairymaid, Sir John, the steward, the ploughman, the keeper, and the Irishwoman, all ran up the park, shouting "Stop thief," in the belief that Tom had at least a thousand pounds' worth of jewels in his empty pockets; and the very magpies and jays followed Tom up, screaking and screaming, as if he were a hunted fox, beginning to droop his brush.

And all the while poor Tom paddled up the park with his little bare feet, like a small black gorilla fleeing to the forest. Alas for

---

1   A comic array of terms for an uproar, commotion.

him! there was no big father gorilla therein to take his part; to scratch out the gardener's inside with one paw, toss the dairymaid into a tree with another, and wrench off Sir John's head with a third, while he cracked the keeper's scull with his teeth, as easily as if it had been a cocoa-nut or a paving-stone.

However, Tom did not remember ever having had a father; so he did not look for one, and expected to have to take care of himself; while as for running, he could keep up for a couple of miles with any stage-coach, if there was the chance of a copper[1] or a cigar-end, and turn coach wheels on his hands and feet ten times following, which is more than you can do. Wherefore his pursuers found it very difficult to catch him; and we will hope that they did not catch him at all.

Tom, of course, made for the woods. He had never been in a wood in his life: but he was sharp enough to know that he might hide in a bush, or swarm up a tree, and, altogether, had more chance there than in the open. If he had not known that, he would have been foolisher than a mouse or a minnow.

But when he got into the wood, he found it a very different sort of place from what he had fancied. He pushed into a thick cover of rhododendrons, and found himself at once caught in a trap. The boughs laid hold of his legs and arms, poked him in his face and his stomach, made him shut his eyes tight (though that was no great loss, for he could not see at best a yard before his nose); and when he got through the rhododendrons, the hassock-grass and sedges tumbled him over, and cut his poor little fingers afterwards most spitefully; the birches birched him as soundly as if he had been a nobleman at Eton, and over the face too (which is not fair swishing, as all brave boys will agree); and the lawyers[2] tripped him up, and tore his shins as if they had sharks' teeth— which lawyers are likely enough to have.

"I must get out of this," thought Tom, "or I shall stay here till somebody comes to help me—which is just what I don't want."

But how to get out was the difficult matter. And indeed I don't think he would ever have got out at all, but have staid there till the cock-robins covered him with leaves, if he had not suddenly run his head against a wall.

Now running your head against a wall is not pleasant, especially if it is a loose wall, with the stones all set on edge, and a

---

1 A penny or halfpenny.
2 Long brambles (*OED*).

sharp-cornered one hits you between the eyes, and makes you see all manner of beautiful stars. The stars are very beautiful, certainly: but unfortunately they go in the twenty-thousandth part of a split second, and the pain which comes after them does not. And so Tom hurt his head; but he was a brave boy, and did not mind that a penny. He guessed that over the wall the cover would end; and up it he went, and over like a squirrel.

And there he was, out on the great grouse-moors, which the country folk called Harthover Fell—heather and bog and rock, stretching away and up, up to the very sky.

Now, Tom was a cunning little fellow—as cunning as an old Exmoor stag. Why not? Though he was but ten years old, he had lived longer than most stags, and had more wits to start with into the bargain.

He knew as well as a stag, that if he backed he might throw the hounds out. So the first thing he did when he was over the wall, was to make the neatest double sharp to his right, and run along under the wall for nearly half a mile.

Whereby Sir John, and the keeper, and the steward, and the gardener, and the ploughman, and the dairy-maid, and all the hue-and-cry together, went on ahead half a mile in the very opposite direction, and inside the wall, leaving him a mile off on the outside, while Tom heard their shouts die away in the wood, and chuckled to himself merrily.

At last he came to a dip in the land, and went to the bottom of it, and then he turned bravely away from the wall, and up the moor; for he knew that he had put a hill between him and his enemies, and could go on without their seeing him.

But the Irishwoman, alone of them all, had seen which way Tom went. She had kept ahead of every one the whole time: and yet she neither walked or ran. She went along quite smoothly and gracefully, while her feet twinkled past each other so fast, that you could not see which was foremost; till every one asked the other who the strange woman was? and all agreed, for want of anything better to say, that she must be in league with Tom.

But when she came to the plantation they lost sight of her; and they could do no less. For she went quietly over the wall after Tom, and followed him wherever he went. Sir John and the rest saw no more of her; and out of sight was out of mind.

And now Tom was right away into the heather, over just such a moor as those in which you have been bred, except that there were rocks and stones lying about everywhere; and that instead of the moor growing flat as he went upwards, it grew more and more broken and hilly: but not so rough but that little Tom could jog along well enough, and find time, too, to stare about at the strange place, which was like a new world to him.

He saw great spiders there, with crowns and crosses marked on their backs, who sat in the middle of their webs, and when they saw Tom coming, shook them so fast that they became invisible. Then he saw lizards, brown, and grey, and green, and thought they were snakes, and would sting him: but they were as much frightened as he, and shot away into the heath. And then, under a rock, he saw a pretty sight—a great brown sharpnosed creature, with a white tag to her brush, and round her, four or five smutty little cubs, the funniest fellows Tom ever saw. She lay on her back, rolling about, and stretching out her legs, and head, and tail in the bright sunshine; and the cubs jumped over her, and ran round her, and nibbled her paws, and lugged her about by the tail; and she seemed to enjoy it mightily. But one selfish little fellow stole away from the rest to a dead crow close by, and dragged it off to hide it, though it was nearly as big as he was. Whereat all his little brothers set off after him in full cry, and saw Tom; and then all ran back, and up jumped Mrs. Vixen, and caught one up in her mouth, and the rest toddled after her, and into a dark crack in the rocks; and there was an end of the show.

And next he had a fright; for as he scrambled up a sandy brow—whirr-poof-poof-cock-cock-kick—something went off in his face, with a most horrid noise. He thought the ground had blown up, and the end of the world come.

And when he opened his eyes (for he shut them very tight), it was only an old cock-grouse, who had been washing himself in sand, like an Arab, for want of water; and who, when Tom had all but trodden on him, jumped up, with a noise like the express train, leaving his wife and children to shift for themselves, like an old coward, and went off, screaming "Cur-ru-u-uck, cur-ru-u-uck—murder, thieves, fire—cur-u-uck-cock-kick —the end of the world is come—kick-kick-cock-kick." He was always fancying that the end of the world was come, when anything happened which was farther off than the end of his own nose. But the end of the world was not come, any more than the twelfth of August[1] was; though the old grouse-cock was quite certain of it.

So the old grouse came back to his wife and family an hour afterwards, and said solemnly, "Cock-cock-kick; my dears, the end of the world is not quite come; but I assure you it is coming

---

1 Opening day of grouse-hunting.

the day after tomorrow—cock." But his wife had heard that so often, that she knew all about it, and a little more. And, beside, she was the mother of a family, and had seven little poults to wash and feed every day; and that made her very practical, and a little sharp-tempered; so all she answered was: "Kick-kick-kick—go and catch spiders, go and catch spiders—kick."

So Tom went on, and on, he hardly knew why: but he liked the great, wide, strange place, and the cool, fresh, bracing air. But he went more and more slowly as he got higher up the hill; for now the ground grew very bad indeed. Instead of soft turf and springy heather, he met great patches of flat limestone rock, just like ill-made pavements, with deep cracks between the stones and ledges, filled with ferns; so he had to hop from stone to stone, and now and then he slipped in between, and hurt his little bare toes, though they were tolerably tough ones: but still he would go on and up, he could not tell why.

What would Tom have said, if he had seen, walking over the moor behind him, the very same Irishwoman who had taken his part upon the road? But whether it was that he looked too little behind him, or whether it was that she kept out of sight behind the rocks and knolls, he never saw her, though she saw him.

And now he began to get a little hungry, and very thirsty; for he had run a long way, and the sun had risen high in heaven, and the rock was as hot as an oven, and the air danced reels over it, as it does over a limekiln, till everything round seemed quivering and melting in the glare.

But he could see nothing to eat anywhere, and still less to drink.

The heath was full of bilberries and whimberries: but they were only in flower yet, for it was June. And as for water, who can find that on the top of a limestone rock? Now and then he passed by a deep dark swallow-hole,[1] going down into the earth, as if it was the chimney of some dwarf's house underground; and more than once, as he passed, he could hear water falling, trickling, tinkling, many many feet below. How he longed to get down to it, and cool his poor baked lips! But, brave little chimney-sweep as he was, he dared not climb down such chimneys as those.

So he went on, and on, till his head spun round with the heat, and he thought he heard church-bells ringing, a long way off.

---

1 "An opening or cavity, such as are common in limestone formations, through which a stream disappears underground" (*OED*).

"Ah!" he thought, "where there is a church, there will be houses and people; and, perhaps, some one will give me a bit and a sup." So he set off again, to look for the church; for he was sure that he heard the bells quite plain.

And in a minute more, when he looked round, he stopped again, and said, "Why, what a big place the world is!"

And so it was; for, from the top of the mountain, he could see—what could he not see?

Behind him, far below, was Harthover, and the dark woods, and the shining salmon river; and on his left, far below, was the town, and the smoking chimneys of the collieries; and far, far away, the river widened to the shining sea; and little white specks, which were ships, lay on its bosom. Before him lay, spread out like a map, great plains, and farms, and villages, amid dark knots of trees. They all seemed at his very feet; but he had sense to see that they were long miles away.

And to his right rose moor after moor, hill after hill, till they faded away, blue into blue sky. But between him and those moors, and really at his very feet, lay something, to which, as soon as Tom saw it, he determined to go, for that was the place for him.

A deep, deep green and rocky valley, very narrow, and filled with wood: but through the wood, hundreds of feet below him, he could see a clear stream glance. Oh, if he could but get down to that stream! Then, by the stream, he saw the roof of a little cottage, and a little garden, set out in squares and beds. And there was a tiny little red thing moving in the garden, no bigger than a fly. As Tom looked down, he saw that it was a woman in a red petticoat. Ah! perhaps she would give him something to eat. And there were the church-bells ringing again. Surely there must be a village down there. Well, nobody would know him, or what had happened at the Place. The news could not have got there yet, even if Sir John had set all the policemen in the county after him; and he could get down there in five minutes.

Tom was quite right about the hue-and-cry not having got thither; for he had come, without knowing it, the best part of ten miles from Harthover: but he was wrong about getting down in five minutes, for the cottage was more than a mile off, and a good thousand feet below.

However, down he went, like a brave little man as he was, though he was very footsore, and tired, and hungry, and thirsty; while the church-bells rang so loud, he began to think that they

must be inside his own head, and the river chimed and tinkled far
below; and this was the song which it sang:—

Clear and cool, clear and cool,
By laughing shallow, and dreaming pool;
Cool and clear, cool and clear,
By shining shingle, and foaming wear;
Under the crag where the ouzel sings,
And the ivied wall where the church-bell rings,
Undefiled, for the undefiled;
Play by me, bathe in me, mother and child.

Dank and foul, dank and foul,
By the smoky town in its murky cowl;
Foul and dank, foul and dank,
By wharf and sewer and slimy bank;
Darker and darker the further I go,
Baser and baser the richer I grow;
Who dare sport with the sin-defiled?
Shrink from me, turn from me, mother and child.

Strong and free, strong and free,
The floodgates are open, away to the sea.
Free and strong, free and strong,
Cleansing my streams as I hurry along,
To the golden sands, and the leaping bar,
And the taintless tide that awaits me afar,
As I lose myself in the infinite main,
Like a soul that has sinned and is pardoned again.
Undefiled, for the undefiled,
Play by me, bathe in me, mother and child.

So Tom went down; and all the while he never saw the Irishwoman going down behind him.

CHAPTER II.

"And is there care in heaven? and is there love
In heavenly spirits to these creatures base
That may compassion of their evils move?
There is:—else much more wretched were the case
Of men than beasts: But oh! the exceeding grace
Of Highest God that loves His creatures so,
And all His works with mercy doth embrace,
That blessed Angels He sends to and fro,
To serve to wicked man, to serve His wicked foe!"[1]

Spenser.

MILE off, and a thousand feet down. So Tom found it; though it seemed as if he could have chucked a pebble on to the back of the woman in the red petticoat who was weeding in the garden, or even across the dale to the rocks beyond.

For the bottom of the valley was just one field broad, and on the other side ran the stream; and above it, grey crag, grey down, grey stair, grey moor, walled up to heaven.

A quiet, silent, rich, happy place; a narrow crack cut deep into the earth; so deep, and so out of the way, that the bad bogies can hardly find it out. The name of the place is Vendale; and if you

---

1 From *The Faerie Queene*, Book 2, Canto 8.

want to see it for yourself, you must go up into the High Craven, and search from Bolland Forest north by Ingleborough, to the Nine Standards and Cross Fell; and if you have not found it, you must turn south, and search the Lake Mountains, down to Scaw Fell and the sea; and then if you have not found it, you must go northward again by merry Carlisle, and search the Cheviots all across, from Annan Water to Berwick Law; and then, whether you have found Vendale or not, you will have found such a country, and such a people, as ought to make you proud of being a British boy.

So Tom went to go down; and first he went down three hundred feet of steep heather, mixed up with loose brown grit-stone, as rough as a file; which was not pleasant to his poor little heels, as he came bump, stump, jump, down the steep. And still he thought he could throw a stone into the garden.

Then he went down three hundred feet of limestone terraces, one below the other, as straight as if Mr. George White[1] had ruled them with his ruler and then cut them out with his chisel. There was no heath there, but—

First, a little grass slope, covered with the prettiest flowers, rockrose and saxifrage, and thyme and basil, and all sorts of sweet herbs.

Then bump down a two-foot step of limestone.

Then another bit of grass and flowers.

Then bump down a one-foot step.

Then another bit of grass and flowers for fifty yards, as steep as the house-roof, where he had to slide down on his dear little tail.

Then another step of stone, ten feet high; and there he had to stop himself, and crawl along the edge to find a crack; for if he had rolled over, he would have rolled right into the old woman's garden, and frightened her out of her wits.

Then, when he had found a dark narrow crack, full of green-stalked fern, such as hangs in the basket in the drawing-room, and had crawled down through it, with knees and elbows, as he would down a chimney, there was another grass slope, and another step, and so on, till—oh, dear me! I wish it was all over; and so did he. And yet he thought he could throw a stone into the old woman's garden.

At last he came to a bank of beautiful shrubs; whitebeam with its great silver-backed leaves, and mountain-ash, and oak; and

1 The gardener at Kingsley's residence in Eversley.

below them cliff and crag, cliff and crag, with great beds of crown-ferns and wood-sedge; while through the shrubs he could see the stream sparkling, and hear it murmur on the white pebbles. He did not know that it was three hundred feet below.

You would have been giddy, perhaps, at looking down: but Tom was not. He was a brave little chimney-sweep; and when he found himself on the top of a high cliff, instead of sitting down and crying for his baba[1] (though he never had had any baba to cry for), he said—"Ah, this will just suit me!" though he was very tired; and down he went, by stock and stone, sedge and ledge, bush and rush, as if he had been born a jolly little black ape, with four hands instead of two.

And all the while, he never saw the Irishwoman coming down behind him.

But he was getting terribly tired now. The burning sun on the fells had sucked him up; but the damp heat of the woody crag sucked him up still more; and the perspiration ran out of the ends of his fingers and toes, and washed him cleaner than he had been for a whole year. But, of course, he dirtied everything terribly as he went. There has been a great black smudge all down the crag ever since. And there have been more black beetles in Vendale since than ever were known before; all, of course, owing to Tom's having blacked the original papa of them all, just as he was setting off to be married, with a sky-blue coat and scarlet leggings, as smart as a gardener's dog with a polyanthus[2] in his mouth.

At last he got to the bottom. But, behold, it was not the bottom—as people usually find when they are coming down a mountain. For at the foot of the crag were heaps and heaps of fallen limestone of every size from that of your head to that of a stage-waggon, with holes between them full of sweet heath-fern; and before Tom got through them, he was out in the bright sunshine again; and then he felt, once for all and suddenly, as people generally do, that he was b-e-a-t, beat.

You must expect to be beat a few times in your life, little man, if you live such a life as a man ought to live, let you be as strong

---

1 An infantile variant of "papa" according to the *OED*, which cites this passage from *The Water-Babies* as its solitary source. In a letter to his young son, Grenville, however, Kingsley writes: "Mind and be a good boy and give Baba my love." *Charles Kingsley, Letters and Memories of his Life* (London: Macmillan, 1891) II, 172. It would seem, then, that "baba" is a variant of "mama."

2 Garden primrose.

and healthy as you may: and when you are, you will find it a very ugly feeling. I hope that that day you may have a stout staunch friend by you who is not beat; for if you have not, you had best lie where you are, and wait for better times, as poor Tom did.

He could not get on. The sun was burning, and yet he felt chill all over. He was quite empty, and yet he felt quite sick. There was but two hundred yards of smooth pasture between him and the cottage, and yet he could not walk down it. He could hear the stream murmuring only one field beyond it, and yet it seemed to him as if it was a hundred miles off.

He lay down on the grass till the beetles ran over him, and the flies settled on his nose. I don't know when he would have got up again, if the gnats and the midges had not taken compassion on him. But the gnats blew their trumpets so loud in his ear, and the midges nibbled so at his hands and face wherever they could find a place free from soot, that at last he woke up, and stumbled away, down over a low wall, and into a narrow road, and up to the cottage door.

And a neat pretty cottage it was, with clipt yew hedges all round the garden, and yews inside too, cut into peacocks and trumpets and teapots and all kinds of queer shapes. And out of the open door came a noise like that of the frogs on the Great-A,[1] when they know that it is going to be scorching hot to-morrow— and how they know that I don't know, and you don't know, and nobody knows.

He came slowly up to the open door, which was all hung round with clematis and roses; and then peeped in, half afraid.

And there sat by the empty fire-place, which was filled with a pot of sweet herbs, the nicest old woman that ever was seen, in her red petticoat, and short dimity[2] bedgown, and clean white cap, with a black silk handkerchief over it, tied under her chin. At her feet sat the grandfather of all the cats; and opposite her sat, on two benches, twelve or fourteen neat rosy chubby little children, learning their Chris-cross-row;[3] and gabble enough they made about it.

---

1   A triangular area of land at Eversley, crossed by a footpath like the bar of the letter "A" (Brian Alderson, ed. *The Water-Babies* [Oxford: Oxford UP, 1995] 205).

2   "A stout cotton fabric, woven with raised stripes or fancy figures; usually employed undyed for beds and bedroom hangings, and some-times for garments" (*OED*).

3   Learning their alphabet.

Such a pleasant cottage it was, with a shiny clean stone floor, and curious old prints on the walls, and an old black oak side-board full of bright pewter and brass dishes, and a cuckoo clock in the corner, which began shouting as soon as Tom appeared: not that it was frightened at Tom, but that it was just eleven o'clock.

All the children started at Tom's dirty black figure; the girls began to cry, and the boys began to laugh, and all pointed at him rudely enough: but Tom was too tired to care for that.

"What art thou, and what dost want?" cried the old dame. "A chimney-sweep! Away with thee. I'll have no sweeps here."

"Water," said poor little Tom, quite faint.

"Water? There's plenty i' the beck," she said, quite sharply.

"But I can't get there; I'm most clemmed[1] with hunger and drought." And Tom sank down upon the door-step, and laid his head against the post.

And the old dame looked at him through her spectacles one minute, and two, and three; and then she said, "He's sick; and a bairn's a bairn,[2] sweep or none."

"Water," said Tom.

"God forgive me!" and she put by her spectacles, and rose, and came to Tom. "Water's bad for thee; I'll give thee milk." And she toddled off into the next room, and brought a cup of milk and a bit of bread.

Tom drank the milk off at one draught, and then looked up, revived.

"Where didst come from?" said the dame.

"Over Fell, there," said Tom, and pointed up into the sky.

"Over Harthover? and down Lewthwaite Crag? Art sure thou art not lying?"

"Why should I?" said Tom, and leant his head against the post.

"And how got ye up there?"

"I came over from the Place," and Tom was so tired and desperate he had no heart or time to think of a story, so he told all the truth in a few words.

"Bless thy little heart! And thou hast not been stealing, then?"

"No."

"Bless thy little heart! and I'll warrant not. Why, God's guided the bairn, because he was innocent! Away from the Place, and

---

1 "To pinch as hunger or fasting does; to waste with hunger, starve. (Also sometimes with reference to thirst)" (*OED*).

2 A child.

over Harthover Fell, and down Lewthwaite Crag! Who ever heard the like, if God hadn't led him? Why dost not eat thy bread?"

"I can't."

"It's good enough, for I made it myself."

"I can't," said Tom, and he laid his head on his knees, and then asked—

"Is it Sunday?"

"No, then; why should it be?"

"Because I hear the church bells ringing so."

"Bless thy pretty heart! The bairn's sick. Come wi' me, and I'll hap thee up somewhere. If thou wert a bit cleaner I'd put thee in my own bed, for the Lord's sake. But come along here."

But when Tom tried to get up, he was so tired and giddy that she had to help him and lead him.

She put him in an outhouse upon soft sweet hay and an old rug, and bade him sleep off his walk, and she would come to him when school was over, in an hour's time.

And so she went in again, expecting Tom to fall fast asleep at once.

But Tom did not fall asleep.

Instead of it he turned and tossed and kicked about in the strangest way, and felt so hot all over that he longed to get into the river and cool himself; and then he fell half asleep, and dreamt that he heard the little white lady crying to him, "Oh, you're so dirty; go and be washed;" and then that he heard the Irishwoman saying, "Those that wish to be clean, clean they will be." And then he heard the church bells ring so loud, close to him, too, that he was sure it must be Sunday, in spite of what the old dame had said; and he would go to church, and see what a church was like inside, for he had never been in one, poor little fellow, in all his life. But the people would never let him come in, all over soot and dirt like that. He must go to the river and wash first. And he said out loud again and again, though being half asleep he did not know it, "I must be clean, I must be clean."

And all of a sudden he found himself, not in the outhouse on the hay, but in the middle of a meadow, over the road, with the stream just before him, saying continually, "I must be clean, I must be clean." He had got there on his own legs, between sleep and awake, as children will often get out of bed, and go about the room, when they are not quite well. But he was not a bit surprised, and went on to the bank of the brook, and lay down on the grass, and looked into the clear clear limestone water, with every pebble at the bottom bright and clean, while the little silver trout dashed about in fright at the sight of his black face; and he dipped his hand in and found it so cool, cool, cool; and he said, "I will be a fish; I will swim in the water; I must be clean, I must be clean."

So he pulled off all his clothes in such haste that he tore some of them, which was easy enough with such ragged old things. And he put his poor hot sore feet into the water; and then his legs; and the further he went in, the more the church bells rang in his head.

"Ah," said Tom, "I must be quick and wash myself; the bells are ringing quite loud now: and they will stop soon, and then the door will be shut, and I shall never be able to get in at all."

Tom was mistaken: for in England the church doors are left open all service time, for everybody who likes to come in, Churchman or Dissenter; ay, even if he were a Turk or a Heathen; and if any man dared to turn him out, as long as he behaved quietly, the good old English law would punish that man, as he deserved, for ordering any peaceable person out of God's house, which belongs to all alike. But Tom did not know that, any more than he knew a great deal more which people ought to know.

And all the while he never saw the Irishwoman: not behind him this time, but before.

For just before he came to the river side, she had stept down into the cool clear water; and her shawl and her petticoat floated off her, and the green water-weeds floated round her sides, and the white water-lilies floated round her head, and the fairies of the stream came up from the bottom, and bore her away and down upon their arms; for she was the Queen of them all; and perhaps of more besides.

"Where have you been?" they asked her.

"I have been smoothing sick folk's pillows, and whispering sweet dreams into their ears; opening cottage casements, to let out the stifling air; coaxing little children away from gutters, and foul pools where fever breeds; turning women from the gin-shop door, and staying men's hands as they were going to strike their wives; doing all I can to help those who will not help themselves: and little enough that is, and weary work for me. But I have brought you a new little brother, and watched him safe all the way here."

Then all the fairies laughed for joy at the thought that they had a little brother coming.

"But mind, maidens, he must not see you, or know that you are here. He is but a savage now, and like the beasts which perish; and from the beasts which perish he must learn. So you must not

play with him, or speak to him, or let him see you: but only keep him from being harmed."

Then the fairies were sad, because they could not play with their new brother, but they always did what they were told.

And their Queen floated away down the river; and whither she went, thither she came. But all this Tom, of course, never saw or heard: and perhaps if he had, it would have made little difference in the story; for he was so hot and thirsty, and longed so to be clean for once, that he tumbled himself as quick as he could into the clear cool stream.

And he had not been in it two minutes before he fell fast asleep, into the quietest, sunniest, cosiest sleep that ever he had in his life; and he dreamt about the green meadows by which he had walked that morning, and the tall elm-trees, and the sleeping cows; and after that he dreamt of nothing at all.

The reason of his falling into such a delightful sleep is very simple; and yet hardly any one has found it out. It was merely that the fairies took him.

Some people think that there are no fairies. Cousin Cramchild[1] tells little folks so in his Conversations. Well, perhaps there are none—in Boston, U.S., where he was raised. There are only a clumsy lot of spirits there, who can't make people hear without thumping on the table: but they get their living thereby, and I suppose that is all they want. And Aunt Agitate,[2] in her Arguments on political economy, says there are none. Well, perhaps there are none—in her political economy. But it is a wide world, my little man—and thank heaven for it, for else, between crinolines and theories, some of us would get squashed—and plenty of room in it for fairies, without people seeing them; unless, of course, they look in the right place. The most wonderful and the strongest things in the world, you know, are just the things which no one can see. There is life in you; and it is the life in you which makes you grow, and move, and think: and yet you can't see it. And there is steam in a steam-engine; and that is what makes it move: and yet you can't see it; and so there may be fairies in the world, and they may be just what makes the world go round to the old tune of

"C'est l'amour, l'amour, l'amour
Qui fait la monde à la ronde:"[3]

and yet no one may be able to see them except those whose hearts are going round to that same tune. At all events, we will make believe that there are fairies in the world. It will not be the last time by many a one that we shall have to make believe. And yet, after all, there is no need for that. There must be fairies; for

---

1 Samuel Griswold Goodrich (1793-1860), an American author and publisher of children's books written under the name "Peter Parley." The Peter Parley books, written in a simple conversational style, were comprised of instructive stories about science and the natural world. His work was imitated in England, where authors used his pseudonym for their own work.

2 Jane Marcet (1769-1858), author of *Conversations on Political Economy* (1816), which presented Classical economic theory in terms of a conversation between a pupil and her tutor.

3 "It is love, love, love/ That makes the world go round." A refrain from a popular French song of the time.

this is a fairy tale: and how can one have a fairy tale if there are no fairies?

You don't see the logic of that? Perhaps not. Then please not to see the logic of a great many arguments exactly like it, which you will hear before your beard is grey.

The kind old dame came back at twelve, when school was over, to look at Tom: but there was no Tom there. She looked about for his footprints; but the ground was so hard that there was no slot,[1] as they say in dear old North Devon. And if you grow up to be a brave healthy man, you may know some day what no slot means, and know, too, I hope, what a slot does mean—a broad slot, with blunt claws, which makes a man put out his cigar, and set his teeth, and tighten his girths, when he sees it; and what his rights mean, if he has them, brow, bay, tray, and points;[2] and see something worth seeing between Haddon Wood and Countisbury Cliff, with good Mr. Palk Collyns[3] to show you the way, and mend your bones as fast as you smash them. Only when that jolly day comes, please don't break your neck: stogged[4] in a mire you never will be, I trust; for you are a heath-cropper[5] bred and born.

So the old dame went in again quite sulky, thinking that little Tom had tricked her with a false story, and shammed ill, and then run away again.

But she altered her mind the next day. For, when Sir John and the rest of them had run themselves out of breath, and lost Tom, they went back again, looking very foolish.

And they looked more foolish still when Sir John heard more of the story from the nurse; and more foolish still, again, when they heard the whole story from Miss Ellie, the little lady in white. All she had seen was a poor little black chimney-sweep, crying and sobbing, and going to get up the chimney again. Of course, she was very much frightened: and no wonder. But that was all. The boy had taken nothing in the room; by the mark of his little sooty feet, they could see that he had never been off

---

1 The track of an animal, especially a deer.

2 The stag's brow, bay and tray antlers are called his rights among Devonshire hunters.

3 Charles Palk Collyns, a surgeon at Dulverton, Somerset and author of *Notes on the Chase of the Wild Red Deer in the Counties of Devon and Somerset* (1862).

4 Stuck or bogged down.

5 One who is able to live off the challenging heath land.

the hearth-rug till the nurse caught hold of him. It was all a mistake.

So Sir John told Grimes to go home, and promised him five shillings if he would bring the boy quietly up to him, without beating him, that he might be sure of the truth. For he took for granted, and Grimes, too, that Tom had made his way home.

But no Tom came back to Mr. Grimes that evening; and he went to the police-office, to tell them to look out for the boy. But no Tom was heard of. As for his having gone over those great fells to Vendale, they no more dreamed of that than of his having gone to the moon.

So Mr. Grimes came up to Harthover next day with a very sour face; but when he got there, Sir John was over the hills and far away; and Mr. Grimes had to sit in the outer servants' hall all day, and drink strong ale to wash away his sorrows; and they were washed away, long before Sir John came back.

For good Sir John had slept very badly that night; and he said to his lady, "My dear, the boy must have got over into the grouse-moors, and lost himself; and he lies very heavily on my conscience, poor little lad. But I know what I will do."

So, at five the next morning up he got, and into his bath, and into his shooting-jacket and gaiters, and into the stable-yard, like a fine old English gentleman, with a face as red as a rose, and a hand as hard as a table, and a back as broad as a bullock's;[1] and bade them bring his shooting pony, and the keeper to come on his pony, and the huntsman, and the first whip, and the second whip, and the under-keeper with the blood-hound in a leash—a great dog as tall as a calf, of the colour of a gravel walk, with mahogany ears and nose, and a throat like a church bell. They took him up to the place where Tom had gone into the wood; and there the hound lifted up his mighty voice, and told them all he knew.

Then he took them to the place where Tom had climbed the wall; and they shoved it down, and all got through.

And then the wise dog took them over the moor, and over the fells, step by step, very slowly; for the scent was a day old, you know, and very light from the heat and drought. But that was why cunning old Sir John started at five in the morning.

And at last he came to the top of Lewthwaite Crag, and there he bayed, and looked up in their faces, as much as to say, "I tell you he is gone down here!"

They could hardly believe that Tom would have gone so far;

---

1 A castrated bull or ox.

and when they looked at that awful cliff, they could never believe that he would have dared to face it. But if the dog said so, it must be true.

"Heaven forgive us!" said Sir John. "If we find him at all, we shall find him lying at the bottom." And he slapped his great hand upon his great thigh, and said—

"Who will go down over Lewthwaite Crag, and see if that boy is alive? Oh that I were twenty years younger, and I would go down myself!" And so he would have done, as well as any sweep in the county. Then he said—

"Twenty pounds to the man who brings me that boy alive!" and as was his way, what he said he meant.

Now among the lot was a little groom-boy, a very little groom indeed; and he was the same who had ridden up the court, and told Tom to come to the Hall; and he said—

"Twenty pounds or none, I will go down over Lewthwaite Crag, if it's only for the poor boy's sake. For he was as civil a spoken little chap as ever climbed a flue."

So down over Lewthwaite Crag he went: a very smart groom he was at the top, and a very shabby one at the bottom; for he tore his gaiters, and he tore his breeches, and he tore his jacket, and he burst his braces, and he burst his boots, and he lost his hat, and what was worst of all, he lost his shirt pin, which he prized very much, for it was gold, and he had won it in a raffle at Malton, and there was a figure at the top of it, of t'ould mare, noble old Beeswing[1] herself, as natural as life; so it was a really severe loss: but he never saw anything of Tom.

And all the while Sir John and the rest were riding round, full three miles to the right, and back again, to get into Vendale, and to the foot of the crag.

When they came to the old dame's school, all the children came out to see. And the old dame came out too; and when she saw Sir John she curtsied very low, for she was a tenant of his.

"Well, dame, and how are you?" said Sir John.

"Blessings on you as broad as your back, Harthover," says she—she didn't call him Sir John, but only Harthover, for that is the fashion in the North country—"and welcome into Vendale: but you're no hunting the fox this time of year?"

---

1 One of the most celebrated of British racehorses. During her racing career, she started 64 times and won 51 races. She won the Newcastle Cup six times, the Craven Stakes and the Fitzwilliam Stakes three times apiece, and the Doncaster Cup four times.

"I am hunting, and strange game too," said he.

"Blessings on your heart, and what makes you look so sad the morn?"

"I'm looking for a lost child, a chimney-sweep, that is run away."

"Oh Harthover, Harthover," says she, "ye were always a just man and a merciful; and ye'll no harm the poor little lad if I give you tidings of him?"

"Not I, not I, dame. I'm afraid we hunted him out of the house all on a miserable mistake, and the hound has brought him to the top of Lewthwaite Crag, and—"

Whereat the old dame broke out crying, without letting him finish his story.

"So he told me the truth after all, poor little dear! Ah, first thoughts are best, and a body's heart'll guide them right, if they will but hearken to it." And then she told Sir John all.

"Bring the dog here, and lay him on," said Sir John, without another word, and he set his teeth very hard.

And the dog opened at once; and went away at the back of the cottage, over the road, and over the meadow, and through a bit of alder copse; and there, upon an alder stump, they saw Tom's clothes lying. And then they knew as much about it all as there was any need to know.

And Tom?

Ah, now comes the most wonderful part of this wonderful story. Tom, when he woke, for of course he woke—children always wake after they have slept exactly as long as is good for them—found himself swimming about in the stream, being about four inches, or—that I may be accurate—3.87902 inches long, and having round the parotid region of his fauces[1] a set of external gills (I hope you understand all the big words) just like those of a sucking eft,[2] which he mistook for a lace frill, till he pulled at them, found he hurt himself, and made up his mind that they were part of himself, and best left alone.

In fact, the fairies had turned him into a water-baby.

A water-baby? You never heard of a water-baby. Perhaps not. That is the very reason why this story was written. There are a great many things in the world which you never heard of; and a great many more which nobody ever heard of; and a great many things, too, which nobody will ever hear of, at least until the

---

1 The area between the ear and the back of the mouth.
2 A salamander or newt.

coming of the Cocqcigrues,[1] when man shall be the measure of all things.

"But there are no such things as water-babies."

How do you know that? Have you been there to see? And if you had been there to see, and had seen none, that would not prove that there were none. If Mr. Garth[2] does not find a fox in Eversley Wood—as folks sometimes fear he never will—that does not prove that there are no such things as foxes. And as is Eversley Wood to all the woods in England, so are the waters we know to all the waters in the world. And no one has a right to say that no water-babies exist, till they have seen no water-babies existing; which is quite a different thing, mind, from not seeing water-babies; and a thing which nobody ever did, or perhaps ever will do.

"But surely if there were water-babies, somebody would have caught one at least?"

Well. How do you know that somebody has not?

"But they would have put it into spirits, or into the Illustrated News, or perhaps cut it into two halves, poor dear little thing, and

1 An indefinitely long time. In Rabelais' *Gargantua and Pantagruel* King Picrochole has been defeated in battle, but is given hope by a self-styled prophetess who tells him that he will recover his lands "at the coming of the Coquecigrues [her term]." "What is become of him since we cannot certainly tell, yet was I told that he is now a porter at Lyons, as testy and pettish in humour as ever he was before, and would be always with great lamentation inquiring at all strangers of the coming of the Cocklicranes, expecting assuredly, according to the old woman's prophecy, that at their coming he shall be re-established in his kingdom." (*Gargantua and Pantagruel.* Book 1, Ch. 49).

2 Thomas Colleton Garth (1821-1907), Deputy Lieutenant for Berkshire and first Master of Fox Hounds in his area. The Master finances the hunt with his private funds and generally presents the riders with the brush (tail), mask (head), and pads (feet).

sent one to Professor Owen, and one to Professor Huxley,[1] to see what they would each say about it."

Ah, my dear little man! that does not follow at all, as you will see before the end of the story.

"But a water-baby is contrary to nature."

Well, but, my dear little man, you must learn to talk about such things, when you grow older, in a very different way from that. You must not talk about "ain't" and "can't" when you speak of this great wonderful world round you, of which the wisest man knows only the very smallest corner, and is, as the great Sir Isaac Newton[2] said, only a child picking up pebbles on the shore of a boundless ocean.

You must not say that this cannot be, or that that is contrary to nature. You do not know what nature is, or what she can do; and nobody knows; not even Sir Roderick Murchison, or Professor Owen, or Professor Sedgwick, or Professor Huxley, or Mr. Darwin, or Professor Faraday, or Mr. Grove,[3] or any other of the

---

1 Thomas Henry Huxley (1825-95), biologist and professor at the Royal College of Surgeons, an advocate of Darwin's theory of evolution; author of *Zoological Evidence as to Man's Place in Nature* (1863).

2 English mathematician and scientist (1642-1727), the inventor of differential calculus and author of the theory of gravitation.

3 Sir Roderick Impey Murchison (1792-1871), noted geologist and president of the Royal Geographic Society, 1843; Adam Sedgwick (1785-1873), professor of geology at Cambridge University; Charles Robert Darwin (1809-82), British naturalist who set forth the theory of evolution through natural selection in his book *Origin of Species* (1859); Michael Faraday (1791-1867), British chemist and physicist who discovered electromagnetism; William Robert Grove (1811-96), scientist and judge, invented the Grove gas voltaic battery. [Owen is noted previously, p. 54.]

great men whom good boys are taught to respect. They are very wise men; and you must listen respectfully to all they say: but even if they should say, which I am sure they never would, "That cannot exist. That is contrary to nature," you must wait a little, and see; for perhaps even they may be wrong. It is only children who read Aunt Agitate's Arguments, or Cousin Cramchild's Conversations; or lads who go to popular lectures, and see a man pointing at a few big ugly pictures on the wall, or making nasty smells with bottles and squirts, for an hour or two, and calling that anatomy or chemistry—who talk about "cannot exist," and "contrary to nature." Wise men are afraid to say that there is any-thing contrary to nature, except what is contrary to mathematical truth; for two and two cannot make five, and two straight lines cannot join twice, and a part cannot be as great as the whole, and so on (at least, so it seems at present): but the wiser men are, the less they talk about "cannot." That is a very rash, dangerous word, that "cannot;" and if people use it too often, the Queen of all the Fairies, who makes the clouds thunder and the fleas bite, and takes just as much trouble about one as about the other, is apt to astonish them suddenly by showing them, that though they say she cannot, yet she can, and what is more, will, whether they approve or not.

And therefore it is, that there are dozens and hundreds of things in the world which we should certainly have said were con-trary to nature, if we did not see them going on under our eyes all day long. If people had never seen little seeds grow into great plants and trees, of quite different shape from themselves, and these trees again produce fresh seeds, to grow into fresh trees, they would have said, "The thing cannot be; it is contrary to nature." And they would have been quite as right in saying so, as in saying that most other things cannot be.

Or suppose again, that you had come, like M. Du Chaillu,[1] a traveller from unknown parts; and that no human being had ever seen or heard of an elephant. And suppose that you described him to people, and said, "This is the shape, and plan, and anatomy of the beast, and of his feet, and of his trunk and of his grinders, and of his tusks, though they are not tusks at all, but two fore teeth run mad; and this is the section of his skull, more like

---

1 Paul Belloni du Chaillu (1835-1903), a French-American who explored the interior of Africa and recorded his adventures in *Explorations in Equatorial Africa* (1861). He brought back the first gorillas to be seen in America (1861) and England (1862).

a mushroom than a reasonable skull of a reasonable or unreasonable beast; and so forth, and so forth; and though the beast (which I assure you I have seen and shot) is first cousin to the little hairy coney of Scripture, second cousin to a pig, and (I suspect) thirteenth or fourteenth cousin to a rabbit, yet he is the wisest of all beasts, and can do everything save read write and cast accounts." People would surely have said, "Nonsense; your elephant is contrary to nature;" and have thought you were telling stories—as the French thought of Le Vaillant[1] when he came back to Paris and said that he had shot a giraffe; and as the king of the Cannibal Islands thought of the English sailor, when he said that in his country water turned to marble, and rain fell as feathers. They would tell you, the more they knew of science, "Your elephant is an impossible monster, contrary to the laws of comparative anatomy, as far as yet known." To which you would answer the less, the more you thought.

Did not learned men, too, hold, till within the last twenty-five years, that a flying dragon was an impossible monster? And do we not now know that there are hundreds of them found fossil up and down the world? People call them Pterodactyles:[2] but that is only because they are ashamed to call them flying dragons, after denying so long that flying dragons could exist. And has not a German, only lately discovered, what is most monstrous of all, that some of these flying dragons, lizards though they are, had feathers?[3] And if that last is not contrary to what people mean by nature now-a-days, one hardly knows what is.

The truth is, that folks' fancy that such and such things cannot be, simply because they have not seen them, is worth no more than a savage's fancy that there cannot be such a thing as a locomotive, because he never saw one running wild in the forest. Wise men know that their business is to examine what is, and not to settle what is not. They know that there are elephants; they know that

---

1 François Levaillant (1753-1824), a pioneering ornithologist and naturalist, whose accounts of his travels to southern Africa in the 1780s were widely read. A flamboyant aristocrat, he hunted lions in his silk clothes and ruffles and traveled widely to find examples of the exotic birds that appear in his books, most of which were illustrated by Jacques Barraband.
2 Prehistoric flying reptiles that existed during the Jurassic and Cretaceous periods.
3 The first edition of *The Water-Babies* contains the following erratum printed before Chapter I: "This was written before Professor Owen's Memoir of November 10, 1862, showing that the Archæopteryx is certainly a bird; and was unfortunately overlooked in correcting the proofs."

there have been flying dragons; and the wiser they are, the less inclined they will be to say positively that there are no water-babies.

No water-babies, indeed? Why, wise men of old said that everything on earth had its double in the water; and you may see that that is, if not quite true, still quite as true as most other theories which you are likely to hear for many a day. There are land-babies—then why not water-babies? Are there not water-rats, water-flies, water-crickets, water-crabs, water-tortoises, water-scorpions, water-tigers and water-hogs, water-cats and water-dogs, sea-lions and sea-bears, sea-horses and sea-elephants, sea-mice and sea-urchins, sea-razors and sea-pens, sea-combs and sea-fans; and of plants, are there not water-grass, and water-crowfoot, water-milfoil, and so on, without end?

"But all these things are only nicknames; the water things are not really akin to the land things."

That's not always true. They are, in millions of cases, not only of the same family, but actually the same individual creatures. Do not even you know that a green drake, and an alder-fly,[1] and a dragon-fly, live under water till they change their skins, just as Tom changed his? And if a water animal can continually change into a land animal, why should not a land animal sometimes change into a water animal? Don't be put down by any of Cousin Cramchild's arguments, but stand up to him like a man, and answer him (quite respectfully, of course) thus:—

If Cousin Cramchild says, that if there are water-babies, they must grow into water men, ask him how he knows that they do not? and then, how he knows that they must, any more than the Proteus of the Adelsberg caverns[2] grows into a perfect newt?

If he says that it is too strange a transformation for a land-baby to turn into a water-baby, ask him if he ever heard of the transformation of Syllis, or the Distomas, or the common jelly-fish, of which M. Quatrefages[3] says excellently well—"who would not

---

1   The green drake is the fisherman's name for the common day-fly; the alder-fly, or orl- fly, is another short-lived fly. All of these insects live in the water as larvae until they surface to hatch as flies.

2   "A genus of tailed amphibians with persistent gills, having four short slender legs and a long eel-like body, found in subterranean caves in Austria" (*OED*).

3   Jean Louis Armand de Quatrefages (1810-92), a French naturalist, whose work ranged over the entire field of zoology, from the annelids and other low organisms to the anthropoids and man. Syllis, or syllid, is a small worm; distoma is a parasitic flatworm.

exclaim that a miracle had come to pass, if he saw a reptile come out of the egg dropped by the hen in his poultry-yard, and the reptile give birth at once to an indefinite number of fishes and birds? Yet the history of the jelly-fish is quite as wonderful as that would be." Ask him if he knows about all this; and if he does not, tell him to go and look for himself; and advise him (very respectfully, of course) to settle no more what strange things cannot happen, till he has seen what strange things do happen every day.

If he says that things cannot degrade, that is, change downwards into lower forms, ask him, who told him that water-babies were lower than land-babies? But even if they were, does he know about the strange degradation of the common goose-barnacles,[1] which one finds sticking on ships' bottoms; or the still stranger degradation of some cousins of theirs, of which one hardly likes to talk, so shocking and ugly it is?

And, lastly, if he says (as he most certainly will) that these transformations only take place in the lower animals, and not in the higher, say that that seems to little boys, and to some grown people, a very strange fancy. For if the changes of the lower animals are so wonderful, and so difficult to discover, why should not there be changes in the higher animals far more wonderful, and far more difficult to discover? And may not man, the crown and flower of all things, undergo some change as much more wonderful than all the rest, as the Great Exhibition[2] is more wonderful than a rabbit-burrow? Let him answer that. And if he says (as he will) that not having seen such a change in his experience, he is not bound to believe it, ask him respectfully where his microscope has been? Does not each of us, in coming into this world, go through a transformation just as wonderful as that of a

---

1   Characterized by their feathery limbs known as "cirri," they derive their name from the fancied resemblance to geese. The parasitic forms attach themselves to other animals. Rhizocephalans, for example, invade the tissues of crabs and other crustaceans and become visible only when a grotesque egg-sac forms under the abdomen of the host. Thus, Kingsley's reference to the "stranger degradation" of their cousins.

2   Conceived by Prince Albert, the Great Exhibition of 1851 was designed to celebrate England's superiority in industry, technology, and the arts. Materials from around the world were displayed in a huge glass structure nicknamed the "Crystal Palace," located in Hyde Park, London. The building was divided into a series of courts depicting the history of art and architecture from ancient Egypt through the Renaissance, as well as exhibits from industry and the natural world.

sea-egg, or a butterfly? and does not reason and analogy, as well as Scripture, tell us that that transformation is not the last? and that, though what we shall be, we know not, yet we are here but as the crawling caterpillar, and shall be hereafter as the perfect fly. The old Greeks, heathens as they were, saw as much as that two thousand years ago; and I care very little for Cousin Cramchild, if he sees even less than they. And so forth, and so forth, till he is quite cross. And then tell him that if there are no water-babies, at least, there ought to be; and that, at least, he cannot answer.

And meanwhile, my dear little man, till you know a great deal more about nature than Professor Owen and Professor Huxley, put together, don't tell me about what cannot be, or fancy that anything is too wonderful to be true. "We are fearfully and wonderfully made,"[1] said old David; and so we are; and so is every thing around us, down to the very deal table. Yes; much more fearfully and wonderfully made, already, is the table, as it stands now, nothing but a piece of dead deal wood, than if, as foxes say, and geese believe, spirits could make it dance, or talk to you by rapping on it.

Am I in earnest? Oh dear no. Don't you know that this is a fairy tale, and all fun and pretence; and that you are not to believe one word of it, even if it is true?

But at all events, so it happened to Tom. And, therefore, the keeper, and the groom, and Sir John, made a great mistake, and were very unhappy (Sir John, at least) without any reason, when they found a black thing in the water, and said it was Tom's body, and that he had been drowned. They were utterly mistaken. Tom was quite alive; and cleaner, and merrier, than he ever had been. The fairies had washed him, you see, in the swift river, so thoroughly, that not only his dirt, but his whole husk and shell had been washed quite off him, and the pretty little real Tom was washed out of the inside of it, and swam away, as a caddis does when its case of stones and silk is bored through, and away it goes on its back, paddling to the shore, there to split its skin, and fly away as a caperer,[2] on four fawn-coloured wings, with long legs and horns. They are foolish fellows, the caperers, and fly into the candle at night, if you leave the door open. We will hope Tom will be wiser, now he has got safe out of his sooty old shell.

---

1   "... I am fearfully and wonderfully made" (*Psalms* 149: 13).

2   The caddis-fly, the larva of the May-fly and other species of Phryganea, which lives in water, and is used as a bait by fishermen. It forms for itself a cylindrical case of hollow stems and small stones.

But good Sir John did not understand all this, not being a fellow of the Linnæan Society;[1] and he took it into his head that Tom was drowned. When they looked into the empty pockets of his shell, and found no jewels there, nor money—nothing but three marbles, and a brass button with a string to it—then Sir John did something as like crying as ever he did in his life, and blamed himself more bitterly than he need have done. So he cried, and the groom-boy cried, and the huntsman cried, and the dame cried, and the little girl cried, and the dairy-maid cried, and the old nurse cried (for it was somewhat her fault), and my lady cried, for though people have wigs, that is no reason why they should not have hearts: but the keeper did not cry, though he had been so good-natured to Tom the morning before; for he was so dried up with running after poachers, that you could no more get tears out of him than milk out of leather: and Grimes did not cry, for Sir John gave him ten pounds, and he drank it all in a week. Sir John sent, far and wide, to find Tom's father and mother: but he might have looked till Doomsday for them, for one was dead, and the other was in Botany Bay. And the little girl would not play with her dolls for a whole week, and never forgot poor little Tom. And soon my lady put a pretty little tombstone over Tom's shell in the little churchyard in Vendale, where the old dalesmen all sleep side by side between the limestone crags. And the dame decked it with garlands every Sunday, till she grew so old that she could not stir abroad; then the little children decked it for her. And always she sung an old old song, as she sat spinning what she called her wedding-dress. The children could not understand it, but they liked it none the less for that; for it was very sweet, and very sad; and that was enough for them. And these are the words of it—

When all the world is young, lad,
  And all the trees are green;
And every goose a swan, lad,
  And every lass a queen;
Then hey for boot and horse, lad,
  And round the world away:
Young blood must have its course, lad,
  And every dog his day.

---

1 James Edward Smith (1759-1828), scientist and collector, founded the Linnean Society in 1788 to promote the study of botany. The society takes its name from the Swedish naturalist Carl Linnaeus (1707-78), who owned a rich botanical and zoological collection and library.

When all the world is old, lad,
  And all the trees are brown;
And all the sport is stale, lad,
  And all the wheels run down;
Creep home, and take your place there,
  The spent and maimed among:
God grant you find one face there,
  You loved when all was young.

Those are the words: but they are only the body of it: the soul of the song was the dear old woman's sweet face, and sweet voice, and the sweet old air to which she sang; and that, alas! one cannot put on paper. And at last she grew so stiff and lame, that the angels were forced to carry her; and they helped her on with her wedding-dress, and carried her up over Harthover Fells, and a long way beyond that too; and there was a new schoolmistress in Vendale, and we will hope that she was not certificated.[1]

And all the while Tom was swimming about in the river, with a pretty little lace-collar of gills about his neck, as lively as a grig,[2] and as clean as a fresh-run salmon.

Now if you don't like my story, then go to the schoolroom and learn your multiplication-table, and see if you like that better. Some people, no doubt, would do so. So much the better for us, if not for them. It takes all sorts, they say, to make a world.

---

1 In order to broaden its educational goals with a minimum of cost, the government sought out bright students from its national school system and prepared them at training centers to be certified teachers. Kingsley felt that this form of education stifled true learning. See the parody of such teachers at the beginning of the next chapter.

2 An extravagantly lively person. The origin of the phrase is ambiguous but may possibly be based upon the quick movements of a swimming eel, known as a grig.

CHAPTER III.

"He prayeth well who loveth well,
Both men and bird and beast;
He prayeth best who loveth best,
All things both great and small:
For the dear God who loveth us,
He made and loveth all."[1]

Coleridge.

OM was now quite amphibious. You do not know what that means? You had better, then, ask the nearest Government pupil-teacher, who may possibly answer you smartly enough, thus—

"Amphibious. Adjective, derived from two Greek words, *amphi*, a fish, and *bios*, a beast. An animal supposed by our ignorant ancestors to be compounded of a fish and a beast; which therefore, like the hippopotamus, can't live on the land, and dies in the water."

However that may be, Tom was amphibious; and what is better still, he was clean. For the first time in his life, he felt how comfortable it was to have nothing on him but himself. But he only enjoyed it: he did not know it, or think about it; just as you enjoy life and health, and yet never think about being alive and healthy: and may it be long before you have to think about it!

He did not remember having ever been dirty. Indeed, he did not remember any of his old troubles, being tired, or hungry, or beaten, or sent up dark chimneys. Since that sweet sleep, he had forgotten all about his master, and Harthover Place, and the little white girl, and in a word, all that had happened to him when he lived before; and what was best of all, he had forgotten all the bad words which he had learnt from Grimes, and the rude boys with whom he used to play.

---

1 From "The Rime of the Ancient Mariner," *Lyrical Ballads* (1798).

That is not strange: for you know, when you came into this world, and became a land-baby, you remembered nothing. So why should he, when he became a water-baby?

Then have you lived before?

My dear child, who can tell? One can only tell that, by remembering something which happened where we lived before; and as we remember nothing, we know nothing about it; and no book, and no man, can ever tell us certainly.

There was a wise man once, a very wise man, and a very good man, who wrote a poem about the feelings which some children have about having lived before; and this is what he said—

> "Our birth is but a sleep and a forgetting;
> The soul that rises with us, our life's star,
>   Hath elsewhere had its setting,
>   And cometh from afar:
>   Not in entire forgetfulness,
>   And not in utter nakedness,
> But trailing clouds of glory, do we come
>   From God, who is our home."[1]

There, you can know no more than that. But if I was you, I would believe that. For then the great fairy Science, who is likely to be queen of all the fairies for many a year to come, can only do you good, and never do you harm; and instead of fancying, with some people, that your body makes your soul, as if a steam-engine could make its own coke; or, with some other people, that your soul has nothing to do with your body, but is only stuck into it like a pin into a pincushion, to fall out with the first shake;—you will believe the one true,

orthodox,	inductive,
rational,	deductive,
philosophical,	seductive,
logical,	productive,
irrefragable,	salutary,
nominalistic,	comfortable,
realistic,	
and on-all-accounts-to-be-received	

---

1   William Wordsworth, "Ode: Intimations of Immortality from Recollections of Early Childhood," (ll. 59-66) first published in 1807.

doctrine of this wonderful fairy tale; which is, that your soul makes your body, just as a snail makes his shell. For the rest, it is enough for us to be sure that whether or not we lived before, we shall live again; though not, I hope, as poor little heathen Tom did. For he went downward into the water: but we, I hope, shall go upward to a very different place.

But Tom was very happy in the water. He had been sadly over-worked in the land-world; and so now, to make up for that, he had nothing but holidays in the water-world for a long, long time to come. He had nothing to do now but enjoy himself, and look at all the pretty things which are to be seen in the cool clear water-world, where the sun is never too hot, and the frost is never too cold.

And what did he live on? Water-cresses, perhaps; or perhaps water-gruel, and water-milk: too many land-babies do so like-wise. But we do not know what one-tenth of the water things eat; so we are not answerable for the water-babies.

Sometimes he went along the smooth gravel water-ways, looking at the crickets which ran in and out among the stones, as rabbits do on land; or he climbed over the ledges of rock, and saw the sand-pipes[1] hanging in thousands, with every one of them a pretty little head and legs peeping out; or he went into a still corner, and watched the caddises eating dead sticks as greedily as you would eat plum-pudding, and building their houses with silk and glue. Very fanciful ladies they were; none of them would keep to the same materials for a day. One would begin with some pebbles; then she would stick on a piece of green weed; then she found a shell, and stuck it on too; and the poor shell was alive, and did not like at all being taken to build houses with: but the caddis did not let him have any voice in the matter, being rude and selfish, as vain people are apt to be; then she stuck on a piece of rotten wood, then a very smart pink stone, and so on, till she was patched all over like an Irishman's coat. Then she found a long straw, five times as long as herself, and said, "Hurrah! my sister has a tail, and I'll have one too;" and she stuck it on her back, and marched about with it quite proud, though it was very inconvenient indeed. And, at that, tails became all the fashion among the caddis-baits[2] in that pool, as they were at the end of

---

1 Worms, which like the caddis, construct habitations out of sand and small stones.
2 Caddis-worms, used as bait, and found close by Kingsley's house at Long Pond, Eversley.

the Long Pond last May, and they all toddled about with long straws sticking out behind, getting between each other's legs, and tumbling over each other, and looking so ridiculous, that Tom laughed at them till he cried, as we did. But they were quite right, you know; for people must always follow the fashion, even if it be spoon-bonnets.[1]

Then sometimes he came to a deep still reach; and there he saw the water-forests. They would have looked to you only little weeds: but Tom, you must remember, was so little that everything looked a hundred times as big to him as it does to you, just as things do to a minnow, who sees and catches the little water-creatures which you can only see in a microscope.

And in the water-forest he saw the water-monkeys and water-squirrels (they had all six legs, though; every thing almost has six legs in the water, except efts and water-babies); and nimbly enough they ran among the branches. There were water-flowers there, too, in thousands; and Tom tried to pick them: but as soon as he touched them, they drew themselves in and turned into knots of jelly; and then Tom saw that they were all alive—bells, and stars, and wheels, and flowers, of all beautiful shapes and colours; and all alive and busy, just as Tom was. So now he found that there was a great deal more in the world than he had fancied at first sight.

There was one wonderful little fellow,[2] too, who peeped out of the top of a house built of round bricks. He had two big wheels, and one little one, all over teeth, spinning round and round like the wheels in a thrashing-machine; and Tom stood and stared at him, to see what he was going to make with his machinery. And what do you think he was doing? Brick-making. With his two big wheels he swept together all the mud which floated in the water: all that was nice in it he put into his stomach and ate; and all the mud he put into the little wheel on his breast, which really was a round hole set with teeth; and there he spun it into a neat hard round brick; and then he took it and stuck it on the top of his house-wall, and set to work to make another. Now was not he a clever little fellow?

Tom thought so: but when he wanted to talk to him, the brick-maker was much too busy and proud of his work to take notice of him.

---

1 A popular style of women's hats in the 1860s shaped like a spoon.
2 Probably a rotifer, a small aquatic organism that employs a wheel-like ring of cilia to draw in a stream of water and food.

Now you must know that all the things under the water talk: only not such a language as ours; but such as horses, and dogs, and cows, and birds talk to each other; and Tom soon learned to understand them and talk to them; so that he might have had very pleasant company if he had only been a good boy. But I am sorry to say, he was too like some other little boys, very fond of hunting and tormenting creatures for mere sport. Some people say that boys cannot help it; that it is nature, and only a proof that we are all originally descended from beasts of prey. But whether it is nature or not, little boys can help it, and must help it. For if they have naughty, low, mischievous tricks in their nature, as monkeys have, that is no reason why they should give way to those tricks like monkeys, who know no better. And therefore they must not torment dumb creatures; for if they do, a certain old lady who is coming will surely give them exactly what they deserve.

But Tom did not know that; and he pecked and howked[1] the poor water things about sadly, till they were all afraid of him, and got out of his way, or crept into their shells; so he had no one to speak to or play with.

The water-fairies, of course, were very sorry to see him so unhappy, and longed to take him, and tell him how naughty he was, and teach him to be good, and to play and romp with him too: but they had been forbidden to do that. Tom had to learn his lesson for himself by sound and sharp experience, as many another foolish person has to do, though there may be many a kind heart yearning over them all the while, and longing to teach them what they can only teach themselves.

At last one day he found a caddis, and wanted it to peep out of its house: but its house-door was shut. He had never seen a caddis with a house-door before: so what must he do, the meddlesome little fellow, but pull it open, to see what the poor lady was doing inside. What a shame! How should you like to have any one breaking your bedroom-door in, to see how you looked when you were in bed? So Tom broke to pieces the door, which was the prettiest little grating of silk, stuck all over with shining bits of crystal; and when he looked in, the caddis poked out her head, and it had turned into just the shape of a bird's. But when Tom spoke to her she could not answer; for her mouth and face were

---

1   Howk or holk: "To hollow out by digging; to excavate; to dig out or up" (*OED*).

tight tied up in a new nightcap of neat pink skin. However, if she didn't answer, all the other caddises did; for they held up their hands and shrieked like the cats in Struwelpeter:[1] "Oh, you nasty horrid boy; there you are at it again! And she had just laid herself up for a fortnight's sleep, and then she would have come out with such beautiful wings, and flown about, and laid such lots of eggs: and now you have broken her door, and she can't mend it because her mouth is tied up for a fortnight, and she will die. Who sent you here to worry us out of our lives?"

So Tom swam away. He was very much ashamed of himself, and felt all the naughtier; as little boys do when they have done wrong, and won't say so.

Then he came to a pool full of little trout, and began tormenting them, and trying to catch them: but they slipt through his fingers, and jumped clean out of water in their fright. But as

---

1 *Der Struwwelpeter* (1845), written and illustrated by Heinrich Hoffman (1809-94), is a collection of morbid cautionary tales for young children. Translated into English in 1848, it includes "The Dreadful Story of Harriet and the Matches," in which Harriet is warned by her mother and her cats not to play with matches. Ignoring the parental and feline advice, she lights the matches and "Then how the pussy-cats did mew–/ What else, poor pussies, could they do?/ They screamed for help, 'twas all in vain!/ So then they said: "We'll scream again;/ Make haste, make haste, me-ow, me-o,/ She'll burn to death; we told her so." And, indeed, she burns to death.

Tom chased them, he came close to a great dark hover[1] under an alder root, and out floushed[2] a huge old brown trout ten times as big as he was, and ran right against him, and knocked all the breath out of his body; and I don't know which was the more frightened of the two.

Then he went on sulky and lonely, as he deserved to be; and under a bank he saw a very ugly dirty creature sitting, about half as big as himself; which had six legs, and a big stomach, and a most ridiculous head with two great eyes and a face just like a donkey's.

"Oh," said Tom, "you are an ugly fellow to be sure!" and he began making faces at him; and put his nose close to him, and halloed at him, like a very rude boy.

When, hey presto! all the thing's donkey-face came off in a moment, and out popped a long arm with a pair of pincers at the end of it, and caught Tom by the nose. It did not hurt him much; but it held him quite tight.

"Yah, ah! Oh, let me go!" cried Tom.

"Then let me go," said the creature. "I want to be quiet. I want to split."

Tom promised to let him alone, and he let go. "Why do you want to split?" said Tom.

"Because my brothers and sisters have all split, and turned into beautiful creatures with wings; and I want to split too. Don't speak to me. I am sure I shall split. I will split!"

Tom stood still, and watched him. And he swelled himself, and puffed, and stretched himself out stiff, and at last—crack, puff, bang—he opened all down his back, and then up to the top of his head.

And out of his inside came the most slender, elegant, soft creature, as soft and smooth as Tom: but very pale and weak, like a little child who has been ill a long time in a dark room. It moved its legs very feebly; and looked about it half ashamed, like a girl when she goes for the first time into a ball-room; and then it began walking slowly up a grass stem to the top of the water.

Tom was so astonished that he never said a word: but he stared with all his eyes. And he went up to the top of the water too, and peeped out to see what would happen.

And as the creature sat in the warm bright sun, a wonderful

---

1 "Any overhanging stone or bank under which a fish can hide" (*OED*).
2 "To come with a heavy splash" (*OED*).

change came over it. It grew strong and firm; the most lovely colours began to show on its body, blue and yellow and black, spots and bars and rings; out of its back rose four great wings of bright brown gauze; and its eyes grew so large that they filled all its head, and shone like ten thousand diamonds.

"Oh, you beautiful creature!" said Tom; and he put out his hand to catch it.

But the thing whirred up into the air, and hung poised on its wings a moment, and then settled down again by Tom quite fearless.

"No!" it said, "you cannot catch me. I am a dragon-fly now, the king of all the flies; and I shall dance in the sunshine, and hawk over the river, and catch gnats, and have a beautiful wife like myself. I know what I shall do. Hurrah!" And he flew away into the air, and began catching gnats.

"Oh! come back, come back," cried Tom, "you beautiful creature. I have no one to play with, and I am so lonely here. If you will but come back I will never try to catch you."

"I don't care whether you do or not," said the dragon fly; "for you can't. But when I have had my dinner, and looked a little about this pretty place, I will come back; and have a little chat about all I have seen in my travels. Why, what a huge tree this is! and what huge leaves on it!"

It was only a big dock: but you know the dragon-fly had never seen any but little water-trees; starwort, and milfoil, and water-crowfoot, and such like; so it did look very big to him. Besides, he was very short-sighted, as all dragon-flies are; and never could see a yard before his nose; any more than a great many other folks, who are not half as handsome as he.

The dragon-fly did come back, and chatted away with Tom. He was a little conceited about his fine colours and his large wings; but you know, he had been a poor dirty ugly creature all his life before; so there were great excuses for him. He was very fond of talking about all the wonderful things he saw in the trees and the meadows; and Tom liked to listen to him, for he had forgotten all about them. So in a little while they became great friends.

And I am very glad to say, that Tom learnt such a lesson that day, that he did not torment creatures for a long time after. And then the caddises grew quite tame, and used to tell him strange stories about the way they built their houses, and changed their skins, and turned at last into winged flies; till Tom began to long to change his skin, and have wings like them some day.

And the trout and he made it up (for trout very soon forget, if they have been frightened and hurt). So Tom used to play with them at hare and hounds, and great fun they had; and he used to try to leap out of the water, head over heels, as they did before a shower came on: but somehow he never could manage it. He liked most, though, to see them rising at the flies, as they sailed round and round under the shadow of the great oak, where the beetles fell flop into the water, and the green cater-pillars let themselves down from the boughs by silk ropes for no reason at all; and then changed their foolish minds for no reason at all either; and hauled themselves up again into the tree, rolling up the rope in a ball between their paws; which is a very clever rope-dancer's trick, and neither Blondin[1] nor

---

1   The stage-name of Jean François Gravelet (1824-97), French tight-rope walker and acrobat. In 1861 Blondin first appeared in London, at the Crystal Palace, performing somersaults on stilts along a rope stretched across the central transept, 170 feet from the ground. Two years earlier he crossed Niagara Falls on a tight-rope.

Leotard[1] could do it: but why they should take so much trouble about it no one can tell; for they cannot get their living, as Blondin and Leotard do, by trying to break their necks on a string.

And very often Tom caught them just as they touched the water; and caught the alder flies, and the caperers, and the cock-tailed duns and spinners, yellow, and brown, and claret, and grey, and gave them to his friends the trout. Perhaps he was not quite kind to the flies; but one must do a good turn to one's friends when one can.

And at last he gave up catching even the flies; for he made acquaintance with one by accident, and found him a very merry little fellow. And this was the way it happened; and it is all quite true.

He was basking at the top of the water one hot day in July, catching duns and feeding the trout, when he saw a new sort, a dark grey little fellow with a brown head. He was a very little fellow indeed: but he made the most of himself, as people ought to do. He cocked up his head, and he cocked up his wings, and he cocked up his tail, and he cocked up the two whisks at his tail-end, and, in short, he looked the cockiest little man of all little men. And so he proved to be; for instead of getting away, he hopped upon Tom's finger, and sat there as bold as nine tailors;[2] and he cried out in the tiniest, shrillest, squeakiest little voice you ever heard.

"Much obliged to you, indeed; but I don't want it yet."

"Want what?" said Tom, quite taken aback by his impudence.

"Your leg, which you are kind enough to hold out for me to sit on. I must just go and see after my wife for a few minutes. Dear me! what a troublesome business a family is!" (though the idle little rogue did nothing at all, but left his poor wife to lay all the eggs by herself.) "When I come back, I shall be glad of it, if you'll be so good as to keep it sticking out just so;" and off he flew.

Tom thought him a very cool sort of personage; and still more so, when in five minutes he came back, and said—"Ah, you were tired waiting? Well, your other leg will do as well."

And he popped himself down on Tom's knee, and began chatting away in his squeaking voice.

---

1 Jules Léotard (1838-70) invented the flying trapeze act. He first performed in London at the Alhambra in May 1861. His name is now associated with the tights he designed for his act.

2 "It takes nine tailors to make a man" is an old proverb.

"So you live under the water? It's a low place. I lived there for some time; and was very shabby and dirty. But I didn't choose that that should last. So I turned respectable, and came up to the top, and put on this grey suit. It's a very business-like suit, you think, don't you?"

"Very neat and quiet indeed," said Tom.

"Yes, one must be quiet, and neat, and respectable, and all that sort of thing for a little, when one becomes a family man. But I'm tired of it, that's the truth. I've done quite enough business, I consider, in the last week, to last me my life. So I shall put on a ball-dress, and go out and be a smart man, and see the gay world, and have a dance or two. Why shouldn't one be jolly if one can?"

"And what will become of your wife?"

"Oh! she is a very plain stupid creature, and that's the truth; and thinks about nothing but eggs. If she chooses to come, why she may; and if not, why I go without her;—and here I go."

And, as he spoke, he turned quite pale, and then quite white.

"Why, you're ill!" said Tom. But he did not answer.

"You're dead," said Tom, looking at him as he stood on his knee as white as a ghost.

"No I ain't!" answered a little squeaking voice over his head. "This is me up here, in my ball-dress: and that's my skin. Ha, ha! you could not do such a trick as that!"

And no more Tom could, nor Houdin,[1] nor Robin,[2] nor Frikell,[3] nor all the conjurors in the world. For the little rogue had jumped clean out of his own skin, and left it standing on Tom's knee, eyes, wings, legs, tails, exactly as if it had been alive.

"Ha, ha!" he said, and he jerked and skipped up and down, never stopping an instant, just as if he had St. Vitus's dance. "Ain't I a pretty fellow now?"

And so he was; for his body was white, and his tail orange, and his eyes all the colours of a peacock's tail. And what was the oddest of all, the whisks at the end of his tail had grown five times as long as they were before.

"Ah!" said he, "now I will see the gay world. My living won't

---

1 Jean Eugène Robert Houdin (1805-71), French conjuror and magician. Harry Houdini named himself after him.

2 Henrik Joseph Donckel (1811-74), a Dutch illusionist. He performed in England during 1850-53, including a command performance at Windsor Castle, and in 1861 at the Egyptian Hall, London.

3 Wiljalba Frikell (1816-1903), a conjuror noted for performing on a simple stage devoid of elaborate apparatus.

cost me much, for I have no mouth, you see, and no inside; so I can never be hungry, nor have the stomach-ache neither."

No more he had. He had grown as dry and hard and empty as a quill, as such silly shallow-hearted fellows deserve to grow.

But, instead of being ashamed of his emptiness, he was quite proud of it, as a good many fine gentlemen are, and began flirting and flipping up and down, and singing—

> "My wife shall dance, and I shall sing,
>   So merrily pass the day;
> For I hold it one of the wisest things,
>   To drive dull care away."

And he danced up and down for three days and three nights, till he grew so tired, that he tumbled into the water, and floated down. But what became of him Tom never knew, and he himself never minded; for Tom heard him singing to the last, as he floated down—

> "To drive dull care away-ay-ay!"

And if he did not care, why nobody else cared either.

But one day Tom had a new adventure. He was sitting on a water-lily leaf, he and his friend the dragon-fly, watching the gnats dance. The dragon-fly had eaten as many as he wanted, and was sitting quite still and sleepy, for it was very hot and bright. The gnats (who did not care the least for their poor brothers' death), danced a foot over his head quite happily, and a large black fly settled within an inch of his nose, and began washing his own face and combing his hair with his paws: but the dragon-fly never stirred, and kept on chatting to Tom about the times when he lived under the water.

Suddenly, Tom heard the strangest noise up the stream; cooing, and grunting, and whining, and squeaking, as if you had put into a bag two stock-doves, nine mice, three guinea-pigs, and a blind puppy, and left them there to settle themselves and make music.

He looked up the water, and there he saw a sight as strange as the noise; a great ball rolling over and over down the stream, seeming one moment of soft brown fur, and the next of shining glass: and yet it was not a ball; for sometimes it broke up and streamed away in pieces, and then it joined again; and all the while the noise came out of it louder and louder.

Tom asked the dragon-fly what it could be: but, of course, with his short sight, he could not even see it, though it was not ten yards away. So he took the neatest little header into the water, and started off to see for himself; and, when he came near, the ball turned out to be four or five beautiful creatures, many times larger than Tom, who were swimming about, and rolling, and diving, and twisting, and wrestling, and cuddling, and kissing, and biting, and scratching, in the most charming fashion that ever was seen. And if you don't believe me, you may go to the Zoological Gardens (for I am afraid that you won't see it nearer, unless, perhaps, you get up at five in the morning, and go down to Cordery's Moor, and watch by the great withy pollard[1] which hangs over the backwater, where the otters breed sometimes), and then say, if otters at play in the water are not the merriest, lithest, gracefullest creatures you ever saw.

But, when the biggest of them saw Tom, she darted out from the rest, and cried in the water-language sharply enough, "Quick, children, here is something to eat, indeed!" and came at poor Tom, showing such a wicked pair of eyes, and such a set of sharp teeth in a grinning mouth, that Tom, who had thought her very handsome, said to himself, Handsome is that handsome does, and slipt in between the water-lily roots as fast as he could, and then turned round and made faces at her.

"Come out," said the wicked old otter, "or it will be worse for you."

But Tom looked at her from between two thick roots, and shook them with all his might, making horrible faces all the while, just as he used to grin through the railings at the old women, when he lived before. It was not quite well-bred, no doubt; but you know, Tom had not finished his education yet.

"Come away, children," said the otter in disgust, "it is not worth eating, after all. It is only a nasty eft, which nothing eats, not even those vulgar pike in the pond."

"I am not an eft!" said Tom; "efts have tails."

"You are an eft," said the otter, very positively; "I see your two hands quite plain, and I know you have a tail."

"I tell you I have not," said Tom. Look here!" and he turned his pretty little self quite round; and, sure enough, he had no more tail than you.

---

1 A tree with a density of new growth after its top branches have been cut back.

The otter might have got out of it by saying that Tom was a frog: but, like a great many other people, when she had once said a thing, she stood to it, right or wrong; so she answered:

"I say you are an eft, and therefore you are, and not fit food for gentlefolk like me and my children. You may stay there till the salmon eat you (she knew the salmon would not, but she wanted to frighten poor Tom). Ha! ha! they will eat you, and we will eat them;" and the otter laughed such a wicked cruel laugh—as you may hear them do sometimes; and the first time that you hear it you will probably think it is bogies.[1]

"What are salmon?" asked Tom.

"Fish, you eft, great fish, nice fish to eat. They are the lords of the fish, and we are the lords of the salmon;" and she laughed again. "We hunt them up and down the pools, and drive them up into a corner, the silly things; they are so proud, and bully the little trout, and the minnows, till they see us coming, and then they are so meek all at once; and we catch them, but we disdain to eat them all; we just bite out their soft throats and suck their sweet juice—Oh, so good!"—(and she licked her wicked lips)—"and then throw them away, and go and catch another. They are coming soon, children, coming soon; I can smell the rain coming up off the sea, and then hurrah for a fresh,[2] and salmon, and plenty of eating all day long."

And the otter grew so proud that she turned head over heels twice, and then stood upright half out of the water, grinning like a Cheshire cat.[3]

"And where do they come from?" asked Tom, who kept himself very close, for he was considerably frightened.

"Out of the sea, eft, the great wide sea, where they might stay and be safe if they liked. But out of the sea the silly things come, into the great river down below, and we come up to watch for them; and when they go down again we go down and follow them. And there we fish for the bass and the pollock,[4] and have

---

1 Evil spirits or hobgoblins.
2 "A rush of water or increase of the stream in a river; a freshet, flood" (*OED*).
3 Although the phrase dates back to the eighteenth century, its appearance here in 1863 may have inspired Lewis Carroll's creation of the Cheshire Cat in *Alice's Adventures in Wonderland* (1865). The character does not appear in Carroll's earlier version of his story, *Alice's Adventures Under Ground*, completed in 1863. A copy of Kingsley's book was in Carroll's library and it appears likely that he had read it.
4 A sea-fish, related to the cod, comprising several species used for food in Europe.

jolly days along the shore, and toss and roll in the breakers, and sleep snug in the warm dry crags. Ah, that is a merry life too, children, if it were not for those horrid men."

"What are men?" asked Tom; but somehow he seemed to know before he asked.

"Two-legged things, eft: and, now I come to look at you, they are actually something like you, if you had not a tail" (she was determined that Tom should have a tail), "only a great deal bigger, worse luck for us; and they catch the fish with hooks and lines, which get into our feet sometimes, and set pots along the rocks to catch lobsters. They speared my poor dear husband as he went out to find something for me to eat. I was laid up among the crags then, and we were very low in the world, for the sea was so rough that no fish would come in shore. But they speared him, poor fellow, and I saw them carrying him away upon a pole. Ah, he lost his life for your sakes, my children, poor dear obedient creature that he was."

And the otter grew so sentimental (for otters can be very sentimental when they choose, like a good many people who are both cruel and greedy, and no good to anybody at all) that she sailed solemnly away down the burn, and Tom saw her no more for that time. And lucky it was for her that she did so; for no sooner was she gone, than down the bank came seven little rough terrier dogs, snuffing and yapping, and grubbing and splashing, in full cry after the otter. Tom hid among the water-lilies till they were gone; for he could not guess that they were the water-fairies come to help him.

But he could not help thinking of what the otter had said about the great river and the broad sea. And, as he thought, he longed to go and see them. He could not tell why; but the more he thought, the more he grew discontented with the narrow little stream in which he lived, and all his companions there; and wanted to get out into the wide wide world,[1] and enjoy all the wonderful sights of which he was sure it was full.

And once he set off to go down the stream. But the stream was very low; and when he came to the shallows he could not keep under water, for there was no water left to keep under. So the sun burnt his back and made him sick; and he went back again and lay quiet in the pool for a whole week more.

And then, on the evening of a very hot day, he saw a sight.

He had been very stupid all day, and so had the trout; for they would not move an inch to take a fly, though there were thousands on the water, but lay dozing at the bottom under the shade of the stones; and Tom lay dozing too, and was glad to cuddle their smooth cool sides, for the water was quite warm and unpleasant.

But toward evening it grew suddenly dark, and Tom looked up and saw a blanket of black clouds lying right across the valley above his head, resting on the crags right and left. He felt not quite frightened, but very still; for everything was still. There was not a whisper of wind, nor a chirp of a bird to be heard; and next a few great drops of rain fell plop into the water, and one hit Tom on the nose and made him pop his head down quickly enough.

And then the thunder roared, and the lightning flashed, and leapt across Vendale and back again, from cloud to cloud, and

---

1 Possibly an allusion to the children's story *The Wide Wide World* (1850) by the American author Susan Bogert Warner. In Chapter VIII Kingsley refers to the story as "the Narrow Narrow World" because he found such tales confining in their sentimentality.

cliff to cliff, till the very rocks in the stream seemed to shake; and Tom looked up at it through the water, and thought it the finest thing he ever saw in his life.

But out of the water he dared not put his head; for the rain came down by bucketsful, and the hail hammered like shot on the stream, and churned it into foam; and soon the stream rose, and rushed down, higher and higher, and fouler and fouler, full of beetles, and sticks, and straws, and worms, and addle-eggs,[1] and wood-lice, and leeches, and odds and ends, and omnium-gatherums,[2] and this, that, and the other, enough to fill nine museums.

Tom could hardly stand against the stream, and hid behind a rock. But the trout did not; for out they rushed from among the stones, and began gobbling the beetles and leeches in the most greedy and quarrelsome way, and swimming about with great worms hanging out of their mouths, tugging and kicking to get them away from each other.

And now, by the flashes of the lightning, Tom saw a new sight—all the bottom of the stream alive with great eels, turning and twisting along, all down stream and away. They had been hiding for weeks past in the cracks of the rocks, and in burrows in the mud; and Tom had hardly ever seen them, except now and then at night: but now they were all out, and went hurrying past him so fiercely and wildly that he was quite frightened. And as they hurried past he could hear them say to each other, "We must run, we must run. What a jolly thunderstorm! Down to the sea, down to the sea!"

And then the otter came by with all her brood, twining and sweeping along as fast as the eels themselves; and she spied Tom as she came by, and said:—

"Now is your time, eft, if you want to see the world. Come along, children, never mind those nasty eels: we shall breakfast on salmon to-morrow. Down to the sea, down to the sea!"

Then came a flash brighter than all the rest, and by the light of it—in the thousandth part of a second they were gone again—but he had seen them, he was certain of it—Three beautiful little white girls, with their arms twined round each other's necks, floating down the torrent, as they sang, "Down to the sea, down to the sea!"

---

1 Rotten eggs.
2 A hodgepodge of items.

"Oh stay! Wait for me!" cried Tom; but they were gone: yet he could hear their voices clear and sweet through the roar of thunder and water and wind, singing as they died away, "Down to the sea!"

"Down to the sea?" said Tom; "everything is going to the sea, and I will go too. Good-bye, trout." But the trout were so busy gobbling worms that they never turned to answer him; so that Tom was spared the pain of bidding them farewell.

And now, down the rushing stream, guided by the bright flashes of the storm; past tall birch-fringed rocks, which shone out one moment as clear as day, and the next were dark as night; past dark hovers under swirling banks, from which great trout rushed out on Tom, thinking him to be good to eat, and turned back sulkily, for the fairies sent them home again with a tremendous scolding, for daring to meddle with a water-baby; on through narrow strids[1] and roaring cataracts, where Tom was deafened and blinded for a moment by the rushing waters; along deep reaches, where the white water-lilies tossed and flapped beneath the wind and hail; past sleeping villages; under dark bridge-arches, and away and away to the sea. And Tom could not stop, and did not care to stop; he would see the great world below, and the salmon, and the breakers, and the wide, wide sea.

And when the daylight came, Tom found himself out in the salmon river.

And what sort of a river was it? Was it like an Irish stream, winding through the brown bogs, where the wild ducks squatter up[2] from among the white water-lilies, and the curlews flit to and fro, crying "Tullie-wheep, mind your sheep;" and Dennis[3] tells you strange stories of the Peishtamore, the great bogy-snake which lies in the black peat pools, among the old pine stems, and puts his head out at night to snap at the cattle as they come down to drink?—But you must not believe all that Dennis tells you, mind; for if you ask him,

"Is there a salmon here, do you think, Dennis?"

"Is it salmon, thin, your honour manes? Salmon? Cartloads it

---

1 Gorges or chasms.

2 "To make one's way among water or wet with much splashing or flapping" (*OED*).

3 An Irish gillie, a parody of the knowledgeable local resident who assists the fisherman. Kingsley later contrasts Dennis with the wise Scottish "gilly:" "He will tell you no fibs, my little man; for he is a Scotchman, and fears God, and not the priest."

is of thim, thin, an' ridgmens, shouldthering ache other out of water, av' ye'd but the luck to see thim."

Then you fish the pool all over, and never get a rise.

"But there can't be a salmon here, Dennis! and, if you'll but think, if one had come up last tide, he'd be gone to the higher pools by now."

"Shure thin, and your honour's the thrue fisherman, and understands it all like a book. Why, ye spake as if ye'd known the wather a thousand years! As I said, how could there be a fish here at all, just now?"

"But you said just now they were shouldering each other out of water?"

And then Dennis will look up at you with his handsome, sly, soft, sleepy, good-natured, untrustable, Irish grey eye, and answer with the prettiest smile:

"Shure, and didn't I think your honour would like a pleasant answer?"

So you must not trust Dennis, because he is in the habit of giving pleasant answers: but, instead of being angry with him, you must remember that he is a poor Paddy, and knows no better; so you must just burst out laughing; and then he will burst out laughing too, and slave for you, and trot about after you, and show you good sport if he can—for he is an affectionate fellow, and as fond of sport as you are—and if he can't, tell you fibs instead, a hundred an hour; and wonder all the while why poor ould Ireland does not prosper like England and Scotland, and some other places, where folk have taken up a ridiculous fancy that honesty is the best policy.

Or was it like a Welsh salmon river, which is remarkable chiefly (at least, till this last year) for containing no salmon, as they have been all poached out by the enlightened peasantry, to prevent the Cythrawl Sassenach[1] (which means you, my little dear, your kith and kin, and signifies much the same as the Chinese Fan Quei)[2] from coming bothering into Wales, with good tackle, and ready money, and civilization, and common honesty, and other like things of which the Cymry[3] stand in no need whatsoever?

Or was it such a salmon stream as I trust you will see among

1 A mixture of Welsh and Gaelic meaning "hostile English" (Alderson, p. 213).
2 The Chinese phrase means "foreign devils" (Alderson, p. 213).
3 The Welsh thought of themselves as Cymry (meaning "fellow country-men") or Britons.

the Hampshire water-meadows before your hairs are grey, under the wise new fishing laws?—when Winchester apprentices shall covenant, as they did three hundred years ago, not to be made to eat salmon more than three days a week; and fresh-run fish[1] shall be as plentiful under Salisbury spire as they are in Hollyhole at Christchurch; in the good time coming, when folks shall see that, of all Heaven's gifts of food, the one to be protected most carefully is that worthy gentleman salmon, who is generous enough to go down to the sea weighing five ounces, and to come back next year weighing five pounds, without having cost the soil or the state one farthing?

Or was it like a Scotch stream, such as Arthur Clough drew in his "Bothie:"—

"Where over a ledge of granite
Into a granite bason the amber torrent descended ...
Beautiful there for the colour derived from green rocks
    under;
Beautiful most of all, where beads of foam uprising
Mingle their clouds of white with the delicate hue of the
    stillness ...
Cliff over cliff for its sides, with rowan and pendant birch
    boughs." ...[2]

Ah, my little man, when you are a big man, and fish such a stream as that, you will hardly care, I think, whether she be roaring down in full spate, like coffee covered with scald cream, while the fish are swirling at your fly as an oar-blade swirls in a boat-race, or flashing up the cataract like silver arrows, out of the fiercest of the foam; or whether the fall be dwindled to a single thread, and the shingle below be as white and dusty as a turnpike road, while the salmon huddle together in one dark cloud in the clear amber pool, sleeping away their time till the rain creeps back again off the sea. You will not care much, if you have eyes and brains; for you will lay down your rod contentedly, and drink in at your eyes the beauty of that glorious place; and listen to the water-ouzel[3] piping on the stones, and watch the yellow roes come down to drink, and look

---

1 Salmon that have recently traveled up from the sea.
2 A rearrangement of lines from sections III and V of *The Bothie of Tober-na-vuolich (1848)* by Arthur Hugh Clough (1819-61). Kingsley has his peculiar spelling of "basons" for Clough's "basins."
3 A bird that dives into swift-moving streams and feeds along the bottom.

up at you with their great soft trustful eyes, as much as to say, "You could not have the heart to shoot at us?" And then, if you have sense, you will turn and talk to the great giant of a gilly who lies basking on the stone beside you. He will tell you no fibs, my little man; for he is a Scotchman, and fears God, and not the priest; and, as you talk with him, you will be surprised more and more at his knowledge, his sense, his humour, his courtesy; and you will find out—unless you have found it out before—that a man may learn from his Bible to be a more thorough gentleman than if he had been brought up in all the drawing-rooms in London.

No. It was none of these, the salmon stream at Harthover. It was such a stream as you see in dear old Bewick;[1] Bewick, who was born and bred upon them. A full hundred yards broad it was, sliding on from broad pool to broad shallow, and broad shallow to broad pool, over great fields of shingle, under oak and ash coverts, past low cliffs of sandstone, past green meadows, and fair parks, and a great house of grey stone, and brown moors above, and here and there against the sky the smoking chimney of a colliery. You must look at Bewick to see just what it was like, for he has drawn it a hundred times with the care and the love of a true north countryman; and, even if you do not care about the salmon river, you ought, like all good boys, to know your Bewick.

At least, so old Sir John used to say, and very sensibly he put it too, as he was wont to do—

"If they want to describe a finished young gentleman in France, I hear, they say of him, 'Il sait son Rabelais.'[2] But if I want to describe one in England, I say, 'He knows his Bewick.' And I think that is the higher compliment."

But Tom thought nothing about what the river was like. All his fancy was, to get down to the wide wide sea.

And after a while he came to a place where the river spread out into broad still shallow reaches, so wide that little Tom, as he put his head out of the water, could hardly see across.

And there he stopped. He got a little frightened. "This must be the sea," he thought. "What a wide place it is. If I go on into it I shall surely lose my way, or some strange thing will bite me. I will stop here and look out for the otter, or the eels, or some one to tell me where I shall go."

---

1 Thomas Bewick (1753-1828), a pioneering wood engraver whose delicate renderings of animal life appear in his *A General History of Quadrupeds* (1790) and the two-volume *History of British Birds* (1797, 1804).
2 "He knows his Rabelais."

So he went back a little way, and crept into a crack of the rock, just where the river opened out into the wide shallows, and watched for some one to tell him his way: but the otter and the eels were gone on miles and miles down the stream.

There he waited, and slept too, for he was quite tired with his night's journey; and, when he woke, the stream was clearing to a beautiful amber hue, though it was still very high. And after a while he saw a sight which made him jump up; for he knew in a moment it was one of the things which he had come to look for.

Such a fish! ten times as big as the biggest trout, and a hundred times as big as Tom, sculling up the stream past him, as easily as Tom had sculled down.

Such a fish! shining silver from head to tail, and here and there a crimson dot; with a grand hooked nose, and grand curling lip, and a grand bright eye, looking round him as proudly as a king, and surveying the water right and left as if it all belonged to him. Surely he must be the salmon, the king of all the fish.

Tom was so frightened that he longed to creep into a hole; but he need not have been; for salmon are all true gentlemen, and, like true gentlemen, they look noble and proud enough, and yet, like true gentlemen, they never harm or quarrel with any one, but go about their own business, and leave rude fellows to themselves.

The salmon looked him full in the face, and then went on without minding him, with a swish or two of his tail which made the stream boil again. And in a few minutes came another, and then four or five, and so on; and all passed Tom, rushing and plunging up the cataract with strong strokes of their silver tails, now and then leaping clean out of water and up over a rock, shining gloriously for a moment in the bright sun; while Tom was so delighted that he could have watched them all day long.

And at last one came up bigger than all the rest; but he came slowly, and stopped, and looked back, and seemed very anxious and busy. And Tom saw that he was helping another salmon, an especially handsome one, who had not a single spot upon it, but was clothed in pure silver from nose to tail.

"My dear," said the great fish to his companion, "you really look dreadfully tired, and you must not over-exert yourself at first. Do rest yourself behind this rock;" and he shoved her gently with his nose, to the rock where Tom sat.

You must know that this was the salmon's wife. For salmon, like other true gentlemen, always choose their lady, and love her, and are true to her, and take care of her, and work for her, and fight for her, as every true gentleman ought; and are not like vulgar chub and roach and pike, who have no high feelings, and take no care of their wives.

Then he saw Tom, and looked at him very fiercely one moment, as if he was going to bite him.

"What do you want here?" he said, very fiercely.

"Oh, don't hurt me!" cried Tom. "I only want to look at you; you are so handsome."

"Ah?" said the salmon, very stately but very civilly. "I really beg your pardon; I see what you are, my little dear. I have met one or two creatures like you before, and found them very agreeable and well-behaved. Indeed, one of them showed me a great kindness lately, which I hope to be able to repay. I hope we shall not be in your way here. As soon as this lady is rested, we shall proceed on our journey.

What a well-bred old salmon he was!

"So you have seen things like me before?" asked Tom.

"Several times, my dear. Indeed, it was only last night that one at the river's mouth came and warned me and my wife of some new stake-nets which had got into the stream, I cannot tell how, since last winter, and showed us the way round them, in the most charmingly obliging way."

"So there are babies in the sea?" cried Tom, and clapped his little hands. "Then I shall have some one to play with there? How delightful!"

"Were there no babies up this stream?" asked the lady salmon.

"No; and I grew so lonely. I thought I saw three last night: but they were gone in an instant, down to the sea. So I went too; for I had nothing to play with but caddises and dragon-flies and trout."

"Ugh!" cried the lady, "what low company!"

"My dear, if he has been in low company, he has certainly not learnt their low manners," said the salmon.

"No, indeed, poor little dear: but how sad for him to live among such people as caddises, who have actually six legs, the nasty things; and dragon-flies, too! why they are not even good to eat; for I tried them once, and they are all hard and empty; and, as for trout, every one knows what they are." Whereon she curled up her lip, and looked dreadfully scornful, while her husband curled up his too, till he looked as proud as Alcibiades.[1]

---

1 Athenian statesman and general (c.450–404 BCE), and friend and follower of Socrates.

"Why do you dislike the trout so?" asked Tom.

"My dear, we do not even mention them, if we can help it; for I am sorry to say they are relations of ours who do us no credit. A great many years ago they were just like us: but they were so lazy, and cowardly, and greedy, that instead of going down to the sea every year to see the world and grow strong and fat, they chose to stay and poke about in the little streams and eat worms and grubs: and they are very properly punished for it; for they have grown ugly and brown and spotted and small; and are actually so degraded in their tastes, that they will eat our children."

"And then they pretend to scrape acquaintance with us again," said the lady. Why, I have actually known one of them propose to a lady salmon, the little impudent little creature."

"I should hope," said the gentleman, "that there are very few ladies of our race who would degrade themselves by listening to such a creature for an instant. If I saw such a thing happen, I should consider it my duty to put them both to death upon the spot." So the old salmon said, like an old blue-blooded hidalgo of Spain: and what is more, he would have done it too. For you must know, no enemies are so bitter against each other as those who are of the same race; and a salmon looks on a trout, as some great folks look on some little folks, as something just too much like himself to be tolerated.

CHAPTER IV.

"Sweet is the lore which Nature brings;
Our meddling intellect
Mis-shapes the beauteous forms of things
We murder to dissect.

Enough of science and of art:
Close up these barren leaves;
Come forth, and bring with you a heart
That watches and receives."[1]

> Wordsworth.

the salmon went up, after Tom had warned them of the wicked old otter; and Tom went down, but slowly and cautiously, coasting along the shore. He was many days about it, for it was many miles down to the sea; and perhaps he would never have found his way, if the fairies had not guided him, without his seeing their fair faces, or feeling their gentle hands.

And, as he went, he had a very strange adventure. It was a clear still September night, and the moon shone so brightly down through the water, that he could not sleep, though he shut his eyes as tight as possible. So at last he came up to the top, and sat upon a little point of rock, and looked up at the broad yellow moon, and wondered what she was, and thought that she looked at him. And he watched the moonlight on the rippling river, and the black heads of the firs, and the silver-frosted lawns, and listened to the owl's hoot, and the snipe's bleat, and the fox's bark, and the otter's laugh; and smelt the soft perfume of the birches, and the wafts of heather honey off the grouse-moor far above; and felt very happy, though he could not well tell

---

1 From "The Tables Turned" (ll. 25-32) from *The Lyrical Ballads* (1798).

why. You, of course, would have been very cold sitting there on a September night, without the least bit of clothes on your wet back; but Tom was a water-baby, and therefore felt cold no more than a fish.

Suddenly, he saw a beautiful sight. A bright red light moved along the river side, and threw down into the water a long tap-root of flame. Tom, curious little rogue that he was, must needs go and see what it was; so he swam to the shore, and met the light as it stopped over a shallow run at the edge of a low rock.

And there, underneath the light, lay five or six great salmon, looking up at the flame with their great goggle eyes, and wagging their tails, as if they were very much pleased at it.

Tom came to the top, to look at this wonderful light nearer, and made a splash.

And he heard a voice say:—

"There was a fish rose."

He did not know what the words meant: but he seemed to know the sound of them, and to know the voice which spoke them; and he saw on the bank three great two-legged creatures, one of whom held the light, flaring and sputtering, and another a long pole. And he knew that they were men, and was frightened, and crept into a hole in the rock, from which he could see what went on.

The man with the torch bent down over the water, and looked earnestly in; and then he said:

"Tak that muckle[1] fellow, lad; he's ower fifteen punds; and haud your hand steady."

Tom felt that there was some danger coming, and longed to warn the foolish salmon, who kept staring up at the light as if he was bewitched. But, before he could make up his mind, down came the pole through the water; there was a fearful splash and struggle, and Tom saw that the poor salmon was speared right through, and was lifted out of the water.

And then, from behind, there sprung on these three men three other men; and there were shouts, and blows, and words which Tom recollected to have heard before; and he shuddered and turned sick at them now, for he felt somehow that they were strange, and ugly, and wrong, and horrible. And it all began to come back to him. They were men; and they were fighting; savage, desperate, up-and-down fighting, such as Tom had seen too many times before.

---

1   Muckle, or mickle, northern English and Scottish dialect for large in size or bulk.

And he stopped his little ears, and longed to swim away; and was very glad that he was a water-baby, and had nothing to do any more with horrid dirty men, with foul clothes on their backs, and foul words on their lips: but he dared not stir out of his hole; while the rock shook over his head with the trampling and struggling of the keepers and the poachers.

All of a sudden there was a tremendous splash, and a frightful flash, and a hissing, and all was still.

For into the water, close to Tom, fell one of the men; he who held the light in his hand. Into the swift river he sank, and rolled over and over in the current. Tom heard the men above run along, seemingly looking for him: but he drifted down into the deep hole below, and there lay quite still, and they could not find him.

Tom waited a long time, till all was quiet; and then he peeped out, and saw the man lying. At last he screwed up his courage, and swam down to him. "Perhaps," he thought, "the water has made him fall asleep, as it did me."

Then he went nearer. He grew more and more curious, he could not tell why. He must go and look at him. He would go very quietly, of course; so he swam round and round him, closer and closer; and, as he did not stir, at last he came quite close and looked him in the face.

The moon shone so bright that Tom could see every feature; and, as he saw, he recollected, bit by bit. It was his old master, Grimes.

Tom turned tail, and swam away as fast as he could.

"Oh dear me!" he thought, "now he will turn into a water-baby. What a nasty troublesome one he will be! And perhaps he will find me out, and beat me again."

So he went up the river again a little way, and lay there the rest of the night under an alder[1] root; but, when morning came, he longed to go down again to the big pool, and see whether Mr. Grimes had turned into a water-baby yet.

So he went very carefully, peeping round all the rocks, and hiding under all the roots. Mr. Grimes lay there still; he had not turned into a water-baby. In the afternoon Tom went back again. He could not rest till he had found out what had become of Mr. Grimes. But this time Mr. Grimes was gone; and Tom made up his mind that he was turned into a water-baby.

---

1 A tree (*Alnus glutinosa*) related to the birch, common in wet areas.

He might have made himself easy, poor little man; Mr. Grimes did not turn into a water-baby, or anything like one at all. But he did not make himself easy; and a long time he was fearful lest he should meet Grimes suddenly in some deep pool. He could not know that the fairies had carried him away, and put him, where they put everything which falls into the water, exactly where it ought to be. But, do you know, what had happened to Mr. Grimes had such an effect on him, that he never poached salmon any more. And it is quite certain that, when a man becomes a confirmed poacher, the only way to cure him is to put him under water for twenty-four hours, like Grimes. So, when you grow to be a big man, do you behave as all honest fellows should; and never touch a fish or a head of game which belongs to another man without his express leave; and then people will call you a gentleman, and treat you like one; and perhaps give you good sport: instead of hitting you into the river, or calling you a poaching snob.[1]

Then Tom went on down, for he was afraid of staying near Grimes; and as he went, all the vale looked sad. The red and yellow leaves showered down into the river; the flies and beetles were all dead and gone; the chill autumn fog lay low upon the hills, and sometimes spread itself so thickly on the river, that he could not see his way. But he felt his way instead, following the flow of the stream, day after day, past great bridges, past boats and barges, past the great town, with its wharfs, and mills, and tall smoking chimneys, and ships which rode at anchor in the stream; and now and then he ran against their hawsers, and wondered what they were, and peeped out, and saw the sailors lounging on board, smoking their pipes; and ducked under again, for he was terribly afraid of being caught by man and turned into a chimney-sweep once more. He did not know that the fairies were close to him always, shutting the sailors' eyes lest they should see him, and turning him aside from millraces, and sewer-mouths, and all foul and dangerous things. Poor little fellow, it was a dreary journey for him; and more than once he longed to be back in Vendale, playing with the trout in the bright summer sun. But it could not be. What has been once can never come over again. And people can be little babies, even water-babies, only once in their lives.

Besides, people who make up their minds to go and see the world, as Tom did, must needs find it a weary journey. Lucky for

---

1 A lower-class fellow.

them if they do not lose heart and stop half way, instead of going on bravely to the end as Tom did. For then they will remain neither boys nor men, neither fish, flesh, nor good red herring; having learnt a great deal too much, and yet not enough; and sown their wild oats, without having the advantage of reaping them.

But Tom was always a brave, determined little English bull-dog, who never knew when he was beaten; and on and on he held, till he saw a long way off the red buoy through the fog. And then he found, to his surprise, the stream turned round, and running up inland.

It was the tide, of course: but Tom knew nothing of the tide. He only knew that in a minute more the water, which had been fresh, turned salt all round him. And then there came a change over him. He felt as strong, and light, and fresh, as if his veins had run champagne; and gave, he did not know why, three skips out of the water, a yard high, and head over heels, just as the salmon do when they first touch the noble rich salt water, which, as some wise men[1] tell us, is the mother of all living things.

He did not care now for the tide being against him. The red buoy was in sight, dancing in the open sea; and to the buoy he would go, and to it he went. He passed great shoals of bass and mullet, leaping and rushing in after the shrimps, but he never heeded them, or they him; and once he passed a great black shining seal, who was coming in after the mullet. The seal put his head and shoulders out of water, and stared at him, looking exactly like a fat old greasy negro with a grey pate. And Tom, instead of being frightened, said, "How d'ye do, sir; what a beautiful place the sea is!" And the old seal, instead of trying to bite him, looked at him with his soft sleepy winking eyes, and said, "Good tide to you, my little man; are you looking for your brothers and sisters? I passed them all at play outside."

"Oh, then," said Tom, "I shall have playfellows at last!" and he swam on to the buoy, and got upon it (for he was quite out of breath) and sat there, and looked round for water-babies: but there were none to be seen.

The sea-breeze came in freshly with the tide, and blew the fog away; and the little waves danced for joy around the buoy, and the

---

1 Thales of Miletus (62?-546? BCE) was the first philosopher to question the originating substance of all natural matter. Aristotle, in his *Metaphysics*, says that Thales believed water to be the primary substance and source of the natural world.

old buoy danced with them. The shadows of the clouds ran races over the bright blue bay, and yet never caught each other up; and the breakers plunged merrily upon the wide white sands, and jumped up over the rocks, to see what the green fields inside were like, and tumbled down and broke themselves all to pieces, and never minded it a bit, but mended themselves and jumped up again. And the terns hovered over Tom like huge white dragon-flies with black heads, and the gulls laughed like girls at play, and the sea-pies,[1] with their red bills and legs, flew to and fro from shore to shore, and whistled sweet and wild. And Tom looked and looked, and listened; and he would have been very happy, if he could only have seen the water-babies. Then, when the tide turned, he left the buoy, and swam round and round in search of them: but in vain. Sometimes he thought he heard them laughing: but it was only the laughter of the ripples. And sometimes he thought he saw them at the bottom: but it was only white and pink shells. And once he was sure he had found one, for he saw two bright eyes peeping out of the sand. So he dived down, and began scraping the sand away, and cried, "Don't hide; I do want some one to play with so much!" And out jumped a great turbot,[2] with his ugly eyes and mouth all awry, and flopped away along the bottom, knocking poor Tom over. And he sat down at the bottom of the sea, and cried salt tears from sheer disappointment.

To have come all this way, and faced so many dangers, and yet to find no water-babies! How hard! Well, it did seem hard: but people, even little babies, cannot have all they want without waiting for it, and working for it too, my little man, as you will find out some day.

And Tom sat upon the buoy long days, long weeks, looking out to sea, and wondering when the water-babies would come back; and yet they never came.

Then he began to ask all the strange things which came in out of the sea if they had seen any; and some said "Yes," and some said nothing at all.

He asked the bass and the pollock; but they were so greedy after the shrimps that they did not care to answer him a word.

Then there came in a whole fleet of purple sea-snails, floating along each on a sponge full of foam, and Tom said, "Where do

---

1 Oyster-catchers, wading birds that feed on oysters, clams, and limpets.
2 European flatfish with a knobby upper skin, prized as food.

you come from, you pretty creatures? and have you seen the water-babies?"

And the sea-snails answered, "Whence we come we know not; and whither we are going, who can tell? We float out our little life in the mid-ocean, with the warm sunshine above our heads, and the warm gulf stream below; and that is enough for us. Yes, perhaps we have seen the water-babies. We have seen many strange things as we sailed along." And they floated away, the happy stupid things, and all went ashore upon the sands.

Then there came in a great lazy sunfish, as big as a fat pig cut in half; and he seemed to have been cut in half too, and squeezed in a clothes-press till he was flat; but to all his big body and big fins he had only a little rabbit's mouth, no bigger than Tom's; and, when Tom questioned him, he answered in a little squeaky, feeble voice:

"I'm sure I don't know, I've lost my way. I meant to go to the Chesapeake, and I'm afraid I've got wrong, somehow. Dear me! it was all by following that pleasant warm water. I'm sure I've lost my way."

And, when Tom asked him again, he could only answer, "I've lost my way. Don't talk to me, I want to think."

But, like a good many other people, the more he tried to think the less he could think; and Tom saw him blundering about all day, till the coast-guardsmen saw his big fin above the water, and rowed out, and struck a boat-hook into him, and took him away. They took him up to the town and showed him for a penny a head, and made a good day's work of it. But of course Tom did not know that.

Then there came by a shoal of porpoises, rolling as they went—papas, and mammas, and little children— and all quite smooth and shiny, because the fairies French-polish[1] them every morning; and they sighed so softly as they came by, that Tom took courage to speak to them: but all they answered was, "Hush, hush, hush;" for that was all they had learnt to say.

And then there came a shoal of basking sharks, some of them as long as a boat, and Tom was frightened at them. But they were very lazy, good-natured fellows, not greedy tyrants, like white sharks and blue sharks and ground sharks and hammer-heads, who eat men, or saw-fish and threshers[2] and ice-sharks, who hunt

---

1 A solution of resin or gum resin in alcohol, used in polishing furniture and woodwork.

2 "A sea-fox or fox-shark, *Alopias vulpes*; so called from the very long upper division of the tail, with which it lashes an enemy. Also called thresher" (*OED*).

the poor old whales. They came and rubbed their great sides against the buoy, and lay basking in the sun with their backfins out of water; and winked at Tom: but he never could get them to speak. They had eaten so many herrings that they were quite stupid; and Tom was glad when a collier brig came by, and frightened them all away; for they did smell most horribly, certainly, and he had to hold his nose tight as long as they were there.

And then there came by a beautiful creature,[1] like a ribbon of pure silver with a sharp head and very long teeth: but it seemed very sick and sad. Sometimes it rolled helpless on its side; and then it dashed away glittering like white fire; and then it lay sick again and motionless.

"Where do you come from?" asked Tom. "And why are you so sick and sad?"

"I come from the warm Carolinas, and the sand-banks fringed with pines; where the great owl-rays leap and flap, like giant bats, upon the tide. But I wandered north and north, upon the treacherous warm gulf stream, till I met with the cold icebergs, afloat in the mid-ocean. So I got tangled among the icebergs, and chilled with their frozen breath. But the water-babies helped me from among them, and set me free again. And now I am mending every day; but I am very sick and sad; and perhaps I shall never get home again to play with the owl-rays any more."

"Oh!" cried Tom. "And you have seen water-babies? Have you seen any near here?"

"Yes; they helped me again last night, or I should have been eaten by a great black porpoise."

How vexatious! The water-babies close to him, and yet he could not find one.

And then he left the buoy, and used to go along the sands and round the rocks, and come out in the night—like the forsaken Merman in Mr. Arnold's beautiful, beautiful poem,[2] which you must learn by heart some day—and sit upon a point of rock, among the shining sea-weeds, in the low October tides, and cry and call for the water-babies: but he never heard a voice call in return. And, at last, with his fretting and crying, he grew quite lean and thin.

But one day among the rocks he found a playfellow. It was not a water-baby, alas! but it was a lobster; and a very distinguished

---

1 Possibly an eel.
2 "The Forsaken Merman," first published in *The Strayed Reveller and Other Poems* (1849). See Appendix B.

lobster he was; for he had live barnacles on his claws, which is a great mark of distinction in lobsterdom, and no more to be bought for money than a good conscience or the Victoria Cross.[1]

Tom had never seen a lobster before; and he was mightily taken with this one; for he thought him the most curious, odd, ridiculous creature he had ever seen; and there he was not far wrong; for all the ingenious men, and all the scientific men, and all the fanciful men, in the world, with all the old German bogy-painters[2] into the bargain, could never invent, if all their wits were boiled into one, anything so curious, and so ridiculous, as a lobster.

He had one claw knobbed and the other jagged; and Tom delighted in watching him hold on to the sea-weed with his knobbed claw, while he cut up salads with his jagged one, and then put them into his mouth, after smelling at them, like a monkey. And always the little barnacles threw out their casting nets and swept the water, and came in for their share of whatever there was for dinner.

But Tom was most astonished to see how he fired himself off—

1 A British military and naval decoration given for bravery in battle.
2 Probably such painters as Matthias Grünewald (c.1475-1528), whose real name was Mathis Gothardt Neithardt, and Hans Baldung, called Grien (1484-1545), German painters noted for their grotesque representations of death, witches, and demons.

snap! like the leap-frogs[1] which you make out of a goose's breast-bone. Certainly he took the most wonderful shots, and backwards, too. For, if he wanted to go into a narrow crack ten yards off, what do you think he did? If he had gone in head foremost, of course he could not have turned round. So he used to turn his tail to it, and lay his long horns, which carry his sixth sense in their tips (and nobody knows what that sixth sense is), straight down his back to guide him, and twist his eyes back till they almost came out of their sockets, and then make ready, present, fire, snap!—and away he went, pop into the hole; and peeped out and twiddled his whiskers, as much as to say, "You couldn't do that."

Tom asked him about water-babies. "Yes," he said. He had seen them often. But he did not think much of them. They were meddlesome little creatures, that went about helping fish and shells which got into scrapes. Well, for his part, he should be ashamed to be helped by little soft creatures that had not even a shell on their backs. He had lived quite long enough in the world to take care of himself.

He was a conceited fellow, the old lobster, and not very civil to Tom; and you will hear how he had to alter his mind before he was done, as conceited people generally have. But he was so funny, and Tom so lonely, that he could not quarrel with him; and they used to sit in holes in the rocks, and chat for hours.

And about this time there happened to Tom a very strange and important adventure—so important, indeed, that he was very near never finding the water-babies at all; and I am sure you would have been sorry for that.

I hope that you have not forgotten the little white lady all this while. At least, here she comes, looking like a clean white good little darling, as she always was, and always will be. For it befel in the pleasant short December days, when the wind always blows from the south-west, till Old Father Christmas comes and spreads the great white table-cloth, ready for little boys and girls to give the birds their Christmas dinner of crumbs—it befel (to go on) in the pleasant December days, that Sir John was so busy hunting that nobody at home could get a word out of him. Four days a week he hunted, and very good sport he had; and the other

---

1 "A home-made toy where a string was attached to the two ends of a goose's breast-bone and then wound tightly on a peg to form a spring. This could be secured with a piece of wax which would 'give' suddenly, causing the apparatus to leap in the air" (Alderson, 215).

two he went to the bench and the board of guardians,[1] and very good justice he did; and, when he got home in time, he dined at five; for he hated this absurd new fashion of dining at eight in the hunting season, which forces a man to make interest with the footman for cold beef and beer as soon as he comes in, and so spoil his appetite, and then sleep in an arm-chair in his bed-room, all stiff and tired, for two or three hours before he can get his dinner like a gentleman. And do you be like Sir John, my dear little man, when you are your own master; and, if you want either to read hard or ride hard, stick to the good old Cambridge hours of breakfast at eight and dinner at five, by which you may get two days' work out of one. But, of course, if you find a fox at three in the afternoon and run him till dark, and leave off twenty miles from home, why you must wait for your dinner till you can get it, as better men than you have done. Only see that, if you go hungry, your horse does not: but give him his warm gruel and beer, and take him gently home, remembering that good horses don't grow on the hedge like blackberries.

It befel (to go on a second time) that Sir John, hunting all day and dining at five, fell asleep every evening, and snored so terribly that all the windows in Harthover shook, and the soot fell down the chimneys. Whereon My Lady, being no more able to get conversation out of him than a song out of a dead nightingale, determined to go off and leave him, and the doctor, and Captain Swinger the agent, to snore in concert every evening to their hearts' content. So she started for the sea-side with all the children, in order to put herself and them into condition by mild applications of iodine.[2] She might as well have stayed at home and used Parry's liquid horse-blister,[3] for there was plenty of it in the stables; and then she would have saved her money, and saved the chance, also, of making all the children ill instead of well (as hundreds are made), by taking them to some nasty smelling undrained lodging, and then wondering how they caught scar-latina and diphtheria: but people won't be wise enough to under-

---

1 As a magistrate, he would be responsible for enforcing the law, and as a board member of the Guardians of the Poor, he would oversee the conditions in the work house.

2 Kingsley is reflecting the current spurious notion that the iodine in the sea air and water promoted good health.

3 A patent medicine which, when applied to a horse with sore muscles or tendons, causes its skin to blister and exude fluid, thereby purging the source of the pain.

stand that till they are all dead of bad smells, and then it will be too late: besides, you see, Sir John did certainly snore very loud.

But where she went to nobody must know, for fear young ladies should begin to fancy that there are water-babies there; and so hunt and howk after them (besides raising the price of lodgings), and keep them in aquariums, as the ladies at Pompeii (as you may see by the paintings) used to keep Cupids in cages. But nobody ever heard that they starved the Cupids, or let them die of dirt and neglect, as English young ladies do by the poor sea-beasts. So nobody must know where My Lady went. Letting water-babies die is as bad as taking singing-birds' eggs; for, though there are thousands, ay, millions, of both of them in the world, yet there is not one too many.

Now it befel that, on the very shore, and over the very rocks, where Tom was sitting with his friend the lobster, there walked one day the little white lady, Ellie herself, and with her a very wise man indeed— Professor Ptthmllnsprts.

His mother was a Dutchwoman, and therefore he was born at Curaçao (of course you have learnt your geography, and therefore know why); and his father a Pole, and therefore he was brought up at Petropaulowski (of course you have learnt your modern politics, and therefore know why): but for all that he was as thorough an Englishman as ever coveted his neighbour's goods. And his name, as I said, was Professor Ptthmllnsprts, which is a very ancient and noble Polish name.

He was, as I said, a very great naturalist, and chief professor of Necrobioneopalæonthydrochthonanthropopithekology in the new university which the king of the Cannibal Islands[1] had founded; and, being a member of the Acclimatisation Society, he had come here to collect all the nasty things which he could find on the coast of England, and turn them loose round the Cannibal Islands, because they had not nasty things enough there to eat what they left.

But he was a very worthy kind good-natured little old gentleman; and very fond of children (for he was not the least a cannibal himself); and very good to all the world as long as it was good to him. Only one fault he had, which cock-robins have likewise, as you may see if you will look out of the nursery window—that, when any one else found a curious worm, he would hop round

---

1   A broadside ballad published and sold in 1858 begins: "Oh, have you heard the news of late, / About a mighty king so great? / If you have not, 'tis in my pate— / The King of the Cannibal Islands."

them, and peck them, and set up his tail, and bristle up his feathers, just as a cock-robin would; and declare that he found the worm first; and that it was his worm: and, if not, that then it was not a worm at all.

He had met Sir John at Scarborough, or Fleetwood, or somewhere or other (if you don't care where, nobody else does), and had made acquaintance with him, and become very fond of his children. Now, Sir John knew nothing about sea-cockyolybirds,[1] and cared less, provided the fishmonger sent him good fish for dinner; and My Lady knew as little: but she thought it proper that the children should know something. For in the stupid old times, you must understand, children were taught to know one thing, and to know it well: but in these enlightened new times they are taught to know a little about everything, and to know it all ill; which is a great deal pleasanter and easier, and therefore quite right.

So Ellie and he were walking on the rocks, and he was showing her about one in ten thousand of all the beautiful and curious things which are to be seen there. But little Ellie was not satisfied with them at all. She liked much better to play with live children, or even with dolls, which she could pretend were alive; and at last she said honestly, "I don't care about all these things, because they can't play with me, or talk to me. If there were little children now in the water, as there used to be, and I could see them, I should like that."

"Children in the water, you strange little duck?" said the professor.

"Yes," said Ellie. "I know there used to be children in the water, and mermaids too, and mermen. I saw them all in a picture at home, of a beautiful lady sailing in a car drawn by dolphins, and babies flying round her, and one sitting in her lap; and the mermaids swimming and playing, and the mermen trumpeting on conch-shells; and it is called 'The Triumph of Galatea;'[2] and there is a burning mountain in the picture behind. It hangs on the great staircase, and I have looked at it ever since I was a baby, and dreamt about it a hundred times; and it is so beautiful, that it must be true."

---

1   "Cockyolly bird, a nursery or pet expression for 'dear little bird'" (*OED*). Similar to dicky-bird.

2   Possibly a conflated memory of Raphael's fresco (c.1514) and Jacques Stella's oil painting of the same name (1650). The latter is more pastoral and charming in tone than Raphael's but neither work reflects all of the details in Kingsley's description.

Ah, you dear little Ellie, fresh out of heaven! when will people understand that one of the deepest and wisest speeches which can come out of a human mouth is that—"It is so beautiful that it must be true."

Not till they give up believing that Mr. John Locke[1] (good man and honest though he was) was the wisest man that ever lived on earth: and recollect that a wiser man than he lived long before him; and that his name was Plato the son of Ariston.[2]

But the professor was not in the least of that opinion. He held very strange theories about a good many things. He had even got up once at the British Association, and declared that apes had hippopotamus majors in their brains just as men have.[3] Which was a shocking thing to say; for, if it were so, what would become of the faith, hope, and charity of immortal millions? You may think that there are other more important differences between you and an ape, such as being able to speak, and make machines, and know right from wrong, and say your prayers, and other little matters of that kind: but that is a child's fancy, my dear. Nothing is to be depended on but the great hippopotamus test. If you have a hippopotamus major in your brain, you are no ape, though you had four hands, no feet, and were more apish than the apes of all aperies. But, if a hippopotamus major is ever discovered in one single ape's brain, nothing will save your great-great-great-great-great-great-great-great-great-great-great-greater-greatest-grand-mother from having been an ape too. No, my dear little man; always remember that the one true, certain, final, and all-impor-

---

1   English philosopher (1632-1704) who argued for the use of reason to search after truth instead of simply relying upon faith or accepting the opinion of authorities.

2   Greek philosopher (427-347 BC), whose concept of a world of pure form and ideas that are unchangeable and perfect resonated with Kingsley's Christian theology.

3   The British Association for the Advancement of Science, founded in 1831, became a lively forum for discussions of Darwinism. Richard Owen, who became president of the Association in 1858, described the anatomy of a newly discovered species of ape, the gorilla, which had only been discovered in 1847. Owen's anti-materialist and anti-Darwin-ian views led him to state that gorillas and other apes lack certain parts of the brain that humans have, specifically a structure known as the hip-pocampus minor. Thus the uniqueness of human brains, Owen argued, showed that humans could not possibly have evolved from apes. Kingsley's satire reflects his own belief in the essential tenets of Darwinism, which he accommodated to his Christian theology.

tant difference between you and an ape is, that you have a hip-popotamus major in your brain, and it has none; and that, there-fore, to discover one in its brain will be a very wrong and dan-gerous thing, at which every one will be very much shocked, as we may suppose they were at the professor. —Though really, after all, it don't much matter: because—as Lord Dundreary[1] and others would put it—nobody but men have hippopotamuses in their brains; so, if a hippopotamus was discovered in an ape's brain, why it would not be one, you know, but something else.

But the professor had gone, I am sorry to say, even further than that; for he had read at the British Association at Mel-bourne, Australia, in the year 1999, a paper, which assured every one who found himself the better or wiser for the news, that there were not, never had been, and could not be, any rational or half-rational beings except men, anywhere, anywhen, or anyhow; that nymphs, satyrs, fauns, inui, dwarfs, trolls, elves, gnomes, fairies, brownies, nixes, wilis, kobolds, leprechaunes, cluricaunes, ban-shees, will-o'-the-wisps, follets, lutins, magots, goblins, afrits, marids, jinns, ghouls, peris, deevs,[2] angels, archangels, imps,

---

1 A foolish character in Tom Taylor's play *Our American Cousin* (1858). In 1861 Kingsley wrote a satire of the debate between Owen and Huxley in "Speech of Lord Dundreary in Section D, on Friday Last, On the Great Hippocampus Question," in which he has Dundreary confuse "hip-pocampus" with "hippopotamus."

2 Spirit creatures from a range of cultures, including: fauns: in Roman mythology, rural deities who are part man and part goat; inui: possibly inua, spirits in Innuit folklore who may be malevolent or benevolent. But it is not clear if Kingsley was familiar with that mythology; nixes (nixie): "In German folklore: a water sprite or nymph having a human torso and the tail of a fish, and able to take on a variety of physical appearances in order to pass unnoticed among humans"(*OED*); wilis: in Austrian mythology, ghostly females who dance around young men until they are dead; kobolds: mischievous household spirits in German folk-lore; cluricaunes: "In Irish mythology, an elf having the appearance of a tiny old man" (*OED*); banshees: in Celtic folklore, female spirits believed to foretell a death in the family by wailing; will-o'-the-wisps: phosphorescent light that hovers over swampy ground; follets: feux follets are spirits who live in bogs and who try to lure travelers into ponds to drown them; lutins: elves in French folklore; magots: possibly the barbary ape, tailless monkeys (*Macaca sylvana*) of Gibraltar and northern Africa; afrits: in Muslim mythology, evil demons or monsters; marids: wicked genii in Muslim mythology; jinns: "In Muslim demonology, an order of spirits lower than the angels, said to have the

bogies, or worse, were nothing at all, and pure bosh and wind. And he had to get up very early in the morning to prove that, and to eat his breakfast overnight: but he did it, at least to his own satisfaction. Whereon a certain great divine, and a very clever divine was he, called him a regular Sadducee; and probably he was quite right. Whereon the professor, in return, called him a regular Pharisee;[1] and probably he was quite right too. But they did not quarrel in the least; for, when men are men of the world, hard words run off them like water off a duck's back. So the professor and the divine met at dinner that evening, and sat together on the sofa afterwards for an hour, and talked over the state of female labour on the antarctic continent (for nobody talks shop after his claret), and each vowed that the other was the best company he ever met in his life. What an advantage it is to be men of the world!

From all which you may guess that the professor was not the least of little Ellie's opinion. So he gave her a succinct compendium of his famous paper at the British Association, in a form suited for the youthful mind. But, as we have gone over his arguments against water-babies once already, which is once too often, we will not repeat them here.

Now little Ellie was, I suppose, a stupid little girl; for, instead of being convinced by Professor Ptthmllnsprts' arguments, she only asked the same question over again.

"But why are there not water-babies?"

I trust and hope that it was because the professor trod at that moment on the edge of a very sharp mussel, and hurt one of his

---

power of appearing in human and animal forms, and to exercise supernatural influence over men" (*OED*); peris: "In Persian Mythology, one of a race of superhuman beings, originally represented as of evil or malevolent character, but subsequently as good genii, fairies, or angels, endowed with grace and beauty" (*OED*); deevs: in Persian mythology, cruel demon fairies who constantly war against the Peries.

1 The Pharisees and the Sadducees were two opposing Jewish sects. The former accepted both the oral and the written forms of Mosaic law, whereas the latter rejected the oral tradition. Kingsley here appears to allude to the famous argument between Samuel Wilberforce, bishop of Oxford, and Thomas Henry Huxley at a meeting of the British Association in Oxford on 30 June 1860. Wilberforce bitterly derided Darwin's *Origin of Species* and Huxley vigorously defended it. At this legendary encounter, Huxley is reported to have said that "he was not ashamed to have a monkey for his ancestor; but he would be ashamed to be connected with a man who used great gifts to obscure the truth."

corns sadly, that he answered quite sharply, forgetting that he was a scientific man, and therefore ought to have known that he couldn't know; and that he was a logician, and therefore ought to have known that he could not prove an universal negative—I say, I trust and hope it was because the mussel hurt his corn, that the professor answered quite sharply—

"Because there ain't."

Which was not even good English, my dear little boy; for, as you must know from Aunt Agitate's Arguments, the professor ought to have said, if he was so angry as to say anything of the kind—Because there are not: or are none: or are none of them; or (if he had been reading Aunt Agitate too), because they do not exist.

And he groped with his net under the weeds so violently, that, as it befel, he caught poor little Tom.

He felt the net very heavy; and lifted it out quickly, with Tom all entangled in the meshes.

"Dear me!" he cried. "What a large pink Holothurian; with hands, too! It must be connected with Synapta."[1]

And he took him out.

"It has actually eyes!" he cried. "Why, it must be a Cephalo-pod![2] This is most extraordinary!"

"No, I ain't!" cried Tom, as loud as he could; for he did not like to be called bad names.

"It is a water-baby!" cried Ellie; and of course it was.

"Water-fiddlesticks, my dear!" said the professor; and he turned away sharply.

There was no denying it. It was a water-baby: and he had said a moment ago that there were none. What was he to do?

He would have liked, of course, to have taken Tom home in a bucket. He would not have put him in spirits. Of course not. He would have kept him alive, and petted him (for he was a very kind old gentleman), and written a book about him, and given him two long names, of which the first would have said a little about Tom, and the second all about himself; for of course he would have called him Hydrotecnon Ptthmllnsprtsianum, or some other long name like that; for they are forced to call everything by long names now, because they have used up all the short ones, ever since they took to making nine species out of one. But—what would all the learned men say to him after his speech at the

---

1 Sea-cucumbers.
2 A mollusk, such as an octopus or cuttlefish.

British Association? And what would Ellie say, after what he had just told her?

There was a wise old heathen[1] once, who said, "Maxima debetur pueris reverentia"—The greatest reverence is due to children; that is, that grown people should never say or do anything wrong before children, lest they should set them a bad example.—Cousin Cramchild says it means, "The greatest respectfulness is expected from little boys." But he was raised in a country[2] where little boys are not expected to be respectful, because all of them are as good as the President:—Well, every one knows his own concerns best; so perhaps they are. But poor Cousin Cramchild, to do him justice, not being of that opinion, and having a moral mission, and being no scholar to speak of, and hard up for an authority—why, it was a very great temptation for him. But some people, and I am afraid the professor was one of them, interpret that in a more strange, curious, one-sided, left-handed, topsy-turvy, inside-out, behind-before fashion, than even Cousin Cramchild; for they make it mean, that you must show your respect for children, by never confessing yourself in the wrong to them, even if you know that you are so, lest they should lose confidence in their elders.

Now, if the professor had said to Ellie, "Yes, my darling, it is a water-baby, and a very wonderful thing it is; and it shows how little I know of the wonders of nature, in spite of forty years' honest labour. I was just telling you that there could be no such creatures: and, behold! here is one come to confound my conceit, and show me that Nature can do, and has done, beyond all that man's poor fancy can imagine. So, let us thank the Maker, and Inspirer, and Lord of Nature for all His wonderful and glorious works, and try and find out something about this one:"—I think that, if the professor had said that, little Ellie would have believed him more firmly, and respected him more deeply, and loved him better, than ever she had done before. But he was of a different opinion. He hesitated a moment. He longed to keep Tom, and yet he half wished he never had caught him; and, at last, he quite longed to get rid of him. So he turned away, and poked Tom with his finger, for want of anything better to do; and said carelessly, "My dear little maid, you must have dreamt of water-babies last night, your head is so full of them."

---

1 Juvenal (c. 60-140 AD), a Roman satirist who, in his 14th Satire, shows how parents teach their children greed by their example.
2 One of several barbs that Kingsley directs at American society.

Now Tom had been in the most horrible and unspeakable fright all the while; and had kept as quiet as he could, though he was called a Holothurian and a Cephalopod; for it was fixed in his little head that if a man with clothes on caught him, he might put clothes on him too, and make a dirty black chimney-sweep of him again. But when the professor poked him, it was more than he could bear; and, between fright and rage, he turned to bay as valiantly as a mouse in a corner, and bit the professor's finger till it bled.

"Oh! ah! yah!" cried he; and glad of an excuse to be rid of Tom, dropped him on to the sea-weed, and thence he dived into the water, and was gone in a moment.

"But it was a water-baby, and I heard it speak!" cried Ellie. "Ah, it is gone!" And she jumped down off the rock to try and catch Tom before he slipt into the sea.

Too late! and what was worse, as she sprang down, she slipped, and fell some six feet, with her head on a sharp rock, and lay quite still.

The professor picked her up, and tried to waken her, and called to her, and cried over her, for he loved her very much: but she would not waken at all. So he took her up in his arms, and carried her to her governess, and they all went home; and little Ellie was put to bed, and lay there quite still; only now and then she woke up, and called out about the water-baby: but no one knew what she meant, and the professor did not tell, for he was ashamed to tell.

And, after a week, one moonlight night, the fairies came flying in at the window, and brought her such a pretty pair of wings, that she could not help putting them on; and she flew with them out of the window, and over the land, and over the sea, and up through the clouds, and nobody heard or saw anything of her for a very long while.

And this is why they say that no one has ever yet seen a water-baby. For my part, I believe that the naturalists get dozens of them when they are out dredging: but they say nothing about them, and throw them overboard again, for fear of spoiling their theories. But, you see the professor was found out, as every one is in due time. A very terrible old fairy found the professor out; she felt his bumps, and cast his nativity, and took the lunars[1] of him carefully inside and out; and so she knew what he would do as well as if she had seen it in a print book, as they say in the dear old west country; and he did it; and so he was found out beforehand, as everybody always is; and the old fairy will find out the naturalists some day, and put them in the Times; and then on whose side will the laugh be?

So the old fairy took him in hand very severely there and then. But she says she is always most severe with the best people, because there is most chance of curing them, and therefore they are the patients who pay her best; for she has to work on the same salary as the Emperor of China's physicians (it is a pity that all do not), no cure, no pay.

So she took the poor professor in hand: and because he was not content with things as they are, she filled his head with things as they are not, to try if he would like them better; and because he did not choose to believe in a water-baby when he saw it, she made him believe in worse things than water-babies—in unicorns, firedrakes, manticoras, basilisks, amphisboenas, griffins,

---

1   She determines his mental abilities by reading the bumps on his skull
    (the pseudo-science of phrenology), determines his future on the basis
    of his birthday, and examines him closely ("lunar: *colloq.* A look," *OED*).

phoeoenixes, rocs, orcs, dogheaded men, three-headed dogs, three-bodied geryons,[1] and other pleasant creatures, which folks think never existed yet, and which folks hope never will exist, though they know nothing about the matter, and never will; and these creatures so upset, terrified, flustered, aggravated, confused, astounded, horrified, and totally flabbergasted the poor professor, that the doctors said that he was out of his wits for three months; and, perhaps, they were right, as they are now and then.

So all the doctors in the county were called in, to make a report on his case; and of course every one of them flatly contradicted the other: else what use is there in being men of science? But at last the majority agreed on a report, in the true medical language, one half bad Latin, the other half worse Greek, and the rest what might have been English, if they had only learnt to write it. And this is the beginning thereof—

"The subanhypaposupernal anastomoses of peritomic diacellurite in the encephalo digital region of the distinguished individual of whose symptomatic phænomena we had the melancholy honour (subsequently to a preliminary diagnostic inspection) of making an inspectorial diagnosis, presenting the interexclusively quadrilateral and antinomian diathesis known as Bumpsterhausen's blue follicles, we proceeded"—

But what they proceeded to do my lady never knew; for she was so frightened at the long words that she ran for her life, and locked herself into her bedroom, for fear of being squashed by the words and strangled by the sentence. A boa constrictor, she said, was bad company enough: but what was a boa constrictor made of paving-stones?

"It was quite shocking! What can they think is the matter with him?" said she to the old nurse.

---

1   In this list of monsters: firedrake: in German mythology, a fire-breathing dragon; manticore: a monster with the head of a man, the body of a lion, and the tail of a scorpion; basilisk: a fabulous serpent whose breath and look was deadly; amphisbæna: a serpent with a head at each end; griffin: a creature with the head and wings of an eagle and the body of a lion; phoenix: in Egyptian mythology, a bird that lives for 500 years, then consumes itself by fire, and later resurrects from its ashes; roc: an enormous mythical bird of prey possessed of great strength; orc: a fierce sea creature; geryon: in Greek mythology, a monster with three bodies killed by Hercules.

"That his wit's just addled; may be wi' unbelief and heathenry," quoth she.

"Then why can't they say so?"

And the heaven, and the sea, and the rocks, and the vales reechoed—"Why indeed?" But the doctors never heard them.

So she made Sir John write to the Times to command the Chancellor of the Exchequer[1] for the time being to put a tax on long words;—

A light tax on words over three syllables, which are necessary evils, like rats: but like them, must be kept down judiciously.

A heavy tax on words over four syllables, as heterodoxy, spontaneity, spiritualism, spuriosity, &c.

And on words over five syllables (of which I hope no one will wish to see any examples), a totally prohibitory tax.

And a similar prohibitory tax on words derived from three or more languages at once; words derived from two languages having become so common, that there was no more hope of rooting out them than of rooting out peth-winds.[2]

The Chancellor of the Exchequer, being a scholar and a man of sense, jumped at the notion; for he saw in it the one and only plan for abolishing Schedule D: but when he brought in his bill, most of the Irish members, and (I am sorry to say) some of the Scotch likewise, opposed it most strongly, on the ground that in a free country no man was bound either to understand himself or to let others understand him. So the bill fell through on the first reading; and the Chancellor, being a philosopher, comforted himself with the thought, that it was not the first time that a woman had hit off a grand idea, and the men turned up their stupid noses thereat.

Now the doctors had it all their own way; and to work they went in earnest, and they gave the poor Professor divers and sundry medicines, as prescribed by the ancients and moderns, from Hippocrates[3] to Feuchtersleben,[4] as below, viz.:—

---

1 Finance minister of the British Government.
2 A twining plant, such as the convolvulus.
3 Greek physician (460?-377? BCE) who established the scientific foundation of medicine.
4 Ernst, Freiherr Von Feuchtersleben (1806-49), an Austrian poet, philosopher and physician, whose seminal study of psychiatry, *The Principles of Medical Psychology* (1845), introduced the terms "psychosis" and "psychiatric" in their modern sense.

1.Hellebore,[1] to wit—

Hellebore of Æta.
Hellebore of Galatia.
Hellebore of Sicily.
And all other Hellebores, after the method of the Helleboriz-ing Helleborists of the Helleboric era. But that would not do. Bumpsterhausen's blue follicles would not stir an inch out of his encephalo digital region.

2. Trying to find out what was the matter with him; after the method of—

Hippocrates.
Aretæus.[2]
Celsus.[3]
Coelius Aurelianus,[4]
And Galen:[5] but they found that a great deal too much trouble, as most people have since; and so had recourse to—

3. Borage.[6]
Cauteries.[7]
Boring a hole in his head to let out fumes, which (says Gor-donius[8]) "will, without doubt, do much good." But it didn't. Bezoar stone.[9]

---

1 "A name given by the ancients to certain plants having poisonous and medicinal properties, and esp. reputed as specifics for mental disease" (*OED*).
2 Aretaeus the Cappadocian, a 2nd century physician who was among the first to study such diseases as asthma, diabetes, diphtheria.
3 Aulus Cornelius Celsus (25 BC-50 AD), a Roman physician whose eight volumes of *De Medicina* described a broad range of illnesses.
4 Caelius Aurelianus, a Roman physician (c.150 AD), the author of a book about chronic and acute diseases.
5 Claudius Galen (c.130-201), a Greek physician whose seminal study of anatomy and physiology provided the foundation for medical science through the Renaissance. He believed that the best doctor was also a philosopher.
6 A bristly European herb having blue, star-shaped flowers.
7 A cautery is an instrument used to burn away abnormal tissue.
8 Bernardus Gordonius (c. 1300 AD), physician, teacher of medicine at the University of Montpellier in France and author of *Lilium Medicinae* (1303).
9 An antidote to poison made from an indigestible mass of matter found in the stomach of animals, especially ruminants.

Diamargaritum.[1]

A ram's brain boiled in spice.

Oil of wormwood.

Water of Nile.

Capers.

Good wine (but there was none to be got).

The water of a smith's forge.

Hops.

Ambergris.[2]

Mandrake pillows.

Dormouse fat.

Hares' ears.

Starvation.

Camphor.

Salts and Senna.[3]

Musk.

Opium.

Strait-waistcoats.

Bullyings.

Bumpings.

Blisterings.

Bleedings.

Bucketings with cold water.

Knockings down.

Kneeling on his chest till they broke it in, &c. &c.; after the mediæval or monkish method: but that would not do. Bumpsterhausen's blue follicles stuck there still. Then—

4. Coaxing.

Kissing.

Champagne and turtle.

Red herrings and soda water.

Good advice.

Gardening.

Croquet.

Musical soirées.

Aunt Sally.[4]

---

1 A medicinal preparation of crushed pearls.

2 A substance formed in the intestines of sperm whales.

3 Dried leaves of a Cassia plant, used as a cathartic.

4 "A game much in vogue at fairs and races, in which the figure of a woman's head with a pipe in its mouth is set up, and the player, throwing sticks from a certain distance, aims at breaking the pipe" (*OED*).

Mild tobacco.

The Saturday Review.[1]

A carriage with outriders,[2] &c. &c. after the modern method. But that would not do.

And if he had but been a convict lunatic, and had shot at the Queen, killed all his creditors to avoid paying them, or indulged in any other little amiable eccentricity of that kind, they would have given him in addition—

The healthiest situation in England, on Easthampstead Plain. Free run of Windsor Forest.

The Times every morning.

A double-barrelled gun and pointers, and leave to shoot three Wellington College[3] boys a week (not more) in case black game[4] were scarce.

But as he was neither mad enough nor bad enough to be allowed such luxuries, they grew desperate, and fell into bad ways, viz.:—

5. Suffumigations[5] of sulphur.

Heerwiggius[6] his "Incomparable drink for madmen:" only they could not find out what it was.

Suffumigation of the liver of the fish only they had forgotten its name, so Dr. Gray[7] could not well procure them a specimen.

---

1 An important Victorian weekly periodical, started in 1855, noted especially for its satire.

2 A person who rides on horseback ahead of or beside the carriage, as an escort.

3 Opened in 1859 and named after the Duke of Wellington, the college was one of the country's great boarding schools. Kingsley's son Maurice was a pupil there.

4 Black grouse.

5 "Fumes or vapours generated by burning herbs" (*OED*).

6 Henningius Michael Herwig, author of "*the art of curing sympathetically or magnetically proved to be most true. ...With a discourse concerning the cure of Madness, and an appendix to prove the reality of Sympathy*" (from the British Library catalog). Written originally in Latin, it was translated into English in 1700.

7 Asa Gray (1810-88), America's foremost botanist, developed the first systematic study of plants at Harvard University and was largely responsible for introducing Darwin's theory of natural selection in the United States.

Metallic tractors.[1]
Holloway's Ointment.[2]
Electro-biology.
Valentine Greatrakes[3] his Stroking Cure.
Spirit-rapping.
Holloway's Pills.
Table-turning.
Morrison's Pills.[4]
Homoeopathy.[5]
Parr's Life Pills.[6]
Mesmerism.
Pure Bosh.
Exorcisms, for which they read Malleus Maleficarum,[7] Nideri

---

1   "Name of a device invented by Elisha Perkins, an American physician
    (died 1799), consisting of a pair of pointed rods of different metals, as
    brass and steel, which were believed to relieve rheumatic or other pain
    by being drawn or rubbed over the skin" (*OED*).

2   One of the most popular patent medicines used in the nineteenth
    century, named after Thomas Holloway, who claimed that his ointment
    and pills could cure anything. He used much of his fortune earned with
    these nostrums to establish in 1886 the Royal Holloway College, one of
    the first women's colleges in England.

3   Valentine Greatrakes (1629-83), an Irishman who served as a lieutenant
    in Oliver Cromwell's army, was purported to cure scrofula by stroking
    the skin of the afflicted.

4   James Morrison (1770-1840), creator of a popular patent medicine. In
    1861 Jenny Marx, in a letter to Frederick Engels, comments that Karl
    [Marx] "now puts his faith on Morrison's pills, that worst of all quack
    medicines."

5   "A system of medical practice founded by Hahnemann of Leipsic about
    1796, according to which diseases are treated by the administration
    (usually in very small doses) of drugs which would produce in a healthy
    person symptoms closely resembling those of the disease treated"
    (*OED*).

6   A popular laxative in the Victorian period. Herbert Ingram and
    Nathaniel Cooke purchased the recipe and marketed it as Parr's Life
    Pills. About this time (1842) Ingram also founded the world's first illus-
    trated weekly newspaper, *The Illustrated London News*.

7   The most influential guide used throughout the Middle Ages for the
    persecution and torture of witches and heretics; written by Heinrich
    Kramer and James Sprenger, two inquisitors of the Dominican order.

Formicarium,[1] Delrio,[2] Wierus,[3] &c., but could not get one that mentioned water-babies.

Hydropathy.

Madame Rachel's[4] Elixir of Youth.

The Poughkeepsie Seer[5] his Prophecies.

The distilled liquor of addle eggs.

Pyropathy,[6] as successfully employed by the old inquisitors to cure the malady of thought, and now by the Persian Mollahs to cure that of rheumatism.

Geopathy, or burying him.

Atmopathy, or steaming him.

Sympathy, after the method of Basil Valentine[7] his Triumph of Antimony, and Kenelm Digby[8] his Weapon-salve, which some call a hair of the dog that bit him.

Hermopathy, or pouring mercury down his throat, to move the animal spirits.

Meteoropathy, or going up to the moon to look for his lost

---

1 Johann Nider (c.1380-1438), a Dominican theologian and inquisitor, whose book, *Formicatius* (1602), contains his account of the trial of Joan of Arc.

2 Martin Antonio Delrio, a Jesuit theologian, author of *Disquisitiones Magicae* (1599-1600), an erudite study of magic and witchcraft.

3 Johann Weyer (aka Wier, Wierus) published *De Praestigiis Daemonum"* (1583), a treatise on witchcraft.

4 Sarah Rachel Russell, the proprietor of a famous beauty salon during the 1860s, who promised everlasting youth to her gullible customers. She spent the last years of her life in jail.

5 Andrew Jackson Davis (1826-1910), spiritualist and author, one of America's foremost writers on psychic phenomena. His book *The Principles of Nature, Her Divine Revelations, and a Voice to Mankind* (1847) was dictated by him over a period of fifteen months during trance states.

6 Kingsley's satiric term for burning a heretic at the stake. The subsequent list of "pathies" are in the same comic vein.

7 Basilius Valentinus, a fifteenth century Benedictine monk who first described in his book, *The Triumphal Chariot of Antimony*, a method for the extraction of antimony from stibnite. The identity of this alchemist is in question.

8 Sir Kenneth Digby (1603-65) author of *Late Discourse... Touching the Cure of Wounds by the Powder of Sympathy* (1658), relating cases of cures by non-medical means, laying hold of the idea of the power of the imagination not only to heal, but also to cause disease. The powder of sympathy was supposed to heal a wound when put on the weapon which had caused it.

wits, as Ruggiero[1] did for Orlando Furioso's: only, having no hippogriff, they were forced to use a balloon; and, falling into the North Sea, were picked up by a Yarmouth herring-boat, and came home much the wiser, and all over scales.

Antipathy, or using him like "a man and a brother."[2]

Apathy, or doing nothing at all.

With all other ipathies and opathies which Noodle has invented, and Foodle tried, since black-fellows chipped flints at Abbeville[3]—which is a considerable time ago, to judge by the Great Exhibition.

But nothing would do; for he screamed and cried all day for a water-baby, to come and drive away the monsters; and of course they did not try to find one, because they did not believe in them, and were thinking of nothing but Bumpsterhausen's blue follicles; having, as usual, set the cart before the horse, and taken the effect for the cause.

So they were forced at last to let the poor professor ease his mind by writing a great book, exactly contrary to all his old opinions; in which he proved that the moon was made of green cheese, and that all the mites in it (which you may see sometimes quite plain through a telescope, if you will only keep the lens dirty enough, as Mr. Weekes[4] kept his voltaic battery) are nothing in

---

1   A character in Ludovico Ariosto's *Orlando Furioso* (1532). Actually it was another character, Astolfo, who flew to the moon on a hippogriff (a winged horse with the head and claws of an eagle) to retrieve Orlando's lost wits.

2   "Am I Not A Man and A Brother?" was an inscription on a medallion commissioned in 1787 by the Society for Effecting the Abolition of the Slave Trade. Josiah Wedgwood, who was a member of the Society, produced the emblem as a jasper-ware cameo. It depicts a kneeling African man with chains around his wrists and legs. The medallion soon became a fashion statement for abolitionists and anti-slavery sympathizers.

3   In 1847 Boucher de Perthes published *Celtic and Antediluvian Antiquities*, which featured engravings of typical flint implements and weapons that he had discovered near Abbeville, in northern France. His discovery helped to establish the early antiquity of man.

4   Robert Chambers in his *Vestiges of the Natural History of Creation* (1844) refers to a "Mr. Weekes, of Sandwich" who combined a current from a voltaic battery with certain chemicals in order to bring about "the aboriginal creation of insects." Chambers notes, however, that the "utmost that can be claimed for [this scientist]... is that he arranged the natural conditions under which the true creative energy—that of the Divine Author of all things—has pleased to work in that instance."

the world but little babies, who are hatching and swarming up there in millions, ready to come down into this world whenever children want a new little brother or sister.

Which must be a mistake, for this one reason: that, there being no atmosphere round the moon (though some one or other says there is, at least on the other side, and that he has been round at the back of it to see, and found that the moon was just the shape of a Bath bun, and so wet that the man in the moon went about on Midsummer-day in Macintoshes[1] and Cording's[2] boots, spearing eels and sneezing); that therefore, I say, there being no atmosphere, there can be no evaporation; and, therefore, the dew-point can never fall below 71.5 below zero of Fahrenheit; and, therefore, it cannot be cold enough there about four o'clock in the morning to condense the babies' mesenteric apophthegms[3] into their left ventricles; and, therefore, they can never catch the hooping-cough; and if they do not have hooping-cough, they cannot be babies at all; and, therefore, there are no babies in the moon.—Q.E.D.

Which may seem a roundabout reason; and so, perhaps, it is: but you will have heard worse ones in your time, and from better men than you are.

But one thing is certain; that, when the good old doctor got his book written, he felt considerably relieved from Bumpsterhausen's blue follicles, and a few things infinitely worse; to wit, from pride and vain-glory, and from blindness and hardness of heart; which are the true causes of Bumpsterhausen's blue follicles, and of a good many other ugly things beside. Whereon the foul flood-water in his brains ran down, and cleared to a fine coffee colour, such as fish like to rise in, till very fine clean fresh-run fish did begin to rise in his brains; and he caught two or three of them (which is exceedingly fine sport, for brain rivers), and anatomized them carefully, and never mentioned what he found out from them, except to little children; and became ever after a sadder and a wiser man; which is a very good thing to become, my dear little boy, even though one has to pay a heavy price for the blessing.

---

1   Charles Macintosh (1766-1843), a Scottish chemist, created the first waterproof cloth out of rubberized cotton. In Britain, a Macintosh became synonymous with a raincoat.

2   A popular boot in the period, advertised as "Cording's Waterproofs, Warranted for all Climates."

3   Literally, a succinct comment about one's intestines; here, simply further satire of the pedantic professor's nonsensical jargon.

CHAPTER V.

"Stern Lawgiver! yet thou dost wear
The Godhead's most benignant grace;
Nor know we anything so fair
As is the smile upon thy face:
Flowers laugh before thee on their beds;
And fragrance in thy footing treads;
Thou dost preserve the stars from wrong;
And the most ancient Heavens, through Thee are fresh and
    strong."[1]

                    Wordsworth.—*Ode to Duty.*

UT what became of little Tom? He slipt away off the rocks into the water, as I said before. But he could not help thinking of little Ellie. He did not remember who she was; but he knew that she was a little girl, though she was a hundred times as big as he. That is not surprising: size has nothing to do with kindred. A tiny weed may be first cousin to a great tree; and a little dog like Vick knows that Lioness is a dog too, though she is twenty times larger than herself. So Tom knew that Ellie was a little girl, and thought about her all that day, and longed to have had her to play with; but he had very soon to think of something else. And here is the account of what happened to him, as it was published next morning in the Waterproof Gazette, on the finest watered paper, for the use of the great fairy, Mrs. Bedonebyas-youdid, who reads the news very carefully every morning, and especially the police cases, as you will hear very soon.

    He was going along the rocks in three-fathom water, watch-

---

1   From *Poems in Two Volumes* (1807).

ing the pollock catch prawns, and the wrasses[1] nibble barnacles off the rocks, shells and all, when he saw a round cage of green withes;[2] and inside it, looking very much ashamed of himself, sat his friend the lobster, twiddling his horns, instead of thumbs.

"What, have you been naughty, and have they put you in the lock-up?" asked Tom.

The lobster felt a little indignant at such a notion, but he was too much depressed in spirits to argue; so he only said, "I can't get out."

"Why did you get in?"

"After that nasty piece of dead fish." He had thought it looked and smelt very nice when he was outside, and so it did, for a lobster: but now he turned round and abused it because he was angry with himself.

"Where did you get in?"

"Through that round hole at the top."

"Then why don't you get out through it?"

"Because I can't;" and the lobster twiddled his horns more fiercely than ever, but he was forced to confess.

"I have jumped upwards, downwards, backwards, and side-ways, at least four thousand times; and I can't get out: I always get up underneath there, and can't find the hole."

Tom looked at the trap, and having more wit than the lobster, he saw plainly enough what was the matter; as you may if you will look at a lobster-pot.

"Stop a bit," said Tom. "Turn your tail up to me, and I'll pull you through hindforemost, and then you won't stick in the spikes."

But the lobster was so stupid and clumsy that he couldn't hit the hole. Like a great many fox-hunters, he was very sharp as long as he was in his own country: but as soon as they get out of it they lose their heads; and so the lobster, so to speak, lost his tail.

Tom reached and clawed down the hole after him, till he caught hold of him; and then, as was to be expected, the clumsy lobster pulled him in head foremost.

"Hullo! here is a pretty business," said Tom. "Now take your great claws, and break the points off those spikes, and then we shall both get out easily."

---

1 Brightly colored fish with thick lips and powerful jaws.
2 Strong supple twigs, especially willows, used for binding things together.

"Dear me, I never thought of that," said the lobster; "and after all the experience of life that I have had!"

You see, experience is of very little good unless a man, or a lobster, has wit enough to make use of it. For a good many people, like old Polonius,[1] have seen all the world, and yet remain little better than children after all.

But they had not got half the spikes away, when they saw a great dark cloud over them; and lo and behold, it was the otter.

How she did grin and girn[2] when she saw Tom. "Yar!" said she, "you little meddlesome wretch, I have you now! I will serve you out for telling the salmon where I was!" And she crawled all over the pot to get in.

Tom was horribly frightened, and still more frightened when she found the hole in the top, and squeezed herself right down through it, all eyes and teeth. But no sooner was her head inside than valiant Mr. Lobster caught her by the nose, and held on.

And there they were all three in the pot, rolling over and over, and very tight packing it was. And the lobster tore at the otter, and the otter tore at the lobster, and both squeezed and thumped poor Tom till he had no breath left in his body; and I don't know what would have happened to him if he had not at last got on the otter's back, and safe out of the hole.

---

1 The tedious old fool in *Hamlet*, father of Ophelia and Laertes.
2 Snarl like a dog.

He was right glad when he got out: but he would not desert his friend who had saved him; and the first time he saw his tail uppermost he caught hold of it, and pulled with all his might.

But the lobster would not let go.

"Come along," said Tom; "don't you see she is dead?" And so she was, quite drowned and dead.

And that was the end of the wicked otter.

But the lobster would not let go.

"Come along, you stupid old stick-in-the-mud," cried Tom, "or the fisherman will catch you!" And that was true, for Tom felt some one above beginning to haul up the pot.

But the lobster would not let go.

Tom saw the fisherman haul him up to the boatside, and thought it was all up with him. But when Mr. Lobster saw the fisherman, he gave such a furious and tremendous snap, that he snapped out of his hand, and out of the pot, and safe into the sea. But he left his knobbed claw behind him; for it never came into his stupid head to let go after all, so he just shook his claw off as the easier method. It was something of a bull,[1] that; but you must know the lobster was an Irish lobster, and was hatched off Island Magee at the mouth of Belfast Lough.

Tom asked the lobster why he never thought of letting go. He said very determinedly that it was a point of honour among lobsters. And so it is, as the mayor of Plymouth found out once to his cost—eight or nine hundred years ago, of course; for if it had happened lately it would be personal to mention it.

For one day he was so tired with sitting on a hard chair, in a grand furred gown, with a gold chain round his neck, hearing one policeman after another come in and sing, "What shall we do with the drunken sailor, so early in the morning?" and answering them each exactly alike—

"Put him in the round house till he gets sober, so early in the morning"—

That, when it was over, he jumped up, and played leap-frog with the town-clerk till he burst his buttons, and then had his luncheon, and burst some more buttons, and then said: "It is a low spring tide; I shall go out this afternoon and cut my capers."[2]

---

1 Self-contradictory behavior, associated with the Irish.
2 Frolic or dance.

Now he did not mean to cut such capers as you eat with boiled mutton. It was the commandant of artillery at Valetta[1] who used to amuse himself with cutting them, and who stuck upon one of the bastions a notice, "No one allowed to cut capers here but me," which greatly edified the midshipmen in port, and the Maltese on the Nix Mangiare stairs.[2] But all that the mayor meant was that he would go and have an afternoon's fun, like any school-boy, and catch lobsters with an iron hook.

So to the Mewstone[3] he went, and for lobsters he looked. And, when he came to a certain crack in the rocks, he was so excited, that, instead of putting in his hook, he put in his hand; and Mr. Lobster was at home, and caught him by the finger, and held on.

"Yah!" said the mayor, and pulled as hard as he dared: but the more he pulled the more the lobster pinched, till he was forced to be quiet.

Then he tried to get his hook in with his other hand; but the hole was too narrow.

Then he pulled again; but he could not stand the pain.

Then he shouted and bawled for help: but there was no one nearer him than the men-of-war inside the breakwater.

Then he began to turn a little pale; for the tide flowed, and still the lobster held on.

Then he turned quite white; for the tide was up to his knees, and still the lobster held on.

Then he thought of cutting off his finger; but he wanted two things to do it with—courage and a knife; and he had got neither.

Then he turned quite yellow; for the tide was up to his waist, and still the lobster held on.

Then he thought over all the naughty things he ever had done: all the sand which he had put in the sugar, and the sloe-leaves in the tea, and the water in the treacle, and the salt in the tobacco (because his brother was a brewer, and a man must help his own kin).

Then he turned quite blue; for the tide was up to his breast, and still the lobster held on.

Then, I have no doubt, he repented fully of all the said naughty things which he had done, and promised to mend his

---

1 The capital of Malta.
2 The name given to some steps in Valetta, Malta, as a consequence of the large number of beggars there crying *nix mangiare* ("nothing to eat" in German-Italian slang).
3 A large rock off the coast of Plymouth, near Wembury Point, noted for its rich marine life that makes it an attractive dive site to this day.

life, as too many do when they think they have no life left to mend. Whereby, as they fancy, they make a very cheap bargain. But the old fairy with the birch rod soon undeceives them.

And then he grew all colours at once, and turned up his eyes like a duck in thunder; for the water was up to his chin, and still the lobster held on.

And then came a man-of-war's boat round the Mewstone, and saw his head sticking up out of the water. One said it was a keg of brandy, and another that it was a cocoanut, and another that it was a buoy loose, and another that it was a black diver, and wanted to fire at it, which would not have been pleasant for the mayor: but just then such a yell came out of a great hole in the middle of it that the midshipman in charge guessed what it was, and bade pull up to it as fast as they could. So somehow or other the Jack-tars got the lobster out, and set the mayor free, and put him ashore at the Barbican.[1] He never went lobster-catching again; and we will hope he put no more salt in the tobacco, not even to sell his brother's beer.

And that is the story of the Mayor of Plymouth, which has two advantages—first, that of being quite true; and second, that of having (as folks say all good stories ought to have) no moral whatsoever: no more, indeed, has any part of this book, because it is a fairy tale, you know.

And now happened to Tom a most wonderful thing; for he had not left the lobster five minutes before he came upon a water-baby.

A real live water-baby, sitting on the white sand, very busy about a little point of rock. And when it saw Tom it looked up for a moment, and then cried, "Why, you are not one of us. You are a new baby! Oh, how delightful!"

And it ran to Tom, and Tom ran to it, and they hugged and kissed each other for ever so long, they did not know why. But they did not want any introductions there under the water.

At last Tom said, "Oh, where have you been all this while? I have been looking for you so long, and I have been so lonely."

"We have been here for days and days. There are hundreds of us about the rocks. How was it you did not see us, or hear us when we sing and romp every evening before we go home?"

Tom looked at the baby again, and then he said:

"Well, this is wonderful! I have seen things just like you again

---

1 Plymouth Barbican, the town's historic heart.

and again, but I thought you were shells, or sea-creatures. I never took you for water-babies like myself."

Now, was not that very odd? So odd, indeed, that you will, no doubt, want to know how it happened, and why Tom could never find a water-baby till after he had got the lobster out of the pot. And, if you will read this story nine times over, and then think for yourself, you will find out why. It is not good for little boys to be told everything, and never to be forced to use their own wits. They would learn, then, no more than they do at Dr. Dulcimer's famous suburban establishment for the idler members of the youthful aristocracy, where the masters learn the lessons, and the boys hear them—which saves a great deal of trouble— for the time being.

"Now," said the baby, "come and help me, or I shall not have finished before my brothers and sisters come, and it is time to go home."

"What shall I help you at?"

"At this poor dear little rock; a great clumsy boulder came rolling by in the last storm, and knocked all its head off, and rubbed off all its flowers. And now I must plant it again with sea-weeds, and coral-line, and anemones, and I will make it the prettiest little rock-garden on all the shore."

So they worked away at the rock, and planted it, and smoothed the sand down round it, and capital fun they had till the tide began to turn. And then Tom heard all the other babies coming, laughing and singing and shouting and romping; and the noise they made was just like the noise of the ripple. So he knew that he had been hearing and seeing the water-babies all along; only he did not know them, because his eyes and ears were not opened.

And in they came, dozens and dozens of them, some bigger than Tom and some smaller, all in the neatest little white bathing dresses; and when they found that he was a new baby they hugged him and kissed him, and then put him in the middle and danced round him on the sand, and there was no one ever so happy as poor little Tom.

"Now then," they cried all at once, "we must come away home, we must come away home, or the tide will leave us dry. We have mended all the broken sea-weed, and put all the rock pools in order, and planted all the shells again in the sand, and nobody will see where the ugly storm swept in last week."

And this is the reason why the rock pools are always so neat and clean; because the water-babies come in shore after every storm, to sweep them out, and comb them down, and put them all to rights again.

Only where men are wasteful and dirty, and let sewers run into the sea, instead of putting the stuff upon the fields like thrifty reasonable souls; or throw herrings' heads, and dead dog-fish, or any other refuse, into the water; or in any way make a mess upon the clean shore, there the water-babies will not come, sometimes not for hundreds of years (for they cannot abide anything smelly or foul): but leave the sea-anemones and the crabs to clear away everything, till the good tidy sea has covered up all the dirt in soft mud and clean sand, where the water-babies can plant live cockles and whelks and razor shells and sea-cucumbers and golden-combs, and make a pretty live garden again, after man's dirt is cleared away. And that, I suppose, is the reason why there are no water-babies at any watering-place which I have ever seen.

And where is the home of the water-babies? In St. Brandan's fairy isle.[1]

Did you never hear of the blessed St. Brandan, how he preached to the wild Irish, on the wild wild Kerry coast; he and five other hermits, till they were weary, and longed to rest? For the wild Irish would not listen to them, or come to confession and to mass, but liked better to brew potheen,[2] and dance the pater o'pee,[3] and knock each other over the head with shillelaghs, and shoot each other from behind turf-dykes, and steal each other's cattle, and burn each other's homes; till St. Brandan and his friends were weary of them, for they would not learn to be peaceable Christians at all.

So St. Brandan went out to the point of old Dunmore,[4] and looked over the tide-way roaring round the Blasquets,[5] at the end of all the world, and away into the ocean, and sighed—"Ah that I had wings as a dove!" And far away, before the setting sun, he saw a blue fairy sea, and golden fairy islands, and he said, "Those are the islands of the blest." Then he and his friends got into a

---

1   St. Brendan of Ardfert and Clonfert, known also as Brendan the Voyager, a sixth-century Irish monk who, according to legend, went with several other monks on a seven-years' quest for the Land of Promise, a beautiful island with luxuriant vegetation.
2   Illegally distilled Irish whisky.
3   A lively Irish dance, also known as the Patre o'Pee, presumably after *Battre au pied*.
4   Dunmore Head, Kerry, the most westerly point in Ireland.
5   A group of islands and rocks off the Kerry coast.

hooker,[1] and sailed away and away to the westward, and were never heard of more. But the people who would not hear him were changed into gorillas, and gorillas they are until this day.[2]

And when St. Brandan and the hermits came to that fairy isle, they found it overgrown with cedars, and full of beautiful birds; and he sat down under the cedars, and preached to all the birds in the air. And they liked his sermons so well that they told the fishes in the sea; and they came, and St. Brandan preached to them; and the fishes told the water-babies, who live in the caves under the isle; and they came up by hundreds every Sunday, and St. Brandan got quite a neat little Sunday-school. And there he taught the water-babies for a great many hundred years, till his eyes grew too dim to see, and his beard grew so long that he dared not walk for fear of treading on it, and then he might have tumbled down. And at last he and the five hermits fell fast asleep under the cedar shades, and there they sleep unto this day. But the fairies took to the water-babies, and taught them their lessons themselves.

And some say that St. Brandan will awake, and begin to teach the babies once more: but some think that he will sleep on, for better for worse, till the coming of the Cocqcigrues. But, on still clear summer evenings, when the sun sinks down into the sea, among golden cloud-capes and cloud-islands, and locks and friths[3] of azure sky, the sailors fancy that they see, away to westward, St. Brandan's fairy isle.

But whether men can see it or not, St. Brandan's Isle once actually stood there; a great land out in the ocean, which has sunk and sunk beneath the waves. Old Plato called it Atlantis,[4] and told strange tales of the wise men who lived therein, and of the wars they fought in the old times. And from off that island came strange flowers, which linger still about this land:—the Cornish heath, and Cornish moneywort,[5] and the delicate Venus's hair,[6]

---

1   "A one-masted fishing smack on the Irish coast and south-west of England" (*OED*).
2   Kingsley here echoes the contemporary prejudice that depicted the Irish as simians.
3   Lochs and friths, namely, lakes and narrow inlets of the sea.
4   In Plato's *Timaeus and Critias*, a lost civilization that was submerged beneath the sea.
5   A trailing plant with rounded leaves and solitary yellow flowers in their axils.
6   A delicate fern having a slender, black and shining stem and branches.

and the London-pride[1] which covers the Kerry mountains, and the little pink butterwort of Devon, and the great blue butterwort[2] of Ireland, and the Connemara heath, and the bristle-fern[3] of the Turk waterfall,[4] and many a strange plant more; all fairy tokens left for wise men and good children from off St. Brandan's Isle.

Now when Tom got there, he found that the isle stood all on pillars, and that its roots were full of caves. There were pillars of black basalt, like Staffa;[5] and pillars of green and crimson serpentine, like Kynance;[6] and pillars ribboned with red and white and yellow sandstone, like Livermead;[7] and there were blue grottoes, like Capri;[8] and white grottoes, like Adelsberg;[9] all curtained and draped with seaweeds, purple and crimson, green and brown; and strewn with soft white sand, on which the water-babies sleep every night. But, to keep the place clean and sweet, the crabs picked up all the scraps off the floor, and ate them like so many monkeys; while the rocks were covered with ten thousand sea-anemones, and corals and madrepores,[10] who scavenged the water all day long, and kept it nice and pure. But, to make up to them for having to do such nasty work, they were not left black and dirty, as poor chimney-sweeps and dustmen are. No; the fairies are more considerate and just than that; and have

---

1 *Saxifraga,* a hardy perennial plant with silver rosettes of foliage and sprays of white, yellow, or pink flowers.
2 Butterworts are carnivorous plants with a rosette of sticky leaves that trap insects.
3 A fern of the genus *Trichomanes* having large, often translucent fronds; most are epiphytic on tree branches and twigs or terrestrial on mossy banks.
4 Torc waterfall, a famous falls close to Killarney.
5 A small island of Scotland's Inner Hebrides, Staffa is famous for the magnificent volcanic rock formations that make up the island.
6 Kynance Cove in Cornwall, a scenic area of white sand, turquoise water and islands of multi-coloured serpentine rock with stacks and arches hidden among the towering cliffs.
7 A sea-side resort in Torquay, Devon, where Kingsley stayed in 1854 while his wife recovered from illness.
8 *Grotta Azzurra,* Capri's famous sea cave, taking its color from the sunlight entering the cave through the water.
9 A town in Carniola, in the mountainous area of Slovenia, noted for its picturesque rock formations.
10 Tiny primitive animals living in colonies and constituted of small size polyps inside a limestone skeleton, the builders of coral reefs.

dressed them all in the most beautiful colours and patterns, till they look like vast flower-beds of gay blossoms. If you think I am talking nonsense, I can only say that it is true; and that an old gentleman named Fourier[1] used to say that we ought to do the same by chimney-sweeps and dustmen, and honour them instead of despising them; and he was a very clever old gentleman: but unfortunately for him and the world, as mad as a March hare.

And, instead of watchmen and policemen to keep out nasty things at night, there were thousands and thousands of water-snakes, and most wonderful creatures they were. They were all named after the Nereids,[2] the sea fairies who took care of them, Eunice and Polynoe, Phyllodoce and Psamathe,[3] and all the rest of the pretty darlings who swim round their Queen Amphitrite,[4] and her car of cameo shell. They were dressed in green velvet, and black velvet, and purple velvet; and were all jointed in rings; and some of them had three hundred brains apiece, so that they must have been uncommonly shrewd detectives; and some had eyes in their tails; and some had eyes in every joint, so that they kept a very sharp look-out; and when they wanted a baby-snake, they just grew one at the end of their own tails, and when it was able to take care of itself it dropped off; so that they brought up their families very cheaply. But if any nasty thing came by, out they rushed upon it; and then out of each of their hundreds of feet there sprang a whole cutler's shop of

Scythes,	Javelins,
Billhooks, ·	Lances,
Pickaxes,	Halberts,

1　Charles Fourier (1772-1837), a Utopian Socialist. Among his mathe-matically-based predictions for the idealized world he hoped to create were the following: the North Pole would be milder than the Mediter-ranean; the seas would lose their salt and become oceans of lemonade; and the world would contain 37 million poets equal to Homer, 37 million mathematicians equal to Newton and 37 million dramatists equal to Molière.

2　In Greek mythology, the fifty daughters of the sea-god Nereus and the sea-nymph Doris. These beautiful women assisted sailors in surviving perilous storms. Thus *Nereididae*, a zoological category of sea worm.

3　These mythological Nereids inspired the zoological names for three classes of sea worms: *Eunicidae*, *Polynoidae*, and *Phyllodocidae*; and a transparent species of shrimp, *Periclimenes psamathe*.

4　A Nereid who was the sea-goddess wife of Poseidon.

Forks,	Gisarines,
Penknives,	Poleaxes,
Rapiers,	Fishhooks,
Sabres,	Bradawls,
Yataghans,	Gimblets,
Creeses,	Corkscrews,
Ghoorka swords,	Pins,
Tucks,	Needles,[1]
And so forth,	

which stabbed, shot, poked, pricked, scratched, ripped, pinked, and crimped those naughty beasts so terribly, that they had to run for their lives, or else be chopped into small pieces and be eaten afterwards. And, if that is not all, every word, true, then there is no Faith in microscopes, and all is over with the Linnæan Society.

And there were the water-babies in thousands, more than Tom, or you either, could count.—All the little children whom the good fairies take to, because their cruel mothers and fathers will not; all who are untaught and brought up heathens, and all who come to grief by ill-usage or ignorance or neglect; all the little children who are overlaid,[2] or given gin when they are young, or are let to drink out of hot kettles, or to fall into the fire; all the little children in alleys and courts, and tumble-down cottages, who die by fever, and cholera, and measles, and scarlatina, and nasty complaints which no one has any business to have, and which no one will have some day, when folks have common sense; and all the little children who have been killed by cruel masters, and wicked soldiers; they were all there, except, of course, the babes of Bethlehem who were killed by wicked King Herod; for they were taken straight to heaven long ago, as everybody knows, and we call them the Holy Innocents.

---

1   In this list, in the comic style of Rabelais: *yataghan*, "a sword of Muslim countries, having a handle without a guard and often a double-curved blade" (*OED*); *creese*, a Malay dagger; Ghoorka swords, a Gurkha sword used by fighters from Nepal; *halbert*, "a military weapon, a kind of combination of spear and battle-axe, consisting of a sharp-edged blade ending in a point, and a spear-head, mounted on a handle five to seven feet long" (*OED*); *gisarine*, or *gisarme*, "a kind of battle-axe, bill, or halberd, having a long blade in line with the shaft, sharpened on both sides and ending in a point" (*OED*); *bradawl*, a small tool used for boring.

2   Suffocated.

But I wish Tom had given up all his naughty tricks, and left off tormenting dumb animals, now that he had plenty of playfellows to amuse him. Instead of that, I am sorry to say, he would meddle with the creatures, all but the water-snakes, for they would stand no nonsense. So he tickled the madrepores, to make them shut up; and frightened the crabs, to make them hide in the sand and peep out at him with the tips of their eyes; and put stones into the anemones' mouths to make them fancy that their dinner was coming.

The other children warned him, and said, "Take care what you are at. Mrs. Bedonebyasyoudid is coming." But Tom never heeded them, being quite riotous with high spirits and good luck, till, one Friday morning early, Mrs. Bedonebyasyoudid came indeed.

A very tremendous lady she was; and when the children saw her, they all stood in a row, very upright indeed, and smoothed down their bathing dresses, and put their hands behind them, just as if they were going to be examined by the inspector.

And she had on a black bonnet, and a black shawl, and no crinoline at all; and a pair of large green spectacles, and a great hooked nose, hooked so much that the bridge of it stood quite up above her eyebrows; and under her arm she carried a great birch-rod. Indeed, she was so ugly, that Tom was tempted to make faces at her: but did not; for he did not admire the look of the birch-rod under her arm.

And she looked at the children one by one, and seemed very much pleased with them, though she never asked them one question about how they were behaving; and then began giving them all sorts of nice sea-things—sea-cakes, sea-apples, sea-oranges, sea-bullseyes,[1] sea-toffee; and to the very best of all she gave sea-ices, made out of sea-cows' cream, which never melt under water.

And, if you don't quite believe me, then just think—What is more cheap and plentiful than sea-rock?[2] Then why should there not be sea-toffee as well? And every one can find sea-lemons (ready quartered too) if they will look for them at low tide; and sea-grapes too sometimes, hanging in bunches; and, if you will go to Nice, you will find the fish-market full of seafruit, which they call "frutta di mare:" though I suppose they call them "fruits de mer" now, out of compliment to that most successful, and there-

---

1 A sweetmeat, a sugared cake shaped in a ball.
2 Hard candy.

fore most immaculate, potentate[1] who is seemingly desirous of inheriting the blessing pronounced on those who remove their neighbours' landmark. And, perhaps, that is the very reason why the place is called Nice, because there are so many nice things in the sea there: at least, if it is not, it ought to be.

Now little Tom watched all these sweet things given away, till his mouth watered, and his eyes grew as round as an owl's. For he hoped that his turn would come at last; and so it did. For the lady called him up, and held out her fingers with something in them, and popped it into his mouth; and, lo and behold, it was a nasty cold hard pebble.

"You are a very cruel woman," said he, and began to whimper.

"And you are a very cruel boy; who puts pebbles into the sea-anemones' mouths, to take them in, and make them fancy that they had caught a good dinner? As you did to them, so I must do to you."

"Who told you that?" said Tom.

"You did yourself, this very minute."

Tom had never opened his lips; so he was very much taken aback indeed.

"Yes; every one tells me exactly what they have done wrong; and that without knowing it themselves. So there is no use trying to hide anything from me. Now go, and be a good boy, and I will put no more pebbles in your mouth, if you put none in other creatures'."

"I did not know there was any harm in it," said Tom.

"Then you know now. People continually say that to me: but I tell them, if you don't know that fire burns, that is no reason that it should not burn you; and if you don't know that dirt breeds fever, that is no reason why the fevers should not kill you. The lobster did not know that there was any harm in getting into the lobster pot; but it caught him all the same."

---

1 Napoleon III in 1860 negotiated with Count Camillo Benso di Cavour the annexation of Nice and Savoy to France.

"Dear me," thought Tom, "she knows everything!" And so she did, indeed.

"And so, if you do not know that things are wrong, that is no reason why you should not be punished for them; though not as much, not as much, my little man" (and, the lady looked very kindly, after all), "as if you did know."

"Well, you are a little hard on a poor lad," said Tom.

"Not at all; I am the best friend you ever had in all your life. But I will tell you; I cannot help punishing people when they do wrong. I like it no more than they do; I am often very, very sorry for them, poor things: but I cannot help it. If I tried not to do it, I should do it all the same. For I work by machinery, just like an engine; and am full of wheels and springs inside; and am wound up very carefully, so that I cannot help going."

"Was it long ago since they wound you up?" asked Tom. For he thought, the cunning little fellow, "She will run down some day: or they may forget to wind her up, as old Grimes used to forget to wind up his watch when he came in from the public-house: and then I shall be safe."

"I was wound up once and for all, so long ago that I forget all about it."

"Dear me," said Tom, "you must have been made a long time!"

"I never was made, my child; and I shall go for ever and ever; for I am as old as Eternity, and yet as young as Time."

And there came over the lady's face a very curious expression—very solemn, and very sad; and yet very, very sweet. And she looked up and away, as if she were gazing through the sea, and through the sky, at something far, far off; and as she did so, there came such a quiet, tender, patient, hopeful smile over her face, that Tom thought for the moment that she did not look ugly at all. And no more she did; for she was like a great many people who have not a pretty feature in their faces, and yet are lovely to behold, and draw little children's hearts to them at once; because, though the house is plain enough, yet from the windows a beautiful and good spirit is looking forth.

And Tom smiled in her face, she looked so pleasant for the moment. And the strange fairy smiled too, and said:

"Yes. You thought me very ugly just now, did you not?"

Tom hung down his head, and got very red about the ears.

"And I am very ugly. I am the ugliest fairy in the world; and I shall be, till people behave themselves as they ought to do. And then I shall grow as handsome as my sister, who is the loveliest fairy in the world; and her name is Mrs. Doasyouwouldbedoneby. So she begins where I end, and I begin where she ends; and those who will not listen to her must listen to me, as you will see. Now, all of you run away, except Tom; and he may stay and see what I am going to do. It will be a very good warning for him to begin with, before he goes to school.

"Now, Tom, every Friday I come down here and call up all who have ill-used little children, and serve them as they served the children."

And at that Tom was frightened, and crept under a stone; which made the two crabs who lived there very angry, and frightened their friend the butter-fish into flapping hysterics: but he would not move for them.

And first she called up all the doctors who give little children so much physic (they were most of them old ones; for the young ones have learnt better, all but a few army surgeons, who still fancy that a baby's inside is much like a Scotch grenadier's), and she set them all in a row; and very rueful they looked; for they knew what was coming.

And first she pulled all their teeth out; and then she bled them all round; and then she dosed them with calomel,[1] and jalap,[2] and salts and senna,[3] and brimstone[4] and treacle;[5] and horrible faces they made; and then she gave them a great emetic of mustard and water, and no basons; and began all over again; and that was the way she spent the morning.

And then she called up a whole troop of foolish ladies, who pinch up their children's waists and toes; and she laced them all up in tight stays, so that they were choked and sick, and their noses grew red, and their hands and feet swelled; and then she crammed their poor feet into the most dreadfully tight boots, and made them all dance, which they did most clumsily indeed; and then she asked them how they liked it; and when they said not at all, she let them go: because they had only done it out of foolish fashion, fancying it was for their children's good, as if wasps'

---

1 A purgative containing a compound of mercury.
2 A purgative made from the tuberous roots of the Mexican plant *Exogonium Purga*, a climber like the morning glory.
3 A purgative made from the dried leaves of *Cassia angustifolia*.
4 Sulfur, used medicinally as a laxative.
5 "A medicinal compound, orig. a kind of salve, composed of many ingredients, formerly in repute as an alexipharmic against and antidote to venomous bites, poisons generally, and malignant diseases" (*OED*).

waists and pigs' toes could be pretty, or wholesome, or of any use to anybody.

Then she called up all the careless nurserymaids, and stuck pins into them all over, and wheeled them about in perambulators with tight straps across their stomachs and their heads and arms hanging over the side, till they were quite sick and stupid, and would have had sun-strokes: but, being under the water, they could only have water-strokes; which, I assure you, are nearly as bad, as you will find if you try to sit under a mill wheel. And mind—when you hear a rumbling at the bottom of the sea, sailors will tell you that it is a ground-swell: but now you know better. It is the old lady wheeling the maids about in perambulators.

And by that time she was so tired, she had to go to luncheon.

And after luncheon she set to work again, and called up all the cruel schoolmasters—whole regiments and brigades of them; and, when she saw them, she frowned most terribly, and set to work in earnest, as if the best part of the day's work was to come. More than half of them were nasty, dirty, frowzy, grubby, smelly old monks, who, because they dare not hit a man of their own size, amused themselves with beating little children instead; as you may see in the picture of old Pope Gregory[1] (good man and true though he was, when he meddled with things which he did understand), teaching children to sing their fa-fa-mi-fa with a cat-o'-nine tails under his chair: but, because they never had any children of their own, they took into their heads (as some folks do still) that they were the only people in the world who knew how to manage children; and they first brought into England, in the old Anglo-Saxon times, the fashion of treating free boys, and girls too, worse than you would treat a dog or a horse: but Mrs. Bedonebyasyoudid has caught them all long ago; and given them many a taste of their own rods; and much good may it do them.

And she boxed their ears, and thumped them over the head with rulers, and pandied their hands with canes, and told them that they told stories, and were this and that bad sort of people; and the more they were very indignant, and stood upon their honour, and declared they told the truth, the more she declared they were not,

---

1 Probably Pope Gregory I (540-604), known as St. Gregory the Great, remembered for his efforts to promote the conversion of the English. Quoting from Gregory's comments on the Book of Job, the Venerable Bede writes: "The Britons, who formerly knew only their own barbaric tongue, have long since begun to cry the Hebrew Alleluia to the praise of God."

and that they were only telling lies; and at last she birched them all round soundly with her great birch rod, and set them each an imposition of three hundred thousand lines of Hebrew to learn by heart before she came back next Friday. And at that they all cried and howled so, that their breaths came all up through the sea like bubbles out of soda-water; and that is one reason of the bubbles in the sea. There are others: but that is the one which principally concerns little boys. And by that time she was so tired that she was glad to stop; and, indeed, she had done a very good day's work.

Tom did not quite dislike the old lady: but he could not help thinking her a little spiteful—and no wonder if she was, poor old soul; for, if she has to wait to grow handsome till people do as they would be done by, she will have to wait a very long time.

Poor old Mrs. Bedonebyasyoudid! she has a great deal of hard work before her, and had better have been born a washerwoman, and stood over a tub all day: but, you see, people cannot always choose their own profession.

But Tom longed to ask her one question; and after all, whenever she looked at him, she did not look cross at all; and now and then there was a funny smile in her face, and she chuckled to herself in a way which gave Tom courage, and at last he said:

"Pray, ma'am, may I ask you a question?"

"Certainly, my little dear."

"Why don't you bring all the bad masters here, and serve them out too? The butties[1] that knock about the poor collier-boys; and the nailers[2] that file off their lads' noses and hammer their fingers; and all the master sweeps, like my master Grimes? I saw him fall into the water long ago; so I surely expected he would have been here. I'm sure he was bad enough to me."

Then the old lady looked so very stern that Tom was quite frightened, and sorry that he had been so bold. But she was not angry with him. She only answered, "I look after them all the week round; and they are in a very different place from this, because they knew that they were doing wrong."

She spoke very quietly; but there was something in her voice which made Tom tingle from head to foot, as if he had got into a shoal of sea-nettles.

---

1 Middlemen between mine owners and workmen, who contract to work the mine and raise coal or ore at so much per ton. They had a reputation for being ruthless.

2 Men who ran nail-making shops, known for their cruelty to the boy apprentices.

"But these people," she went on, "did not know that they were doing wrong: they were only stupid and impatient; and therefore I only punish them till they become patient, and learn to use their common sense like reasonable beings. But as for chimney-sweeps, and collier-boys, and nailer lads, my sister has set good people to stop all that sort of thing; and very much obliged to her I am; for if she could only stop the cruel masters from ill-using poor children, I should grow handsome at least a thousand years sooner. And now do you be a good boy, and do as you would be done by, which they did not; and then, when my sister, Madame Doasyouwouldbedoneby, comes on Sunday, perhaps she will take notice of you, and teach you how to behave. She understands that better than I do." And so she went.

Tom was very glad to hear that there was no chance of meeting Grimes again, though he was a little sorry for him, considering that he used sometimes to give him the leavings of the beer: but he determined to be a very good boy all Saturday; and he was; for he never frightened one crab, nor tickled any live corals, nor put stones into the sea-anemones' mouths, to make them fancy they had got a dinner; and, when Sunday morning came, sure enough, Mrs. Doasyouwouldbedoneby came too. Whereat all the little children began dancing and clapping their hands, and Tom danced too with all his might.

And as for the pretty lady, I cannot tell you what the colour of her hair was, or of her eyes: no more could Tom; for, when any one looks at her, all they can think of is, that she has the sweetest, kindest, tenderest, funniest, merriest face they ever saw, or want to see. But Tom saw that she was a very tall woman, as tall as her sister: but instead of being gnarly, and horny, and scaly, and prickly, like her, she was the most nice, soft, fat, smooth, pussy, cuddly, delicious creature who ever nursed a baby; and she understood babies thoroughly, for she had plenty of her own, whole rows and regiments of them, and has to this day. And all her delight was, whenever she had a spare moment, to play with babies, in which she showed herself a woman of sense; for babies are the best company, and the pleasantest playfellows, in the world; at least, so all the wise people in the world think. And therefore when the children saw her, they naturally all caught hold of her, and pulled her till she sat down on a stone, and climbed into her lap, and clung round her neck, and caught hold of her hands; and then they all put their thumbs into their mouths, and began cuddling and purring like so many kittens, as they ought to have done. While those who could get nowhere else sat down on the sand, and cuddled her feet—for no one, you know, wears shoes in the water, except horrid old bathing-women,[1] who are afraid of the water-babies pinching their horny toes. And Tom stood staring at them; for he could not understand what it was all about.

"And who are you, you little darling?" she said.

"Oh, that is the new baby!" they all cried, pulling their thumbs out of their mouths; "and he never had any mother," and they all put their thumbs back again, for they did not wish to lose any time.

"Then I will be his mother, and he shall have the very best place; so get out all of you, this moment."

And she took up two great armfuls of babies—nine hundred under one arm, and thirteen hundred under the other—and threw them away, right and left, into the water. But they minded it no more than the naughty boys in Struwelpeter[2] minded when St. Nicholas dipped them in his inkstand; and did not even take their thumbs out of their mouths, but came paddling and wriggling back to her like so many tadpoles, till you could see nothing of her from head to foot for the swarm of little babies.

But she took Tom in her arms, and laid him in the softest place of all, and kissed him, and patted him, and talked to him, tenderly and low, such things as he had never heard before in his life; and Tom looked up into her eyes, and loved her, and loved, till he fell fast asleep from pure love.

And when he woke, she was telling the children a story. And what story did she tell them? One story she told them, which begins every Christmas Eve, and yet never ends at all for ever and ever; and, as she went on, the children took their thumbs out of their mouths, and listened quite seriously; but not sadly at all; for she never told them anything sad; and Tom listened too, and never grew tired of listening. And he listened so long that he fell fast asleep again, and, when he woke, the lady was nursing him still.

---

1 Women who would attend to the upper-class tourists at sea-side resorts. Philip Henry Gosse, a friend of Kingsley and fellow-naturalist, gives an equally unpleasant image of them in his essay "Seaside Pleasures": "the busy bathing-women—uncouth, uncorsetted figures—in blue serge gowns with a fringe of rags below."

2 In Heinrich Hoffmann's "Story of the Inky Boys" St. Nicholas punishes three boys by dropping them into an ink pot "Because they set up such a roar,/ And teas'd the harmless black-a-moor."

"Don't go away," said little Tom. "This is so nice. I never had anyone to cuddle me before."

"Don't go away," said all the children; "you have not sung us one song."

"Well, I have time for only one. So what shall it be?"

"The doll you lost! The doll you lost!" cried all the babies at once.

So the strange fairy sang:—

> I once had a sweet little doll, dears,
>   The prettiest doll in the world;
> Her cheeks were so red and so white, dears,
>   And her hair was so charmingly curled.
> But I lost my poor little doll, dears,
>   As I played in the heath one day;
> And I cried for her more than a week, dears;
>   But I never could find where she lay.
>
> I found my poor little doll, dears,
>   As I played in the heath one day:
> Folks say she is terribly changed, dears,
>   For her paint is all washed away,
> And her arm trodden off by the cows, dears,
>   And her hair not the least bit curled:
> Yet for old sakes' sake she is still, dears,
>   The prettiest doll in the world.

What a silly song for a fairy to sing!

And what silly water-babies to be quite delighted at it!

Well, but you see they have not the advantage of Aunt Agitate's Arguments in the sea-land down below.

"Now," said the fairy to Tom, "will you be a good boy for my sake, and torment no more sea-beasts, till I come back?"

"And you will cuddle me again?" said poor little Tom.

"Of course I will, you little duck. I should like to take you with me, and cuddle you all the way, only I must not;" and away she went.

So Tom really tried to be a good boy, and tormented no sea-beasts after that, as long as he lived; and he is quite alive, I assure you, still.

Oh, how good little boys ought to be, who have kind pussy mammas to cuddle them and tell them stories; and how afraid they ought to be of growing naughty, and bringing tears into their mammas' pretty eyes!

CHAPTER VI.

"Thou little child, yet glorious in the might
Of heaven-born freedom on thy Being's height,
Why with such earnest pains dost thou provoke
The Years to bring the inevitable yoke—
Thus blindly with thy blessedness at strife?
Full soon thy soul shall have her earthly freight,
And custom lie upon thee with a weight
Heavy as frost, and deep almost as life."[1]

Wordsworth.

ERE I come to the very saddest part of all my story. I know some people will only laugh at it, and call it much ado about nothing. But I know one man who would not; and he was an officer with a pair of grey moustaches as long as your arm, who said once in company, that two of the most heartrending sights in the world, which moved him most to tears, which he would do anything to prevent or remedy, were a child over a broken toy, and a child stealing sweets.

The company did not laugh at him; his moustaches were too long and too grey for that: but, after he was gone, they called him sentimental, and so forth, all but one dear little old quaker lady with a soul as white as her cap, who was not, of course, generally partial to soldiers; and she said very quietly, like a quaker:

"Friends, it is borne upon my mind that that is a truly brave man."

Now you may fancy that Tom was quite good, when he had everything that he could want or wish: but you would be very

---

1   From "Ode: Intimations of Immortality from Recollections of Early Childhood" (1807).

much mistaken. Being quite comfortable is a very good thing; but it does not make people good. Indeed, it sometimes makes them naughty, as it has made the people in America; and as it made the people in the Bible, who waxed fat and kicked,[1] like horses overfed and underworked. And I am very sorry to say that this happened to little Tom. For he grew so fond of the sea-bull's-eyes and sea-lollipops, that his foolish little head could think of nothing else: and he was always longing for more, and wondering when the strange lady would come again and give him some, and what she would give him, and how much, and whether she would give him more than the others. And he thought of nothing but lollipops by day, and dreamt of nothing else by night— and what happened then?

That he began to watch the lady to see where she kept the sweet things; and began hiding, and sneaking, and following her about, and pretending to be looking the other way, or going after something else, till he found out that she kept them in a beautiful mother-of-pearl cabinet, away in a deep crack of the rocks.

And he longed to go to the cabinet, and yet he was afraid; and then he longed again, and was less afraid; and at last, by continual thinking about it, he longed so violently, that he was not afraid at all. And one night, when all the other children were asleep, and he could not sleep for thinking of lollipops, he crept away among the rocks, and got to the cabinet, and behold! it was open.

But, when he saw all the nice things inside, instead of being delighted, he was quite frightened, and wished he had never come there. And then he would only touch them, and he did; and then he would only taste one, and he did; and then he would only eat one, and he did; and then he would only eat two, and then three, and so on; and then he was terrified lest she should come and catch him, and began gobbling them down so fast that he did not taste them, or have any pleasure in them; and then he felt sick, and would have only one more; and then only one more again; and so on till he had eaten them all up.

And all the while, close behind him, stood Mrs. Bedonebyas-youdid.

Some people may say, But why did she not keep her cupboard locked? Well, I know.—It may seem a very strange thing, but she

---

1 *Deuteronomy* 32:15: "But Jeshurun waxed fat, and kicked: thou art waxen fat, thou art grown thick."

never does keep her cupboard locked; every one may go and taste for themselves, and fare accordingly. It is very odd, but so it is; and I am quite sure that she knows best. Perhaps she wishes people to keep their fingers out of the fire, by having them burnt.

She took off her spectacles, because she did not like to see too much; and in her pity she arched up her eyebrows into her very hair, and her eyes grew so wide that they would have taken in all the sorrows of the world, and filled with great big tears, as they too often do.

But all she said was:

"Ah, you poor little dear! you are just like all the rest."

But she said it to herself, and Tom neither heard nor saw her. Now, you must not fancy that she was sentimental at all. If you do, and think that she is going to let off you, or me, or any human being when we do wrong, because she is too tender-hearted to punish us, then you will find yourself very much mistaken, as many a man does every year and every day.

But what did the strange fairy do when she saw all her lollipops eaten?

Did she fly at Tom, catch him by the scruff of the neck, hold him, howk him, hump him, hurry him, hit him, poke him, pull him, pinch him, pound him, put him in the corner, shake him, slap him, set him on a cold stone to reconsider himself, and so forth?

Not a bit. You may watch her at work, if you know where to find her. But you will never see her do that. For, if she had, she knew quite well, Tom would have fought, and kicked, and bit, and said bad words, and turned again that moment into a naughty little heathen chimney-sweep, with his hand, like Ishmael's[1] of old, against every man, and every man's hand against him.

Did she question him, hurry him, frighten him, threaten him, to make him confess? Not a bit. You may see her, as I said, at her work often enough, if you know where to look for her: but you will never see her do that. For if she had, she would have tempted him to tell lies in his fright; and that would have been worse for him, if possible, than even becoming a heathen chimney-sweep again.

No. She leaves that for anxious parents and teachers (lazy ones, some call them), who, instead of giving children a fair trial,

---

1 *Genesis* 16:11-12: "He [Ishmael] shall be a wild ass of a man, his hand against every man and every man's hand against him; and he shall dwell over against all his kinsmen."

such as they would expect and demand for themselves, force them by fright to confess their own faults—which is so cruel and unfair, that no judge on the bench dare do it to the wickedest thief or murderer, for the good British law forbids it—ay, and even punish them to make them confess, which is so detestable a crime, that it is never committed now, save by Inquisitors, and Kings of Naples,[1] and a few other wretched people of whom the world is weary. And then they say, "We have trained up the child in the way he should go, and when he grew up he has departed from it. Why then did Solomon[2] say that he would not depart from it?" But perhaps the way of beating, and hurrying, and frightening, and questioning, was not the way that the child should go; for it is not even the way in which a colt should go, if you want to break it in, and make it a quiet serviceable horse.

Some folks may say, "Ah! but the Fairy does not need to do that, if she knows everything already." True. But if she did not know, she would not surely behave worse than a British judge and jury; and no more should parents and teachers either.

So she just said nothing at all about the matter, not even when Tom came next day with the rest for sweet things. He was horribly afraid of coming: but he was still more afraid of staying away, lest any one should suspect him. He was dreadfully afraid, too, lest there should be no sweets—as was to be expected, he having eaten them all—and lest then the fairy should inquire who had taken them. But, behold! she pulled out just as many as ever, which astonished Tom, and frightened him still more.

And, when the fairy looked him full in the face, he shook from head to foot: however, she gave him his share like the rest, and he thought within himself that she could not have found him out.

But, when he put the sweets into his mouth, he hated the taste of them; and they made him so sick, that he had to get away as fast as he could; and terribly sick he was, and very cross and unhappy, all the week after.

Then, when next week came, he had his share again; and again the fairy looked him full in the face; but more sadly than she had ever looked. And he could not bear the sweets: but took them again in spite of himself.

---

1   Especially Ferdinand II (1810-59), King of the Two Sicilies (1830-59), whose despotic rule angered European liberals and conservatives alike.
2   "Train up a child in the way he should go: and when he is old, he will not depart from it" (*Prov.* 22: 6).

And, when Mrs. Doasyouwouldbedoneby came, he wanted to be cuddled like the rest; but she said very seriously:

"I should like to cuddle you; but I cannot, you are so horny and prickly."

And Tom looked at himself: and he was all over prickles, just like a sea-egg.[1]

Which was quite natural; for you must know and believe that people's souls make their bodies, just as a snail makes its shell (I am not joking, my little man; I am in serious, solemn earnest). And, therefore, when Tom's soul grew all prickly with naughty tempers, his body could not help growing prickly too, so that nobody would cuddle him, or play with him, or even like to look at him.

What could Tom do now, but go away and hide in a corner, and cry? For nobody would play with him, and he knew full well why.

And he was so miserable all that week that, when the ugly fairy came, and looked at him once more full in the face, more seriously and sadly than ever, he could stand it no longer, and thrust the sweetmeats away, saying, "No, I don't want any; I can't bear them now," and then burst out crying, poor little man, and told Mrs. Bedonebyasyoudid every word as it happened.

He was horribly frightened when he had done so; for he expected her to punish him very severely. But, instead, she only took him up and kissed him, which was not quite pleasant, for her chin was very bristly indeed; but he was so lonely-hearted, he thought that rough kissing was better than none.

"I will forgive you, little man," she said. "I always forgive every one the moment they tell me the truth of their own accord."

"Then you will take away all these nasty prickles?"

"That is a very different matter. You put them there yourself, and only you can take them away."

"But how can I do that?" asked Tom, crying afresh.

"Well, I think it is time for you to go to school; so I shall fetch you a schoolmistress, who will teach you how to get rid of your prickles." And so she went away.

Tom was frightened at the notion of a schoolmistress; for he thought she would certainly come with a birch-rod or a cane; but he comforted himself, at last, that she might be something like the old woman in Vendale—which she was not in the least; for, when the fairy brought her, she was the most beautiful little girl

---

1 A large sea-urchin.

that ever was seen, with long curls floating behind her like a golden cloud, and long robes floating all round her like a silver one.

"There he is," said the fairy; "and you must teach him to be good, whether you like or not."

"I know," said the little girl; but she did not seem quite to like, for she put her finger in her mouth, and looked at Tom under her brows; and Tom put his finger in his mouth, and looked at her under his brows, for he was horribly ashamed of himself.

The little girl seemed hardly to know how to begin; and perhaps she would never have begun at all, if poor Tom had not burst out crying, and begged her to teach him to be good, and help him to cure his prickles; and at that she grew so tender-hearted, that she began teaching him as prettily as ever child was taught in the world.

And what did the little girl teach Tom? She taught him, first, what you have been taught ever since you said your first prayers at your mother's knees; but she taught him much more simply. For the lessons in that world, my child, have no such hard words in them as the lessons in this, and therefore the water-babies like them better than you like your lessons, and long to learn them more and more; and grown men cannot puzzle nor quarrel over their meaning, as they do here on land; for those lessons all rise clear and pure, like the Test out of Overton Pool,[1] out of the everlasting ground of all life and truth.

So she taught Tom every day in the week; only on Sundays she always went away home, and the kind fairy took her place. And, before she had taught Tom many Sundays, his prickles had vanished quite away, and his skin was smooth and clean again.

"Dear me!" said the little girl; "why, I know you now. You are the very same little chimney-sweep who came into my bedroom."

"Dear me!" cried Tom. "And I know you, too, now. You are the very little white lady whom I saw in bed." And he jumped at her, and longed to hug and kiss her; but did not, remembering that she was a lady born; so he only jumped round and round her, till he was quite tired.

And then they began telling each other all their story—how he had got into the water, and she had fallen over the rock; and how he had swam down to the sea, and how she had flown out of the window; and how this, that, and the other, till it was all talked out: and then they both began over again, and I can't say which of the two talked fastest.

And then they set to work at their lessons again, and both liked them so well, that they went on well till seven full years were past and gone.

You may fancy that Tom was quite content and happy all those seven years; but the truth is, he was not. He had always one thing on his mind, and that was—where little Ellie went, when she went home on Sundays.

To a very beautiful place, she said.

But what was the beautiful place like, and where was it?

Ah! that is just what she could not say. And it is strange, but true, that no one can say; and that those who have been oftenest in it, or even nearest to it, can say least about it, and make people understand least what it is like. There are a good many folks about the Other-end-of-Nowhere (where Tom went afterwards), who pretend to know it from north to south as well as if they had been penny postmen there; but, as they are safe at the Other-end-of-Nowhere, nine hundred and ninety-nine million miles away, what they say cannot concern us.

But the dear, sweet, loving, wise, good, self-sacrificing people, who really go there, can never tell you anything about it, save that

---

1   The River Test is famous for its high quality fly-fishing sites. Its water, which bubbles up through chalk formations, is so clean that it is used to wash the paper used for British bank notes at Overton.

it is the most beautiful place in all the world; and, if you ask them more, they grow modest, and hold their peace, for fear of being laughed at; and quite right they are.

So all that good little Ellie could say was, that it was worth all the rest of the world put together. And of course that only made Tom the more anxious to go likewise.

"Miss Ellie," he said, at last, "I will know why I cannot go with you when you go home, on Sundays, or I shall have no peace, and give you none either."

"You must ask the fairies that."

So when the fairy, Mrs. Bedonebyasyoudid, came next, Tom asked her.

"Little boys who are only fit to play with sea-beasts cannot go there," she said. "Those who go there must go first where they do not like, and do what they do not like, and help somebody they do not like."

"Why, did Ellie do that?"

"Ask her."

And Ellie blushed, and said, "Yes, Tom; I did not like coming here at first; I was so much happier at home, where it is always Sunday. And I was afraid of you, Tom, at first, because— because—"

"Because I was all over prickles? But I am not prickly now, am I, Miss Ellie?"

"No," said Ellie. "I like you very much now; and I like coming here, too."

"And perhaps," said the fairy, "you will learn to like going where you don't like, and helping some one that you don't like, as Ellie has."

But Tom put his finger in his mouth, and hung his head down; for he did not see that at all.

So when Mrs. Doasyouwouldbedoneby came, Tom asked her; for he thought in his little head, She is not so strict as her sister, and perhaps she may let me off more easily.

Ah, Tom, Tom, silly fellow! and yet I don't know why I should blame you, while so many grown people have got the very same notion in their heads.

But, when they try it, they get just the same answer as Tom did. For, when he asked the second fairy, she told him just what the first did, and in the very same words.

Tom was very unhappy at that. And, when Ellie went home on Sunday, he fretted and cried all day, and did not care to listen to the fairy's stories about good children, though they were prettier than ever. Indeed, the more he overheard of them, the less he liked to listen, because they were all about children who did what they did not like, and took trouble for other people, and worked to feed their little brothers and sisters, instead of caring only for their play. And, when she began to tell a story about a holy child in old times, who was martyred by the heathen because it would not worship idols, Tom could bear no more, and ran away and hid among the rocks.

And, when Ellie came back, he was shy with her, because he fancied she looked down on him, and thought him a coward. And then he grew quite cross with her, because she was superior to him, and did what he could not do. And poor Ellie was quite surprised and sad; and at last Tom burst out crying; but he would not tell her what was really in his mind.

And all the while he was eaten up with curiosity to know where Ellie went to; so that he began not to care for his playmates, or for the sea-palace, or anything else. But perhaps that made matters all the easier for him; for he grew so discontented with everything round him, that he did not care to stay, and did not care where he went.

"Well," he said, at last, "I am so miserable here, I'll go; if only you will go with me?"

"Ah!" said Ellie, "I wish I might; but the worst of it is, that the fairy says, that you must go alone, if you go at all. Now don't poke that poor crab about, Tom (for he was feeling very naughty and mischievous), or the fairy will have to punish you."

Tom was very nearly saying, "I don't care if she does;" but he stopped himself in time.

"I know what she wants me to do," he said, whining most dolefully. "She wants me to go after that horrid old Grimes. I don't like him, that's certain. And if I find him, he will turn me into a chimney-sweep again, I know. That's what I have been afraid of all along."

"No, he won't—I know as much as that. Nobody can turn water-babies into sweeps, or hurt them at all, as long as they are good."

"Ah," said naughty Tom, "I see what you want; you are persuading me all along to go, because you are tired of me, and want to get rid of me."

Little Ellie opened her eyes very wide at that, and they were all brimming over with tears.

"Oh, Tom, Tom!" she said, very mournfully—and then she cried, "Oh, Tom! where are you?"

And Tom cried, "Oh, Ellie, where are you?"

For neither of them could see each other—not the least. Little Ellie vanished quite away, and Tom heard her voice calling him, and growing smaller and smaller, and fainter and fainter, till all was silent.

Who was frightened then but Tom? He swam up and down among the rocks, into all the halls and chambers, faster than ever he swam before, but could not find her. He shouted after her, but she did not answer; he asked all the other children, but they had not seen her; and at last he went up to the top of the water and began crying and screaming for Mrs. Doasyouwouldbeoneby, but she did not come. Then he began crying and screaming for Mrs. Bedonebyasyoudid—which perhaps was the best thing to do—for she came in a moment.

"Oh!" said Tom. "Oh dear, oh dear! I have been naughty to Ellie, and I have killed her—I know I have killed her."

"Not quite that," said the fairy; "but I have sent her away home, and she will not come back again for I do not know how long."

And at that Tom cried so bitterly, that the salt sea was swelled with his tears, and the tide was .3,954,620,819 of an inch higher than it had been the day before: but perhaps that was owing to the waxing of the moon. It may have been so; but it is considered right in the new philosophy,[1] you know, to give spiritual causes for physical phenomena—especially in parlour-tables; and, of course, physical causes for spiritual ones, like thinking, and praying, and knowing right from wrong. And so they odds it till it comes even, as folks say down in Berkshire.

"How cruel of you to send Ellie away!" sobbed Tom. "However, I will find her again, if I go to the world's end to look for her."

The fairy did not slap Tom, and tell him to hold his tongue: but she took him on her lap very kindly, just as her sister would have done; and put him in mind how it was not her fault, because she was wound up inside, like watches, and could not help doing things whether she liked or not. And then she told him how he

---

1 Spiritualism, popularized by the Scottish-American medium Daniel
   Dunglas Home (1833-86) in England during the1850s. In his drawing
   room séances furniture moved with no apparent cause, ghostly hands
   appeared, and furniture would levitate in the air. Kingsley also pokes fun
   at the assumption of scientific materialism, namely, that the only thing
   that exists is matter; even mental states are reducible to matter.

had been in the nursery long enough, and must go out now and see the world, if he intended ever to be a man; and how he must go all alone by himself, as every one else that ever was born has to go, and see with his own eyes, and smell with his own nose, and make his own bed and lie on it, and burn his own fingers if he put them into the fire. And then she told him how many fine things there were to be seen in the world, and what an odd, curious, pleasant, orderly, respectable, well-managed, and, on the whole successful (as, indeed, might have been expected) sort of a place it was, if people would only be tolerably brave and honest and good in it; and then she told him not to be afraid of anything he met, for nothing would harm him if he remembered all his lessons, and did what he knew was right. And at last she comforted poor little Tom so much, that he was quite eager to go, and wanted to set out that minute. "Only," he said, "if I might see Ellie once before I went!"

"Why do you want that?"

"Because—because I should be so much happier if I thought she had forgiven me."

And in the twinkling of an eye there stood Ellie, smiling, and looking so happy that Tom longed to kiss her; but was still afraid it would not be respectful, because she was a lady born.

"I am going, Ellie!" said Tom. "I am going, if it is to the world's end. But I don't like going at all, and that's the truth."

"Pooh! pooh! pooh!" said the fairy. "You will like it very well indeed, you little rogue, and you know that at the bottom of your heart. But if you don't I will make you like it. Come here, and see what happens to people who do only what is pleasant."

And she took out of one of her cupboards (she had all sorts of mysterious cupboards in the cracks of the rocks) the most wonderful waterproof book, full of such photographs as never were seen. For she had found out photography[1] (and this is a fact) more than 13,598,000 years before anybody was born; and, what is more, her photographs did not merely represent light and shade, as ours do, but colour also, and all colours, as you may see if you look at a black-cock's tail, or a butterfly's wing, or, indeed, most things that are or can be, so to speak. And, therefore, her

---

1 The photographic processes invented by William Henry Fox Talbot (1800-77), an Englishman, and Louis Jacques Mande Daguerre (1787-1851), a Frenchman, made the popular hobby of photography possible by the 1860s. Colour film was not available until 1907, when the Lumiere brothers produced their Autochrome plates.

photographs were very curious and famous, and the children looked with great delight for the opening of the book.

And on the title-page was written, "The History of the great and famous nation of the Doasyoulikes, who came away from the country of Hardwork, because they wanted to play on the Jews'-harp all day long."

In the first picture they saw these Doasyoulikes living in the land of Readymade, at the foot of the Happygolucky Mountains, where flapdoodle grows wild; and if you want to know what that is, you must read Peter Simple.[1]

They lived very much such a life as those jolly old Greeks in Sicily, whom you may see painted on the ancient vases, and really there seemed to be great excuses for them, for they had no need to work.

Instead of houses, they lived in the beautiful caves of tufa, and

---

1 A novel by Frederick Marryat (1792-1848) published in 1834. One of the sailors in the novel explains the term: "It's my opinion, Peter, that the gentleman has eaten no small quantity of flapdoodle in his lifetime." "What's that, O'Brien?" replied I; "I never heard of it." "Why, Peter," rejoined he, "it's the stuff they feed fools on" (Ch. 28).

bathed in the warm springs three times a day; and, as for clothes, it was so warm there that the gentlemen walked about in little beside a cocked hat and a pair of straps, or some light summer tackle of that kind; and the ladies all gathered gossamer in autumn (when they were not too lazy) to make their winter dresses.

They were very fond of music, but it was too much trouble to learn the piano or the violin; and, as for dancing, that would have been too great an exertion. So they sat on ant-hills all day long and played on the Jews'-harp; and, if the ants bit them, why they just got up and went to the next ant-hill, till they were bitten there likewise.

And they sat under the flapdoodle-trees, and let the flapdoodle drop into their mouths; and under the vines, and squeezed the grape-juice down their throats; and, if any little pigs ran about ready roasted, crying, "Come and eat me," as was their fashion in that country, they waited till the pigs ran against their mouths, and then took a bite, and were content, just as so many oysters would have been.

They needed no weapons, for no enemies ever came near their land; and no tools, for everything was readymade to their hand; and the stern old fairy Necessity never came near them to hunt them up, and make them use their wits, or die.

And so on, and so on, and so on, till there were never such comfortable, easy-going, happy-go-lucky people in the world.

"Well, that is a jolly life," said Tom.

"You think so?" said the fairy. "Do you see that great peaked mountain there behind," said the fairy, "with smoke coming out of its top?"

"Yes."

"And do you see all those ashes, and slag, and cinders, lying about?"

"Yes."

"Then turn over the next five hundred years, and you will see what happens next."

And behold the mountain had blown up like a barrel of gunpowder, and then boiled over like a kettle; whereby one-third of the Doasyoulikes were blown into the air, and another third were smothered in ashes; so that there was only one-third left.

"You see," said the fairy, "what comes of living on a burning mountain."

"Oh, why did you not warn them?" said little Ellie.

"I did warn them all that I could. I let the smoke come out of the mountain; and wherever there is smoke there is fire. And I laid the ashes and cinders all about; and wherever there are cinders, cinders may be again. But they did not like to face facts, my dears, as very few people do; and so they invented a cock-and-bull story, which, I am sure, I never told them, that the smoke was the breath of a giant, whom some gods or other had buried under the mountain; and that the cinders were what the dwarfs roasted the little pigs whole with; and other nonsense of that kind. And, when folks are in that humour, I cannot teach them, save by the good old birch-rod."

And then she turned over the next five hundred years: and there were the remnant of the Doasyoulikes, doing as they liked, as before. They were too lazy to move away from the mountain; so they said, If it has blown up once, that is all the more reason that it should not blow up again. And they were few in number: but they only said, The more the merrier, but the fewer the better fare. However, that was not quite true; for all the flapdoodle-trees were killed by the volcano, and they had eaten all the roast pigs, who, of course, could not be expected to have little ones. So they had to live very hard, on nuts and roots which they scratched out of the ground with sticks. Some of them talked of sowing corn, as their ancestors used to do, before they came into the land of Readymade; but they had forgotten how to make ploughs (they had forgotten even how to make Jews'-harps by this time), and had eaten all the seed-corn which they brought out of the land of Hardwork years since; and of course it was too much trouble to go away and find more. So they lived miserably on roots and nuts, and all the weakly little children had great stomachs, and then died.

"Why," said Tom, "they are growing no better than savages."

"And look how ugly they are all getting," said Ellie.

"Yes; when people live on poor vegetables instead of roast beef and plum-pudding, their jaws grow large, and their lips grow coarse, like the poor Paddies who eat potatoes."

And she turned over the next five hundred years. And there they were all living up in trees, and making nests to keep off the rain. And underneath the trees lions were prowling about.

"Why," said Ellie, "the lions seem to have eaten a good many of them, for there are very few left now."

"Yes," said the fairy; "you see it was only the strongest and most active ones who could climb the trees, and so escape."

"But what great, hulking, broad-shouldered chaps they are," said Tom; "they are a rough lot as ever I saw."

"Yes, they are getting very strong now; for the ladies will not marry any but the very strongest and fiercest gentlemen, who can help them up the trees out of the lions' way."

And she turned over the next five hundred years. And in that they were fewer still, and stronger, and fiercer; but their feet had changed shape very oddly, for they laid hold of the branches with their great toes, as if they had been thumbs, just as a Hindoo tailor uses his toes to thread his needle.

The children were very much surprised, and asked the fairy whether that was her doing.

"Yes, and no," she said, smiling. "It was only those who could use their feet as well as their hands who could get a good living: or, indeed, get married; so that they got the best of everything, and starved out all the rest; and those who are left keep up a regular breed of toe-thumb-men, as a breed of shorthorns, or skye-terriers, or fancy pigeons is kept up."

"But there is a hairy one among them," said Ellie.

"Ah!" said the fairy, "that will be a great man in his time, and chief of all the tribe."

And, when she turned over the next five hundred years, it was true.

For this hairy chief had hairy children, and they hairier children still; and every one wished to marry hairy husbands, and have hairy children too; for the climate was growing so damp that none but the hairy ones could live: all the rest coughed and sneezed, and had sore throats, and went into consumptions, before they could grow up to be men and women.

Then the fairy turned over the next five hundred years. And they were fewer still.

"Why, there is one on the ground picking up roots," said Ellie, "and he cannot walk upright."

No more he could; for in the same way that the shape of their feet had altered, the shape of their backs had altered also.

"Why," cried Tom, "I declare they are all apes."

"Something fearfully like it, poor foolish creatures," said the fairy. "They are grown so stupid now, that they can hardly think: for none of them have used their wits for many hundred years. They have almost forgotten, too, how to talk. For each stupid child forgot some of the words it heard from its stupid parents, and had not wits enough to make fresh words for itself. Beside, they are grown so fierce and suspicious and brutal that they keep out of each other's way, and mope and sulk in the dark forests, never hearing each other's voice, till they have forgotten almost what speech is like. I am afraid they will all be apes very soon, and all by doing only what they liked."

And in the next five hundred years they were all dead and gone, by bad food and wild beasts and hunters; all except one tremendous old fellow with jaws like a jack, who stood full seven feet high; and M. Du Chaillu[1] came up to him, and shot him, as he stood roaring and thumping his breast. And he remembered that his ancestors had once been men, and tried to say, "Am I not a man and a brother?"[2] but had forgotten how to use his tongue; and then he had tried to call for a doctor, but he had forgotten the word for one. So all he said was, "Ubboboo!" and died.

And that was the end of the great and jolly nation of the Doasyoulikes. And, when Tom and Ellie came to the end of the book, they looked very sad and solemn; and they had good reason so to do, for they really fancied that the men were apes, and never thought, in their simplicity, of asking whether the creatures had hippopotamus majors in their brains or not; in which case, as you have been told already, they could not possibly have been apes, though they were more apish than the apes of all aperies.

"But could you not have saved them from becoming apes?" said little Ellie, at last.

"At first, my dear; if only they would have behaved like men, and set to work to do what they did not like. But the longer they waited, and behaved like the dumb beasts, who only do what they like, the stupider and clumsier they grew; till at last they were past all cure, for they had thrown their own wits away. It is such things as this that help to make me so ugly, that I know not when I shall grow fair."

"And where are they all now?" asked Ellie.

"Exactly where they ought to be, my dear.

"Yes!" said the fairy, solemnly, half to herself, as she closed the wonderful book. "Folks say now that I can make beasts into men, by circumstance, and selection, and competition, and so forth. Well, perhaps they are right; and perhaps, again, they are wrong. That is one of the seven things which I am forbidden to tell, till the coming of the Cocqcigrues; and, at all events, it is no concern of theirs. Whatever their ancestors were, men they are; and I advise them to behave as such, and act accordingly. But let them recollect this, that there are two sides to every question, and a downhill as well as an uphill road; and, if I can turn beasts into

---

1 See note 1, p. 79.
2 See note 2, p. 137.

men, I can, by the same laws of circumstance, and selection, and competition, turn men into beasts.[1] You were very near being turned into a beast once or twice, little Tom. Indeed, if you had not made up your mind to go on this journey, and see the world, like an Englishman, I am not sure but that you would have ended as an eft in a pond."

"Oh, dear me!" said Tom; "sooner than that, and be all over slime, I'll go this minute, if it is to the world's end."

---

1 Kingsley grants Mrs. Doasyouwouldbedoneby the power to reverse the Darwinian world of evolution that accounts for the survival of the species through natural selection of the fittest creatures.

CHAPTER VII.

"And Nature, the old Nurse, took
  The child upon her knee,
Saying 'Here is a story book
  Thy father hath written for thee.

'Come wander with me' she said,
  'Into regions yet untrod,
And read what is still unread
  In the Manuscripts of God.'

And he wandered away and away
  With Nature, the dear old Nurse,
Who sang to him night and day
  The rhymes of the universe."[1]
                   Longfellow.

"NOW," said Tom, "I am ready to be off, if it's to the world's end."

"Ah!" said the fairy, "that is a brave, good boy. But you must go further than the world's end, if you want to find Mr. Grimes; for he is at the Other-end-of-Nowhere. You must go to Shiny Wall, and through the white gate that never was opened; and then you will come to Peacepool, and Mother Carey's Haven, where the good whales go when they die. And there Mother Carey will tell you the way to the Other-end-of-Nowhere, and there you will find Mr. Grimes."

"Oh, dear!" said Tom. "But I do not know my way to Shiny Wall, or where it is at all."

---

1   From "The Fiftieth Birthday of Agassiz. May 28, 1857." Louis Agassiz (1807-73) was America's leading scientist in the mid-nineteenth century, whose work had a profound influence upon Charles Darwin.

"Little boys must take the trouble to find out things for themselves, or they will never grow to be men; so that you must ask all the beasts in the sea and the birds in the air, and if you have been good to them, some of them will tell you the way to Shiny Wall."

"Well," said Tom, "it will be a long journey, so I had better start at once. Good-bye, Miss Ellie; you know I am getting a big boy, and I must go out and see the world."

"I know you must," said Ellie; "but you will not forget me, Tom. I shall wait here till you come."

And she shook hands with him, and bade him good-bye. Tom longed very much again to kiss her; but he thought it would not be respectful, considering she was a lady born; so he promised not to forget her: but his little whirl-about of a head was so full of the notion of going out to see the world, that it forgot her in five minutes: however, though his head forgot her, I am glad to say his heart did not.

So he asked all the beasts in the sea, and all the birds in the air, but none of them knew the way to Shiny Wall. For why? He was still too far down south.

Then he met a ship, far larger than he had ever seen—a gallant ocean-steamer, with a long cloud of smoke trailing behind; and he wondered how she went on without sails, and swam up to her to see. A school of dolphins were running races round and round her, going three feet for her one, and Tom asked them the way to Shiny Wall: but they did not know. Then he tried to find out how she moved, and at last he saw her screw, and was so delighted with it that he played under her quarter all day, till he nearly had his nose knocked off by the fans, and thought it time to move. Then he watched the sailors upon deck, and the ladies, with their bonnets and parasols: but none of them could see him, because their eyes were not opened—as, indeed, most people's eyes are not.

At last there came out into the quarter-gallery a very pretty lady, in deep black widow's weeds, and in her arms a baby. She leaned over the quarter-gallery, and looked back and back toward England far away; and as she looked she sang:

I.

"Soft soft wind, from out the sweet south sliding,
Waft thy silver cloud-webs athwart the summer sea;
Thin thin threads of mist on dewy fingers twining
Weave a veil of dappled gauze to shade my babe and me.

II.

"Deep deep Love, within thine own abyss abiding,
Pour Thyself abroad, O Lord, on earth and air and sea;
  Worn weary hearts within Thy holy temple hiding,
Shield from sorrow, sin, and shame my helpless babe and me."

Her voice was so soft and low, and the music of the air so sweet, that Tom could have listened to it all day. But as she held the baby over the gallery-rail, to show it the dolphins leaping and the water gurgling in the ship's wake, lo! and behold, the baby saw Tom.

He was quite sure of that; for when their eyes met, the baby smiled and held out its hands; and Tom smiled and held out his hands too; and the baby kicked and leaped, as if it wanted to jump overboard to him.

"What do you see, my darling?" said the lady; and her eyes followed the baby's till she too caught sight of Tom, swimming about among the foam-beads below.

She gave a little shriek and start; and then she said, quite quietly, "Babies in the sea? Well, perhaps it is the happiest place for them," and waved her hand to Tom, and cried, "Wait a little, darling, only a little: and perhaps we shall go with you and be at rest."

And at that an old nurse, all in black, came out and talked to her, and drew her in. And Tom turned away northward, sad and wondering; and watched the great steamer slide away into the dusk, and the lights on board peep out one by one, and die out again, and the long bar of smoke fade away into the evening mist, till all was out of sight.

And he swam northward again, day after day, till at last he met the King of the Herrings, with a currycomb growing out of his nose, and a sprat in his mouth for a cigar, and asked him the way to Shiny Wall; so he bolted his sprat head foremost, and said:

"If I were you, young gentleman, I should go to the Allalone-stone, and ask the last of the Gairfowl.[1] She is of a very ancient clan, very nearly as ancient as my own; and knows a good deal which these modern upstarts don't, as ladies of old houses are likely to do."

Tom asked his way to her, and the King of the Herrings told him very kindly; for he was a courteous old gentleman of the old

---

1 The Gare-fowl, or Great Auk, is a large flightless seabird that was native to northern Atlantic coasts until it was hunted to extinction in the middle of the nineteenth century.

school, though he was horribly ugly, and strangely bedizened too, like the old dandies who lounge in the club-house windows.

But just as Tom had thanked him and set off, he called after him: "Hi! I say, can you fly?"

"I never tried," says Tom. "Why?"

"Because, if you can, I should advise you to say nothing to the old lady about it. There; take a hint. Good-bye."

And away Tom went for seven days and seven nights due north-west, till he came to a great codbank, the like of which he never saw before. The great cod lay below in tens of thousands, and gobbled shellfish all day long; and the blue sharks roved above in hundreds, and gobbled them when they came up. So they ate, and ate, and ate each other, as they had done since the making of the world; for no man had come here yet to catch them, and find out how rich old Mother Carey is.

And there he saw the last of the Gairfowl, standing up on the Allalonestone, all alone. And a very grand old lady she was, full three feet high, and bolt upright, like some old Highland chieftain-ess. She had on a black velvet gown, and a white pinner and apron, and a very high bridge to her nose (which is a sure mark of high breeding), and a large pair of white spectacles on it, which made her look rather odd: but it was the ancient fashion of her house.

And instead of wings, she had two little feathery arms, with which she fanned herself, and complained of the dreadful heat; and she kept on crooning an old song to herself, which she learnt when she was a little baby-bird, long ago—

"Two little birds, they sat on a stone,
One swam away, and then there was one;
　　With a fal-lal-la-lady.

The other swam after, and then there was none,
And so the poor stone was left all alone;
　　With a fal-lal-la-lady."[1]

It was "flew" away, properly, and not "swam" away: but, as she could not fly, she had a right to alter it. However, it was a very fit song for her to sing, because she was a lady herself.

1　Kingsley's variation on the nursery rhyme in *Mother Goose's Melody* (1795): "There were two birds sat on a stone,/ Fa, la, la, la, lal, de;/ One flew away, and then there was one,/ Fa, la, la, la, lal, de;/ The other bird flew after,/ And then there was none,/ Fa, la, la, la, lal, de;/ And so the stone/ Was left alone,/ Fa la, la, la, lal, de."

Tom came up to her very humbly, and made his bow; and the first thing she said was—

"Have you wings? Can you fly?"

"Oh dear, no, ma'am; I should not think of such a thing," said cunning little Tom.

"Then I shall have great pleasure in talking to you, my dear. It is quite refreshing nowadays to see anything without wings. They must all have wings, forsooth, now, every new upstart sort of bird, and fly. What can they want with flying, and raising themselves above their proper station in life? In the days of my ancestors no birds ever thought of having wings, and did very well without; and

now they all laugh at me because I keep to the good old fashion. Why, the very marrocks[1] and dovekies[2] have got wings, the vulgar creatures, and poor little ones enough they are; and my own cousins too, the razor-bills, who are gentlefolk born, and ought to know better than to ape their inferiors."

And so she was running on, while Tom tried to get in a word edgeways; and at last he did, when the old lady got out of breath, and began fanning herself again; and then he asked if she knew the way to Shiny Wall.

"Shiny Wall? Who should know better than I? We all came from Shiny Wall, thousands of years ago, when it was decently cold, and the climate was fit for gentlefolk; but now, what with the heat, and what with these vulgar-winged things who fly up and down and eat everything, so that gentlepeople's hunting is all spoilt, and one really cannot get one's living, or hardly venture off the rock for fear of being flown against by some creature that would not have dared to come within a mile of one a thousand

1 Marrots, auks or razorbills.
2 Arctic birds, the Black Guillemots.

years ago—what was I saying? Why, we have quite gone down in the world, my dear, and have nothing left but our honour. And I am the last of my family. A friend of mine and I came and settled on this rock when we were young, to be out of the way of low people. Once we were a great nation, and spread over all the Northern Isles. But men shot us so, and knocked us on the head, and took our eggs—why, if you will believe it, they say that on the coast of Labrador the sailors used to lay a plank from the rock on board the thing they called their ship, and drive us along the plank by hundreds, till we tumbled down into the ship's waist in heaps; and then, I suppose, they ate us, the nasty fellows! Well—but—what was I saying? At last there were none of us left, except on the old Gairfowlskerry,[1] just off the Iceland coast, up which no man could climb. Even there we had no peace; for one day, when I was quite a young girl, the land rocked, and the sea boiled, and the sky grew dark, and all the air was filled with smoke and dust, and down tumbled the old Gairfowlskerry into the sea. The dovekies and marrocks, of course, all flew away; but we were too proud to do that. Some of us were dashed to pieces, and some drowned; and those who were left got away to Eldey, and the dovekies tell me they are all dead now, and that another Gairfowlskerry has risen out of the sea close to the old one, but that it is such a poor flat place that it is not safe to live on: and so here I am left alone."

This was the Gairfowl's story, and, strange as it may seem, it is every word of it true.

"If you only had had wings!" said Tom; "then you might all have flown away too."

"Yes, young gentleman: and if people are not gentlemen and ladies, and forget that *noblesse oblige*,[2] they will find it as easy to get on in the world as other people who don't care what they do. Why, if I had not recollected that *noblesse oblige*, I should not have been all alone now." And the poor old lady sighed.

"How was that, ma'am?"

"Why, my dear, a gentleman came hither with me, and after we had been here some time, he wanted to marry—in fact, he actually proposed to me. Well, I can't blame him; I was young,

---

1 The Geirfuglasker Skerries (rugged sea rocks), located off the coast of Iceland, were among the last refuges for the Great Auk when they submerged after a volcanic eruption in 1830.

2 Honorable behavior considered the responsibility of someone of noble birth.

and very handsome then, I don't deny: but you see, I could not hear of such a thing, because he was my deceased sister's husband, you see?"[1]

"Of course not, ma'am," said Tom; though, of course, he knew nothing about it. "She was very much diseased, I suppose?"

"You do not understand me, my dear. I mean, that being a lady, and with right and honourable feelings, as our house always has had, I felt it my duty to snub him, and howk him, and peck him continually, to keep him at his proper distance; and, to tell the truth, I once pecked him a little too hard, poor fellow, and he tumbled backwards off the rock, and—really, it was very unfortunate, but it was not my fault—a shark coming by saw him flapping, and snapped him up. And since then I have lived all alone—

With a fal-lal-la-lady.

And soon I shall be gone, my little dear, and nobody will miss me; and then the poor stone will be left all alone."

"But, please, which is the way to Shiny Wall?" said Tom.

"Oh, you must go, my little dear—you must go. Let me see— I am sure—that is—really, my poor old brains are getting quite puzzled. Do you know, my little dear, I am afraid, if you want to know, you must ask some of these vulgar birds about, for I have quite forgotten."

And the poor old Gairfowl began to cry tears of pure oil; and Tom was quite sorry for her; and for himself too, for he was at his wit's end whom to ask.

But by there came a flock of petrels,[2] who are Mother Carey's own chickens; and Tom thought them much prettier than Lady Gairfowl, and so perhaps they were; for Mother Carey had had a great deal of fresh experience between the time that she invented the Gairfowl and the time that she invented them. They flitted along like a flock of black swallows, and hopped and skipped from wave to wave, lifting up their little feet behind them so daintily, and whistling to each other so tenderly, that Tom fell in love with them at once, and called them to know the way to Shiny Wall.

"Shiny Wall? Do you want Shiny Wall? Then come with us, and we will show you. We are Mother Carey's own chickens, and she

---

1   The Marriage Act of 1835 made it illegal for a man to marry the sister of his deceased wife.

2   Small black-and-white sea-birds with long wings, also known as Stormy Petrels.

sends us out over all the seas, to show the good birds the way home."

Tom was delighted, and swam off to them, after he had made his bow to the Gairfowl. But she would not return his bow: but held herself bolt upright, and wept tears of oil as she sang:

> "And so the poor stone was left all alone;
>   With a fal-lal-la-lady."

But she was wrong there; for the stone was not left all alone: and the next time that Tom goes by it, he will see a sight worth seeing.

The old Gairfowl is gone already: but there are better things come in her place; and when Tom comes he will see the fishing-smacks anchored there in hundreds, from Scotland, and from Ireland, and from the Orkneys, and the Shetlands, and from all the Northern ports, full of the children of the old Norse Vikings, the masters of the sea. And the men will be hauling in the great cod by thousands, till their hands are sore from the lines; and they will be making cod-liver oil and guano,[1] and salting down the fish; and there will be a man-of-war steamer there to protect them, and a lighthouse to show them the way; and you and I, perhaps, shall go some day to the Allalonestone to the great summer sea-fair, and dredge strange creatures such as man never saw before; and we shall hear the sailors boast that it is not the worst jewel in Queen Victoria's crown, for there are eighty miles of codbank, and food for all the poor folk in the land. That is what Tom will see, and perhaps you and I shall see it too. And then we shall not be sorry because we cannot get a Gairfowl to stuff, much less find gairfowl enough to drive them into stone pens and slaughter them, as the old Norsemen did, or drive them on board along a plank till the ship was victualled with them, as the old English and French rovers used to do, of whom dear old Hakluyt[2] tells: but we shall remember what Mr. Tennyson says, how

---

1 A natural manure made from the excrement of sea-fowl found along the coasts.

2 Richard Hakluyt (1552-1616), a lecturer in geography at Oxford University and author of *The Principal Navigations, Voyages and Discoveries of the English Nation* (1589). In these recorded adventures of the Elizabethan sailors Kingsley discovered a heroic model for his own age.

"The old order changeth, giving place to the new,
And God fulfils Himself in many ways."[1]

And now Tom was all agog to start for Shiny Wall; but the petrels said no. They must go first to Allfowlsness, and wait there for the great gathering of all the seabirds, before they start for their summer breeding-places far away in the Northern isles; and there they would be sure to find some birds which were going to Shiny Wall: but where Allfowlsness was, he must promise never to tell, lest men should go there and shoot the birds, and stuff them, and put them into stupid museums, instead of leaving them to play and breed and work in Mother Carey's water-garden, where they ought to be.

So where Allfowlsness is nobody must know; and all that is to be said about it is, that Tom waited there many days; and as he waited, he saw a very curious sight. On the rabbit burrows on the shore there gathered hundreds and hundreds of hoodiecrows,[2] such as you see in Cambridgeshire. And they made such a noise, that Tom came on shore and went up to see what was the matter.

And there he found them holding their great caucus,[3] which they hold every year in the North; and all their stump-orators were speechifying; and for a tribune, the speaker stood on an old sheep's skull.

And they cawed and cawed, and boasted of all the clever things they had done; how many lambs' eyes they had picked out, and how many dead bullocks they had eaten, and how many young grouse they had swallowed whole, and how many grouse-eggs they had flown away with, stuck on the point of their bills, which is the hoodiecrow's particularly clever feat, of which he is as proud as a gipsy is of doing the hokany-baro;[4] and what that is, I won't tell you.

And at last they brought out the prettiest, neatest young lady-crow that ever was seen, and set her in the middle, and all began

---

1 From "Morte d'Arthur," published in *Poems* (1842). The lines should read "The old order changeth, yielding place to new,/ And God fulfils Himself in many ways."
2 The Hooded or Royston Crow, marked by its two-colour plumage: the body is a dirty grey, while the wings, tail, head and bib are black.
3 A political meeting of party members.
4 *Hokkano baro*, or the Great Trick. The term refers to various Gypsy methods of duping credulous *gorgios* (non-gypsies).

abusing and vilifying, and rating,[1] and bullyragging[2] at her, because she had stolen no grouse-eggs, and had actually dared to say that she would not steal any. So she was to be tried publicly by their laws (for the hoodies always try some offenders in their great yearly parliament). And there she stood in the middle, in her black gown and grey hood, looking as meek and as neat as a quakeress, and they all bawled at her at once—

And it was in vain that she pleaded

That she did not like grouse-eggs;
That she could get her living very well without them;
That she was afraid to eat them, for fear of the gamekeepers;
That she had not the heart to eat them, because the grouse were such pretty, kind, jolly birds;
And a dozen reasons more.

For all the other scaul-crows set upon her, and pecked her to death there and then, before Tom could come to help her; and then flew away, very proud of what they had done.

Now, was not this a scandalous transaction?

But they are true republicans, these hoodies, who do every one just what he likes, and make other people do so too; so that, for any freedom of speech, thought, or action, which is allowed among them, they might as well be American citizens of the new school.[3]

But the fairies took the good crow, and gave her nine new sets of feathers running, and turned her at last into the most beautiful bird of paradise with a green velvet suit and a long tail, and sent her to eat fruit in the Spice Islands, where cloves and nutmegs grow.

And Mrs. Bedonebyasyoudid settled her account with the wicked hoodies. For, as they flew away, what should they find but a nasty dead dog?—on which they all set to work, pecking and

---

1 Chiding or reproving.
2 Harassing or scolding.
3 The Republican Party and its abolitionist platform that took power in 1861. Kingsley did not think Lincoln was fit to be president. In a letter to his son Henry, dated 1862, Kingsley wrote that the war in America might likely prove "a blessing for the whole world by breaking up an insolent and aggressive republic of rogues" (quoted in Margaret Thorp's *Charles Kingsley* [Princeton: Princeton UP, 1937], 150).

gobbling and cawing and quarrelling, to their hearts' content. But the moment afterwards, they all threw up their bills into the air, and gave one screech; and then turned head over heels backward, and fell down dead, one hundred and twenty-three of them at once. For why? The fairy had told the gamekeeper in a dream, to fill the dead dog full of strychnine; and so he did.

And after a while the birds began to gather at Allfowlsness, in thousands and tens of thousands, blackening all the air; swans and brant geese,[1] harlequins[2] and eiders,[3] harelds[4] and garganeys,[5] smews[6] and goosanders,[7] divers and loons, grebes[8] and

---

1 Small, dark wild geese that breed in the Arctic.
2 A northern species of duck with variegated plumage.
3 A species of duck found especially in Arctic regions.
4 A sea duck.
5 A species of teal, a freshwater duck.
6 A saw-billed duck, also known as the white nun.
7 A fish-eating duck with a serrated bill.
8 Short-bodied, almost tailless diving birds.

dovekies, auks and razorbills, gannets[1] and petrels, skuas[2] and terns, with gulls beyond all naming or numbering; and they paddled and washed and splashed and combed and brushed themselves on the sand, till the shore was white with feathers; and they quacked and clucked and gabbled and chattered and screamed and whooped as they talked over matters with their friends, and settled where they were to go and breed that summer, till you might have heard them ten miles off; and lucky it was for them that there was no one to hear them but the old keeper, who lived all alone upon the Ness,[3] in a turf hut thatched with heather and fringed round with great stones slung across the roof by bent-ropes, lest the winter gales should blow the hut right away. But he never minded the birds nor hurt them, because they were not in season: indeed, he minded but two things in the whole world, and those were, his Bible and his grouse; for he was as good an old Scotchman as ever knit stockings on a winter's night: only, when all the birds were going, he toddled out, and took off his cap to them, and wished them a merry journey and a safe return; and then gathered up all the feathers which they had left, and cleaned them to sell down south, and make feather-beds for stuffy people to lie on.

Then the petrels asked this bird and that whether they would take Tom to Shiny Wall: but one set was going to Sutherland,[4] and one to the Shetlands,[5] and one to Norway, and one to Spitzbergen,[6] and one to Iceland, and one to Greenland: but none would go to Shiny Wall. So the good-natured petrels said that they would show him part of the way themselves, but they were only going as far as Jan Mayen's land;[7] and after that he must shift for himself.

And then all the birds rose up, and streamed away in long black lines, north, and north-east, and north-west, across the

---

1   The Solan goose: a large sea-fowl resembling a goose, found on the small islands of Britain, the Faeroes, Iceland, and Canada.
2   Predatory gulls that breed in the Shetlands, the Faeroes, and Iceland.
3   A promontory or headland.
4   A county in the north of Scotland.
5   The Shetland Islands, an archipelago of northern Scotland in the Atlantic Ocean northeast of the Orkney Islands.
6   One of the islands between the Arctic Ocean, Barents Sea, Greenland Sea, and Norwegian Sea, north of Norway.
7   An island between the Greenland Sea and the Norwegian Sea, northeast of Iceland.

bright blue summer sky; and their cry was like ten thousand packs of hounds, and ten thousand peals of bells. Only the puffins stayed behind, and killed the young rabbits, and laid their eggs in the rabbit-burrows; which was rough practice, certainly: but a man must see to his own family.

And, as Tom and the petrels went north-eastward, it began to blow right hard; for the old gentleman in the grey great-coat, who looks after the big copper boiler in the gulf of Mexico, had got behind-hand with his work; so Mother Carey had sent an electric message to him for more steam; and now the steam was coming, as much in an hour as ought to have come in a week, puffing and roaring and swishing and swirling, till you could not see where the sky ended and the sea began. But Tom and the petrels never cared, for the gale was right abaft, and away they went over the crests of the billows, as merry as so many flying-fish.

And at last they saw an ugly sight—the black side of a great ship, water-logged in the trough of the sea. Her funnel and her masts were overboard, and swayed and surged her lee; her decks were swept as clean as a barn floor, and there was no living soul on board.

The petrels flew up to her, and wailed round her; for they were very sorry indeed, and also they expected to find some salt pork; and Tom scrambled on board of her and looked round, frightened and sad.

And there, in a little cot, lashed tight under the bulwark, lay a baby fast asleep; the very same baby, Tom saw at once, which he had seen in the singing lady's arms.

He went up to it, and wanted to wake it: but behold, from under the cot out jumped a little black and tan terrier dog and began barking and snapping at Tom, and would not let him touch the cot.

Tom knew the dog's teeth could not hurt him: but at least it could shove him away, and did; and he and the dog fought and struggled, for he wanted to help the baby, and did not want to throw the poor dog overboard: but, as they were struggling, there came a tall green sea, and walked in over the weather side of the ship, and swept them all into the waves.

"Oh, the baby, the baby!" screamed Tom: but the next moment he did not scream at all; for he saw the cot settling down through the green water, with the baby smiling in it, fast asleep; and he saw fairies come up from below, and carry baby and cradle gently down in their soft arms; and then he knew it was all right, and that there would be a new water-baby in St. Brandan's Isle.

And the poor little dog?

Why, after he had kicked and coughed a little, he sneezed so hard, that he sneezed himself clean out of his skin, and turned into a water-dog, and jumped and danced round Tom, and ran over the crests of the waves, and snapped at the jelly-fish and the mackerel, and followed Tom the whole way to the Other-end-of-Nowhere.

Then they went on again, till they began to see the peak of Jan Mayen's Land, standing up like a white sugar-loaf, two miles above the clouds.

And there they fell in with a whole flock of mollymocks,[1] who were feeding on a dead whale.

"These are the fellows to show you the way," said Mother Carey's chickens; "we cannot help you further north. We don't like to get among the ice pack, for fear it should nip our toes; but the mollys dare fly anywhere."

So the petrels called to the mollys: but they were so busy and greedy, gobbling and pecking and spluttering and fighting over the blubber, that they did not take the least notice.

"Come, come," said the petrels, "you lazy greedy lubbers, this young gentleman is going to Mother Carey, and if you don't attend on him, you won't earn your discharge from her, you know."

"Greedy we are," says a great fat old molly, "but lazy we ain't; and, as for lubbers, we're no more lubbers than you. Let's have a look at the lad."

And he flapped right into Tom's face, and stared at him in the most impudent way (for the mollys are audacious fellows, as all whalers know), and then asked him where he hailed from, and what land he sighted last.

And, when Tom told him, he seemed pleased, and said he was a good plucked one to have got so far.

"Come along, lads," he said to the rest, "and give this little chap a cast over the pack, for Mother Carey's sake. We've eaten blubber enough for to-day, and we'll e'en work out a bit of our time by helping the lad."

So the mollys took Tom up on their backs, and flew off with him, laughing and joking—and oh, how they did smell of train oil!

"Who are you, you jolly birds?" asked Tom.

---

1 Smoky gray, gull-like sea-birds, also known as fulmar petrels.

"We are the spirits of the old Greenland skippers (as every sailor knows), who hunted here, right whales and horse-whales, full hundreds of years agone. But, because we were saucy and greedy, we were all turned into mollys, to eat whale's blubber all our days. But lubbers we are none, and could sail a ship now against any man in the North Seas, though we don't hold with this newfangled steam. And it's a shame of those black imps of petrels to call us so; but because they're her grace's pets, they think they may say anything they like."

"And who are you?" asked Tom of him, for he saw that he was the king of all the birds.

"My name is Hendrick Hudson,[1] and a right good skipper was I; and my name will last to the world's end, in spite of all the wrong I did. For I discovered Hudson River, and I named Hudson's Bay; and many have come in my wake that dared not have shown me the way. But I was a hard man in my time, that's truth, and stole the poor Indians off the coast of Maine, and sold them for slaves down in Virginia; and at last I was so cruel to my sailors, here in these very seas, that they set me adrift in an open boat, and I never was heard of more. So now I'm the king of all the mollys, till I've worked out my time."

And now they came to the edge of the pack, and beyond it they could see Shiny Wall looming, through mist, and snow, and storm. But the pack rolled horribly upon the swell, and the ice giants fought and roared, and leapt upon each other's backs, and ground each other to powder, so that Tom was afraid to venture among them, lest he should be ground to powder too. And he was the more afraid, when he saw lying among the ice pack the wrecks of many a gallant ship; some with masts and yards all standing, some with the seamen frozen fast on board.

---

1 Henry Hudson (c. 1570-1611), English explorer who, in his search for the Northwest Passage, discovered the Hudson River in 1609 during an expedition sponsored by the Dutch East India Company. His crew mutinied when they found out he intended to extend his explorations in order to search for a western outlet from James Bay. They left him, his son, and seven loyal crewmen in a small boat to be heard of never again. There is no evidence, however, that Hudson ever captured Indians and sold them as slaves. Kingsley may have confused Hudson with Captain Thomas Hunt, an English colonizer, who, in 1614, kidnaped 24 Indians from the Cape Cod area and sold them as slaves. An account of the kidnapping is recorded in Cotton Mather's *The Story of Squanto* (c. 1698).

Alas, alas, for them! They were all true English hearts; and they came to their end like good knights-errant, in searching for the white gate that never was opened yet.

But the good mollys took Tom and his dog up, and flew with them safe over the pack and the roaring ice giants, and set them down at the foot of Shiny Wall.

"And where is the gate?" asked Tom.

"There is no gate," said the mollys.

"No gate?" cried Tom aghast.

"None; never a crack of one, and that's the whole of the secret, as better fellows, lad, than you have found to their cost; and if there had been, they'd have killed by now every right whale that swims the sea."

"What am I to do, then?"

"Dive under the floe, to be sure, if you have pluck."

"I've not come so far to turn now," said Tom; "so here goes for a header."

"A lucky voyage to you, lad," said the mollys; "we knew you were one of the right sort. So good-bye."

"Why don't you come too?" asked Tom.

But the mollys only wailed sadly, "We can't go yet, we can't go yet," and flew away over the pack.

So Tom dived under the great white gate which never was opened yet, and went on in black darkness, at the bottom of the sea, for seven days and seven nights. And yet he was not a bit frightened. Why should he be? He was a brave English lad, whose business is to go out and see all the world.

And at last he saw the light, and clear clear water overhead; and up he came a thousand fathoms, among clouds of sea-moths,[1] which fluttered round his head. There were moths with pink heads and wings and opal bodies, that flapped about slowly; moths with brown wings that flapped about quickly; yellow shrimps that hopped and skipped most quickly of all; and jellies of all the colours in the world, that neither hopped nor skipped, but only dawdled and yawned, and would not get out of his way. The dog snapped at them till his jaws were tired: but Tom hardly minded them at all, he was so eager to get to the top of the water, and see the pool where the good whales go.

And a very large pool it was, miles and miles across, though the air was so clear that the ice cliffs on the opposite side looked

---

1   Sea moth, or sea robin, small fish with armored bodies and large wing-like pectoral fins. They are closely related to pipe-fishes and seahorses.

as if they were close at hand. All round it the ice cliffs rose, in walls and spires and battlements, and caves and bridges, and stories and galleries, in which the ice-fairies live, and drive away the storms and clouds, that Mother Carey's pool may lie calm from year's end to year's end. And the sun acted policeman, and walked round outside every day, peeping just over the top of the ice wall, to see that all went right; and now and then he played conjuring tricks, or had an exhibition of fireworks, to amuse the ice-fairies. For he would make himself into four or five suns at once, or paint the sky with rings and crosses and crescents of white fire, and stick himself in the middle of them, and wink at the fairies; and I dare say they were very much amused; for anything's fun in the country.

And there the good whales lay, the happy sleepy beasts, upon the still oily sea. They were all right whales, you must know, and finners, and razor-backs, and bottle-noses, and spotted sea-unicorns with long ivory horns. But the sperm whales are such raging, ramping, roaring, rumbustious fellows, that, if Mother Carey let them in, there would be no more peace in Peacepool. So she packs them away in a great pond by themselves at the South Pole, two hundred and sixty-three miles south-south east of Mount Erebus,[1] the great volcano in the ice; and there they butt each other with their ugly noses, day and night from year's end to year's end. And if they think that sport—why, so do their American cousins.

But here there were only good quiet beasts, lying about like the black hulls of sloops, and blowing every now and then jets of white steam, or sculling round with their huge mouths open, for the sea-moths to swim down their throats. There were no threshers[2] there to thresh their poor old backs, or sword-fish to stab their stomachs, or saw-fish to rip them up, or ice-sharks to bite lumps out of their sides, or whalers to harpoon and lance them. They were quite safe and happy there; and all they had to do was to wait quietly in Peacepool, till Mother Carey sent for them to make them out of old beasts into new.

Tom swam up to the nearest whale, and asked the way to Mother Carey.

"There she sits in the middle," said the whale.

---

1 A volcano on Ross Island, Antarctica, discovered by the British explorer James C. Ross in 1841 and named after one of his two ships.

2 "A sea-fox or fox-shark, *Alopias vulpes*; so called from the very long upper division of the tail, with which it lashes an enemy" (*OED*).

Tom looked; but he could see nothing in the middle of the pool, but one peaked iceberg: and he said so.

"That's Mother Carey," said the whale, "as you will find when you get to her. There she sits making old beasts into new all the year round."

"How does she do that?"

"That's her concern, not mine," said the old whale; and yawned so wide (for he was very large) that there swam into his mouth 943 sea-moths, 13,846 jellyfish no bigger than pins' heads, a string of salpæ[1] nine yards long, and forty-three little ice-crabs, who gave each other a parting pinch all round, tucked their legs under their stomachs, and determined to die decently, like Julius Cæsar.

"I suppose," said Tom, "she cuts up a great whale like you into a whole shoal of porpoises?"

---

1   A genus of transparent, tubular, free-swimming oceanic tunicates, such as the sea-squirt, found abundantly in all the warmer latitudes.

At which the old whale laughed so violently that he coughed up all the creatures; who swam away again very thankful at having escaped out of that terrible whalebone net of his, from which bourne no traveller returns;[1] and Tom went on to the iceberg, wondering.

And, when he came near it, it took the form of the grandest old lady he had ever seen—a white marble lady, sitting on a white marble throne. And from the foot of the throne there swum away, out and out into the sea, millions of new-born creatures, of more shapes and colours than man ever dreamed. And they were Mother Carey's children, whom she makes out of the sea-water all day long.

He expected, of course—like some grown people who ought to know better—to find her snipping, piecing, fitting, stitching, cobbling, basting, filing, planing, hammering, turning, polishing, moulding, measuring, chiselling, clipping, and so forth, as men do when they go to work to make anything.

But, instead of that, she sat quite still with her chin upon her hand, looking down into the sea with two great grand blue eyes, as blue as the sea itself. Her hair was white as the snow—for she was very very old—in fact, as old as any thing which you are likely to come across, except the difference between right and wrong.

And, when she saw Tom, she looked at him very kindly.

"What do you want, my little man? It is long since I have seen a water-baby here."

Tom told her his errand, and asked the way to the Other-end-of-Nowhere.

"You ought to know yourself, for you have been there already."

"Have I, ma'am? I'm sure I forget all about it."

"Then look at me."

And, as Tom looked into her great blue eyes, he recollected the way perfectly.

Now, was not that strange?

"Thank you, ma'am," said Tom. "Then I won't trouble your ladyship any more; I hear you are very busy."

"I am never more busy than I am now," she said, without stirring a finger.

---

1 *Hamlet*, III, I, 56: "The undiscover'd country from whose bourn/ No traveller returns." The whalebone net refers to the fringed plates in the mouth of the baleen whale that filters the plankton from the sea water.

"I heard, ma'am, that you were always making new beasts out of old."

"So people fancy. But I am not going to trouble myself to make things, my little dear. I sit here and make them make themselves."[1]

"You are a clever fairy, indeed," thought Tom. And he was quite right.

That is a grand trick of good old Mother Carey's, and a grand answer, which she has had occasion to make several times to impertinent people.

There was once, for instance, a fairy who was so clever that she found out how to make butterflies. I don't mean sham ones; no: but real live ones, which would fly, and eat, and lay eggs, and do everything that they ought; and she was so proud of her skill that she went flying straight off to the North Pole, to boast to Mother Carey how she could make butterflies.

But Mother Carey laughed.

"Know, silly child," she said, "that any one can make things, if they will take time and trouble enough: but it is not every one who, like me, can make things make themselves."

But people do not yet believe that Mother Carey is as clever as all that comes to; and they will not till they, too, go the journey to the Other-end-of-Nowhere.

"And now, my pretty little man," said Mother Carey, "you are sure you know the way to the Other-end-of-Nowhere?"

Tom thought; and behold, he had forgotten it utterly.

"That is because you took your eyes off me."

Tom looked at her again, and recollected; and then looked away, and forgot in an instant.

"But what am I to do, ma'am? For I can't keep looking at you when I am somewhere else."

"You must do without me, as most people have to do, for nine hundred and ninety-nine thousandths of their lives; and look at the dog instead; for he knows the way well enough, and will not

---

1 In *Glaucus; or, The Wonders of the Shore* (1855) Kingsley attributes this power to God: "Ought God to appear less or more august in our eyes if we discover that the means [of creation] are even simpler than we supposed? We held Him to be Almighty and All-wise. Are we to reverence Him less or more if we find Him to be so much mightier, so much wiser, than we dreamed, that He can not only make all things, but—the very perfection of creative power—MAKE ALL THINGS MAKE THEMSELVES?"

forget it. Besides, you may meet some very queer-tempered people there, who will not let you pass without this passport of mine, which you must hang round your neck and take care of; and, of course, as the dog will always go behind you, you must go the whole way backward."

"Backward!" cried Tom. "Then I shall not be able to see my way."

"On the contrary, if you look forward, you will not see a step before you, and be certain to go wrong; but, if you look behind you, and watch carefully whatever you have passed, and especially keep your eye on the dog, who goes by instinct, and therefore can't go wrong, then you will know what is coming next as plainly as if you saw it in a looking-glass."

Tom was very much astonished: but he obeyed her, for he had learnt always to believe what the fairies told him.

"So it is, my dear child," said Mother Carey; "and I will tell you a story, which will show you that I am perfectly right, as it is my custom to be."

"Once on a time, there were two brothers. One was called Prometheus, because he always looked before him, and boasted that he was wise beforehand. The other was called Epimetheus,[1] because he always looked behind him, and did not boast at all; but said humbly, like the Irishman, that he had sooner prophesy after the event.

"Well, Prometheus was a very clever fellow, of course, and invented all sorts of wonderful things. But, unfortunately, when they were set to work, to work was just what they would not do: wherefore very little has come of them, and very little is left of them; and now nobody knows what they were, save a few archæo-

---

1   Prometheus and Epimetheus were brothers and sons of the Titan Iapetus and Gæa (Earth). Their names mean "forethought" and "afterthought." Prometheus is usually depicted as an heroic figure, one who brought fire and the arts to humankind. Epimetheus, on the other hand, is portrayed as careless and responsible for man's weakness. Although warned by his brother not to accept any gifts from Zeus, Epimetheus accepts Pandora as his wife and she, in turn, opens a box that frees all manner of evils to inflict the world. Prometheus is punished by Zeus for his defiance in stealing fire from the gods by being chained to a rock and having an eagle endlessly tear away his liver, which regenerates each night. Oddly, Kingsley here views Epimetheus as the superior brother, someone practical, down-to-earth, experienced, and sanguine. Prometheus, by contrast, is seen as an over-reaching romantic, a theorist whose prophetic fantasies preclude the real world in which he lives.

logical old gentlemen who scratch in queer corners, and find little there save Ptinum Furem, Blaptem Mortisagam, Acarum Horridum, and Tineam Laciniarum.[1]

"But Epimetheus was a very slow fellow, certainly, and went among men for a clod, and a muff, and a milksop, and a slow-coach,[2] and a bloke, and a boodle,[3] and so forth. And very little he did, for many years: but what he did, he never had to do over again.

"And what happened at last? There came to the two brothers the most beautiful creature that ever was seen, Pandora by name; which means, All the gifts of the Gods. But because she had a strange box in her hand, this fanciful, forecasting, suspicious, prudential, theoretical, deductive, prophesying Prometheus, who was always settling what was going to happen, would have nothing to do with pretty Pandora and her box.

"But Epimetheus took her and it, as he took everything that came; and married her for better for worse, as every man ought, whenever he has even the chance of a good wife. And they opened the box between them, of course, to see what was inside: for, else, of what possible use could it have been to them?

"And out flew all the ills which flesh is heir to; all the children of the four great bogies, Self-will, Ignorance, Fear, and Dirt—for instance:

Measles,	Famines,
Monks,	Quacks,
Scarlatina,	Unpaid bills,
Idols,	Tight stays,
Hooping-coughs,	Potatoes,
Popes,	Bad Wine,
Wars,	Despots,
Peacemongers,	Demagogues,

And, worst of all, Naughty Boys and Girls:
But one thing remained at the bottom of the box, and that was, Hope.

"So Epimetheus got a great deal of trouble, as most men do in this world: but he got the three best things in the world into the

---

1 A nonsense list of what appear to be various esoteric chemicals.
2 An idle or indolent person.
3 "A stupid noodle" (*OED*, which cites Kingsley as the sole reference for this rather odd definition).

bargain—a good wife, and experience, and hope: while Prometheus had just as much trouble, and a great deal more (as you will hear), of his own making; with nothing beside, save fancies spun out of his own brain, as a spider spins her web out of her stomach.

"And Prometheus kept on looking before him so far ahead, that as he was running about with a box of lucifers (which were the only useful things he ever invented, and do as much harm as good), he trod on his own nose, and tumbled down (as most deductive philosophers do), whereby he set the Thames on fire; and they have hardly put it out again yet. So he had to be chained to the top of a mountain, with a vulture by him to give him a peck whenever he stirred, lest he should turn the whole world upside down with his prophecies and his theories.

"But stupid old Epimetheus went working and grubbing on, with the help of his wife Pandora, always looking behind him to see what had happened, till he really learnt to know now and then what would happen next; and understood so well which side his bread was buttered, and which way the cat jumped, that he began to make things which would work, and go on working, too; to till and drain the ground, and to make looms, and ships, and rail-roads, and steam ploughs, and electric telegraphs, and all the things which you see in the Great Exhibition; and to foretell famine, and bad weather, and the price of stocks, and the end of President Lincoln's policy; till at last he grew as rich as a Jew, and as fat as a farmer; and people thought twice before they meddled with him, but only once before they asked him to help them; for, because he earned his money well, he could afford to spend it well likewise.

"And his children are the men of science, who get good lasting work done in the world: but the children of Prometheus are the fanatics, and the theorists, and the bigots, and the bores, and the noisy windy people, who go telling silly folk what will happen, instead of looking to see what has happened already."

Now, was not Mother Carey's a wonderful story? And, I am happy to say, Tom believed it every word.

For so it happened to Tom likewise. He was very sorely tried; for though, by keeping the dog to heels (or rather to toes, for he had to walk backward), he could see pretty well which way the dog was hunting, yet it was much slower work to go backwards than to go forwards. But, what was more trying still, no sooner had he got out of Peacepool, than there came running to him all the conjurors, fortune-tellers, astrologers, prophesiers, projectors, prestigiators, as many as were in those parts (and there are too many of them everywhere), Old Mother Shipton[1] on her broomstick, with Merlin,[2] Thomas the Rhymer,[3] Gerbertus,[4] Rabanus Maurus,[5] Nostradamus,[6] Zadkiel,[7] Raphael Moore,[8] Old Nixon,[9] and a good many in black coats and white ties who might have known better, considering in what century they were born, all bawling and screaming at him, "Look a-head, only look a-head; and we will show you what man never saw before, and right away to the end of the world!"

But I am proud to say that, though Tom had not been at Cambridge—for, if he had, he would have certainly been senior wrangler[10]—he was such a little dogged, hard, gnarly, foursquare brick of an English boy, that he never turned his head round once all the way from Peacepool to the Other-end-of-Nowhere: but kept his eye on the dog, and let him pick out the scent, hot or cold, straight or crooked, wet or dry, up hill or down dale; by which means he never made a single mistake, and saw all the wonderful and hitherto by-no-mortal-man-imagined things, which it is my duty to relate to you in the next chapter.

---

1 Ursula Southeil, a fifteenth century British prophetess who lived in a Yorkshire cave where she wrote her prophetic verses.

2 Magician and prophet in Arthurian legend.

3 Thomas Learmont, a thirteenth century poet and seer who lived in Erceldoune, Scotland; also known as "True Thomas," because he could never lie after eating a magical apple given him by an elf queen. His story is recorded in the popular "Ballad of Thomas Rhymer."

4 Gerbert of Aurillac, a tenth century French pope, Sylvester II (999-1002) who, according to legend, had traveled to Spain as a young man where he became the apprentice of a Muslim magician of wondrous powers.

5 Rabanus Maurus Magnentius (c.780-856), German scholar and theologian.

6 Michel de Nostradame (1503-66), French physician, astrologist, and seer.

7 Pseudonym of Richard James Morrison (1794–1874), English astrologer and inventor. After service in the Royal Navy (1806–29) he started a best-selling astrological almanac in 1831.

8 Pseudonym of Robert Cross Smith (1795-1832), a British astrologer and author of *Raphael's Ephemeris* (1832), a set of tables showing the position of the sun, moon and all the planets as they travel through the sky; the book is updated and published to this day.

9 Robert Nixon, the Cheshire prophet, worked as a plowboy during the late fifteenth century. Though considered insane, he was believed to have prophesied the death of Richard III and the crowning of Henry VII.

10 "The head of the 'wranglers', i.e., of the first class of those who are successful in the Mathematical Tripos at Cambridge" (*OED*).

CHAPTER VIII. AND LAST.

"Come to me, O ye children!
  For I hear you at your play;
And the questions that perplexed me
  Have vanished quite away.

"Ye open the Eastern windows,
  That look towards the sun,
Where thoughts are singing swallows,
  And the brooks of morning run.

"For what are all our contrivings
  And the wisdom of our books,
When compared with your caresses,
  And the gladness of your looks?

"Ye are better than all the ballads
  ·That ever were sung or said;
For ye are living poems,
  And all the rest are dead."[1]

Longfellow.

ERE begins the never-to-be-too-much-studied account of the nine-hundred-and-ninety-ninth part of the wonderful things which Tom saw, on his journey to the Other-end-of-Nowhere; which all good little children are requested to read; that, if ever they get to the Other-end-of-Nowhere, as they may very probably do, they may not burst out laughing, or try to run way, or do any other silly vulgar thing which may offend Mrs. Bedonebyasyoudid.

Now, as soon as Tom had left Peace-pool, he came to the white lap of the great sea-mother, ten thousand fathoms

---

1 From "Children," in *Birds of Passage*, "Flight the First" (1858).

deep; where she makes world-pap all day long, for the steam-giants to knead, and the fire-giants to bake, till it has risen and hardened into mountain-loaves and island-cakes.

And there Tom was very near being kneaded up in the world-pap, and turned into a fossil water-baby; which would have astonished the Geological Society of New Zealand some hundreds of thousands of years hence.

For, as he walked along in the silence of the sea-twilight, on the soft white ocean floor, he was aware of a hissing, and a roaring, and thumping, and a pumping, as of all the steam-engines in the world at once. And, when he came near, the water grew boiling hot; not that that hurt him in the least: but it also grew as foul as gruel; and every moment he stumbled over dead shells, and fish, and sharks, and seals, and whales, which had been killed by the hot water.

And at last he came to the great sea-serpent himself, lying dead at the bottom; and, as he was too thick to scramble over, Tom had to walk round him three-quarters of a mile and more, which put him out of his path sadly; and, when he had got round, he came to the place called Stop. And there he stopped, and just in time.

For he was on the edge of a vast hole in the bottom of the sea, up which was rushing and roaring clear steam enough to work all the engines in the world at once; so clear, indeed, that it was quite light at moments; and Tom could see almost up to the top of the water above, and down below into the pit for nobody knows how far.

But, as soon as he bent his head over the edge, he got such a rap on the nose from pebbles, that he jumped back again; for the steam, as it rushed up, rasped away the sides of the hole, and hurled it up into the sea in a shower of mud and gravel and ashes; and then it spread all around, and sank again, and covered in the dead fish so fast, that before Tom had stood there five minutes he was buried in silt up to his ancles, and began to be afraid that he should have been buried alive.

And perhaps he would have been, but that while he was thinking, the whole piece of ground on which he stood was torn off and blown upwards, and away flew Tom a mile up through the sea, wondering what was coming next.

At last he stopped—thump! and found himself tight in the legs of the most wonderful bogy which he had ever seen.

It had I don't know how many wings, as big as the sails of a windmill, and spread out in a ring like them; and with them it hovered over the steam which rushed up, as a ball hovers over the top of a fountain. And for every wing above it had a leg below, with a claw like a comb at the tip, and a nostril at the root; and in the middle it had no stomach and one eye; and as for its mouth, that was all on one side, as the madreporiform tubercle[1] in a star-fish is. Well, it was a very strange beast; but no stranger than some dozens which you may see.

"What do you want here," it cried quite peevishly, "getting in my way?" and it tried to drop Tom: but he held on tight to its claws, thinking himself safer where he was.

So Tom told him who he was, and what his errand was. And the thing winked its one eye, and sneered:

"I am too old to be taken in in that way. You are come after gold—I know you are."

"Gold! What is gold?" And really Tom did not know; but the suspicious old bogy would not believe him.

But after a while Tom began to understand a little. For, as the vapours came up out of the hole, the bogy smelt them with his nostrils, and combed them and sorted them with his combs; and then, when they steamed up through them against his wings, they were changed into showers and streams of metal. From one wing fell gold-dust, and from another silver, and from another copper, and from another tin, and from another lead, and so on, and sank into the soft mud, into veins and cracks, and hardened there. Whereby it comes to pass that the rocks are full of metal.

But, all of a sudden, somebody shut off the steam below, and the hole was left empty in an instant: and then down rushed the water into the hole, in such a whirlpool that the bogy spun round and round as fast as a tee-totum. But that was all in his day's work, like a fair fall with the hounds; so all he did was to say to Tom—

"Now is your time, youngster, to get down, if you are in earnest, which I don't believe."

"You'll soon see," said Tom; and away he went, as bold as Baron Munchausen,[2] and shot down the rushing cataract like a salmon at Ballisodare.[3]

---

1 "A pore or perforated plate in echinoderms by which seawater enters the stone canal of the water-vascular system" (*OED*).

2 *The Adventures of Baron Munchausen* by Rudolf Erich Raspe (1737-94) recounts the stories told by Karl Friedrich von Münchhausen (1720-97), a retired army captain, noted for his exaggerated accounts of his war adventures and hunting experiences.

3 A river in Sligo, Ireland, famous for its wide array of fish.

And, when he got to the bottom, he swam till he was washed on shore safe upon the Other-end-of-Nowhere; and he found it, to his surprise, as most other people do, much more like This-End-of-Somewhere than he had been in the habit of expecting.

And first he went through Waste-paper-land, where all the stupid books lie in heaps, up hill and down dale, like leaves in a winter wood; and there he saw people digging and grubbing among them, to make worse books out of bad ones, and thrashing chaff to save the dust of it; and a very good trade they drove thereby, especially among children.

Then he went by the sea of slops, to the mountain of messes, and the territory of tuck,[1] where the ground was very sticky, for it was all made of bad toffee (not Everton toffee,[2] of course), and full of deep cracks and holes choked with wind-fallen fruit, and green goose-berries, and sloes, and crabs, and whinberries, and hips and haws,[3] and all the nasty things which little children will eat if they can get them. But the fairies hide them out of the way in that country as fast as they can, and very hard work they have, and of very little use it is. For as fast as they hide away the old trash, foolish and wicked people make fresh trash full of lime and poisonous paints, and actually go and steal receipts out of old Madame Science's big book to invent poisons for little children, and sell them at wakes and fairs and tuck-shops. Very well. Let them go on. Dr. Letheby and Dr. Hassall[4] cannot catch them, though they are setting traps for them all day long. But the Fairy with the birch-rod will catch them all in time, and make them begin at one corner of their shops, and eat their way out at the other: by which time they will have got such stomach-aches as will cure them of poisoning little children.

Next he saw all the little people in the world, writing all the little books in the world, about all the other little people in the world; probably because they had no great people to write about:

---

1 A slang term for sweets, such as jam or pastry.
2 Everton mints, produced by the confectioner Barker & Dobson in the Liverpool district of Everton, were a popular black-and-white striped sweet with a chewy toffee center.
3 The fruit of the wild rose and hawthorn.
4 Henry Letheby (1816-76), British chemist, became Medical Officer of Health for the City of London in 1849. Arthur Hill Hassall (1817-94), British physician and chemist, was an authority on public health and hygiene. He published several works dealing with sanitation, clean water and the adulteration of food, drink, and drugs.

and if the names of the books were not Squeeky, nor the Pump-lighter, nor the Narrow Narrow World, nor the Hills of the Chattermuch, nor the Children's Twaddeday,[1] why then they were something else. And all the rest of the little people in the world read the books, and thought themselves each as good as the President; and perhaps they were right, for every one knows his own business best. But Tom thought he would sooner have a jolly good fairy tale, about Jack the Giant-killer or Beauty and the Beast, which taught him something that he didn't know already.

And next he came to the centre of Creation (the hub, they call it there), which lies in latitude 42.21 south, and longitude 108.56 east.

And there he found all the wise people instructing mankind in the science of spirit-rapping, while their house was burning over their heads: and when Tom told them of the fire, they held an indignation meeting forthwith, and unanimously determined to hang Tom's dog for coming into their country with gunpowder in his mouth. Tom couldn't help saying that though they did fancy they had carried all the wit away with them out of Lincolnshire two hundred years ago, yet if they had had one such Lincolnshire nobleman among them as good old Lord Yarborough,[2] he would have called for the fire-engines before he hanged other people's dogs. But it was of no use, and the dog was hanged: and Tom couldn't even have his carcase; for they had abolished the have-his-carcase act in that country, for fear lest when rogues fell out, honest men should come by their own. And so they would have succeeded perfectly, as they always do, only that (as they also

---

1 Kingsley parodies the names of immensely popular sentimental novels by contemporary American women. *Queechy*, *The Wide Wide World*, and *The Hills of Shatemuc* were written by Susan Bogert Warner (1819-85) under the name Elizabeth Wetherwell. *The Lamplighter* was by Maria Susanna Cummins (1827-66). These works bear a resemblance to the Sunday school books of the period, with their evangelical themes of instruction and conversion. What book the "Children's Twaddeday" refers to is unclear, but its name carries Kingsley's view that all of the mentioned stories are mere twaddle. In 1855, Nathaniel Hawthorne expressed a similar distaste for these authors: "America is now wholly given over to a d—d mob of scribbling women and I should have no chance of success while the public taste is occupied with their trash—and should be ashamed of myself if I did succeed."

2 Charles Anderson Worsley Anderson Pelham, 2nd Earl of Yarborough (1809-62). He is now remembered for giving his name to a hand of cards dealt in bridge that has no card higher than a nine.

always do) they failed in one little particular, viz. that the dog would not die, being a water-dog, but bit their fingers so abominably that they were forced to let him go, and Tom likewise, as British subjects. Whereon they recommenced rapping for the spirits of their fathers; and very much astonished the poor old spirits were when they came, and saw how, according to the laws of Mrs. Bedonebyasyoudid, their descendants had weakened their constitution by hard living.

Then came Tom to the Island of Polupragmosyne,[1] which some call Rogues' Harbour (but they are wrong; for that is in the middle of Bramshill Bushes,[2] and the country police have cleared it out long ago). There everyone knows his neighbour's business better than his own; and a very noisy place it is, as might be expected, considering that all the inhabitants are ex-officio on the wrong side of the house in the "Parliament of Man, and the Federation of the World;"[3] and are always making wry mouths, and crying that the fairies' grapes were sour.

There Tom saw ploughs drawing horses, nails driving hammers, birds' nests taking boys, books making authors, bulls keeping china-shops, monkeys shaving cats, dead dogs drilling live lions, blind brigadiers shelfed as principals of colleges, play-actors not in the least shelfed as popular preachers; and, in short, every one set to do something which he had not learnt, because in what he had learnt, or pretended to learn, he had failed.

There stands the Pantheon of the Great Unsuccessful, from the builders of the Tower of Babel to those of the Trafalgar Fountains;[4] in which politicians lecture on the constitutions which ought to have marched, conspirators on the revolutions which ought to have succeeded, economists on the schemes which ought to have made every one's fortune, projectors on the discoveries which ought to have set the Thames on fire; and (in due time) presidents on the union which ought to have re-united, and

---

1 Usually spelled *Polupragmosune,* an Athenian legal term that literally means "one who conducts much business." In Kingsley's context, however, it suggests a busy-body or meddler.
2 A wooded area near Kingsley's home in Eversley.
3 From Tennyson's "Locksley Hall" (1842). Those who are on the wrong side of the house in this metaphorical parliament are the opponents of the glorious future imagined by the speaker in the poem.
4 Designed by Sir Charles Barry, red granite fountains were installed in Trafalgar Square in 1845. One wag described them as "mean enough to have been bought at any shop in the Paddington Road."

secretaries of state on the greenbacks which ought to have done just as well as hard money. There cobblers lecture on orthopedy[1] (whatsoever that may be) because they cannot sell their shoes; and poets on Æsthetics (whatsoever that may be) because they cannot sell their poetry. There philosophers demonstrate that England would be the freest and richest country in the world, if she would only turn Papist again; penny-a-liners abuse the Times, because they have not wit enough to get on its staff; and young ladies walk about with lockets of Charles the First's hair (or of somebody else's, when the Jews' genuine stock is used up), inscribed with the neat and appropriate legend—which indeed is popular through all that land, and which, I hope, you will learn to translate in due time and to perpend likewise:—

"Victrix causa diis placuit, sed victa puellis."[2]

When he got into the middle of the town, they all set on him at once, to show him his way; or rather, to show him that he did not know his way; for as for asking him what way he wanted to go, no one ever thought of that.

But one pulled him hither, and another poked him thither, and a third cried—

"You mustn't go west, I tell you; it is destruction to go west."

"But I am not going west, as you may see," said Tom.

And another, "The east lies here, my dear; I assure you this is the east."

"But I don't want to go east," said Tom.

"Well then at all events, whichever way you are going, you are going wrong," cried they all with one voice—which was the only thing which they ever agreed about; and all pointed at once to all the thirty-and-two points of the compass, till Tom thought all the sign-posts in England had got together, and fallen fighting.

And whether he would have ever escaped out of the town, it is hard to say, if the dog had not taken it into his head that they were going to pull his master in pieces, and tackled them so sharply about the gastrocnemius muscle,[3] that he gave them

---

1 The art of curing physical deformities.

2 A play on a line from Lucan's Civil War epic, *Pharsalia*: "*victrix causa diis placuit, sed victa Catoni*" ("The victorious cause pleased the gods but the defeated one pleased Cato.") Kingsley's version translates: "The victorious cause pleased the gods but the defeated one pleased the girls."

3 The large muscle that runs down the calf of the leg.

some business of their own to think of at last; and while they were rubbing their bitten calves, Tom and the dog got safe away.

On the borders of that island he found Gotham,[1] where the wise men live; the same who dragged the pond because the moon had fallen into it, and planted a hedge round the cuckoo, to keep spring all the year. And he found them bricking up the town gate, because it was so wide that little folks could not get through. And, when he asked why, they told him they were expanding their liturgy. So he went on; for it was no business of his: only he could not help saying that in his country, if the kitten could not get in at the same hole as the cat, she might stay outside and mew.

But he saw the end of such fellows, when he came to the island of the Golden Asses,[2] where nothing but thistles grow. For there they were all turned into mokes[3] with ears a yard long, for meddling with matters which they do not understand, as Lucius did in the story. And like him, mokes they must remain, till, by the laws of development, the thistles develop into roses. Till then, they must comfort themselves with the thought, that the longer their ears are, the thicker their hides; and so a good beating don't hurt them.

Then came Tom to the great land of Hearsay, in which are no less than thirty and odd kings, beside half a dozen Republics, and perhaps more by next mail.

And there he fell in with a deep, dark, deadly, and destructive war, waged by the princes and potentates of those parts, both spiritual and temporal, against what do you think? One thing I am sure of. That unless I told you, you would never know; nor how they waged that war either; for all their strategy and art military consisted in the safe and easy process of stopping their ears and screaming, "Oh, don't tell us!" and then running away.

So when Tom came into that land, he found them all, high and

---

1   *The Merry Tales of the Mad Men of Gotham* (c.1540), of uncertain authorship, depicted the village of Gotham in Nottinghamshire as comprised of mad men, or fools. The stories were so popular they continued to be re-published almost unchanged to the end of the nineteenth century. They were even exported to America by Washington Irving, who coined the title of "Gotham City" for his native New York.

2   Lucius Apuleius (c.124-70), a Roman philosopher whose *Asinus Aureus* (later called *Metamorphoses)* narrates the adventures of Lucius, who is transformed into an ass and later regains his human form with the help of the goddess Isis.

3   Donkeys.

low, man, woman and child, running for their lives day and night continually, and entreating not to be told they didn't know what: only the land being an island, and they having a dislike to the water (being a musty lot for the most part) they ran round and round the shore for ever, which (as the island was exactly of the same circumference as the planet on which we have the honour of living) was hard work, especially to those who had business to look after. But before them, as bandmaster and fugleman,[1] ran a gentleman shearing a pig; the melodious strains of which animal led them for ever, if not to conquest, still to flight; and kept up their spirits mightily with the thought that they would at least have the pig's wool for their pains.

And running after them, day and night, came such a poor, lean, seedy, hard-worked old giant, as ought to have been cockered up, and had a good dinner given him, and a good wife found him, and been set to play with little children; and then he would have been a very presentable old fellow after all; for he had a heart, though it was considerably overgrown with brains.

He was made up principally of fish bones and parchment, put together with wire and Canada balsam; and smelt strongly of spirits, though he never drank anything but water: but spirits he used somehow, there was no denying. He had a great pair of spectacles on his nose, and a butterfly-net in one hand, and a geological hammer in the other; and was hung all over with pockets, full of collecting boxes, bottles, microscopes, telescopes, barometers, ordnance maps, scalpels, forceps, photographic apparatus, and all other tackle for finding out everything about everything, and a little more too. And, most strange of all, he was running not forwards but backwards, as fast as he could.

Away all the good folks ran from him, except Tom, who stood his ground and dodged between his legs; and the giant, when he had passed him, looked down, and cried, as if he was quite pleased and comforted,—

"What? who are you? And you actually don't run away, like all the rest?" But he had to take his spectacles off, Tom remarked, in order to see him plainly.

Tom told him who he was; and the giant pulled out a bottle and a cork instantly, to collect him with.

But Tom was too sharp for that, and dodged between his legs and in front of him; and then the giant could not see him at all.

---

1   A well-trained soldier placed at the front of a regiment as a role model.

"No, no, no!" said Tom, "I've not been round the world, and through the world, and up to Mother Carey's haven, beside being caught in a net and called a Holothurian and a Cephalopod, to be bottled up by any old giant like you."

And when the giant understood what a great traveller Tom had been, he made a truce with him at once, and would have kept him there to this day to pick his brains, so delighted was he at finding any one to tell him what he did not know before.

"Ah, you lucky little dog!" said he at last, quite simply—for he was the simplest, pleasantest, honestest, kindliest old Dominie Sampson[1] of a giant that ever turned the world upside down without intending it— "Ah, you lucky little dog! If I had only been where you have been, to see what you have seen!"

"Well," said Tom, "if you want to do that, you had best put your head under water for a few hours, as I did, and turn into a water-baby, or some other baby, and then you might have a chance."

"Turn into a baby, eh? If I could do that, and know what was happening to me for but one hour, I should know everything then, and be at rest. But I can't; I can't be a little child again; and I suppose if I could, it would be no use, because then I should know nothing about what was happening to me. Ah, you luckly little dog!" said the poor old giant.

"But why do you run after all these poor people?" said Tom, who liked the giant very much.

"My dear, it's they that have been running after me, father and son, for hundreds and hundreds of years, throwing stones at me till they have knocked off my spectacles fifty times, and calling me a malignant and a turbaned Turk, who beat a Venetian and traduced the state[2]—goodness only knows what they mean, for I never read poetry—and hunting me round and round—though catch me they can't, for every time I go over the same ground, I go the faster, and grow the bigger. While all I want is to be friends with them, and to tell them something to their advantage, like Mr. Joseph Ady:[3] only somehow they are so strangely afraid of

---

1 A village schoolmaster and scholar in Sir Walter Scott's *Guy Mannering* (1815) noted for his generous and simple spirit.

2 From *Othello*: "Set you down this,/ And say besides that in Aleppo once,/ Where a malignant and a turbaned Turk/ Beat a Venetian and traduced the state,/ I took by the throat the circumcisèd dog,/ And smote him, thus." (v, ii)

3 A notorious imposter, who bilked gullible Victorians by circulating letters promising, on the receipt of a suitable fee, to inform those whom he addressed of "something to their advantage."

hearing it. But, I suppose I am not a man of the world, and have no tact."

"But why don't you turn round and tell them so?"

"Because I can't. You see, I am one of the sons of Epimetheus, and must go backwards, if I am to go at all."

"But why don't you stop, and let them come up to you?"

"Why, my dear, only think. If I did, all the butterflies and cock-yolybirds would fly past me, and then I could catch no more new species, and should grow rusty and mouldy, and die. And I don't intend to do that, my dear; for I have a destiny before me, they say: though what it is I don't know, and don't care."

"Don't care?" said Tom.

"No. Do the duty which lies nearest you, and catch the first beetle you come across, is my motto; and I have thriven by it for some hundred years. Now I must go on. Dear me, while I have been talking to you, at least nine new species have escaped me."

And on went the giant, behind before, like a bull in a china shop, till he ran into the steeple of the great idol temple (for they are all idolaters in those parts, of course, else they would never be afraid of giants), and knocked the upper half clean off, hurting himself horribly about the small of the back.

But little he cared; for as soon as the ruins of the steeple were well between his legs, he poked and peered among the falling stones, and shifted his spectacles, and pulled out his pocket-magnifier, and cried—

"An entirely new Oniscus, and three obscure Podurellæ![1] Beside a moth which M. le Roi des Papillons[2] (though he, like all Frenchmen, is given to hasty inductions) says is confined to the limits of the Glacial Drift. This is most important!"

And down he sat on the nave of the temple (not being a man of the world) to examine his Podurellæ. Whereon (as was to be expected) the roof caved in bodily, smashing the idols, and sending the priests flying out of doors and windows, like rabbits out of a burrow when a ferret goes in.

But he never heeded; for out of the dust flew a bat, and the giant had him in a moment.

---

1   *Oniscus asellus,* a woodlouse commonly found under stones and rotting logs. *Podurellæ* (*Poduridae Latreille*): springtails, small wingless hexapods that dwell in the soil and litter, preferring wet or damp surroundings.
2   "King of the Butterflies": Pierre André Latreille (1762-1833), a priest and foremost entomologist of his time, and author of *Genera Crustaceorum et Insectorum* (4 vols., 1806-09).

"Dear me! This is even more important! Here is a cognate species to that which Macgilliwaukie Brown insists is confined to the Buddhist Temples of Little Thibet; and now when I look at it, it may be only a variety produced by difference of climate!"

And having bagged his bat, up he got, and on he went; while all the people ran, being in none the better humour for having their temple smashed for the sake of three obscure species of Podurella, and a Buddhist bat.

"Well," thought Tom; "this is a very pretty quarrel, with a good deal to be said on both sides. But it is no business of mine."

And no more it was; because he was a water-baby, and had the original sow by the right ear; which you will never have, unless you be a baby, whether of the water, the land, or the air, matters not, provided you can only keep on continually being a baby.

So the giant ran round after the people, and the people ran round after the giant, and they are running unto this day for aught I know, or do not know; and will run till either he, or they, or both, turn into little children. And then, as Shakspeare says (and therefore it must be true)—

"Jack shall have Gill
Nought shall go ill
The man shall have his mare again, and all go well."[1]

Then Tom came to a very famous island, which was called, in the days of the great traveller Captain Gulliver, the Isle of Laputa.[2] But Mrs. Bedonebyasyoudid has named it over again, the Isle of Tomtoddies, all heads and no bodies.

And when Tom came near it, he heard such a grumbling and grunting and growling and wailing and weeping and whining that he thought people must be ringing little pigs, or cropping puppies' ears, or drowning kittens: but when he came nearer still, he began to hear words among the noise; which was the Tomtoddies' song which they sing morning and evening, and all night too, to their great idol Examination—

"I can't learn my lesson: the examiner's coming!"

---

1 From Shakespeare's *A Midsummer Night's Dream*. The correct lines, spoken by Puck, are: "Jack shall have Jill;/ Nought shall go ill;/ The man shall have his mare again, and all shall be well." (Act 3, Scene 2)

2 In Jonathan Swift's *Gulliver's Travels* (1726), the Isle of Laputa is inhabited by people obsessed with mathematics and the science of music to the detriment of imagination and common sense.

And that was the only song which they knew.

And when Tom got on shore the first thing he saw was a great pillar, on one side of which was inscribed, "Playthings not allowed here;" at which he was so shocked that he would not stay to see what was written on the other side. Then he looked round for the people of the island: but instead of men, women, and children, he found nothing but turnips and radishes, beet and mangold wurzel, without a single green leaf among them, and half of them burst and decayed, with toadstools growing out of them. Those which were left began crying to Tom, in half a dozen different languages at once, and all of them badly spoken, "I can't learn my lesson; do come and help me!" And one cried, "Can you show me how to extract this square-root?"

And another, "Can you tell me the distance between α Lyræ[1] and β Camelopardalis?"[2]

And another, "What is the latitude and longitude of Snooksville, in Noman's County, Oregon, U.S.?"

And another, "What was the name of Mutius Scævola's[3] thirteenth cousin's grandmother's maid's cat?"

And another, "How long would it take a school-inspector of average activity to tumble head over heels from London to York?"

And another, "Can you tell me the name of a place that nobody ever heard of, where nothing ever happened, in a country which has not been discovered yet?"

And another, "Can you show me how to correct this hopelessly corrupt passage of Graidiocolosyrtus Tabenniticus,[4] on the cause why crocodiles have no tongues?"

And so on, and so on, and so on, till one would have thought they were all trying for tide-waiters'[5] places, or cornetcies[6] in the heavy dragoons.

---

1   A white star of the first magnitude, called Alpha Lyræ, or Vega, in the northern constellation Lyra.

2   A constellation in the Northern Hemisphere.

3   Quintus Mucius Scaevola (d. 82 BCE), a Roman jurist.

4   In his novel *Hypatia* (1853), Kingsley first created this nonsensical volume: "The remainder of his history it seems better to extract from an unpublished fragment of the Hagiologia Nilotica of Graidiocolosyrtus Tabenniticus, the greater part of which valuable work was destroyed at the taking of Alexandria under Amrou, AD 640."

5   Customs officers who awaited the arrival of ships and boarded them to assure that customs regulations were enforced.

6   Soldiers who carried the colors in a troop of cavalry.

"And what good on earth will it do you if I did tell you?" quoth Tom.

Well, they didn't know that: all they knew was the examiner was coming.

Then Tom stumbled on the hugest and softest nimblecome-quick turnip you ever saw filling a hole in a crop of swedes,[1] and it cried to him, "Can you tell me anything at all about anything you like?"

"About what?" says Tom.

"About anything you like; for as fast as I learn things I forget them again. So my mamma says that my intellect is not adapted for methodic science, and says that I must go in for general information."

Tom told him that he did not know general information, nor any officers in the army; only he had a friend once that went for a drummer: but he could tell him a great many strange things which he had seen in his travels.

So he told him prettily enough, while the poor turnip listened very carefully; and the more he listened, the more he forgot, and the more water ran out of him.

Tom thought he was crying: but it was only his poor brains running away, from being worked so hard; and as Tom talked, the unhappy turnip streamed down all over with juice, and split and shrank till nothing was left of him but rind and water; whereat Tom ran away in a fright, for he thought he might be taken up for killing the turnip.

But, on the contrary, the turnip's parents were highly delighted, and considered him a saint and a martyr, and put up a long inscription over his tomb about his wonderful talents, early development, and unparalleled precocity. Were they not a foolish couple? But there was a still more foolish couple next to them, who were beating a wretched little radish, no bigger than my thumb, for sullenness and obstinacy and wilful stupidity, and never knew that the reason why it couldn't learn or hardly even

---

1 A variety of turnips.

speak was, that there was a great worm inside it eating out all its brains. But even they are no foolisher than some hundred score of papas and mammas, who fetch the rod when they ought to fetch a new toy, and send to the dark cupboard instead of to the doctor.

Tom was so puzzled and frightened with all he saw, that he was longing to ask the meaning of it; and at last he stumbled over a respectable old stick lying half covered with earth.

But a very stout and worthy stick it was, for it belonged to good Roger Ascham[1] in old time, and had carved on its head King Edward the Sixth, with the Bible in his hand.

"You see," said the stick, "there were as pretty little children once as you could wish to see, and might have been so still if they had been only left to grow up like human beings, and then handed over to me; but their foolish fathers and mothers, instead of letting them pick flowers, and make dirt-pies, and get birds' nests, and dance round the gooseberry bush, as little children should, kept them always at lessons, working, working, working, learning weekday lesson all weekdays, and Sunday lessons all Sunday, and weekly examinations every Saturday, and monthly examinations every month, and yearly examinations every year, everything seven times over, as if once was not enough, and enough as good as a feast—till their brains grew big, and their bodies grew small, and they were all changed into turnips, with little but water inside; and still their foolish parents actually pick the leaves off them as fast as they grow, lest they should have anything green about them."

"Ah!" said Tom, "if dear Mrs. Doasyouwouldbedoneby knew of it she would send them a lot of tops, and balls, and marbles, and ninepins, and make them all as jolly as sand-boys."[2]

"It would be no use," said the stick. "They can't play now, if they tried. Don't you see how their legs have turned to roots and grown into the ground, by never taking any exercise, but sapping and moping always in the same place? But here comes the Exam-

---

1   English Renaissance scholar (1515-68), tutor to Edward VI and author of a treatise on education entitled *The Scholemaster*, published posthumously in 1570. Kingsley's own view of education resonates with Ascham's thesis: "In writing this booke, I haue had earnest respecte to three speciall pointes, trothe of Religion, honestie in liuing, right order in learning" (from "A Præface to the Reader," *The Scholemaster*).

2   Street urchins who sell sand. "Happy or jolly as a sand-boy" is a proverbial phrase.

iner-of-all-Examiners. So you had better get away, I warn you, or he will examine you and your dog into the bargain, and set him to examine all the other dogs, and you to examine all the other water-babies. There is no escaping out of his hands, for his nose is nine thousand miles long, and can go down chimneys and through keyholes, upstairs, downstairs, in my lady's chamber, examining all little boys, and the little boys' tutors likewise. But when he is thrashed—so Mrs. Bedonebyasyoudid has promised me —I shall have the thrashing of him: and if I don't lay it on with a will it's a pity."

Tom went off: but rather slowly and surlily; for he was somewhat minded to face this same Examiner-of-all-Examiners, who came striding among the poor turnips, binding heavy burdens and grievous to be borne, and laying them on little children's shoulders, like the Scribes and Pharisees[1] of old, and not touching the same with one of his fingers; for he had plenty of money, and a fine house to live in, and so forth; which was more than the poor little turnips had.

But when he got near, he looked so big and burly and dictatorial, and shouted so loud to Tom to come and be examined, that Tom ran for his life, and the dog too. And really it was time; for the poor turnips, in their hurry and fright, crammed themselves so fast to be ready for the Examiner, that they burst and popped by dozens all round him, till the place sounded like Aldershott[2] on a field-day, and Tom thought he should be blown into the air, dog and all.

As he went down to the shore he passed the poor turnip's new tomb. But Mrs. Bedonebyasyoudid had taken away the epitaph about talents and precocity and development, and put up one of her own instead which Tom thought much more sensible:—

"Instruction sore long time I bore,
  And cramming was in vain;
Till Heaven did please my woes to ease,
  By water on the brain."

---

1 "The scribes and the Pharisees sit in Moses' seat: All therefore whatsoever they bid you observe, observe and do; but do not ye after their works: for they say, and do not. For they bind heavy burdens and grievous to be borne, and lay them on men's shoulders; but they themselves will not move them with one of their fingers" (Matthew 23: 2-4).
2 A military training camp set up in 1854 for soldiers returning from the Crimean War.

So Tom jumped into the sea, and swam on his way, singing:—

"Farewell, Tomtoddies all; I thank my stars
That nought I know save those three royal r's:
Reading and riting sure, with rithmetick,
Will help a lad of sense through thin and thick."

Whereby you may see that Tom was no poet: but no more was John Bunyan,[1] though he was as wise a man as you will meet in a month of Sundays.

And next he came to Oldwivesfabledom, where the folks were all heathens, and worshipped a howling ape.

And there he found a little boy sitting in the middle of the road, and crying bitterly.

"What are you crying for?" said Tom.

"Because I am not as frightened as I could wish to be."

"Not frightened? You are a queer little chap: but, if you want to be frightened, here goes—Boo!"

"Ah," said the little boy, "that is very kind of you; but I don't feel that it has made any impression."

Tom offered to upset him, punch him, stamp on him, fettle[2] him over the head with a brick, or anything else whatsoever which would give him the slightest comfort.

But he only thanked Tom very civilly, in fine long words which he had heard other folk use, and which, therefore, he thought were fit and proper to use himself; and cried on till his papa and mamma came, and sent off for the Powwow man immediately. And a very good-natured gentleman and lady they were, though they were heathens; and talked quite pleasantly to Tom about his travels, till the Powwow man arrived, with his thunderbox[3] under his arm.

---

1 An English preacher and writer (1628-88), best remembered for his *Pilgrim's Progress* (1678, 1684). His poetry for children, however, is remarkably bad, as seen in these lines from "Meditations Upon an Egg": "But chicks from rotten eggs do not proceed,/ Nor is a hypocrite a saint indeed./ The rotten egg, though underneath the hen,/ If crack'd, stinks, and is loathsome unto men" (*A Book for Boys and Girls or Temporal Things Spritualized*, 1701).

2 Beat.

3 American rifles, such as the blunderbuss, were prized by the Natives, especially the Quapaws. Blunderbuss means "thunder box" in Dutch and refers to the noise made when the gun is fired. The context of the story, however, suggests a magical box that contains, in addition to thunder, all sorts of spirits and devices that spring out with a deafening noise.

And a well-fed, ill-favoured gentleman he was, as ever served her Majesty at Portland.[1] Tom was a little frightened at first; for he thought it was Grimes. But he soon saw his mistake: for Grimes always looked a man in the face; and this fellow never did. And when he spoke, it was fire and smoke; and when he sneezed, it was squibs and crackers; and when he cried (which he did whenever it paid him), it was boiling pitch; and some of it was sure to stick.

"Here we are again!" cried he, like the clown in a pantomime. "So you can't feel frightened, my little dear—eh? I'll do that for you. I'll make an impression on you! Yah! Boo! Whirroo! Hullabaloo!"

And he rattled, thumped, brandished his thunderbox, yelled, shouted, raved, roared, stamped, and danced corrobory[2] like any black fellow; and then he touched a spring in the thunderbox, and out popped turnipghosts and magic-lanthorns and pasteboard bogies and spring-heeled Jacks and sallabalas, with such a horrid din, clatter, clank, roll, rattle, and roar, that the little boy turned up the whites of his eyes, and fainted right away.

And at that his poor heathen papa and mamma were as much delighted as if they had found a gold mine; and fell down upon their knees before the Powwow man, and gave him a palanquin[3] with a pole of solid silver and curtains of cloth of gold; and carried him about in it on their own backs: but as soon as they had taken him up, the pole stuck to their shoulders, and they could not set him down any more, but carried him on willy-nilly, as Sinbad[4] carried the old man of the sea: which was a pitiable sight to see; for the father was a very brave officer, and wore two swords and a blue button; and the mother was as pretty a lady as ever had pinched feet like a Chinese. But you see, they had

---

1 The Isle of Portland in Dorset, where convicts from a local prison worked in the Admiralty Quarries.

2 "The native dance of the Australian aborigines; it is held at night by moonlight or a bush fire, and is either of a festive or warlike character" (*OED*).

3 "A covered conveyance, usually for one person, consisting of a large box carried on two horizontal poles by four or six (rarely two) bearers" (*OED*).

4 In Sinbad's fifth voyage in *The Arabian Nights* he meets the Old Man of the Sea, who persuades him to carry him on his shoulders. He keeps Sinbad captive with his grip until Sinbad gets him so drunk that he drops off.

chosen to do a foolish thing just once too often; so by the laws of Mrs. Bedonebyasyoudid, they had to go on doing it whether they chose or not, till the coming of the Coqcigrues.

Ah! don't you wish that some one would go and convert those poor heathens, and teach them not to frighten their little children into fits?

"Now, then," said the Powwow man to Tom, wouldn't you like to be frightened, my little dear? For I can see plainly that you are a very wicked, naughty, graceless, reprobate boy."

"You're another," quoth Tom, very sturdily. And when the man ran at him, and cried "Boo!" Tom ran at him in return, and cried "Boo!" likewise, right in his face, and set the little dog upon him; and at his legs the dog went.

At which, if you will believe it, the fellow turned tail, thunder-box and all, with a "Woof!" like an old sow on the common; and ran for his life, screaming, "Help! thieves! murder! fire! He is going to kill me! I am a ruined man! He will murder me; and break, burn, and destroy my precious and invaluable thunderbox; and then you will have no more thunder showers in the land. Help! help! help!"

At which the papa and mamma and all the people of Old-wivesfabledom, flew at Tom, shouting, "Oh, the wicked, impudent, hard-hearted, graceless boy! Beat him, kick him, shoot him, drown him, hang him, burn him!" and so forth: but luckily they had nothing to shoot, hang, or burn him with, for the fairies had hid all the killing-tackle out of the way a little while before; so they could only pelt him with stones; and some of the stones went clean through him, and came out the other side. But he did not mind that a bit; for the holes closed up again as fast as they were made, because he was a water-baby. However, he was very glad when he was safe out of the country, for the noise there made him all but deaf.

Then he came to a very quiet place, called Leaveheavenalone. And there the sun was drawing water out of the sea to make steam-threads, and the wind was twisting them up to make cloud-patterns, till they had worked between them the loveliest wedding veil of Chantilly lace, and hung it up in their own Crystal Palace[1] for any one to buy who could afford it; while the good old sea never grudged, for she knew they would pay her

---

1 The Crystal Palace, a huge building made of iron and glass, was built to house the Great Exhibition of the Industry of All Nations in Hyde Park, London, in 1851.

back honestly. So the sun span, and the wind wove, and all went well with the great steam-loom; as is likely, considering—and considering—and considering—

And at last, after innumerable adventures, each more wonderful than the last, he saw before him a huge building, much bigger, and—what is most surprising— a little uglier than a certain new lunatic asylum,[1] but not built quite of the same materials. None of it, at least—or, indeed, for aught that I ever saw, any part of any other building whatsoever—is cased with nine-inch brick inside and out, and filled up with rubble between the walls, in order that any gentleman who has been confined during her Majesty's pleasure may be unconfined during his own pleasure, and take a walk in the neighbouring park to improve his spirits, after an hour's light and wholesome labour with his dinner-fork or one of the legs of his iron bedstead. No. The walls of this building were built on an entirely different principle, which need not be described, as it has not yet been discovered.

Tom walked towards this great building, wondering what it was, and having a strange fancy that he might find Mr. Grimes inside it, till he saw running toward him, and shouting "Stop!" three or four people, who, when they came nearer, were nothing else than policemen's truncheons, running along without legs or arms.

Tom was not astonished. He was long past that. Besides, he had seen the naviculæ[2] in the water move nobody knows how, a hundred times, without arms, or legs, or anything to stand in their stead. Neither was he frightened; for he had been doing no harm.

So he stopped; and, when the foremost truncheon came up and asked his business, he showed Mother Carey's pass; and the truncheon looked at it in the oddest fashion; for he had one eye in the middle of his upper end, so that when he looked at anything, being quite stiff, he had to slope himself, and poke himself, till it was a wonder why he did not tumble over; but, being quite

---

1   The Colney Hatch Lunatic Asylum, north of London, one of the most famous and dreaded institutions for the mad, opened in 1850. Constructed of brick and decorated with stone, its Italianate design was the work of architect Samuel Whitfield Daulkes (1811-80).

2   Diatoms of the common genus *Navicula*. Recent science has partially explained their movement by noting that these single-cell creatures contain a raphe, a narrow slit running their length, through which a slime is produced and exuded, thereby affording them motion.

full of the spirit of justice (as all policemen, and their truncheons, ought to be), he was always in a position of stable equilibrium, whichever way he put himself.

"All right—pass on," said he at last. And then he added: "I had better go with you, young man." And Tom had no objection, for such company was both respectable and safe; so the truncheon coiled its thong neatly round its handle, to prevent tripping itself up—for the thong had got loose in running—and marched on by Tom's side.

"Why have you no policeman to carry you?" asked Tom, after a while.

"Because we are not like those clumsy-made truncheons in the land-world, which cannot go without having a whole man to carry them about. We do our own work for ourselves; and do it very well, though I say it who should not."

"Then why have you a thong to your handle?" asked Tom.

"To hang ourselves up by, of course, when we are off duty."

Tom had got his answer, and had no more to say, till they came up to the great iron door of the prison. And there the truncheon knocked twice, with its own head.

A wicket in the door opened, and out looked a tremendous old brass blunderbuss charged up to the muzzle with slugs, who was the porter; and Tom started back a little at the sight of him.

"What case is this?" he asked in a deep voice, out of his broad bell-mouth.

"If you please, sir, it is no case; only a young gentleman from her ladyship, who wants to see Grimes the master-sweep."

"Grimes?" said the blunderbuss. And he pulled in his muzzle, perhaps to look over his prison-lists.

"Grimes is up chimney No. 345," he said from inside. "So the young gentleman had better go on to the roof."

Tom looked up at the enormous wall, which seemed at least ninety miles high, and wondered how he should ever get up: but, when he hinted that to the truncheon, it settled the matter in a moment. For it whisked round, and gave him such a shove behind as sent him up to the roof in no time, with his little dog under his arm.

And there he walked along the leads, till he met another truncheon, and told him his errand.

"Very good," it said. "Come along: but it will be of no use. He is the most unremorseful, hard-hearted, foul-mouthed fellow I have in charge; and thinks about nothing but beer and pipes, which are not allowed here, of course."

So they walked along over the leads, and very sooty they were, and Tom thought the chimneys must want sweeping very much. But he was surprised to see that the soot did not stick to his feet, or dirty them in the least. Neither did the live coals, which were lying about in plenty, burn him; for, being a water-baby, his radical humours were of a moist and cold nature, as you may read at large in Lemnius,[1] Cardan,[2] Van Helmont,[3] and other gentlemen, who knew as much as they could, and no man can know more.

And at last they came to chimney No. 345. Out of the top of it, his head and shoulders just showing, stuck poor Mr. Grimes; so sooty, and bleared, and ugly, that Tom could hardly bear to look at him. And in his mouth was a pipe: but it was not a-light, though he was pulling at it with all his might.

"Attention, Mr. Grimes," said the truncheon; "here is a gentleman come to see you."

But Mr. Grimes only said bad words; and kept grumbling, "My pipe won't draw. My pipe won't draw."

"Keep a civil tongue, and attend!" said the truncheon; and popped up just like Punch, hitting Grimes such a crack over the head with itself, that his brains rattled inside like a dried walnut in its shell. He tried to get his hands out, and rub the place: but he could not, for they were stuck fast in the chimney.

Now he was forced to attend.

"Hey!" he said, "why, it's Tom! I suppose you have come here to laugh at me, you spiteful little atomy?"[4]

Tom assured him he had not, but only wanted to help him.

"I don't want anything except beer, and that I can't get; and a light to this bothering pipe, and that I can't get either."

---

1 Simon Lemnius (c. 1505-50), a German humanist and poet. He produced a play depicting Martin Luther as a lustful monk, thereby earning the reformer's enmity.

2 Girolamo Cardano (1501-76), an Italian philosopher, physician, mathematician, and astrologer. His greatest mathematical work *Ars Magna* (1545) provides the methods of solution of the cubic and quartic equation.

3 Jean Baptist van Helmont (1579-1644), a Belgian physician and chemist who coined the word "gas." He identified four gases: carbon dioxide, carbon monoxide, nitrous oxide, and methane, and was the first to take the melting point of ice and the boiling point of water as standards for temperature.

4 A diminutive or tiny being, a mite, a pigmy (*OED*).

"I'll get you one," said Tom; and he took up a live coal (there were plenty lying about) and put it to Grimes's pipe: but it went out instantly.

"It's no use," said the truncheon, leaning itself up against the chimney, and looking on. "I tell you, it is no use. His heart is so cold that it freezes everything that comes near him. You will see that presently, plain enough."

"Oh, of course, it's my fault. Everything's always my fault," said Grimes. "Now don't go to hit me again (for the truncheon started upright, and looked very wicked); you know, if my arms were only free, you daren't hit me then."

The truncheon leant back against the chimney, and took no notice of the personal insult, like a well-trained policeman as it was, though he was ready enough to avenge any transgression against morality or order.

"But can't I help you in any other way? Can't I help you to get out of this chimney?" said Tom.

"No," interposed the truncheon; "he has come to the place where everybody must help themselves; and he will find it out, I hope, before he is done with me."

"Oh, yes," said Grimes, "of course it's me. Did I ask to be brought here into the prison? Did I ask to be set to sweep your foul chimneys? Did I ask to have lighted straw put under me to make me go up? Did I ask to stick fast in the very first chimney of all, because it was so shamefully clogged up with soot? Did I ask to stay here—I don't know how long—a hundred years, I do believe, and never get my pipe, nor my beer, nor nothing fit for a beast, let alone a man."

"No," answered a solemn voice behind. "No more did Tom, when you behaved to him in the very same way."

It was Mrs. Bedonebyasyoudid. And, when the truncheon saw her, it started bolt upright—Attention!—and made such a low bow, that if it had not been full of the spirit of justice, it must have tumbled on its end, and probably hurt its one eye. And Tom made his bow too.

"Oh, ma'am," he said, "don't think about me; that's all past and gone, and good times and bad times and all times pass over. But may not I help poor Mr. Grimes? Mayn't I try and get some of these bricks away, that he may move his arms?"

"You may try, of course," she said.

So Tom pulled and tugged at the bricks: but he could not move one. And then he tried to wipe Mr. Grimes's face: but the soot would not come off.

"Oh, dear!" he said, "I have come all this way, through all these terrible places, to help you, and now I am of no use after all."

"You had best leave me alone," said Grimes; "you are a good-natured forgiving little chap, and that's truth; but you'd best be off. The hail's coming on soon, and it will beat the eyes out of your little head."

"What hail?"

"Why hail that falls every evening here; and, till it comes close to me, it's like so much warm rain: but then it turns to hail over my head, and knocks me about like small shot."

"That hail will never come any more," said the strange lady. "I have told you before what it was. It was your mother's tears, those which she shed when she prayed for you by her bedside; but your cold heart froze it into hail. But she is gone to heaven now, and will weep no more for her graceless son."

Then Grimes was silent a while; and then he looked very sad.

"So my old mother's gone, and I never there to speak to her! Ah! a good woman she was, and might have been a happy one, in her little school there in Vendale, if it hadn't been for me and my bad ways."

"Did she keep the school in Vendale?" asked Tom. And then he told Grimes all the story of his going to her house, and how she could not abide the sight of a chimney-sweep, and then how kind she was, and how he turned into a water-baby.

"Ah!" said Grimes, "good reason she had to hate the sight of a chimney-sweep. I ran away from her and took up with the sweeps, and never let her know where I was, nor sent her a penny to help her, and now it's too late—too late!" said Mr. Grimes.

And he began crying and blubbering like a great baby, till his pipe dropped out of his mouth, and broke all to bits.

"Oh dear, if I was but a little chap in Vendale again, to see the clear beck, and the apple-orchard, and the yew-hedge, how different I would go on! But it's too late now. So you go along, you kind little chap, and don't stand to look at a man crying, that's old enough to be your father, and never feared the face of man, nor of worse neither. But I'm beat now, and beat I must be. I've made my bed, and I must lie on it. Foul I would be, and foul I am, as an Irishwoman said to me once; and little I heeded it. It's all my own fault: but it's too late." And he cried so bitterly that Tom began crying too.

"Never too late," said the fairy, in such a strange soft new voice that Tom looked up at her; and she was so beautiful for the moment, that Tom half fancied she was her sister.

No more was it too late. For, as poor Grimes cried and blubbered on, his own tears did what his mother's could not do, and Tom's could not do, and nobody's on earth could do for him; for they washed the soot off his face and off his clothes; and then they washed the mortar away from between the bricks; and the chimney crumbled down; and Grimes began to get out of it.

Up jumped the truncheon, and was going to hit him on the crown a tremendous thump, and drive him down again like a cork into a bottle. But the strange lady put it aside.

"Will you obey me if I give you a chance?"

"As you please, ma'am. You're stronger than me, that I know too well, and wiser than me, I know too well also. And, as for being my own master, I've fared ill enough with that as yet. So whatever your ladyship pleases to order me; for I'm beat, and that's the truth."

"Be it so then—you may come out. But remember, disobey me again, and into a worse place still you go."

"I beg pardon, ma'am, but I never disobeyed you that I know of. I never had the honour of setting eyes upon you till I came to these ugly quarters."

"Never saw me? Who said to you, Those that will be foul, foul they will be?"

Grimes looked up; and Tom looked up too; for the voice was that of the Irishwoman who met them the day that they went out together to Harthover. "I gave you your warning then: but you gave it yourself a thousand times before and since. Every bad word that you said—every cruel and mean thing that you did—every time that you got tipsy—every day that you went dirty—you were disobeying me, whether you knew it or not."

"If I'd only known, ma'am—"

"You knew well enough that you were disobeying something, though you did not know it was me. But come out and take your chance. Perhaps it may be your last."

So Grimes stept out of the chimney, and, really, if it had not been for the scars on his face, he looked as clean and respectable as a master-sweep need look.

"Take him away," said she to the truncheon, "and give him his ticket-of-leave."[1]

"And what is he to do, ma'am?"

"Get him to sweep out the crater of Etna; he will find some very steady men working out their time there, who will teach him his business: but mind, if that crater gets choked again, and there is an earthquake in consequence, bring them all to me, and I shall investigate the case very severely."

So the truncheon marched off Mr. Grimes, looking as meek as a drowned worm.

And for aught I know, or do not know, he is sweeping the crater of Etna to this very day.

"And now," said the fairy to Tom, "your work here is done. You may as well go back again."

"I should be glad enough to go," said Tom, "but how am I to get up that great hole again, now the steam has stopped blowing?"

"I will take you up the backstairs: but I must bandage your eyes first; for I never allow anybody to see those backstairs of mine."

---

1   A document given to convicts when granting them limited freedom
    before their sentence expired or they were pardoned.

"I am sure I shall not tell anybody about them, ma'am, if you bid me not."

"Aha! So you think, my little man. But you would soon forget your promise if you got back into the land-world. For, if people only once found out that you had been up my backstairs, you would have all the fine ladies kneeling to you, and the rich men emptying their purses before you, and statesmen offering you place and power; and young and old, rich and poor, crying to you, 'Only tell us the great backstairs secret, and we will be your slaves; we will make you lord, king, emperor, bishop, archbishop, pope, if you like—only tell us the secret of the backstairs. For thousands of years we have been paying, and petting, and obeying, and worshipping quacks who told us they had the key of the backstairs, and could smuggle us up them; and in spite of all our disappointments, we will honour, and glorify, and adore, and beatify, and translate, and apotheosize you likewise, on the chance of your knowing something about the backstairs, that we may all go on pilgrimage to it; and, even if we cannot get up it, lie at the foot of it, and cry—

'Oh backstairs,
precious backstairs,
invaluable backstairs,   aristocratic backstairs,
requisite backstairs,   respectable backstairs,
necessary backstairs,   gentlemanlike backstairs,
good-natured backstairs,   ladylike backstairs,
cosmopolitan backstairs,   commercial backstairs,
comprehensive backstairs,   economical backstairs,
accommodating backstairs,   practical backstairs,
well-bred backstairs,   logical backstairs,
comfortable backstairs,   deductive backstairs,
humane backstairs,   orthodox backstairs,
reasonable backstairs,   probable backstairs,
long-sought backstairs,   credible backstairs,
coveted backstairs,   demonstrable backstairs,
potent backstairs,   irrefragable backstairs,
all-but-omnipotent backstairs,
&C.

Save us from the consequences of our own actions, and from the cruel fairy, Mrs. Bedonebyasyoudid!' Do not you think that you would be a little tempted then to tell what you know, laddie?"

Tom thought so certainly. "But why do they want so to know about the backstairs?" asked he, being a little frightened at the long words, and not understanding them the least; as, indeed, he was not meant to do, or you either.

"That I shall not tell you. I never put things into little folks' heads which are but too likely to come there of themselves. So come—now I must bandage your eyes." So she tied the bandage on his eyes with one hand, and with the other she took it off.

"Now," she said, "you are safe up the stairs." Tom opened his eyes very wide, and his mouth too; for he had not, as he thought, moved a single step. But, when he looked round him, there could be no doubt that he was safe up the backstairs, whatsoever they may be, which no man is going to tell you, for the plain reason that no man knows.

The first thing which Tom saw was the black cedars, high and sharp against the rosy dawn; and St. Brandan's Isle reflected double in the still broad silver sea.

The wind sang softly in the cedars, and the water sang among the caves; the sea-birds sang as they streamed out into the ocean, and the land-birds as they built among the boughs; and the air was so full of song that it stirred St. Brandan and his hermits, as they slumbered in the shade; and they moved their good old lips, and sang their morning hymn amid their dreams. But among all the songs one came across the water more sweet and clear than all; for it was the song of a young girl's voice.

And what was the song which she sang? Ah, my little man, I am too old to sing that song, and you too young to understand it. But have patience, and keep your eye single, and your hands clean, and you will learn some day to sing it yourself, without needing any man to teach you.

And as Tom neared the island, there sat upon a rock the most graceful creature that ever was seen, looking down, with her chin upon her hand, and paddling with her feet in the water. And when they came to her she looked up, and behold it was Ellie.

"Oh, Miss Ellie," said he, "how you are grown!"

"Oh, Tom," said she, "how you are grown, too!"

And no wonder; they were both quite grown up—he into a tall man, and she into a beautiful woman.

"Perhaps I may be grown," she said. "I have had time enough; for I have been sitting here waiting for you many a hundred years, till I thought you were never coming."

"Many a hundred years?" thought Tom; but he had seen so much in his travels that he had quite given up being astonished;

and, indeed, he could think of nothing but Ellie. So he stood and looked at Ellie, and Ellie looked at him; and they liked the employment so much that they stood and looked for seven years more, and neither spoke or stirred.

At last they heard the fairy say: "Attention, children! Are you never going to look at me again?"

"We have been looking at you all this while," they said. And so they thought they had been.

"Then look at me once more," said she.

They looked—and both of them cried out at once, "Oh, who are you, after all?"

"You are our dear Mrs. Doasyouwouldbedoneby."

"No, you are good Mrs. Bedonebyasyoudid; but you are grown quite beautiful now!"

"To you," said the fairy. "But look again."

"You are Mother Carey," said Tom, in a very low, solemn voice; for he had found out something which made him very happy, and yet frightened him more than all that he had ever seen.

"But you are grown quite young again."

"To you," said the fairy. "Look again."

"You are the Irishwoman who met me the day I went to Harthover!"

And when they looked she was neither of them, and yet all of them at once.

"My name is written in my eyes, if you have eyes to see it there."

And they looked into her great, deep, soft eyes, and they changed again and again into every hue, as the light changes in a diamond.

"Now read my name," said she, at last.

And her eyes flashed, for one moment, clear, white, blazing light: but the children could not read her name; for they were dazzled, and hid their faces in their hands.

"Not yet, young things, not yet," said she, smiling; and then she turned to Ellie.

"You may take him home with you now on Sundays, Ellie. He has won his spurs in the great battle, and become fit to go with you, and be a man; because he has done the thing he did not like."

So Tom went home with Ellie on Sundays, and sometimes on week-days, too; and he is now a great man of science, and can plan railroads, and steam-engines, and electric telegraphs, and rifled guns, and so forth; and knows everything about everything, except why a hen's egg don't turn into a crocodile, and two or three other little things which no one will know till the coming of the Cocqcigrues. And all this from what he learnt when he was a water-baby, underneath the sea.

"And of course Tom married Ellie?"

My dear child, what a silly notion! Don't you know that no one ever marries in a fairy tale, under the rank of a prince or a princess?

"And Tom's dog?"

Oh, you may see him any clear night in July; for the old dog-star was so worn out by the last three hot summers that there have been no dog-days[1] since; so that they had to take him down and put Tom's dog up in his place. Therefore, as new brooms sweep clean, we may hope for some warm weather this year. And that is the end of my story.

MORAL.

And now, my dear little man, what should we learn from this parable?

We should learn thirty-seven or thirty-nine things,[2] I am not exactly sure which: but one thing, at least, we may learn, and that is this—when we see efts in the ponds, never to throw stones at them, or catch them with crooked pins, or put them into vivariums[3] with sticklebacks,[4] that the sticklebacks may prick them in their poor little stomachs, and make them jump out of the glass into somebody's workbox, and so come to a bad end. For these efts are nothing else but the water-babies who are stupid and dirty, and will not learn their lessons and keep themselves clean;

---

1   In the summer the dog-star Sirius (the brightest star in Canis Major) rises and sets with the sun. During late July, Sirius is in conjunction with the sun, and the ancients believed that its heat added to the heat of the sun, thereby creating the spell of hot and sultry weather known as "dog-days."

2   An allusion to the Thirty-Nine Articles of Faith of the Church of England. Subscription to them by the clergy was ordered by act of Parliament in 1571.

3   An indoor enclosure for keeping and raising living animals or fish.

4   "A small spiny-finned fish, of the genus *Gasterosteus*" (*OED*).

and, therefore (as comparative anatomists will tell you fifty years hence, though they are not learned enough to tell you now), their skulls grow flat, their jaws grow out, and their brains grow small, and their tails grow long, and they lose all their ribs (which I am sure you would not like to do), and their skins grow dirty and spotted, and they never get into the clear rivers, much less into the great wide sea, but hang about in dirty ponds, and live in the mud, and eat worms, as they deserve to do.

But that is no reason why you should ill-use them: but only why you should pity them, and be kind to them, and hope that some day they will wake up, and be ashamed of their nasty, dirty, lazy, stupid life, and try to amend, and become something better once more. For, perhaps, if they do so, then after 379,423 years, nine months, thirteen days, two hours, and twenty-one minutes (for aught that appears to the contrary), if they work very hard and wash very hard all that time, their brains may grow bigger, and their jaws grow smaller, and their ribs come back, and their tails wither off, and they will turn into water-babies again, and, perhaps, after that into land-babies; and after that, perhaps, into grown men.

You know they won't? Very well, I dare say you know best. But, you see, some folks have a great liking for those poor little efts. They never did anybody any harm, or could if they tried; and their only fault is, that they do no good—any more than some thousands of their betters. But what with ducks, and what with pike, and what with sticklebacks, and what with water-beetles, and what with naughty boys, they are "sae sair haddened doun,"[1] as the Scotsmen say, that it is a wonder how they live; and some folks can't help hoping, with good Bishop Butler,[2] that they may have another chance, to make things fair and even, somewhere, somewhen, somehow.

Meanwhile, do you learn your lessons, and thank God that you have plenty of cold water to wash in; and wash in it too, like a true English man. And then, if my story is not true, something

---

1   "So cruelly held down."
2   Joseph Butler (1692-1752), Bishop of Bristol and later Durham, argued that conscience was the supreme and universal center of a virtuous and moral life, and that it is through one's conscience that God makes his presence felt. Butler's most famous work is *Analogy of Religion, Natural and Revealed, to the Constitution and Nature* (1736).

better is; and if I am not quite right, still you will be, as long as you stick to hard work and cold water.

But remember always, as I told you at first, that this is all a fairy tale, and only fun and pretence; and, therefore, you are not to believe a word of it, even if it is true.

Appendix A: William Blake, "The Chimney Sweeper," from Songs of Innocence and Songs of Experience (1789, 1794)

[Blake's outcry against the spiritual, physical, and emotional abuse of children was clearly ahead of its time. In 1804, more than a decade after Blake published his two sweeper poems, a bill to stop the use of children under ten as chimney sweeps was defeated by the House of Lords. Only in 1864, after many years of sporadic and ineffectual legislation, was an Act of Parliament finally approved by the House of Lords to outlaw the use of children under age sixteen for cleaning chimneys. Lord Shaftesbury's Act for the Regulation of Chimney Sweepers established a penalty of £10 for offenders. For the times, this was a large amount of money, and the law, with the support of the police and the public, brought an end to the practice. It seems hardly coincidental that Kingsley's Tom appeared only a couple of years before the Lords, under public pressure, came to grips with this long-standing abuse of children.]

The Chimney Sweeper (*Songs of Innocence*, 1789)

When my mother died I was very young.
And my father sold me while yet my tongue,
Could scarcely cry weep weep weep weep.
So your chimneys I sweep & in soot I sleep.

Theres little Tom Dacre, who cried when his head
That curl'd like a lambs back, was shav'd, so I said,
Hush Tom never mind it, for when your head's bare,
You know that the soot cannot spoil your white hair.

And so he was quiet, & that very night,
As Tom was a sleeping he had such a sight,
That thousands of sweepers Dick, Joe Ned & Jack
Were all of them lock'd up in coffins of black,

And by came an Angel who had a bright key
And he open'd the coffins & set them all free.
Then down a green plain leaping laughing they run
And wash in a river and shine in the Sun.

Then naked & white, all their bags left behind,
They rise upon clouds, and sport in the wind.
And the Angel told Tom if he'd be a good boy,
He'd have God for his father & never want joy.

And so Tom awoke and we rose in the dark
And got with our bags & our brushes to work,
Tho' the morning was cold, Tom was happy & warm
So if all do their duty, they need not fear harm.

The Chimney Sweeper (*Songs of Experience*, 1794)

A little black thing among the snow:
Crying weep, weep, in notes of woe!
Where are thy father & mother! say!
They are both gone up to the church to pray.

Because I was happy upon the heath,
And smil'd among the winters snow:
They clothed me in the clothes of death,
And taught me to sing the notes of woe.

And because I am happy, & dance & sing,
They think they have done me no injury:
And are gone to praise God & his Priest & King
Who make up a heaven of our misery.

Appendix B: Matthew Arnold, "The Forsaken Merman," from The Strayed Reveller and Other Poems (1849)

[In Chapter IV of *The Water-Babies* Kingsley describes how Tom "left the buoy, and used to go along the sands and round the rocks, and come out in the night—like the forsaken Merman in Mr. Arnold's beautiful, beautiful poem, which you {Kingsley's son, Grenville} must learn by heart some day—and sit upon a point of rock, among the shining sea-weeds, in the low October tides, and cry and call for the water-babies: but he never heard a voice call in return. And, at last, with his fretting and crying, he grew quite lean and thin."]

The Forsaken Merman

Come, dear children, let us away;
Down and away below!
Now my brothers call from the bay,
Now the great winds shoreward blow,
Now the salt tides seaward flow;
Now the wild white horses play,
Champ and chafe and toss in the spray.
Children dear, let us away!
This way, this way!

Call her once before you go—
Call once yet!
In a voice that she will know:
"Margaret! Margaret!"
Children's voices should be dear
(Call once more) to a mother's ear;
Children's voices, wild with pain—
Surely she will come again!
Call her once and come away;
This way, this way!
"Mother dear, we cannot stay!
The wild white horses foam and fret."
Margaret! Margaret!

Come, dear children, come away down;
Call no more!
One last look at the white-wall'd town,
And the little grey church on the windy shore;
Then come down!
She will not come though you call all day;
Come away, come away!

Children dear, was it yesterday
We heard the sweet bells over the bay?
In the caverns where we lay,
Through the surf and through the swell,
The far-off sound of a silver bell?
Sand-strewn caverns, cool and deep,
Where the winds are all asleep;
Where the spent lights quiver and gleam,
Where the salt weed sways in the stream,
Where the sea-beasts, ranged all round,
Feed in the ooze of their pasture-ground;
Where the sea-snakes coil and twine,
Dry their mail and bask in the brine;
Where great whales come sailing by,
Sail and sail, with unshut eye,
Round the world for ever and aye?
When did music come this way?
Children dear, was it yesterday?

Children dear, was it yesterday
(Call yet once) that she went away?
Once she sate with you and me,
On a red gold throne in the heart of the sea,
And the youngest sate on her knee.
She comb'd its bright hair, and she tended it well,
When down swung the sound of a far-off bell.
She sigh'd, she look'd up through the clear green sea;
She said: "I must go, for my kinsfolk pray
In the little grey church on the shore to-day.
'Twill be Easter-time in the world—ah me!
And I lose my poor soul, Merman! here with thee."
I said: "Go up, dear heart, through the waves;
Say thy prayer, and come back to the kind sea-caves!"
She smiled, she went up through the surf in the bay.
Children dear, was it yesterday?

Children dear, were we long alone?
"The sea grows stormy, the little ones moan;
Long prayers," I said, "in the world they say;
Come!" I said; and we rose through the surf in the bay.
We went up the beach, by the sandy down
Where the sea-stocks bloom, to the white-wall'd town;
Through the narrow paved streets, where all was still,
To the little grey church on the windy hill.
From the church came a murmur of folk at their prayers,
But we stood without in the cold blowing airs.
We climb'd on the graves, on the stones worn with rains,
And we gazed up the aisle through the small leaded panes.
She sate by the pillar; we saw her clear:
"Margaret, hist! come quick, we are here!
Dear heart," I said, "we are long alone;
The sea grows stormy, the little ones moan."
But, ah, she gave me never a look,
For her eyes were seal'd to the holy book!
Loud prays the priest; shut stands the door.
Come away, children, call no more!
Come away, come down, call no more!

Down, down, down!
Down to the depths of the sea!
She sits at her wheel in the humming town,
Singing most joyfully.
Hark what she sings: "O joy, O joy,
For the humming street, and the child with its toy!
For the priest, and the bell, and the holy well;
For the wheel where I spun,
And the blessed light of the sun!"
And so she sings her fill,
Singing most joyfully,
Till the spindle drops from her hand,
And the whizzing wheel stands still.
She steals to the window, and looks at the sand,
And over the sand at the sea;
And her eyes are set in a stare;
And anon there breaks a sigh,
And anon there drops a tear,
From a sorrow-clouded eye,
And a heart sorrow-laden,
A long, long sigh;

For the cold strange eyes of a little Mermaiden
And the gleam of her golden hair.

Come away, away children;
Come children, come down!
The hoarse wind blows coldly;
Lights shine in the town.
She will start from her slumber
When gusts shake the door;
She will hear the winds howling,
Will hear the waves roar.
We shall see, while above us
The waves roar and whirl,
A ceiling of amber,
A pavement of pearl.
Singing: "Here came a mortal,
But faithless was she!
And alone dwell for ever
The kings of the sea."

But, children, at midnight,
When soft the winds blow,
When clear falls the moonlight,
When spring-tides are low;
When sweet airs come seaward
From heaths starr'd with broom,
And high rocks throw mildly
On the blanch'd sands a gloom;
Up the still, glistening beaches,
Up the creeks we will hie,
Over banks of bright seaweed
The ebb-tide leaves dry.
We will gaze, from the sand-hills,
At the white, sleeping town;
At the church on the hill-side—
And then come back down.
Singing: "There dwells a loved one,
But cruel is she!
She left lonely for ever
The kings of the sea."

Appendix C: From Heinrich Hoffman, Struwwelpeter (New York: Frederick Warne, 1845)

[Dr. Heinrich Hoffman (1809-94), a general practitioner in Frankfurt, Germany, authored several books on medicine and psychiatry, but his fame derives from his children's book *Der Struwwelpeter* (1845). Translated into over thirty languages (including an English version by Mark Twain), *Struwwelpeter* (Shockhead Peter or Slovenly Peter) was conceived after Hoffman failed to find a suitable book for his son Carl as a Christmas gift. He illustrated his own book, which is comprised of humorously macabre poems designed to scare children into civilized behavior. Like Kingsley, he found contemporary children's books to be too artificial, moralistic, and out of touch with a child's psychology. In Chapter III of *The Water-Babies*, Tom breaks open the home of a caddis. The mother caddis, having on a tight nightcap, cannot speak, but the other caddises "held up their hands and shrieked like the cats in Struwelpeter [sic.]. "Oh, you horrid nasty boy; there you are at it again!" Tom later learns his lesson not to mistreat these creatures when he is abandoned by some of the sea folk and is left with no playmates. The punishment most reminiscent of that meted out to Hoffman's bad children, however, comes in Chapter VI when Tom steals some lollipops from Mrs. Doasyouwouldbedoneby's cupboard. This misbehavior causes his entire body to become covered with horny prickles.]

The Dreadful Story of Harriet and the Matches

It almost makes me cry to tell
What foolish Harriet befell.
Mamma and Nurse went out one day
And left her all alone at play.
Now, on the table close at hand,
A box of matches chanced to stand;
And kind Mamma and Nurse had told her,
That, if she touched them, they would scold her.
But Harriet said: "Oh, what a pity!
For, when they burn, it is so pretty;

They crackle so, and spit, and flame:
Mamma, too, often does the same."

The pussy-cats heard this,
And they began to hiss,
And stretch their claws,
And raise their paws;
"Me-ow," they said, "me-ow, me-o,
You'll burn to death, if you do so."

But Harriet would not take advice:
She lit a match, it was so nice!
It crackled so, it burned so clear—
Exactly like the picture here.
She jumped for joy and ran about
And was too pleased to put it out.

The Pussy-cats saw this
And said: "Oh, naughty, naughty Miss!"
And stretched their claws,
And raised their paws:
"'Tis very, very wrong, you know,
Me-ow, me-o, me-ow, me-o,
You will be burnt, if you do so."

And see! oh, what dreadful thing!
The fire has caught her apron-string;
Her apron burns, her arms, her hair—
She burns all over everywhere.

Then how the pussy-cats did mew—
What else, poor pussies, could they do?
They screamed for help, 'twas all in vain!
So then they said: "We'll scream again;
Make haste, make haste, me-ow, me-o,
She'll burn to death; we told her so."

So she was burnt, with all her clothes,
And arms, and hands, and eyes, and nose;
Till she had nothing more to lose
Except her little scarlet shoes;
And nothing else but these was found
Among her ashes on the ground.

And when the good cats sat beside
The smoking ashes, how they cried!
"Me-ow, me-oo, me-ow, me-oo,
What will Mamma and Nursey do?"
Their tears ran down their cheeks so fast,
They made a little pond at last.

The Story of Little Suck-a-Thumb

One day Mamma said "Conrad dear,
I must go out and leave you here.
But mind now, Conrad, what I say,
Don't suck your thumb while I'm away.
The great tall tailor always comes
To little boys who suck their thumbs;
And ere they dream what he's about,
He takes his great sharp scissors out,
And cuts their thumbs clean off—and then,
You know, they never grow again."

Mamma had scarcely turned her back,
The thumb was in, Alack! Alack!

The door flew open, in he ran,
The great, long, red-legged scissor-man.
Oh! children, see! the tailor's come
And caught out little Suck-a-Thumb.
Snip! Snap! Snip! the scissors go;
And Conrad cries out "Oh! Oh! Oh!"
Snip! Snap! Snip! They go so fast,
That both his thumbs are off at last.

Mamma comes home: there Conrad stands,
And looks quite sad, and shows his hands;
"Ah!" said Mamma, "I knew he'd come
To naughty little Suck-a-Thumb."

[Source: Heinrich Hoffman, *Struwwelpeter* (New York: Frederick
Warne, n.d.) 6-7, 15-16.]

Appendix D: From Lewis Carroll, "The Mock-Turtle's Story" in Alice's Adventures in Wonderland (1865)

[Published shortly after *The Water-Babies*, *Alice's Adventures in Wonderland* introduces a parallel universe, located under ground rather than under water. Carroll had read Kingsley's *Alton Locke* in 1856 and *Hypatia* in 1857. Although there is no direct evidence that he read *The Water-Babies*, it seems likely that he had, given some similarities between the two tales. Furthermore, Kingsley's story was very popular and was sure to have caught Carroll's interest. Carroll's friendship with Kingsley's brother, Henry, might also have made the book known to him. In 1894 Carroll went to see an adaptation of *The Water-Babies* by E.W. Bowles. He found this operatic extravaganza to be vulgar, coarse, and profane, and wrote the acting manager a complaint that the work was indecent. He later tried to keep the play from being licensed to other theaters. Lacking the particulars of Bowles's adaptation, it is impossible to say why Carroll found the production so offensive. It is unfortunate that he left behind no comment on Kingsley's book.

Carroll's playful treatment of the education of young people in "The Mock-Turtle's Story" has an interesting antecedent in Chapter VIII of *The Water-Babies*, where Tom comes upon the pathetic turnip children and the threatening Examiner-of-all-Examiners.]

"The Mock-Turtle's Story"

They had not gone far before they saw the Mock Turtle in the distance, sitting sad and lonely on a little ledge of rock, and, as they came nearer, Alice could hear him sighing as if his heart would break. She pitied him deeply. "What is his sorrow?" she asked the Gryphon. And the Gryphon answered, very nearly in the same words as before, "It's all his fancy, that: he hasn't got no sorrow, you know. Come on!"

So they went up to the Mock Turtle, who looked at them with large eyes full of tears, but said nothing.

"This here young lady," said the Gryphon, "she wants for to know your history, she do."

"I'll tell it her," said the Mock Turtle in a deep, hollow tone. "Sit down, both of you, and don't speak a word till I've finished."

So they sat down, and nobody spoke for some minutes. Alice thought to herself "I don't see how he can *ever* finish, if he doesn't begin." But she waited patiently.

"Once," said the Mock Turtle at last, with a deep sigh, "I was a real Turtle."

These words were followed by a very long silence, broken only by an occasional exclamation of "Hjckrrh!" from the Gryphon, and the constant heavy sobbing of the Mock Turtle. Alice was very nearly getting up and saying, "Thank you, Sir, for your interesting story," but she could not help thinking there *must* be more to come, so she sat still and said nothing.

"When we were little," the Mock Turtle went on at last, more calmly, though still sobbing a little now and then, "we went to school in the sea. The master was an old Turtle—we used to call him Tortoise—"

"Why did you call him Tortoise, if he wasn't one?" Alice asked.

"We called him Tortoise because he taught us," said the Mock Turtle angrily. "Really you are very dull!"

"You ought to be ashamed of yourself for asking such a simple question," added the Gryphon; and then they both sat silent and looked at poor Alice, who felt ready to sink into the earth. At last the Gryphon said to the Mock Turtle "Drive on, old fellow! Don't be all day about it!," and he went on in these words:—

"Yes, we went to school in the sea, though you mayn't believe it—"

"I never said I didn't!" interrupted Alice.

"You did," said the Mock Turtle.

"Hold your tongue!" added the Gryphon, before Alice could speak again. The Mock Turtle went on.

"We had the best of educations—in fact, we went to school every day—"

"*I've* been to a day-school, too," said Alice. "You needn't be so proud as all that."

"With extras?" asked the Mock Turtle, a little anxiously.

"Yes," said Alice: "we learned French and music."

"And washing?" said the Mock Turtle. "Certainly not!" said Alice indignantly.

"Ah! Then yours wasn't a really good school," said the Mock

Turtle in a tone of great relief. "Now, at *ours*, they had, at the end of the bill, 'French, music, *and washing*—extra.'"[1]

"You couldn't have wanted it much," said Alice; "living at the bottom of the sea."

"I couldn't afford to learn it," said the Mock Turtle with a sigh. "I only took the regular course."

"What was that?" inquired Alice.

"Reeling and Writing, of course, to begin with,"[2] the Mock Turtle replied; "and then the different branches of Arithmetic—Ambition, Distraction, Uglification, and Derision."

"I never heard of 'Uglification,'" Alice ventured to say. "What is it?"

The Gryphon lifted up both its paws in surprise. "Never heard of uglifying!" it exclaimed. "You know what to beautify is, I suppose?"

"Yes," said Alice doubtfully: "it means—to—make—any-thing—prettier."

"Well, then," the Gryphon went on, "if you don't know what to uglify is, you *are* a simpleton."

Alice did not feel encouraged to ask anymore questions about it: so she turned to the Mock Turtle, and said "What else had you to learn?"

"Well, there was Mystery," the Mock Turtle replied, counting off the subjects on his flappers,—"Mystery, ancient and modern, with Seaography: then Drawling—the Drawling-master was an old conger-eel, that used to come once a week: he taught us Drawling, Stretching, and Fainting in Coils."

"What was *that* like?" said Alice.

"Well, I ca'n't show it you, myself," the Mock Turtle said: "I'm too stiff. And the Gryphon never learnt it."

"Hadn't time," said the Gryphon: "I went to the Classical master, though. He was an old crab, *he* was."

---

1 According to Martin Gardner (*Annotated Alice*) the phrase "French, music, and washing—extra" often appeared on boarding school bills. The meaning is simply that there was an extra charge to teach French and music, and to have one's clothes washed by the school. The Mock Turtle, however, asks Alice if washing was one of the subjects taught at her school, an idea obviously repugnant to her middle-class assumptions.

2 All of the Mock Turtle's subjects are puns on traditional courses of study: reading, writing, addition, subtractions, multiplication, division, history, geography, drawing, sketching, painting in oils, Latin, and Greek.

"I never went to him," the Mock Turtle said with a sigh. "He taught Laughing and Grief, they used to say."

"So he did, so he did," said the Gryphon, sighing in his turn; and both creatures hid their faces in their paws.

"And how many hours a day did you do lessons?" said Alice, in a hurry to change the subject.

"Ten hours the first day," said the Mock Turtle: "nine the next, and so on."

"What a curious plan!" exclaimed Alice.

"That's the reason they're called lessons," the Gryphon remarked: "because they lessen from day to day."

This was quite a new idea to Alice, and she thought it over a little before she made her next remark. "Then the eleventh day must have been a holiday?"

"Of course it was," said the Mock Turtle.

"And how did you manage on the twelfth?"[1] Alice went on eagerly.

"That's enough about lessons," the Gryphon interrupted in a very decided tone. "Tell her something about the games now."

[Source: Lewis Carroll, *Alice's Adventures in Wonderland*, ed. Richard Kelly (Ontario, Canada: Broadview Press, 2000) 127-31.]

---

1 The eleventh day was a holiday because the hours have been reduced to zero. The Gryphon ends the discussion when Alice asks about the twelfth day because, as Martin Gardner points out (*More Annotated Alice*), she introduces the possibility of mysterious negative numbers, something of a mind boggler in the context of diminishing lessons.

Appendix E: From Margaret Gatty, "Whereunto?" Parables From Nature (1861)

[Margaret Scott Gatty (1809-73), known as Mrs. Alfred Gatty, was an editor, writer of children's books, and landscape artist. In 1866 she became editor of *Aunt Judy's Magazine*, and remained editor until her death in 1873. *Parables from Nature* was published in five series between 1855 and 1871. Gatty possessed a scientific interest in the natural world, so that her tales are full of wondrous creatures.

"Whereunto," which was first published with the third series in 1861, illustrates her interest in the popular science of the seashore. She was a great enthusiast for marine biology, and published a textbook, *The History of British Seaweeds* (1863). Like Kingsley, who was clearly inspired by her keen observations of the natural world, she enjoyed collecting shells, rocks, seaweed, and other specimens from the sea. Also like Kingsley, she humanizes her sea creatures, in this instance a starfish and a crab, and suggests that spiritual insights can be derived from the close examination of nature. The interdependence of sea life, shown by the protective role of seaweed in this story, clearly carries an important ecological and moral message to both children and adults.]

Whereunto?

        I see in part
That all, as in some piece of art,
    Is toil co-operant to an end.
            Tennyson[1]

"THIS is dreadful! What can I do?"

"Why, follow me, to be sure! Here! quick! sideways! to the left! into this crevice of the rock! there! all's right!"

"Oh, it's easy to talk, when people can trip away as lightly as you do. But look at me with the ground slipping away wherever I try to lay hold."

---

1 *In Memoriam*, 128, ll. 22-24.

"Come along; all's right," repeated the Crab (for such was the speaker) from his crevice in the rock.

And all was right certainly, as far as he was concerned; but as for the poor Star-fish, who was left on the sand, all was as wrong as possible, for he was much too hot; and no wonder.

It was a low tide—a spring tide—and even for a spring tide, a particularly low one; for there was very little wind astir, and what there was, blew off the shore.

So the rocks were uncovered now, which seldom tasted the air, and the stems of the great oarweed, or tangle, which grew from them, were bent into a half-circle by the weight of their broad leathery fronds, as, no longer buoyed up by the sea, they lay trailing on the sands.

What a day it was, to be sure! one of those rare, serene ones, when there is not a cloud in the delicate blue sky, and when the sea lies so calm and peaceful under it, that one might almost be persuaded to believe nothing would ever again ruffle its surface. The white-sailed vessels in the distance, too, looked as if they had nothing in the world to do for ever, but to float from one beautiful end of the world to the other, in security and joy. Yet delicious—unspeakably delicious—as the day was, it brought discomfort to some who lived under it. The numberless star-fishes, for instance, who had been unexpectedly left stranded on the shore by the all-too-gently-retreating waves, how could they rejoice in the beautiful sunshine, when it was streaming so pitilessly on their helpless limbs, and scorching them by its dry cruel heat? And as for the jelly-fishes, who had shared a similar fate, they had died almost at once from the shock, as the wave cast them ashore; so of the merits of the delicious day they knew nothing at all.

All creatures did not suffer, of course. The Crab, for instance, who had given such good advice to his friend (if he could but have followed it), did very well. In the first place, he liked the air nearly as well as the water, so that being left high and dry on the shore now and then was quite to his taste. Moreover, he could scuttle off and hide in a crevice of the rocks whenever he chose. Or he could shelter under the large sea-weeds, and because of his hard coat was even able to take a short walk from time to time, to see how matters went on, and observe how far the tide had gone down; and if the sun did happen to bake him a little too much, he had only to run off to a pool and take a bath, and then was as fresh as ever in a minute.

And now, just as the tide was at the lowest, where it was likely to beat about for some time without much change, two other creatures appeared on the sands, and approached the very spot where the Star-fish lay in his distress, and near which the Crab was hid. Now there was a ledge of rocks here, which would have furnished seats for dozens of human beings, and from the front of it grew almost a forest of oarweed plants.

What the creatures were who came up to this place and stopped to observe it, I shall not say; but one of them remarked to the other, "Here again, you see; the same old story as before. Wasted life and wasted death, and all within a few inches of each other! Useless, lumbering plants, not seen half-a-dozen times in the year; and helpless, miserable sea-creatures, dying in health and strength, one doesn't know why."

As the creature who spoke said this, it lifted up two or three tangle fronds with a stick it carried in its hand, and then let them flop suddenly down on the sand; after which it used the end of the same stick to chuck the unhappy Star-fish into the air, who, tumbling by a lucky accident under the shelter of the tangle, was hid for a time from sight.

"And so we go up, and so we go down, ourselves," continued the creature; "a good many of us, with no more end in life, and of no more use, that one can see, than these vile useless seaweeds; coming into the world, in fact, for no earthly purpose but to go out of it, in some such wretched manner as this!"

And here the creature kicked three or four more stranded star-fishes across the narrow sands, till he had fairly kicked them into the sea; muttering as he did so, "What did you come into the world for, I wonder, and you, and you, and you? Purposeless life and purposeless death—the fate of thousands. And I for one as useless as any of them, but at any rate having the grace to acknowledge that the world would get on quite as cleverly without me as with! Whereunto, whereunto, whereunto? Answer it if you can!" As the creature finished speaking, the two moved on together; but what the companion answered was never exactly known; for though the voice sounded as if in dispute, what was said was not heard by those who were left behind, for they began at once to chatter among themselves.

And first out popped the head of the Crab from the crevice he had taken shelter in; and he cocked his eyes knowingly, first to one side, and then to the other, and began to talk; for he had always plenty to say for himself, and was remarkably bold when there was no danger. "Miserable sea-creatures!" was his first exclamation, repeating what the land-creature had said. "I suppose I am included in that elegant compliment. I say! where are you, old

Lilac-legs? Have you contrived to crawl away after all? Come out of your corner, or wherever you are, for a bit. Who was the creature that was talking such nonsense just now? Only let me come across him, that's all! Helpless sea-creatures, indeed! I should like to have seen him hiding in a crevice as nimbly as I can do! He'd better not come within reach of me any more, I can tell him!"

It was all very well for the Crab to sit outside the rock looking so fierce, and brushing his mouth so boldly with his whisker-like feelers, now that there was nobody to fight with. How he would have scuttled away sideways into his hole, if the creature had re-appeared, everybody can guess.

"You happy fellow!" answered the meek voice of the Star-fish, Lilac-legs; "you can afford to joke about everything, and can do whatever you please. You have so many things in your favour— your stiff coat, and your jointed legs, and your claws with pincers at their ends; and your large eyes. Dear me, what advantages! and yet I have an advantage too, and that a very great one, over you all, so I shall not grumble, especially not now that I am in the shade. That sun was very unpleasant, certainly; I felt something between scalded and baked. Horrible! but I am sheltered now. And how did that come to pass, do you think?"

The Star-fish paused for an answer; but the Crab declared he couldn't think—had no time for thinking; it was too slow work to suit him. So Lilac-legs told him how she had been chucked into the air by the stick, and how she had come down in the midst of the tangle, and fallen under shelter. "So you see," added she in conclusion, "that you were quite right in saying what nonsense the creature talked. Why, he said he was as useless as these vile useless sea-weeds, and had come into the world, like them, for nothing; whereas, don't you see, he was born to save me, which was something to be born for, at any rate, that's quite clear; and so was the vile useless sea-weed, as he called it, too. I, with my advantages, can tell them both that!"

"You go in and out, and in and out, over people's remarks, till you make me quite giddy, I get so puzzled," replied the Crab; "and then you are always talking of your advantages," he contin-ued, whisking his feelers backwards and forwards conceitedly as he spoke, "and I can't make out what they are. I wish you would say at once what you mean."

"Oh, my advantages, you want to know about?" answered Lilac-legs. "Well, I certainly have one in each leg, near the end, with which I—but I don't think I can describe it exactly. You have several advantages yourself, as I told you just now, and we have one or two in common; for instance, the loss of a leg or two is nothing to either of us; they grow again so quickly; but still I am very helpless now and then, I must admit! on the sand, for instance—it is so soft—and the more I try to lay hold, the more it slips away. Still these advantages in my legs make amends for a good deal, for at any rate I know my own superiority, and there's a great comfort in that; I can't explain, but you may safely take it for granted, that with my advantages, I know a good deal more than you give me credit for. I know, for instance, that the poor ignorant creature need not consider himself useless, since he was the means of chucking me here, and that this fine old tangle hasn't lived for nothing, since it is sheltering me."

"How conceited some people are with their advantages!" murmured a silver voice from one of the tangle fronds. "If the tangle had come into the world for nothing but to shelter you, there would have been a fuss to very little purpose indeed! Can't your advantages tell you there are other creatures in the world quite as important as yourself, if not more so, you poor helpless Lilac-legs? Do you know who is speaking? It is the blue-eyed limpet, I beg to say—the Patella pellucida, if you please. I have an advantage or two myself! My coat is harder even than the crab's, and it is studded with a row of azure spots, as bright as the turquoise itself. That is something to reflect upon in one's solitude, I can assure you! and the tangle plants are the natural home and food of our lovely race. The creature was ignorant enough in calling them useless, therefore, of course; but you were not much wiser in thinking they were put into the world to shelter you. I flatter myself I have said enough! To be the home and the food of beings like us, is cause sufficient—almost more than sufficient, I venture to think—for the existence of any vegetable that fringes these shores. And while they live for us, our turquoise-gemmed backs are, in return, their highest ornament and pride. The whole thing is perfect and complete. Anybody with half an eye, and a grain of understanding, may see that!"

"Oh, the narrow-mindedness of people who live under a shell!" murmured a score of whispers, in unison, from another tangle frond close by. "Oh, the assurance of you poor moveable limpets in talking about your home, when you do but stick to first one part of these vast leaves and then another, moving from place to place, and never fairly settling anywhere! Home, indeed; you call it? What sort of a home is it, when an unlucky chance can force you off at any moment, or some passing creature pick you from your hold? The pretension would be disgusting, if it were not so absurd. Think of mere travellers, as one may say, talking of their lodging-house as if it were their own, and belonged to them by a natural right!—how ridiculous, if not wrong! We can afford to speak—we, of whose dwelling-places it is the foundation and support. Talk of the useless tangle, indeed! Yes, the creature was ignorant indeed who said so. Little he knew that it was the basis of the lives of millions. Little he knew of the silver net-work we spread over it from year to year, or of the countless inhabitants of the beautiful web—a fairy-land of beings, so small, that the crab can scarcely see us, yet spreading so far and wide, and accomplishing so much; but that is because we work in unison, of course. We never quarrel among ourselves, as some folks do—not altogether unlike the crab in the crevice yonder. We work to one end, so that we are sure to continue strong. Useless tangles, forsooth! when they have been the foundations of colonies like ours from the beginning of the world! Of course the thing is clear enough to those who choose to look into it; any one who knows us, can tell people what the tangle is in the world for, I should think!"

"Hear how they talk," murmured another shell-fish, no distant relation of the blue-eyed limpet who had spoken before, and who lay hidden in the midst of the twisted roots by which the tangle stem held fast to the rock; "hear how the poor scurfy creatures talk, to be sure, as if there was nobody in the world but themselves. But anything can talk, which has so many mouths to talk with. I could say a good deal myself, if I chose to try, with only one; but I don't care to let out my secrets into everybody's foolish ears. Much better hold my tongue, than let certain people, not a hundred miles off, know I am here. I don't fancy being sucked at by star-fishes, or picked out of my place by crab's claws. Of course I know what the tangle is in the world for, as well as anybody else. For while they are fighting merely about his flapping leathery ends, here I sit in the very heart of the matter; safe in the roots themselves, knowing what's what with the cleverest of them. Useless tangle, the creature said—useless enough, perhaps, as far as he could tell, who only looked at the long, loose, rubbishy leaves; but those who want to know the truth of the matter, must use their eyes to a little more purpose, and find out what's going on at the roots. Ah, they'd soon see then what the tangle is for! I don't speak of myself alone, though of course I know one very sufficient reason why the tangle is in the world, if I chose to say. Am I right, little Silver-tuft, in the corner there, with the elegant doors to your house?"

Now, little Silver-tuft, the coralline, piqued herself particularly on the carving of the curious doors which guarded the front of every one of the numberless cells in which her family lived; so she was flattered by the compliment, and owned that the limpet was right in the main. She was, nevertheless, rather cool in her manner, for, thought she to herself, "The rough fellow forgets that he is but a lodger here, as the sea-mat said of his blue-eyed cousin; whereas everybody knows that I am a bonâ-fide inhabitant, though with a little more freedom of movement than people who stick to their friends so closely as to cover them up! No offence to the sea-mat, or anybody who can't help himself. Nevertheless, my fibres being firmly interlaced with the roots, I am here by right for ever. These limpets may talk as they please, but nobody in their senses can suppose the tangle came into the world merely to accommodate chance travellers like them, even though they may now and then spend their lives in the place. But vanity blinds the judgment, that's very clear. Roots and plants have to grow for such as myself and my silver-tuft cousins, however; but that's quite another affair. There's a reason in that—a necessity, I may say; we want them, and of course, therefore, they are here. The thing is as straightforward and plain to anybody of sense, as—"

But, unfortunately, the simile was lost; for a wave of the now-returning tide interrupted Silver-tuft's speech, by breaking suddenly over the tangle with a noisy splash. It drew back again for a bit immediately after; but, meantime, both plants and animals were revelling in the delicious moisture, and for a few moments thought of nothing else. And just then, hurrying along the narrow strip of sand that yet remained exposed, as fast as their legs could carry them, came the land-creature and its companion.

Before, however, they had passed the spot where they had stopped to talk when the tide was low, another wave was seen coming; to avoid which, the friends sprang together on the ledge of rock, and from thence watched the gathering water, as it fell tumbling over the forest of tangle plants. And again and again this happened, and they remained to observe it, and see how the huge fronds surged up like struggling giants, as the waves rushed in below; and how by degrees, as the tide rose higher and higher, their curved stems unbent, so that they resumed their natural position, till at last they were bending and bowing in graceful undulations to the swell of the water, as was their wont.

And, "Look at them!" cried the creature's companion. "For the existence of even these poor plants in the world, I could give you a hundred reasons, and believe that as many more might be found. Of their use, I could tell you a hundred instances in proof; there is not one of them but what gives shelter to the helpless, food to the hungry, a happy home to as many as desire it, and vigour and health to the element in which it lives. Purposeless life you talk of! Such a thing exists nowhere. Come, I will explain. To begin—but see, we must move on, for the wind as well as the tide is rising, and we might chance to be caught. Follow me quick, for even we might be missed; and, besides, it is cowardly to shirk one's appointed share of work and well-doing before one's time. For if the vile sea-weeds are able to do good in the world, how much more—"

But here, too, the discourse was cut short by the roar of a breaking wave, which carried the conclusion out of hearing.

People talk of the angry sea; was he angry now at what he had heard? No, he was only loud and in earnest, after all. But undoubtedly he and the risen wind between them contrived to make a great noise over the tangle beds. And he gave his opinion pretty strongly on the subject in hand. For, cried he, "You foolish creatures, one and all! what is all this nonsense about? Who dares to talk of useless sea-weeds while I am here to throw their folly in their face? And you, poor little worms and wretches, who have been talking your small talk together, as if it was in your power to form the least idea of anything an inch beyond your own noses— well, well, well, I won't undeceive you! There, there! believe what you like about yourselves and your trumpery little comforts and lives; but if any really philosophical inquirer wants to know what sea-weeds are in the world for, and what good they do, I will roar them the true answer all day long, if they please—to keep me, the great sea, pure, and sweet, and healthy! There, now, that's the reply! They suck in my foul vapours as food, and give me back life-supporting vapours in return. Vile and useless! What fool has called anything so? Only let me catch him—thus—"

Bang!—with what a roar that wave came down! and yet it did no harm—didn't even dislodge the Crab from the new crevice he had squeezed himself into for the present. And as to Star-fish Lilac-legs, she was spreading herself out in the rocking water, rejoicing in her regained freedom, and telling all her friends of her wonderful escape, and of the creature who had been born into the world on purpose to save her from an untimely death.

It was a very fine story indeed; and the longer she told it, the more pathetic she made it, till at last there was not a creature in the sea who could listen to it with dry eyes.

[Source: Margaret Gatty, "Whereunto?" in *Parables from Nature*, (London: T. Nelson & Sons, n.d.).]

Appendix F: From Maria Susanna Cummins, The Lamplighter (1854)

[Educated at home and at a private girls' school in Lenox, Massachusetts, Maria Cummins (1827-66) published her first novel, *The Lamplighter*, in 1854. The book was an immediate success, selling 40,000 copies in a few weeks and 70,000 in a year. It went on to sell 100,000 copies in England alone. The enormous sales of Cummins's novel and Susan Warner's *Wide, Wide World* (1850) led Nathaniel Hawthorne to complain: "America is now wholly given over to a d____d mob of scribbling women, and I have no chance of success while the public taste is occupied with their trash.... What is the mystery of these innumerable editions of the Lamplighter, and other books neither better nor worse?—worse they could not be, and better they need not be, when they sell by the 100,000.[1]

Kingsley shared Hawthorne's dislike of these sentimental works of domestic fiction. In Chapter VIII of *The Water-Babies* he writes: "Next he [Tom] saw all the little people in the world, writing all the little books in the world: probably because they had no great people to write about: and if the names of the books were not Squeeky, nor the Pumplighter, nor the Narrow Narrow World, nor the Hills of the Chattermuch, nor the Children's Twaddleday, why then they were something else." "Squeeky" and "the Hills of the Chattermuch" refer to Susan Warner's two novels, *Queechy* (1852) and *The Hills of the Shatemuc* (1856).

The heroine of *The Lamplighter* is Gertrude Flint, an abused orphan rescued at the age of eight by Trueman Flint, a lamplighter, from her cruel guardian, Nan Grant. Trueman's neighbours, Mrs. Sullivan and her son, Willie, help Gertrude to overcome her anger, learn the elements of domesticity, and join the Christian fold. Later, Emily Graham, a wealthy, blind, and devout young woman, becomes her financial and spiritual benefactor. Through her self-reliance and her faith in God, Gertrude endures and overcomes many hardships in subsequent years. She leaves the supportive world of her benefactor to earn a living on her own. Having sustained her virtue and piety, despite many

---

1 *Letters of Hawthorne to William D. Ticknor* (Newark, NJ: Carteret Book Club, 1910).

temptations and obstacles, Gertrude is finally rewarded with marriage to her childhood friend, Willie Sullivan, and a reunion with her long-lost father. Abiding by Christian principles and accepting the social and economic strictures of the time, Gertrude rises from the seemingly hopeless slums to achieve happiness as a citizen of the middle class.]

The Lamplighter

Chapter 1

It was growing dark in the city. Out in the open country it would be light for half an hour or more; but within the close streets where my story leads me it was already dusk. Upon the wooden door-step of a low-roofed, dark, and unwholesome-looking house, sat a little girl, who was gazing up the street with much earnestness. The house-door, which was open behind her, was close to the side-walk; and the step on which she sat was so low that her little unshod feet rested on the cold bricks. It was a chilly evening in November, and a light fall of snow, which had made everything look bright and clean in the pleasant open squares, near which the fine houses of the city were built, had only served to render the narrow streets and dark lanes dirtier and more cheerless than ever; for, mixed with the mud and filth which abound in those neighborhoods where the poor are crowded together, the beautiful snow had lost all its purity.

A great many people were passing to and fro, bent on their various errands of duty or of pleasure; but no one noticed the little girl, for there was no one in the world who cared for her. She was scantily clad, in garments of the poorest description. Her hair was long and very thick; uncombed and unbecoming, if anything could be said to be unbecoming to a set of features which, to a casual observer, had not a single attraction,—being thin and sharp, while her complexion was sallow, and her whole appearance unhealthy.

She had, to be sure, fine, dark eyes; but so unnaturally large did they seem, in contrast to her thin, puny face, that they only increased the peculiarity of it, without enhancing its beauty. Had any one felt any interest in her (which nobody did), had she had a mother (which, alas! she had not), those friendly and partial eyes would perhaps have found something in her to praise. As it was, however, the poor little thing was told, a dozen times a day, that she was the worst-looking child in the world; and, what was more, the worst-behaved. No one loved her, and she loved no one; no one treated her kindly; no one tried to make her happy, or cared whether she were so. She was but eight years old, and all alone in the world.

There was one thing, and one only, which she found pleasure in. She loved to watch for the coming of the old man who lit the street-lamp in front of the house where she lived; to see the bright torch he carried flicker in the wind; and then, when he ran up his ladder, lit the lamp so quickly and easily, and made the whole place seem cheerful, one gleam of joy was shed on a little desolate heart, to which gladness was a stranger; and, though he had never seemed to see, and certainly had never spoken to her, she almost felt, as she watched for the old lamplighter, as if he were a friend.

"Gerty," exclaimed a harsh voice within, "have you been for the milk?"

The child made no answer, but, gliding off the door-step, ran quickly round the corner of the house, and hid a little out of sight.

"What's become of that child?" said the woman from whom the voice proceeded, and who now showed herself at the door.

A boy who was passing, and had seen Gerty run,—a boy who had caught the tone of the whole neighborhood, and looked upon her as a sort of imp, or spirit of evil,—laughed aloud, pointed to the corner which concealed her, and, walking off with his head over his shoulder, to see what would happen next, exclaimed to himself, as he went, "She'll catch it! Nan Grant'll fix her!"

In a moment more, Gerty was dragged from her hiding-place, and, with one blow for her ugliness and another for her impudence (for she was making up faces at Nan Grant with all her might), she was despatched down a neighboring alley with a kettle for the milk.

She ran fast, for she feared the lamplighter would come and go in her absence, and was rejoiced, on her return, to catch sight of him, as she drew near the house, just going up his ladder. She stationed herself at the foot of it, and was so engaged in watching the bright flame, that she did not observe when the man began to descend; and, as she was directly in his way, he hit against her, as he sprang to the ground, and she fell upon the pavement. "Hollo, my little one!" exclaimed he, "how's this?" as he stooped to lift her up.

She was upon her feet in an instant; for she was used to hard knocks, and did not much mind a few bruises. But the milk!—it was all spilt.

"Well! now, I declare!" said the man, "that's too bad!— what'll mammy say?" and, for the first time looking full in Gerty's face, he here interrupted himself with, "My! what an oddfaced child!— looks like a witch!" Then, seeing that she looked apprehensively at the spilt milk, and gave a sudden glance up at the house, he added, kindly, "She won't be hard on such a mite of a thing as you are, will she? Cheer up, my ducky! never mind if she does scold you a little. I'll bring you something, to-morrow, that I think you'll like, may be; you're such a lonesome sort of a looking thing. And, mind, if the old woman makes a row, tell her I did it.—But didn't I hurt you? What was you doing with my ladder?"

"I was seeing you light the lamp," said Gerty, "and I an't hurt a bit; but I wish I hadn't spilt the milk."

At this moment Nan Grant came to the door, saw what had happened, and commenced pulling the child into the house, amidst blows, threats, and profane and brutal language. The lamplighter tried to appease her; but she shut the door in his face. Gerty was scolded, beaten, deprived of the crust which she usually got for her supper, and shut up in her dark attic for the night. Poor little child! Her mother had died in Nan Grant's house, five years before; and she had been tolerated there since, not so much because when Ben Grant went to sea he bade his wife be sure and keep the child until his return (for he had been gone so long that no one thought he would ever come back), but because Nan had reasons of her own for doing so; and, though she considered Gerty a dead weight upon her hands, she did not care to excite inquiries by trying to dispose of her elsewhere.

When Gerty first found herself locked up for the night in the dark garret (Gerty hated and feared the dark), she stood for a minute perfectly still; then suddenly began to stamp and scream, tried to beat open the door, and shouted, "I hate you, Nan Grant! Old Nan Grant, I hate you!" But nobody came near her; and, after a while, she grew more quiet, went and threw herself down on her miserable bed, covered her face with her little thin hands, and sobbed and cried as if her heart would break. She wept until she was utterly exhausted; and then gradually, with only now and then a low sob and catching of the breath, she grew quite still. By and by she took away her hands from her face, clasped them together in a convulsive manner, and looked up at a little glazed window by the side of the bed. It was but three panes of glass unevenly stuck together, and was the only chance of light the room had. There was no moon; but, as Gerty looked up, she saw through the window shining down upon her one bright star. She thought she had never seen anything half so beautiful. She had often been out of doors when the sky was full of stars, and had not noticed them much; but this one, all alone, so large, so bright, and yet so soft and pleasant-looking, seemed to speak to her; it seemed to say, "Gerty! Gerty! poor little Gerty!" She thought it seemed like a kind face, such as she had a long time ago seen or dreamt about. Suddenly it flashed through her mind, "Who lit it? Somebody lit it! Some good person, I know! O! how could he get up so high!" And Gerty fell asleep, wondering who lit the star.

Poor little, untaught, benighted soul! Who shall enlighten thee? Thou art God's child, little one! Christ died for thee. Will he not send man or angel to light up the darkness within, to kindle a light that shall never go out, the light that shall shine through all eternity!

Chapter 2

Gerty awoke the next morning, not as children wake who are roused by each other's merry voices, or by a parent's kiss, who have kind hands to help them dress, and know that a nice break-fast awaits them. But she heard harsh voices below; knew, from the sound, that the men who lived at Nan Grant's (her son and two or three boarders) had come in to breakfast, and that her only chance of obtaining any share of the meal was to be on the spot when they had finished, to take that portion of what remained which Nan might chance to throw or shove towards her. So she crept down stairs, waited a little out of sight until she smelt the smoke of the men's pipes as they passed through the passage, and, when they had all gone noisily out, she slid into the room, looking about her with a glance made up of fear and defi-ance. She met but a rough greeting from Nan, who told her she had better drop that ugly, sour look; eat some breakfast, if she wanted it, but take care and keep out of her way, and not come near the fire, plaguing round where she was at work, or she'd get another dressing, worse than she had last night.

Gerty had not looked for any other treatment, so there was no disappointment to bear; but, glad enough of the miserable food left for her on the table, swallowed it eagerly, and, waiting no second bidding to keep herself out of the way, took her little old hood, threw on a ragged shawl, which had belonged to her mother, and which had long been the child's best protection from the cold, and, though her hands and feet were chilled by the sharp air of the morning, ran out of the house.

Back of the building where Nan Grant lived, was a large wood and coal yard; and beyond that a wharf, and the thick muddy water of a dock. Gerty might have found playmates enough in the neighborhood of this place. She sometimes did mingle with the troops of boys and girls, equally ragged with herself, who played about in the yard; but not often,—there was a league against her among the children of the place. Poor, ragged and miserably cared for, as most of them were, they all knew that Gerty was still more neglected and abused. They had often seen her beaten, and daily heard her called an ugly, wicked child, told that she belonged to nobody, and had no business in any one's house. Children as they were, they felt their advantage, and scorned the little outcast. Perhaps this would not have been the case if Gerty had ever mingled freely with them, and tried to be on friendly terms. But, while her mother lived there with her, though it was but a short time, she did her best to keep her little girl away from the rude herd. Perhaps that habit of avoidance, but still more a something in the child's nature, kept her from joining in their rough sports, after her mother's death had left her to do as she liked. As it was, she seldom had any intercourse with them. Nor did they venture to abuse her, otherwise than in words; for, singly, they dared not cope with her;—spirited, sudden and violent, she had made herself feared, as well as disliked. Once a band of them had united in a plan to tease and vex her; but, Nan Grant coming up at the moment when one of the girls was throwing the shoes, which she had pulled from Gerty's feet, into the dock, had given the girl a sound whipping, and put them all to flight. Gerty had not had a pair of shoes since; but Nan Grant, for once, had done her good service, and the children now left her in peace.

It was a sunshiny, though a cold day, when Gerty ran away from the house, to seek shelter in the wood-yard. There was an immense pile of timber in one corner of the yard, almost out of sight of any of the houses. Of different lengths and unevenly placed, the planks formed, on one side, a series of irregular steps, by means of which it was easy to climb up. Near the top was a little sheltered recess, overhung by some long planks, and forming a miniature shed, protected by the wood on all sides but one, and from that looking out upon the water.

This was Gerty's haven of rest, her sanctum, and the only place from which she never was driven away. Here, through the long summer days, the little, lonesome child sat, brooding over her griefs, her wrongs and her ugliness; sometimes weeping for hours. Now and then, when the course of her life had been smooth for a few days (that is, when she had been so fortunate as to offend no one, and had escaped whipping, or being shut up in the dark), she would get a little more cheerful, and enjoy watching the sailors belonging to a schooner hard by, as they labored on board their vessel, or occasionally rowed to and fro in a little boat. The warm sunshine was so pleasant, and the men's voices at their work so lively, that the poor little thing would for a time forget her woes.

But summer had gone; the schooner, and the sailors, who had been such pleasant company, had gone too. The weather was now cold, and for a few days it had been so stormy, that Gerty had been obliged to stay in the house. Now, however, she made the best of her way to her little hiding-place; and, to her joy, the sunshine had reached the spot before her, dried up the boards, so that they felt warm to her bare feet, and was still shining so bright and pleasant, that Gerty forgot Nan Grant, forgot how cold she had been, and how much she dreaded the long winter. Her thoughts rambled about some time; but, at last, settled down upon the kind look and voice of the old lamplighter; and then, for the first time since the promise was made, it came into her mind, that he had engaged to bring her something the next time he came. She could not believe he would remember it; but still, he might, he seemed to be so good-natured, and sorry for her fall.

What could he mean to bring? Would it be something to eat? O, if it were only some shoes! But he wouldn't think of that. Perhaps he did not notice but she had some.

At any rate, Gerty resolved to go for her milk in season to be back before it was time to light the lamp, so that nothing should prevent her seeing him.

The day seemed unusually long, but darkness came at last; and with it came True——or rather Trueman—Flint, for that was the lamplighter's name.

Gerty was on the spot, though she took good care to elude Nan Grant's observation.

True was late about his work that night, and in a great hurry. He had only time to speak a few words in his rough way to Gerty; but they were words coming straight from as good and honest a heart as ever throbbed. He put his great, smutty hand on her head in the kindest way, told her how sorry he was she got hurt, and said "It was a plaguy shame she should have been whipped too, and all for a spill o' milk, that was a misfortin', and no crime."

"But here," added he, diving into one of his huge pockets, "here's the critter I promised you. Take good care on't; don't 'buse it; and, I'm guessin', if it's like the mother that I've got at home, 't won't be a little ye'll be likin' it, 'fore you're done. Good-by, my little gal;" and he shouldered his ladder and went off, leaving in Gerty's hands a little gray-and-white kitten.

Gerty was so taken by surprise, on finding in her arms a live kitten, something so different from what she had anticipated, that she stood for a minute irresolute what to do with it. There were a great many cats, of all sizes and colors, inhabitants of the neigh-boring houses and yard; frightened-looking creatures, which, like Gerty herself, crept or scampered about, and often hid them-selves among the wood and coal, seeming to feel, as she did, great doubts about their having a right to be anywhere. Gerty had often felt a sympathy for them, but never thought of trying to catch one, carry it home and tame it; for she knew that food and shelter were most grudgingly accorded to herself, and would not cer-tainly be extended to her pets. Her first thought, therefore, was to throw the kitten down and let it run away.

But, while she was hesitating, the little animal pleaded for itself in a way she could not resist. Frightened by its long impris-onment and journey in True Flint's pocket, it crept from Gerty's arms up to her neck, clung there tight, and, with its low, feeble cries, seemed to ask her to take care of it. Its eloquence prevailed over all fear of Nan Grant's anger. She hugged pussy to her bosom, and made a childish resolve to love it, feed it, and, above all, keep it out of Nan's sight.

How much she came in time to love that kitten, no words can tell. Her little, fierce, untamed, impetuous nature had hitherto only expressed itself in angry passion, sullen obstinacy, and even hatred. But there were in her soul fountains of warm affection yet unstirred, a depth of tenderness never yet called out, and a warmth and devotion of nature that wanted only an object to expend themselves upon.

So she poured out such wealth of love on the little creature that clung to her for its support as only such a desolate little heart has to spare. She loved the kitten all the more for the care she was obliged to take of it, and the trouble and anxiety it gave her. She kept it, as much as possible, out among the boards, in her own favorite haunt. She found an old hat, in which she placed her own hood, to make a bed for pussy. She carried it a part of her own scanty meals; she braved for it what she would not have done for herself; for she almost every day abstracted from the kettle, when she was returning with the milk for Nan Grant, enough for pussy's supper; running the risk of being discovered and punished, the only risk or harm the poor ignorant child knew or thought of, in connection with the theft and deception; for her ideas of abstract right and wrong were utterly undeveloped. So she would play with her kitten for hours among the boards, talk to it, and tell it how much she loved it. But, when the days were very cold, she was often puzzled to know how to keep herself warm out of doors, and the risk of bringing the kitten into the house was great. She would then hide it in her bosom, and run with it into the little garret-room where she slept; and, taking care to keep the door shut, usually eluded Nan's eyes and ears. Once or twice, when she had been off her guard, her little playful pet had escaped from her, and scampered through the lower room and passage. Once Nan drove it out with a broom; but in that thickly-peopled region, as we have said, cats and kittens were not so uncommon as to excite inquiry.

It may seem strange that Gerty had leisure to spend all her time at play. Most children living among the poorer class of people learn to be useful even while they are very young. Numbers of little creatures, only a few years old, may be seen in our streets, about the yards and doors of houses, bending under the weight of a large bundle of sticks, a basket of shavings, or, more frequently yet, a stout baby, nearly all the care of which devolves upon them. We have often pitied such little drudges, and thought their lot a hard one. But, after all, it was not the worst thing in the world; they were far better off than Gerty, who had nothing to do at all, and had never known the satisfaction of helping anybody. Nan Grant had no babies; and, being a very active woman, with but a poor opinion of children's services, at the best, she never tried to find employment for Gerty, much better satisfied if she would only keep out of her sight; so that, except her daily errand for the milk, Gerty was always idle,—a fruitful source of unhappiness and discontent, if she had suffered from no other.

Nan was a Scotchwoman, no longer young, and with a temper which, never good, became worse and worse as she grew older. She had seen life's roughest side, had always been a hard-working woman, and had the reputation of being very smart and a driver. Her husband was a carpenter by trade; but she made his home so uncomfortable, that for years he had followed the sea. She took in washing, and had a few boarders; by means of which she earned what might have been an ample support for herself, had it not been for her son, an unruly, disorderly young man, spoilt in early life by his mother's uneven temper and management, and who, though a skilful workman when he chose to be industrious, always squandered his own and a large part of his mother's earnings. Nan, as we have said, had reasons of her own for keeping Gerty, though they were not so strong as to prevent her often having half a mind to rid herself of the encumbrance.

[Source: Maria Susanna Cummins, *The Lamplighter* (Boston: Houghton Mifflin, 1902), 1-10.]

Appendix G: From Samuel G. Goodrich, Peter Parley's Method of Telling About Geography to Children *(1831)*

[Born in Ridgefield, Connecticut, Samuel Griswold Goodrich (1793-1860) was the first widely-read American author of secular children's literature. He wrote over 100 books under the pen name of "Peter Parley" and edited *Parley's Magazine*. His books and articles, designed for children age ten and up, were mostly short instructive moral tales about science and the natural world, written in a simple colloquial style, and illustrated by the author. He found contemporary children's literature to be too coarse, vulgar, and grotesque. Although his books were very popular in England, British authors and critics, especially those interested in resurrecting old nursery books, thought his work dull and excessively didactic.

Kingsley refers to Goodrich in *The Water-Babies* as "Cousin Cramchild," suggesting that the American author was too determined to cram children's heads with facts instead of appealing to their imaginations and moral instincts. Recognizing the influence of John Locke's rationalism upon Griswold's stories, Kingsley accuses "Cousin Cramchild" of denying the existence of fairies and water-babies, thereby putting him in the same category as Professor Ptthmllnsprts, Kingsley's satiric character who takes rationalism to foolish extremes, and Dickens's Thomas Gradgrind in *Hard Times* (1854), whose educational philosophy is summarized in his comment: "Facts alone are wanted in life."]

Geography for Children

———

Lesson First.
General Description of the Earth.

1. Here is a picture of the World, or the Earth we live upon. It is round you see, and seems to swing in the air like a great ball. It is surrounded by the heavens, or a sky and stars. [An illustration of the globe is presented in the original text.]

2. The surface of the world is divided into land and water, as you will see by the picture. Men live on the land, and build towns and cities upon it; animals of various kinds also live on the land; vessels sail on the water, and fish live in the water.

3. Vessels sail around the world on all sides of it, as a fly would crawl around an apple. If you look at the picture, you will see vessels sailing in various directions.

4. Men and animals live on the land on all sides of the world. They have a sky and stars above them, let them be in what part of the world they may. If you were to go to Asia, or Africa, or any other country, there would still be stars over your head.

———

The only purpose of the engraving that faces this page, is to convey the general idea that the earth is a globe or ball, and that we inhabit its surface. Of course, nothing like the relative proportion of the objects is attempted in the representation.

———

5. Now geography is a description of the world; it tells us of its shape, and how it is divided; and it describes the men and animals that live upon it. Geography is therefore a very useful and interesting study.

I am now going to ask you some questions to see if you remember what I have told you.

Questions.

1. What is the shape of the world or earth?
What does it seem to swing in the air like?
What is the earth surrounded by?

2. What is the surface of the earth divided into?
What live on the land?
What sail on the water?

3. Like what do vessels sail around the earth?
What can you see in the picture sailing on all sides of the earth?

4. Do men and animals live only on one side of the world, or on all sides of it?
What do men see above them, in all parts of the world?
If you were to go to Asia, or Africa, what would you see above you?

5. What is geography?
What does geography tell of?
What does geography describe?
Is geography a useful and interesting study?

———

Note. One of the first things to be taught a child in Geography is, that the world is round, and that men and animals inhabit its surface. Simple as the idea seems to be, it is one not easily received by children; and therefore at the end of this lesson, the teacher or parent should make the pupil understand it, and correct at the outset the crude and erroneous fancies which he will be apt to form. The use of an artificial globe will make this a very easy matter.

———

... I hope you will recollect what I have told you, but, lest you should forget, I will put it into rhyme, and you may learn it by heart.

Geographical Rhymes.
To Be Prepared by the Pupil.

The world is round, and like a ball
Seems swinging in the air,
A sky extends around it all,
And stars are shining there.
Water and land upon the face
Of this round world we see,
The land is man's safe dwelling place,
But ships sail on the sea.
Two mighty continents there are,
And many islands too,
And mountains, hills, and valleys there,

With level plains we view.
The oceans, like the broad blue sky,
Extend around the sphere,
While seas, and lakes, and rivers, lie
Unfolded, bright, and clear.
Around the earth on every side
Where hills and plains are spread,
The various tribes of men abide
White, black, and copper red.
And animals and plants there be
Of various name and form,
And in the bosom of the sea
All sorts of fishes swarm.
And now geography doth tell,
Of these full many a story,
And if you learn your lessons well,
I'll set them all before you

[Source: Samuel G. Goodrich, *Peter Parley's Method of Telling About Geography to Children With Nine Maps and Seventy-Five Engravings. Principally for the Use of Schools.* (Hartford: H. and F.J. Huntington, 1831) 10-12, 20-21.]

Appendix H: Reflections of Charles Kingsley on Nature and Sanitation

[Kingsley wrote *Glaucus* in the hope that sea-side visitors would be inspired to discover the wonders of the shore and come to understand that Darwinian evolution need not be a threat to their religious beliefs. He asks, "Are we to reverence Him less or more if we find Him to be so much mightier, so much wiser, than we dreamed, that He can not only make all things, but—the very perfection of creative power—MAKE ALL THINGS MAKE THEMSELVES?" In this book Kingsley celebrates the glory of the natural world and the changeless God who allows natural selection to bring forth more perfect life forms. This same celebration is extended into *The Water Babies* as Tom explores the streams, rivers, and ocean, experiences the wonders of sea life, and learns of the mysterious power of Mother Carey to "make things make themselves."

In *Madame How and Lady Why* Kingsley's chief lesson is that we must learn about the world through careful observation and realize that scientific knowledge has strict limitations. Thus the schoolhouse of the natural world belongs to Madame How and it is here that we learn how things work. It is equally important to realize that why things work in a certain way may never be understood. Lady Why, who is the mistress of Madam How, oversees the mysterious design in the natural world, and her province is infused with the spiritual and the gospels. This duality is apparent throughout *The Water-Babies* as Tom comes to understand his water world and it various creatures but places blind faith in Mother Carey's instructions to walk backwards guided by the instincts of a dog towards the Other-end-of-Nowhere and redemption.

Kingsley's obsession with hygiene and sanitation arose out of his personal illness and his public concern about cholera, and the filthy water and air that plagued London. "Air-Mothers" critiques the foul conditions in London from the view point of a ghostly emperor of ancient Rome: "But if you wish me to consider you a civilised nation: let me hear that you have brought a great river from the depths of the earth, be they a thousand fathoms deep, of from your nearest mountains, be they five hundred miles away; and have washed out London's dirt—and your own shame. Till then, abstain from judging too harshly a

Constantine, or even a Caracalla; for they, whatever were their sins, built baths, and kept their people clean." Kingsley's view of cleanliness and water, however, goes beyond the physical and encompasses a spiritual purgation. In *The Water-Babies* Tom has the soot cleansed from his body in the river but more importantly, his immersion is a baptism that opens him to the spiritual realm.]

1. From Charles Kingsley, *Glaucus; or, The Wonders of the Shore* (1855)

Let no one think that this same Natural History is a pursuit fitted only for effeminate or pedantic men. I should say, rather, that the qualifications required for a perfect naturalist are as many and as lofty as were required, by old chivalrous writers, for the perfect knight-errant of the Middle Ages: for (to sketch an ideal, of which I am happy to say our race now affords many a fair realization) our perfect naturalist should be strong in body; able to haul a dredge, climb a rock, turn a boulder, walk all day, uncertain where he shall eat or rest; ready to face sun and rain, wind and frost, and to eat or drink thankfully anything, however coarse or meagre; he should know how to swim for his life, to pull an oar, sail a boat, and ride the first horse which comes to hand; and, finally, he should be a thoroughly good shot, and a skilful fisherman; and, if he go far abroad, be able on occasion to fight for his life.

For his moral character, he must, like a knight of old, be first of all gentle and courteous, ready and able to ingratiate himself with the poor, the ignorant, and the savage; not only because foreign travel will be often otherwise impossible, but because he knows how much invaluable local information can be only obtained from fishermen, miners, hunters, and tillers of the soil. Next, he should be brave and enterprising, and withal patient and undaunted; not merely in travel, but in investigation; knowing (as Lord Bacon[1] might have put it) that the kingdom of Nature, like the kingdom of heaven, must be taken by violence, and that only to those who knock long and earnestly does the great mother open the doors of her sanctuary. He must be of a reverent turn of mind also; not rashly discrediting any reports,

---

1 Francis Bacon, Baron Verulam (1561-1626), English philosopher, writer, and statesman.

however vague and fragmentary; giving man credit always for some germ of truth, and giving Nature credit for an inexhaustible fertility and variety, which will keep him his life long always reverent, yet never superstitious; wondering at the commonest, but not surprised by the most strange; free from the idols of size and sensuous loveliness; able to see grandeur in the minutest objects, beauty, in the most ungainly; estimating each thing not carnally, as the vulgar do, by its size or its pleasantness to the senses, but spiritually, by the amount of Divine thought revealed to Man therein; holding every phenomenon worth the noting down; believing that every pebble holds a treasure, every bud a revelation; making it a point of conscience to pass over nothing through laziness or hastiness, lest the vision once offered and despised should be withdrawn; and looking at every object as if he were never to behold it again.

Moreover, he must keep himself free from all those perturbations of mind which not only weaken energy, but darken and confuse the inductive faculty; from haste and laziness, from melancholy, testiness, pride, and all the passions which make men see only what they wish to see. Of solemn and scrupulous reverence for truth; of the habit of mind which regards each fact and discovery, not as our own possession, but as the possession of its Creator, independent of us, our tastes, our needs, or our vain-glory, I hardly need to speak; for it is the very essence of a nature's faculty—the very tenure of his existence: and without truthfulness science would be as impossible now as chivalry would have been of old.

And last, but not least, the perfect naturalist should have in him the very essence of true chivalry, namely, self-devotion; the desire to advance, not himself and his own fame or wealth, but knowledge and mankind. He should have this great virtue; and in spite of many shortcomings (for what man is there who liveth and sinneth not?), naturalists as a class have it to a degree which makes them stand out most honourably in the midst of a self-seeking and mammonite generation, inclined to value everything by its money price, its private utility. The spirit which gives freely, because it knows that it has received freely; which communicates knowledge without hope of reward, without jealousy and rivalry, to fellow-students and to the world; which is content to delve and toil comparatively unknown, that from its obscure and seemingly worthless results others may derive pleasure, and even build up great fortunes, and change the very face of cities and lands, by the practical use of some stray talisman which the poor student has invented in his laboratory; —this is the spirit which is abroad among our scientific men, to a greater degree than it ever has been among any body of men for many a century past; and might well be copied by those who profess deeper purposes and a more exalted calling, than the discovery of a new zoophyte, or the classification of a moorland crag.

And it is these qualities, however imperfectly they may be realized in any individual instance, which make our scientific men, as a class, the wholesomest and pleasantest of companions abroad, and at home the most blameless, simple, and cheerful, in all domestic relations; men for the most part of manful heads, and yet of childlike hearts, who have turned to quiet study, in these late piping times of peace, an intellectual health and courage which might have made them, in more fierce and troublous times, capable of doing good service with very different instruments than the scalpel and the microscope.

I have been sketching an ideal: but one which I seriously recommend to the consideration of all parents; for, though it be impossible and absurd to wish that every young man should grow up a naturalist by profession, yet this age offers no more wholesome training, both moral and intellectual, than that which is given by instilling into the young an early taste for outdoor physical science. The education of our children is now more than ever a puzzling problem, if by education we mean the development of the whole humanity, not merely of some arbitrarily chosen part of it. How to feed the imagination with wholesome food, and teach it to despise French novels, and that sugared slough of sentimental poetry, in comparison with which the old fairy-tales and ballads were manful and rational; how to counteract the tendency to shallowed and conceited sciolism, engendered by hearing popular lectures on all manner of subjects, which can only be really learnt by stern methodic study; how to give habits of enterprise, patience, accurate observation, which the counting-house or the library will never bestow; above all, how to develop the physical powers, without engendering brutality and coarseness—are questions becoming daily more and more puzzling, while they need daily more and more to be solved, in an age of enterprise, travel, and emigration, like the present. For the truth must be told, that the great majority of men who are now distinguished by commercial success, have had a training the directly opposite to that which they are giving to their sons. They are for the most part men who have migrated from the country to the town, and had in their youth all the advantages of a sturdy and manful hill-side or sea-side training; men whose bodies were developed, and their lungs fed on pure breezes, long before they brought to work in the city the bodily and mental strength which they had gained by loch and moor. But it is not so with their sons. Their business habits are learnt in the counting-house; a good school, doubtless, as far as it goes: but one which will expand none but the lowest intellectual faculties; which will make them accurate accountants, shrewd computers and competitors, but never the originators of daring schemes, men able and willing to go forth to replenish the earth and subdue it. And in the hours of relaxation, how much of their time is thrown away, for want of anything better, on frivolity, not to say on secret profligacy, parents know too well; and often shut their eyes in very despair to evils which they know not how to cure. A frightful majority of our middle-class young men are growing up effeminate, empty of all knowledge but what tends directly to the making of a fortune; or rather, to speak correctly, to the keeping up the fortunes which their fathers have made for them; while of the minority, who are indeed thinkers and readers, how many women as well as men have we seen wearying their souls with study undirected, often misdirected; craving to learn, yet not knowing how or what to learn; cultivating, with unwholesome energy, the head at the expense of the body and the heart; catching up with the most capricious self-will one mania after another, and tossing it away again for some new phantom; gorging the memory with facts which no one has taught them to arrange, and the reason with problems which they have no method for solving; till they fret themselves in a chronic fever of the brain, which too often urge them on to plunge, as it were, to cool the inward fire, into the ever-restless seas of doubt or of superstition. It is a sad picture. There are many who may read these pages whose hearts will tell them that it is a true one. What is wanted in these cases is a methodic and scientific habit of mind; and a class of objects on which to exercise that habit, which will fever neither the speculative intellect nor the moral sense; and those physical science will give, as nothing else can give it.

★ ★ ★

Geology has disproved the old popular belief that the universe was brought into being as it now exists by a single fiat. We know that the work has been gradual; that the earth

"In tracts of fluent heat began,
The seeming prey of cyclic storms,
The home of seeming random forms,
Till, at the last, arose the man."[1]

And we know, also, that these forms, "seeming random" as they are, have appeared according to a law which, as far as we can judge, has been on the whole one of progress,—lower animals (though we cannot yet say, the lowest) appearing first, and man, the highest mammal, "the roof and crown of things," one of the latest in the series. We have no more right, let it be observed, to say that man, the highest, appeared last, than that the lowest appeared first. It was probably so, in both cases; but there is as yet no positive proof of either; and as we know that species of animals lower than those which already existed appeared again and again during the various eras, so it is quite possible that they may be appearing now, and may appear hereafter: and that for every extinct Dodo or Moa,[2] a new species may be created, to keep up the equilibrium of the whole. This is but a surmise: but it may be wise, perhaps, just now, to confess boldly, even to insist on, its possibility, lest any should fancy, from our unwillingness to allow it, that there would be ought in it, if proved, contrary to sound religion.

I am, I must honestly confess, more and more unable to perceive anything which an orthodox Christian may not hold, in those physical theories of "evolution," which are gaining more and more the assent of our best zoologists and botanists. All that they ask us to believe is, that "species" and "families," and indeed the whole of organic nature, have gone through, and may still be going through, some such development from a lowest germ, as we know that every living individual, from the lowest zoophyte to man himself, does actually go through. They apply to the whole of the living world, past, present, and future, the law which is undeniably at work on each individual of it. They may be wrong, or they may be right: but what is there in such a conception contrary to any doctrine—at least of the Church of England? To say that this cannot be true; that species cannot vary, because God,

---

1   Alfred, Lord Tennyson, *In Memoriam*, 118, 9-12.
2   The dodo was a flightless bird, once a native of the island of Mauritius. It was discovered in 1598 and extinct by 1681. The Moa was another large flightless bird, native to New Zealand, where it was hunted to extinction.

at the beginning, created each thing "according to its kind," is really to beg the question; which is—Does the idea of "kind" include variability or not? and if so, how much variability? Now, "kind," or "species," as we call it, is defined nowhere in the Bible. What right have we to read our own definition into the word?— and that against the certain fact, that some "kinds" do vary, and that widely,—mankind, for instance, and the animals and plants which he domesticates. Surely that latter fact should be significant, to those who believe, as I do, that man was created in the likeness of God. For if man has the power, not only of making plants and animals vary, but of developing them into forms of higher beauty and usefulness than their wild ancestors possessed, why should not the God in whose image he is made possess the same power? If the old theological rule be true—"There is nothing in man which was not first in God" (sin, of course, excluded)—then why should not this imperfect creative faculty in man be the very guarantee that God possesses it in perfection?

Such at least is the conclusion of one who, studying certain families of plants, which indulge in the most fantastic varieties of shape and size, and yet through all their vagaries retain—as do the Palms, the Orchids, the Euphorbiaceae[1]—one organ, or form of organs, peculiar and highly specialized, yet constant throughout the whole of each family, has been driven to the belief that each of these three families, at least, has "sported off" from one common ancestor—one archetypal Palm, one archetypal Orchid, one archetypal Euphorbia, simple, it may be, in itself, but endowed with infinite possibilities of new and complex beauty, to be developed, not in it, but in its descendants. He has asked himself, sitting alone amid the boundless wealth of tropic forests, whether even then and there the great God might not be creating round him, slowly but surely, new forms of beauty? If he chose to do it, could He not do it? That man found himself none the worse Christian for the thought. He has said—and must be allowed to say again, for he sees no reason to alter his words—in speaking of the wonderful variety of forms in the Euphorbiaceae, from the weedy English Euphorbias, the Dog's Mercuries,[2] and the Box,[3] to the prickly-stemmed Scarlet Euphorbia of Madagascar, the

---

1 The *Euphorbiaceae* are mostly monoecious herbs, shrubs, and trees, sometimes succulent and cactus-like, comprising one of the largest families of plants with about 300 genera and 7,500 species.

2 A perennial weedy plant with greenish flowers.

3 An evergreen shrub.

succulent Cactus-like Euphorbias of the Canaries and elsewhere; the Gale-like Phyllanthus;[1] the many-formed Crotons;[2] the Hemp-like Maniocs,[3] Physic-nuts,[4] Castor-oils,[5] the scarlet Poinsettia, the little pink and yellow Dalechampia,[6] the poisonous Manchineel,[7] and the gigantic Hura,[8] or sandbox tree,[9] of the West Indies,—all so different in shape and size, yet all alike in their most peculiar and complex fructification, and in their acrid milky juice,—"What if all these forms are the descendants of one original form? Would that be one whit the more wonderful than the theory that they were, each and all, with the minute, and often imaginary, shades of difference between certain cognate species among them, created separately and at once? But if it be so—which I cannot allow—what would the theologian have to say, save that God's works are even more wonderful than he always believed them to be? As for the theory being impossible— that is to be decided by men of science, on strict experimental grounds. As for us theologians, who are we, that we should limit, ... priori, the power of God? 'Is anything too hard for the Lord?' asked the prophet of old; and we have a right to ask it as long as the world shall last. If it be said that 'natural selection,' or, as Mr. Herbert Spencer[10] better defines it, the 'survival of the fittest,' is too simple a cause to produce such fantastic variety—that, again, is a question to be settled exclusively by men of science, on their own grounds. We, meanwhile, always knew that God works by

---

1 An herb found in central and southern India, used in medicine.
2 *Codiaeum Variegatum* are colorful plants native to Southeast Asia.
3 Also known as cassave, a root with a crisp white flesh, used to make cassreep and tapioca.
4 A small tropical American tree yielding purple dye and a tanning extract and bearing physic nuts containing a purgative oil.
5 Derived from the seeds of the castor bean, the fatty oil is used as a purgative.
6 Evergreen, perennial shrubs or vines from tropical regions worldwide, flowering with colored bracts throughout the year.
7 A tropical American tree, having poisonous fruit and a milky sap that causes skin blisters on contact.
8 A tropical tree that reaches heights of 130 feet, with a spiny trunk and spreading branches.
9 A tropical American tree having an irritating milky juice, a spiny trunk, and large woody seed capsules that split explosively when ripe.
10 Herbert Spencer (1820-1903), a British philosopher and sociologist, and one of the principal proponents of evolutionary theory in the mid-nineteenth century.

very simple, or seemingly simple, means; that the universe, as far as we could discern it, was one organization of the most simple means. It was wonderful—or should have been—in our eyes, that a shower of rain should make the grass grow, and that the grass should become flesh, and the flesh food for the thinking brain of man. It was—or ought to have been—more wonderful yet to us that a child should resemble its parents, or even a butterfly resemble, if not always, still usually, its parents likewise. Ought God to appear less or more august in our eyes if we discover that the means are even simpler than we supposed? We held Him to be Almighty and All-wise. Are we to reverence Him less or more if we find Him to be so much mightier, so much wiser, than we dreamed, that He can not only make all things, but—the very perfection of creative power—MAKE ALL THINGS MAKE THEMSELVES?[1] We believed that His care was over all His works; that His providence worked perpetually over the universe. We were taught—some of us at least—by Holy Scripture, that without Him not a sparrow fell to the ground, and that the very hairs of our head were all numbered; that the whole history of the universe was made up, in fact, of an infinite network of special providences. If, then, that should be true which a great natural-ist[2] writes, 'It may be metaphorically said that natural selection is daily and hourly scrutinizing, throughout the world, every varia-tion, even the slightest; rejecting that which is bad, preserving and adding up all that is good; silently and insensibly working, whenever and wherever opportunity offers, at the improvement of each organic being, in relation to its organic and inorganic conditions of life,'—if this, I say, were proved to be true, ought God's care and God's providence to seem less or more magnifi-cent in our eyes? Of old it was said by Him without whom nothing is made—'My Father worketh hitherto, and I work.'[3] Shall we quarrel with physical science, if she gives us evidence that those words are true?"

And—understand it well—the grand passage I have just

---

1 With this idea, Kingsley weds his Christian theology with the Darwinian concept of evolution and echoes Mother Carey's comment to Tom in *The Water-Babies*: "I am not going to trouble myself to make things, my little dear. I sit here and make them make themselves." The phrase "make all things make themselves" does not appear in the first edition of *Glaucus* (1855).

2 Charles Darwin, in *Origin of Species* (1859).

3 John 5: 17.

quoted need not be accused of substituting "natural selection for God." In any case natural selection would be only the means or law by which God works, as He does by other natural laws. We do not substitute gravitation for God, when we say that the planets are sustained in their orbits by the law of gravitation. The theory about natural selection may be untrue, or imperfect, as may the modern theories of the "evolution and progress" of organic forms: let the man of science decide that. But if true, the theories seem to me perfectly to agree with, and may be perfectly explained by, the simple old belief which the Bible sets before us, of a LIVING GOD: not a mere past will, such as the Koran sets forth, creating once and for all, and then leaving the universe, to use Goethe's simile, "to spin round his finger;" nor again, an "all-pervading spirit," words which are mere contradictory jargon, concealing, from those who utter them, blank Materialism: but One who works in all things which have obeyed Him to will and to do of His good pleasure, keeping His abysmal and self-perfect purpose, yet altering the methods by which that purpose is attained, from aeon to aeon, ay, from moment to moment, for ever various, yet for ever the same. This great and yet most blessed paradox of the Changeless God, who yet can say "It repenteth me," and "Behold, I work a new thing on the earth," is revealed no less by nature than by Scripture; the changeableness, not of caprice or imperfection, but of an Infinite Maker and "Poietes,"[1] drawing ever fresh forms out of the inexhaustible treasury of His primaeval Mind; and yet never throwing away a conception to which He has once given actual birth in time and space, (but to compare reverently small things and great) lovingly repeating it, re-applying it; producing the same effects by endlessly different methods; or so delicately modifying the method that, as by the turn of a hair, it shall produce endlessly diverse effects; looking back, as it were, ever and anon over the great work of all the ages, to retouch it, and fill up each chasm in the scheme, which for some good purpose had been left open in earlier worlds; or leaving some open (the forms, for instance, necessary to connect the bimana and the quadrumana)[2] to be filled up perhaps hereafter when the world needs them; the handiwork,

---

1 Greek term for creator or maker.
2 Bimana: animals with two hands. Quadrumana: animals such as apes and monkeys, whose hind feet are usually prehensile, and whose great toes are opposable.

in short, of a living and loving Mind, perfect in His own eternity, but stooping to work in time and space, and there rejoicing Himself in the work of His own hands, and in His eternal Sabbaths ceasing in rest ineffable, that He may look on that which He hath made, and behold it is very good.

★ ★ ★

But, in the meanwhile, there are animals in which results so strange, fantastic, even seemingly horrible, are produced, that fallen man may be pardoned, if he shrinks from them in disgust. That, at least, must be a consequence of our own wrong state; for everything is beautiful and perfect in its place. It may be answered, "Yes, in its place; but its place is not yours. You had no business to look at it, and must pay the penalty for intermeddling." I doubt that answer; for surely, if man have liberty to do anything, he has liberty to search out freely his heavenly Father's works; and yet every one seems to have his antipathic animal; and I know one bred from his childhood to zoology by land and sea, and bold in asserting, and honest in feeling, that all without exception is beautiful, who yet cannot, after handling and petting and admiring all day long every uncouth and venomous beast, avoid a paroxysm of horror at the sight of the common house-spider. At all events, whether we were intruding or not, in turning this stone, we must pay a fine for having done so; for there lies an animal as foul and monstrous to the eye as "hydra, gorgon, or chimaera dire," and yet so wondrously fitted to its work, that we must needs endure for our own instruction to handle and to look at it. Its name, if you wish for it, is Nemertes;[1] probably N. Borlasii; a worm of very "low" organization, though well fitted enough for its own work. You see it? That black, shiny, knotted lump among the gravel, small enough to be taken up in a dessert spoon. Look now, as it is raised and its coils drawn out. Three feet—six—nine, at least: with a capability of seemingly endless expansion; a slimy tape of living caoutchouc,[2] some eighth of an inch in diameter, a dark chocolate-black, with paler longitudinal lines. Is it alive? It hangs, helpless and motionless, a mere velvet string across the hand. Ask the

---

1 Voracious predators, these marine worms are characterized by a unique eversible proboscis.
2 Latex from trees.

neighbouring Annelids[1] and the fry of the rock fishes, or put it into a vase at home, and see. It lies motionless, trailing itself among the gravel; you cannot tell where it begins or ends; it may be a dead strip of sea-weed, Himanthalia lorea,[2] perhaps, or Chorda filum;[3] or even a tarred string. So thinks the little fish who plays over and over it, till he touches at last what is too surely a head. In an instant a bell-shaped sucker mouth has fastened to his side. In another instant, from one lip, a concave double proboscis, just like a tapir's (another instance of the repetition of forms), has clasped him like a finger; and now begins the struggle: but in vain. He is being "played" with such a fishing-line as the skill of a Wilson[4] or a Stoddart[5] never could invent; a living line, with elasticity beyond that of the most delicate fly-rod, which follows every lunge, shortening and lengthening, slipping and twining round every piece of gravel and stem of sea-weed, with a tiring drag such as no Highland wrist or step could ever bring to bear on salmon or on trout. The victim is tired now; and slowly, and yet dexterously, his blind assailant is feeling and shifting along his side, till he reaches one end of him; and then the black lips expand, and slowly and surely the curved finger begins packing him end-foremost down into the gullet, where he sinks, inch by inch, till the swelling which marks his place is lost among the coils, and he is probably macerated to a pulp long before he has reached the opposite extremity of his cave of doom. Once safe down, the black murderer slowly contracts again into a knotted heap, and lies, like a boa with a stag inside him, motionless and blest.

[Source: *Glaucus; or, The Wonders of the Shore* (London: Macmillan, 1890) 43-51, 93-104, 135-38. This edition is much revised from the first edition, published in 1855 by Macmillan (London) and Ticknor and Fields (Boston). In 1854, Kingsley published an anonymous essay, "The Wonders of the Shore," in the *North British Review*. It served as the basis for his book in the following year.]

---

1 The Phylum *Annelida* consists of such segmented worms as earthworms and their relatives, leeches.
2 A blackish seaweed found on the northern coasts of the Atlantic.
3 A brown sea weed found along the coasts of England and Ireland. Also known as sea lace or dead man's rope.
4 John Wilson (1785-1854) a.k.a. "Christopher North," a reviewer, essayist and sportsman, who wrote several pieces on angling.
5 Thomas Staddard (1810-80), an angler, poet, and author of *Angler's Companion to the Rivers and Lakes of Scotland* (1847).

2. From Charles Kingsley, *Madame How and Lady Why or, First Lessons in Earth Lore for Children* (1870)

Dedication

To my son Grenville Arthur, and to his school-fellows at Winton House
This little book is dedicated.

Preface

My dear boys,—When I was your age, there were no such children's books as there are now. Those which we had were few and dull, and the pictures in them ugly and mean: while you have your choice of books without number, clear, amusing, and pretty, as well as really instructive, on subjects which were only talked of fifty years ago by a few learned men, and very little understood even by them. So if mere reading of books would make wise men, you ought to grow up much wiser than us old fellows. But mere reading of wise books will not make you wise men: you must use for yourselves the tools with which books are made wise; and that is—your eyes, and ears, and common sense.

Now, among those very stupid old-fashioned boys' books was one which taught me that; and therefore I am more grateful to it than if it had been as full of wonderful pictures as all the natural history books you ever saw. Its name was *Evenings at Home*;[1] and in it was a story called "Eyes and no Eyes;" a regular old-fashioned, prim, sententious story; and it began thus:—

"Well, Robert, where have you been walking this afternoon?" said Mr. Andrews to one of his pupils at the close of a holiday.

Oh—Robert had been to Broom Heath, and round by Camp Mount, and home through the meadows. But it was very dull. He hardly saw a single person. He had much rather have gone by the turnpike-road.

Presently in comes Master William, the other pupil, dressed, I suppose, as wretched boys used to be dressed forty years ago, in a frill collar, and skeleton monkey-jacket, and tight trousers buttoned over it, and hardly coming down to his ancles; and low

1 *Evenings at Home, or, the Juvenile Budget Opened*, by John Aikin (1747-1822) and his sister Anna Laetitia Barbauld (1743-1825). A popular series of six volumes (1792-95), translated into almost every European language, they provided elementary family reading.

shoes, which always came off in sticky ground; and terribly dirty and wet he is: but he never (he says) had such a pleasant walk in his life; and he has brought home his handkerchief (for boys had no pockets in those days much bigger than key-holes) full of curiosities.

He has got a piece of mistletoe, wants to know what it is; and he has seen a woodpecker, and a wheat-ear, and gathered strange flowers on the heath; and hunted a peewit because he thought its wing was broken, till of course it led him into a bog, and very wet he got. But he did not mind it, because he fell in with an old man cutting turf, who told him all about turf-cutting, and gave him a dead adder. And then he went up a hill, and saw a grand prospect; and wanted to go again, and make out the geography of the country from Cary's old county maps,[1] which were the only maps in those days. And then, because the hill was called Camp Mount, he looked for a Roman camp, and found one; and then he went down to the river, saw twenty things more; and so on, and so on, till he had brought home curiosities enough, and thoughts enough, to last him a week.

Whereon Mr. Andrews, who seems to have been a very sensible old gentleman, tells him all about his curiosities: and then it comes out—if you will believe it—that Master William has been over the very same ground as Master Robert, who saw nothing at all.

Whereon Mr. Andrews says, wisely enough, in his solemn old-fashioned way,—

"So it is. One man walks through the world with his eyes open, another with his eyes shut; and upon this difference depends all the superiority of knowledge which one man acquires over another. I have known sailors who had been in all the quarters of the world, and could tell you nothing but the signs of the tippling-houses, and the price and quality of the liquor. On the other hand, Franklin[2] could not cross the Channel without making observations useful to mankind. While many a vacant thoughtless youth is whirled through Europe without gaining a single idea worth crossing the street for, the observing eye and

---

1 John Cary (c.1754-1835), a London cartographer and engraver. His *New and Correct English Atlas* was published in 1787.
2 Benjamin Franklin (1706-90) proposed the use of airborne kites to propel ships across a large body of water, such as the English Channel. His keen observations also led to an understanding of the Gulf Stream and its value to navigation.

inquiring mind find matter of improvement and delight in every ramble. You, then, William, continue to use your eyes. And you, Robert, learn that eyes were given to you to use."

So said Mr. Andrews: and so I say, dear boys—and so says he who has the charge of you—to you. Therefore I beg all good boys among you to think over this story, and settle in their own minds whether they will be eyes or no eyes; whether they will, as they grow up, look and see for themselves what happens: or whether they will let other people look for them, or pretend to look; and dupe them, and lead them about—the blind leading the blind, till both fall into the ditch.

I say "good boys;" not merely clever boys, or prudent boys: because using your eyes, or not using them, is a question of doing Right or doing Wrong. God has given you eyes; it is your duty to God to use them. If your parents tried to teach you your lessons in the most agreeable way, by beautiful picture-books, would it not be ungracious, ungrateful, and altogether naughty and wrong, to shut your eyes to those pictures, and refuse to learn? And is it not altogether naughty and wrong to refuse to learn from your Father in Heaven, the Great God who made all things, when he offers to teach you all day long by the most beautiful and most wonderful of all picture-books, which is simply all things which you can see, hear, and touch, from the sun and stars above your head to the mosses and insects at your feet? It is your duty to learn His lessons: and it is your interest. God's Book, which is the Universe, and the reading of God's Book, which is Science, can do you nothing but good, and teach you nothing but truth and wisdom. God did not put this wondrous world about your young souls to tempt or to mislead them. If you ask Him for a fish, he will not give you a serpent. If you ask Him for bread, He will not give you a stone.

So use your eyes and your intellect, your senses and your brains, and learn what God is trying to teach you continually by them. I do not mean that you must stop there, and learn nothing more. Anything but that. There are things which neither your senses nor your brains can tell you; and they are not only more glorious, but actually more true and more real than any things which you can see or touch. But you must begin at the beginning in order to end at the end, and sow the seed if you wish to gather the fruit. God has ordained that you, and every child which comes into the world, should begin by learning something of the world about him by his senses and his brain; and the better you learn what they can teach you, the more fit you will be to learn what they cannot teach you. The more you try now to understand *things*, the more you will be able hereafter to understand men, and That which is above men. You began to find out that truly Divine mystery, that you had a mother on earth, simply by lying soft and warm upon her bosom; and so (as Our Lord told the Jews of old) it is by watching the common natural things around you, and considering the lilies of the field, how they grow, that you will begin at least to learn that far Diviner mystery, that you have a Father in Heaven. And so you will be delivered (if you will) out of the tyranny of darkness, and distrust, and fear, into God's free kingdom of light, and faith, and love; and will be safe from the venom of that tree which is more deadly than the fabled upas[1] of the East. Who planted that tree I know not, it was planted so long ago: but surely it is none of God's planting, neither of the Son of God: yet it grows in all lands and in all climes, and sends its hidden suckers far and wide, even (unless we be watchful) into your hearts and mine. And its name is the Tree of Unreason, whose roots are conceit and ignorance, and its juices folly and death. It drops its venom into the finest brains; and makes them call sense, nonsense; and nonsense, sense; fact, fiction; and fiction, fact. It drops its venom into the tenderest hearts, alas! and makes them call wrong, right; and right, wrong; love, cruelty; and cruelty, love. Some say that the axe is laid to the root of it just now, and that it is already tottering to its fall: while others say that it is growing stronger than ever, and ready to spread its upas-shade over the whole earth. For my part, I know not, save that all shall be as God wills. The tree has been cut down already again and again; and yet has always thrown out fresh shoots and dropped fresh poison from its boughs. But this at least I know: that any little child, who will use the faculties God has given him, may find an antidote to all its poison in the meanest herb beneath his feet.

There, you do not understand me, my boys; and the best prayer I can offer for you is, perhaps, that you should never need to understand me: but if that sore need should come, and that poison should begin to spread its mist over your brains and hearts, then you will be proof against it; just in proportion as you have used the eyes and the common sense which God has

---

1 The Bohun Upas, a Southeast Asian tree of the mulberry family that yields a poisonous latex used by natives on the tips of their arrows. Early legend claimed that anyone who fell asleep beneath the shade of the Upas would never awaken.

given you, and have considered the lilies of the field, how they grow.

Chapter I—The Glen

You find it dull walking up here upon Hartford Bridge Flat this sad November day? Well, I do not deny that the moor looks somewhat dreary, though dull it need never be. Though the fog is clinging to the fir-trees, and creeping among the heather, till you cannot see as far as Minley Corner, hardly as far as Bramshill woods—and all the Berkshire hills are as invisible as if it was a dark midnight—yet there is plenty to be seen here at our very feet. Though there is nothing left for you to pick, and all the flowers are dead and brown, except here and there a poor half-withered scrap of bottle-heath, and nothing left for you to catch either, for the butterflies and insects are all dead too, except one poor old Daddy-long-legs, who sits upon that piece of turf, boring a hole with her tail to lay her eggs in, before the frost catches her and ends her like the rest: though all things, I say, seem dead, yet there is plenty of life around you, at your feet, I may almost say in the very stones on which you tread. And though the place itself be dreary enough, a sheet of flat heather and a little glen in it, with banks of dead fern, and a brown bog between them, and a few fir-trees struggling up—yet, if you only have eyes to see it, that little bit of glen is beautiful and wonderful,—so beautiful and so wonderful and so cunningly devised, that it took thousands of years to make it; and it is not, I believe, half finished yet.

How do I know all that? Because a fairy told it me; a fairy who lives up here upon the moor, and indeed in most places else, if people have but eyes to see her. What is her name? I cannot tell. The best name that I can give her (and I think it must be something like her real name, because she will always answer if you call her by it patiently and reverently) is Madam How. She will come in good time, if she is called, even by a little child. And she will let us see her at her work, and, what is more, teach us to copy her. But there is another fairy here likewise, whom we can hardly hope to see. Very thankful should we be if she lifted even the smallest corner of her veil, and showed us but for a moment if it were but her finger tip—so beautiful is she, and yet so awful too. But that sight, I believe, would not make us proud, as if we had had some great privilege. No, my dear child: it would make us feel smaller, and meaner, and more stupid and more ignorant than we had ever felt in our lives before; at the same time it would make us wiser than ever we were in our lives before—that one glimpse of the great glory of her whom we call Lady Why.

But I will say more of her presently. We must talk first with Madam How, and perhaps she may help us hereafter to see Lady Why. For she is the servant, and Lady Why is the mistress; though she has a Master over her again—whose name I leave for you to guess. You have heard it often already, and you will hear it again, for ever and ever.

But of one thing I must warn you, that you must not confound Madam How and Lady Why. Many people do it, and fall into great mistakes thereby,—mistakes that even a little child, if it would think, need not commit. But really great philosophers sometimes make this mistake about Why and How; and therefore it is no wonder if other people make it too, when they write children's books about the wonders of nature, and call them "Why and Because," or "The Reason Why." The books are very good books, and you should read and study them: but they do not tell you really "Why and Because," but only "How and So." They do not tell you the "Reason Why" things happen, but only "The Way in which they happen." However, I must not blame these good folks, for I have made the same mistake myself often, and may do it again: but all the more shame to me. For see—you know perfectly the difference between How and Why, when you are talking about yourself. If I ask you, "Why did we go out to-day?" You would not answer, "Because we opened the door." That is the answer to "How did we go out?" The answer to Why did we go out is, "Because we chose to take a walk." Now when we talk about other things beside ourselves, we must remember this same difference between How and Why. If I ask you, "Why does fire burn you?" you would answer, I suppose, being a little boy, "Because it is hot;" which is all you know about it. But if you were a great chemist, instead of a little boy, you would be apt to answer me, I am afraid, "Fire burns because the vibratory motion of the molecules of the heated substance communicates itself to the molecules of my skin, and so destroys their tissue;" which is, I dare say, quite true: but it only tells us how fire burns, the way or means by which it burns; it does not tell us the reason why it burns.

But you will ask, "If that is not the reason why fire burns, what is?" My dear child, I do not know. That is Lady Why's business, who is mistress of Mrs. How, and of you and of me; and, as I think, of all things that you ever saw, or can see, or even dream. And what her reason for making fire burn may be I cannot tell. But I believe on excellent grounds that her reason is a very good one. If I dare to guess, I should say that one reason, at least, why fire burns, is that you may take care not to play with it, and so not only scorch your finger, but set your whole bed on fire, and perhaps the house into the bargain, as you might be tempted to do if putting your finger in the fire were as pleasant as putting sugar in your mouth.

My dear child, if I could once get clearly into your head this difference between Why and How, so that you should remember them steadily in after life, I should have done you more good than if I had given you a thousand pounds.

But now that we know that How and Why are two very different matters, and must not be confounded with each other, let us look for Madam How, and see her at work making this little glen; for, as I told you, it is not half made yet. One thing we shall see at once, and see it more and more clearly the older we grow; I mean her wonderful patience and diligence. Madam How is never idle for an instant. Nothing is too great or too small for her; and she keeps her work before her eye in the same moment, and makes every separate bit of it help every other bit. She will keep the sun and stars in order, while she looks after poor old Mrs. Daddy-long-legs there and her eggs. She will spend thousands of years in building up a mountain, and thousands of years in grinding it down again; and then carefully polish every grain of sand which falls from that mountain, and put it in its right place, where it will be wanted thousands of years hence; and she will take just as much trouble about that one grain of sand as she did about the whole mountain. She will settle the exact place where Mrs. Daddy-long-legs shall lay her eggs, at the very same time that she is settling what shall happen hundreds of years hence in a star millions of miles away. And I really believe that Madam How knows her work so thoroughly, that the grain of sand which sticks now to your shoe, and the weight of Mrs. Daddy-long-legs' eggs at the bottom of her hole, will have an effect upon suns and stars ages after you and I are dead and gone. Most patient indeed is Madam How. She does not mind the least seeing her own work destroyed; she knows that it must be destroyed. There is a spell upon her, and a fate, that everything she makes she must unmake again: and yet, good and wise woman as she is, she never frets, nor tires, nor fudges her work, as we say at school. She takes just as much pains to make an acorn as to make a peach. She takes just as much pains about the acorn which the pig eats, as about the acorn which will grow into a tall oak, and help to build a great ship. She took just as much pains, again, about the acorn which you crushed under your foot just now, and which you fancy will never come to anything. Madam How is wiser than that. She knows that it will come to something. She will find some use for it, as she finds a use for everything. That acorn which you crushed will turn into mould, and that mould will go to feed the roots of some plant, perhaps next year, if it lies where it is; or perhaps it will be washed into the brook, and then into the river, and go down to the sea, and will feed the roots of some plant in some new continent ages and ages hence: and so Madam How will have her own again. You dropped your stick into the river yesterday, and it floated away. You were sorry, because it had cost you a great deal of trouble to cut it, and peel it, and carve a head and your name on it. Madam How was not sorry, though she had taken a great deal more trouble with that stick than ever you had taken. She had been three years making that stick, out of many things, sunbeams among the rest. But when it fell into the river, Madam How knew that she should not lose her sunbeams nor anything else: the stick would float down the river, and on into the sea; and there, when it got heavy with the salt water, it would sink, and lodge, and be buried, and perhaps ages hence turn into coal; and ages after that some one would dig it up and burn it, and then out would come, as bright warm flame, all the sunbeams that were stored away in that stick: and so Madam How would have her own again. And if that should not be the fate of your stick, still something else will happen to it just as useful in the long run; for Madam How never loses anything, but uses up all her scraps and odds and ends somehow, somewhere, somewhen, as is fit and proper for the Housekeeper of the whole Universe. Indeed, Madam How is so patient that some people fancy her stupid, and think that, because she does not fall into a passion every time you steal her sweets, or break her crockery, or disarrange her furniture, therefore she does not care. But I advise you as a little boy, and still more when you grow up to be a man, not to get that fancy into your head; for you will find that, however good-natured and patient Madam How is in most matters, her keeping silence and not seeming to see you is no sign that she has forgotten. On the contrary, she bears a grudge (if one may so say, with all respect to her) longer than any one else does; because she will always have her own again. Indeed, I sometimes think that if it were not for Lady Why, her mistress, she might bear some of her grudges for ever and ever. I have seen men ere now damage some of Madam How's property when they were little boys, and be punished by her all their lives long, even though she had mended the broken pieces, or turned them to some other use. Therefore I say to you, beware of Madam How. She will teach you more kindly, patiently, and tenderly than any mother, if you want to learn her trade. But if, instead of learning her trade, you damage her materials and play with her tools, beware lest she has her own again out of you.

Some people think, again, that Madam How is not only stupid, but ill-tempered and cruel; that she makes earthquakes and storms, and famine and pestilences, in a sort of blind passion, not caring where they go or whom they hurt; quite heedless of who is in the way, if she wants to do anything or go anywhere. Now, that Madam How can be very terrible there can be no doubt: but there is no doubt also that, if people choose to learn, she will teach them to get out of her way whenever she has business to do which is dangerous to them. But as for her being cruel and unjust, those may believe it who like. You, my dear boys and girls, need not believe it, if you will only trust to Lady Why; and be sure that Why is the mistress and How the servant, now and for ever. That Lady Why is utterly good and kind I know full well; and I believe that, in her case too, the old proverb holds, "Like mistress, like servant;" and that the more we know of Madam How, the more we shall be content with her, and ready to submit to whatever she does: but not with that stupid resignation which some folks preach who do not believe in lady Why— that is no resignation at all. That is merely saying—

> "What can't be cured
> Must be endured,"

like a donkey when he turns his tail to a hail-storm,—but the true resignation, the resignation which is fit for grown people and children alike, the resignation which is the beginning and the end of all wisdom and all religion, is to believe that Lady Why knows best, because she herself is perfectly good; and that as she is mistress over Madam How, so she has a Master over her, whose name—I say again—I leave you to guess.

[Source: *Madam How and Lady Why or, First Lessons in Earth Lore for Children* (London: Bell and Daldy, 1870) vii-xv; 1-11. The work originally appeared in *Good Words for the Young*, 1868-70.]

3. From Charles Kingsley, "Air-Mothers," in *Sanitary and Social Lectures and Essays* (1880)

I have often amused myself, by fancying one question which an old Roman emperor would ask, were he to rise from his grave and visit the sights of London under the guidance of some minister of state. The august shade would, doubtless, admire our railroads and bridges, our cathedrals and our public parks, and much more of which we need not be ashamed. But after awhile, I think, he would look round, whether in London or in most of our great cities, inquiringly and in vain, for one class of buildings, which in his empire were wont to be almost as conspicuous and as splendid, because, in public opinion, almost as necessary, as the basilicas and temples: "And where," he would ask, "are your public baths?" And if the minister of state who was his guide should answer: "Oh great Caesar, I really do not know. I believe there are some somewhere at the back of that ugly building which we call the National Gallery; and I think there have been some meetings lately in the East End, and an amateur concert at the Albert Hall, for restoring, by private subscriptions, some baths and wash-houses in Bethnal Green,[1] which had fallen to decay. And there may be two or three more about the metropolis; for parish vestries have powers by Act of Parliament to establish such places, if they think fit, and choose to pay for them out of the rates." Then, I think, the august shade might well make answer: "We used to call you, in old Rome, northern barbarians. It seems that you have not lost all your barbarian habits. Are you aware that, in every city in the Roman empire, there were, as a matter of course, public baths open, not only to the poorest freeman, but to the slave, usually for the payment of the smallest current coin, and often gratuitously? Are you aware that in Rome itself, millionaire after millionaire, emperor after emperor, from Menenius Agrippa[2] and Nero[3] down to Diocletian[4] and Constantine,[5] built baths, and yet more baths; and connected with them gymnasia

---

1 Bethnal Green is located in the heart of London's East End. Known in the early nineteenth century for its market gardens and silk-weaving trade, the area degenerated into a crowded slum by the end of the century.

2 A Roman consul in 503 BC.

3 Roman emperor (54-68 AD).

4 Roman emperor (284-305 AD).

5 Roman emperor (306-337 AD).

for exercise, lecture-rooms, libraries, and porticoes, wherein the people might have shade, and shelter, and rest? I remark, by-the-bye, that I have not seen in all your London a single covered place in which the people may take shelter during a shower. Are you aware that these baths were of the most magnificent architecture, decorated with marbles, paintings, sculptures, fountains, what not? And yet I had heard, in Hades down below, that you prided yourselves here on the study of the learned languages; and, indeed, taught little but Greek and Latin at your public schools?"

Then, if the minister should make reply: "Oh yes, we know all this. Even since the revival of letters in the end of the fifteenth century a whole literature has been written—a great deal of it, I fear, by pedants who seldom washed even their hands and faces—about your Greek and Roman baths. We visit their colossal ruins in Italy and elsewhere with awe and admiration; and the discovery of a new Roman bath in any old city of our isles sets all our antiquaries buzzing with interest."

"Then why," the shade might ask, "do you not copy an example which you so much admire? Surely England must be much in want, either of water, or of fuel to heat it with?"

"On the contrary, our rainfall is almost too great; our soil so damp that we have had to invent a whole art of subsoil drainage unknown to you; while, as for fuel, our coal-mines make us the great fuel-exporting people of the world."

What a quiet sneer might curl the lip of a Constantine as he replied: "Not in vain, as I said, did we call you, some fifteen hundred years ago, the barbarians of the north. But tell me, good barbarian, whom I know to be both brave and wise—for the fame of your young British empire has reached us even in the realms below, and we recognise in you, with all respect, a people more like us Romans than any which has appeared on earth for many centuries—how is it you have forgotten that sacred duty of keeping the people clean, which you surely at one time learnt from us? When your ancestors entered our armies, and rose, some of them, to be great generals, and even emperors, like those two Teuton peasants, Justin[1] and Justinian,[2] who, long after my days, reigned in my own Constantinople: then, at least, you saw baths, and used them; and felt, after the bath, that you were civilised men, and not 'sordidi ac foetentes,'[3] as we used to call

---

1   Justin I (c.450-527), emperor and military leader.
2   Roman emperor (527-565 AD), nephew of Justin I.
3   Filthy and stinking.

you when fresh out of your bullock-waggons[1] and cattle-pens. How is it that you have forgotten that lesson?"

The minister, I fear, would have to answer that our ancestors were barbarous enough, not only to destroy the Roman cities, and temples, and basilicas, and statues, but the Roman baths likewise; and then retired, each man to his own freehold in the country, to live a life not much more cleanly or more graceful than that of the swine which were his favourite food. But he would have a right to plead, as an excuse, that not only in England, but throughout the whole of the conquered Latin empire, the Latin priesthood, who, in some respects, were—to their honour—the representatives of Roman civilisation and the protectors of its remnants, were the determined enemies of its cleanliness; that they looked on personal dirt—like the old hermits of the Thebaid[2]—as a sign of sanctity; and discouraged—as they are said to do still in some of the Romance countries of Europe—the use of the bath, as not only luxurious, but also indecent.

At which answer, it seems to me, another sneer might curl the lip of the august shade, as he said to himself: "This, at least, I did not expect, when I made Christianity the state religion of my empire. But you, good barbarian, look clean enough. You do not look on dirt as a sign of sanctity?"

"On the contrary, sire, the upper classes of our empire boast of being the cleanliest—perhaps the only perfectly cleanly—people in the world: except, of course, the savages of the South Seas. And dirt is so far from being a thing which we admire, that our scientific men—than whom the world has never seen wiser—have proved to us, for a whole generation past, that dirt is the fertile cause of disease and drunkenness, misery, and recklessness."

"And, therefore," replies the shade, ere he disappears, "of discontent and revolution: followed by a tyranny endured, as in Rome and many another place, by men once free; because tyranny will at least do for them what they are too lazy, and cowardly, and greedy, to do for themselves. Farewell, and prosper; as you seem likely to prosper, on the whole. But if you wish me to consider you a civilised nation: let me hear that you have brought

---

1 Wagons drawn by oxen.
2 The upper part of the Nile valley under Roman domination. During the fourth to fifth centuries it was the chosen land of the monks.

a great river from the depths of the earth, be they a thousand fathoms deep, or from your nearest mountains, be they five hundred miles away; and have washed out London's dirt—and your own shame. Till then, abstain from judging too harshly a Constantine, or even a Caracalla;[1] for they, whatever were their sins, built baths, and kept their people clean. But do your gymnasia—your schools and universities, teach your youth naught about all this?"

[Source: *Sanitary and Social Lectures and Essays* (London: Macmillan, 1880) 158-63. The essay "Air-Mothers" originally appeared in *Good Words for the Young* in 1870.]

---

1 Marcus Aurelius Severus Antonius (211-217 AD), cruel and treacherous emperor of Rome who ascended to sole power by having his brother murdered.

Appendix I: Joseph Noel Paton's Illustrations for the First Edition of The Water-Babies *(1863)*

Appendix J: Reviews of The Water-Babies

1. *The Anthropological Review*: Vol. 1, No. 3 (November 1863): 472-76

[The Anthropological Society of London was founded in 1863 by Richard Francis Burton and Dr. James Hunt. Kingsley was an honorary fellow of the Society. The Society broke away from the existing Ethnological Society of London, founded in 1842, and defined itself in opposition to the older society, arguing against Darwin's theory of natural selection. Instead, they proposed studying the natural laws and cultural forces that contributed to the diversity of nature. The Society was also outspoken on the "Negro Question." Hunt believed that Africans belonged to a species distinctly inferior to Caucasians, and that slavery was their proper condition. This anonymous review was published under the auspices of The Anthropological Society of London.]

In these days, when Anthropology seems to be reviving from the prolonged torpor in which it has placidly rested since the time of the publication of the sedative works of Prichard,[1] while the great doctrine of the subordination of the actions of each individual, his birth, his life, and his death, to the operation of uniform dynamical laws which govern the entirety of external nature, is now receiving universal acceptance, the publication of the above work [*The Water-Babies*] marks the period of an epoch in our biological literature.

Great changes in the thoughts of mankind have often been distinguished by the publication of poetical or satirical effusions. Since the time when Aristophanes satirized the nascent biological truths which were then scarce yet cropping out amongst the thoughts of Hellenic inquirers, and ignorantly confused them with Socratic speculations; since the time when the painters of the Egyptian papyri, often, in the exercise of their sportive skill,

---

1 James Cowles Prichard (1786-1848), an English physician and ethnologist, argued that mankind evolved from common black ancestors. In 1843 he published *The Natural History of Man,* in which he set forth the doctrine of monogenesis, the unitary origin of man, a view in direct opposition of Hunt and his associates, who believed in polygenesis.

depicted the various known animals in ridiculous or ludicrous positions; since the time when the beetle-hunter and butterfly-preserver of Pope's *Dunciad*[1] were regarded as beings beneath the notice of the poet or the reciter of "smart things;" down to the period when authors who profess to investigate the history of England sneer at the "most intense study of entomology" as something almost incompatible with the attainment of correct information, exalted ideas, or noble sentiments, great changes have taken place in the world's thoughts. We have to deal at the present time with the advocates of the inductive method, with the disciples of a philosophy founded on the observance of the constancy of the laws of nature, and consonant with, if it may not be directing, the cause of the state of European science at the present time. To those who may wish to emulate the reputation of some of those quasi-scientific writers, who have no notion of any more lofty conception of the science of life than the inspection of a series of disconnected objects, each exhibiting "evidences of design," and nothing more, and who are characterized by the lines which have been applied or misapplied to the poet Göethe:[2]—

"The lessons he taught mankind were few,
And none that could make them good or true,"

to those who regard the whole universe as subordinated to man, who creates the laws by which the inferior beings live or die; or to those who may, while they thoroughly comprehend the systematic and classificatory productions of zoology, be wholly ignorant of the great conclusions to which the conception of such system and classification leads us, Professor Kingsley's "Water Babies" will open a new vista of contemplation wholly at variance with the habitual and unrefreshing thoughts which may have left feeble impressions on their plastic minds.

The style of the work is throughout in pure English—such English as Kingsley always writes—clear, manly, and to the point. In this it may fairly bear comparison with any of Professor Kingsley's previous publications. The superficial reader will merely be struck with the flashes of wit and humour which are scattered

---

1 Alexander Pope (1688-1744) first published *The Dunciad* in 1728, in which he satirized the follies of British society.
2 Johann Wolfgang von Goethe (1749-1832), German poet, novelist, and playwright.

throughout the book; the "land babies," for which it is ostensibly destined, must, however, attain a competent knowledge of biological controversy before they can hope to comprehend it, while the disciples of the false philosophies which it satirizes, will hardly relish the castigation administered. The description of such remedial agents as life-pills, homœpathy, mesmerism, pure bosh, the distilled liquor of addle eggs; "antipathy, or using the subject like a man and a brother; apathy, or doing nothing at all; with all other ipathies and opathies which Noodle has invented, and Foodie tried, since black fellows chipped flints at Abbeville, which is a considerable time ago, to judge by the Great Exhibition," should be carefully read and studied by those medical practitioners who may feel disposed to commence a heterodox practice. The pure anthropologist has, however, more interesting matter afforded him. That destructive school of scientific thinkers who, like the giant in the great land of Hearsay, would smash in the temple of the land for the sake of three obscure species of Podurellæ[1] and a Buddhist bat, the latter cognate with that which is said to be confined to the Buddhist temples of Little Thibet, meet with due notice in the work.

We regret that the exigencies of our space preclude us from the reproduction of the inimitable passage in which Professor Kingsley applies the Darwinian laws to the supposed "degradation" of the ape from the human species. The career of the Doasyoulike nation, whose neglect of the physical laws conditional on their existence reduced them ultimately to gorillas, is no doubt familiar to many of our readers, and upon the supposition, therefore, of their familiarity with the work, we feel bound to point out that the great flaw in the Darwinian theory, which Professor Kingsley, to a certain extent, we believe, advocates, is admirably illustrated in this passage. According to our interpretation, when the Doasyoulikes had once ascended the trees, and the weaker individuals had been all eaten up by the lions, the felines would have had nothing to eat. They would consequently have been hungry, and unless their structure was modified to catch something else—and Professor Kingsley telling us of no other carnivorous or herbivorous animal, upon which to prey—they must, in the long run, have died of inanition. Then, when the lions were all dead, the Doasyoulikes might have safely descended the trees, and the further transmutation of the scansorial[2] man into the ape would have been rendered functionally unnecessary.

---

1 Springtails, small wingless hexapods that dwell in the soil and litter.
2 Having limbs adapted for climbing.

Or, we are as much at liberty to suppose plasticity in the organization of the lion as of the man. The organization of the lion being slightly plastic, those individuals with the most powerful claws, and in whom the scapular arch was most mobile, let the difference be ever so small, would be slightly favoured, and would tend to live longer, and to survive during the time of the year when the food was scarcest; they would also rear more young, which would tend to inherit these slight peculiarities. The less scansorial ones would be rigidly destroyed. The consequence would be, that the lions would be transformed into tigers, leopards, or other climbing cats, and would ascend the trees and eat up the men, unless from the *homines* the smaller and lighter individuals were selected, who might have descended along the flexible boughs, as Friday[1] did, when the bear pursued him, and so reached the ground in safety. Then, if there were any terrestrial lions left, the men would stand an equal chance of being devoured; or the scansorial lions might come down at leisure, modify their organization, and commence the game afresh. The "selective process" would thus bring us precisely to the point whence we started.

Another great feature in Professor Kingsley's work is the extreme liberality with which his scientific opinions are characterized. The contempt which he bestows on the "Cousin Cramchild's arguments" of the anti-scientific school of thinkers, is exemplified by his description of the land of Oldwifesfabledom, where the people were not so frightened as they wish to be; the narrative of Tom's journey to the other end of Nowhere, to attain which he was told to "go to Shiny Wall, and through the white gate that never was opened; and then you will come to Peacepool and Mother Carey's haven, where the good whales go when they die;" and his delightfully minute account of the signification of many things "which nobody will ever hear of, at least until the coming of the Cocqeigruess [*sic*], when man shall be the measure of all things," contain ideas which we must recommend to the attention of every sincere thinker.

Superficial and limited knowledge is especially visited with Professor Kingsley's severe condemnation. The adventures of the old cock-grouse, who "was always fancying that the end of the world was come when anything happened which was farther off than the end of his own nose," and on finding an hour afterwards

---

1 Servant of Robinson Crusoe.

that the end of the world was not quite come, gravely announced that "it was coming the day after to-morrow," justly parallels the words of the far-seeing writer who, a short time ago, regarded the formation of the Anthropological Society as a sign of the "last days."

The finest passage of the work, however, is the plea for possible degradation of mankind into a perennibranchiate amphibian, *i.e.*, a water baby. We must commend the following argument to M. de Castelnau,[1] who advocates the existence of men with tails in Equatorial America:—"No one has a right to say that no water babies exist, till they have seen no water babies existing, which is quite a different thing, mind, from not seeing water babies, and a thing which nobody ever did, or perhaps ever will do." The argument is certainly a fair specimen of reasoning, and would have been accepted in the middle ages, when men reasoned better and knew less than they do now. After Professor Kingsley has exhausted every argument in favour of the existence of water babies, he triumphantly clenches the matter by telling Cousin Cramchild, his adversary, "that if there are no water babies, at least there ought to be; and that at least he cannot answer."

The whole episode relating to Professor Ptthmllnsprts, the chief professor of necrobioneopalæonthydrochthonanthropopithekology, in the new university which the King of the Cannibal Islands has founded, should be perused by every *savant*, especially by every anthropologist. We must pass it over here, as well as many other brilliant passages. Careful perusal, and a thorough scientific education, are preliminaries to the study of this work, which, like the Gargantua of Rabelais,[2] or the Sueños of Quevedo[3] (especially the latter, in Sir Roger l'Estrange's inimitable translation), inculcates lessons of the highest import in language which must gratify every one who has reflected on the generalizations to which modern science has arrived.

---

1   Francis-Louis de Castelnau (1812-80), a French naturalist who, between the years 1843-47, explored the regions of South America from Rio de Janeiro to Lima.

2   François Rabelais (c.1495-1553), a French Benedictine monk, physician, and humanist scholar. *Gargantua and Pantagruel,* a panoramic folk epic, satirizes medieval scholasticism and superstition and extols secular learning and the richness of human nature.

3   Don Francisco de Quevedo (1580-1645), Spanish satirical novelist and poet. *Los Sueños* [visions] (1627) is a brilliant and bitterly satiric account of the inhabitants of hell, modeled after Dante.

2. *New York Times* (25 December 1863)

The Professor of Modern History at Cambridge furnishes with equal grace and readiness milk for babes as well as strong meat for men. This charming little book is a fantasia of the wildest character, and as such, will delight those for whom it is written. But there are hints of a deeper significance behind. In the words of the dedication to the Professor's youngest son "and all other good boys," where he says:

"Come read my riddle, my good little man,
   If you cannot read it, no grown-up folks can."

Grown-up folks may possibly discover in it a sharp satire on some prominent scientific notions, not forgetting the Darwinian theory of development. Viewed in any light, it is a book that no one but Mr. Kingsley could have written.

3. *The Times* (26 January 1864): 6

Mr. Kingsley has written a very pleasant story, which Mr. Macmillan has rightly deemed worthy of being issued in all the glories of a gift-book. That the *Water-Babies* will outlive many generations of ordinary gift-books would probably be no unsafe prophecy; those ephemeræ live their season and depart to that lumber-room of the universe where the old moons, superannuated donkeys and octogenarian postboys take their rest; but Mr. Kingsley's babies, after being the playfellows of the wee things of 1864, will by express permission, remain young to gambol with children yet unborn. All the more fitting is it that the book which tells us of them should be honoured with tone paper, with Mr. Clay's best printing, and with Mr. Noel Paton's best designs. Mr. Paton has evidently taken to his task as to a labour of love; and if we cannot accept his illustrations as perfectly satisfactory, we must in justice add that we know of no one who could have attained a greater degree of excellence.... Mr. Paton may defy rivalry in his babies; they are excellent and by far the best of his designs. We may object to the fairy in the frontispiece, whose hair flies about like flickering fire-light—she is too much earnest and proper; but we must acknowledge the admirable manner in which the children suck their thumbs; they do it with gravity but without obstinacy.

It is amusing to note the reception which the *Water-Babies* met with when they first appeared in *Macmillan's Magazine*. A sort of douce sobriety generally reigns throughout that periodical; it has a grave character; and some weak digestions, spoilt by the sweets and trifles in which they habitually indulge, have not scrupled to call it heavy. It is only necessary to remember the performances of the Messrs. Kingsley in it to see how unjust is this epithet. The reverend Professor and Mr. Henry Kingsley appear and reappear with delightful but confusing activity. Like a pair of bounding brothers they dazzle the unaccustomed sight, and when you finally think the elder or the younger, as the case may be, is the actor, it is the other who is throwing somersaults. Nevertheless, quite sober people favoured *Macmillan*, and were a good deal puzzled and a little scandalized when the *Water-Babies* began to tumble about in it like so many porpoises. *Water-Babies* were pure nonsense. The whole story was absurd, without rhyme or reason, beginning or end, and a sort of thing that no man could understand. "What does it all mean?" was the question they asked; a question which we forbear from answering, partly because we are not sure that we altogether know. Indeed, we may as well confess frankly that we have a very vague conception of what a peth-wind[1] may be, and as to Mr. George White,[2] "who rules things straight with his ruler and then cuts them out with his chisel," he is, no doubt, an excellent man; but we never met him. We need not tell the reader of the *Water-Babies* that until we are acquainted with peth-winds and Mr. White our explanation of the book must be incomplete and unsatisfactory. But withal we have called the story a very pleasant one, and we intend to stick to our opinion. It is by no means necessary to understand a book to know whether or not it is agreeable; and it is, perhaps, true that the pleasantest things of life are as a rule unintelligible to us until we have lost them.

The *Water-Babies* appear to indicate a real advance in Mr. Kingsley's literary progress. His powers have matured without abating aught of their energy. His humour is richer and more mellow than we could have anticipated from his earlier works. How pleasant it is to watch this development can be felt only by those who have had to note the dismal lapse from strength to weakness. We have heard of a man who drew in his youth a strong picture of University life, and in after-life rubbed it all out, and

---

1 A twining plant, such as the convolvulus.
2 The gardener at Kingsley's residence in Eversley.

put in its place a namby-pamby sketch as weak as anything ever executed by a disciple of Overbeck.[1] Nothing in this decline can we trace in the *Water-Babies*. There are some faults of the author which remain; they are inextricably intertwined with his merits, and the one cannot be removed without destroying the other, but the faults are less obtrusive than they were, while his merits have not diminished. There is in Mr. Kingsley's mind a certain one-sidedness, we might almost call it narrowness, closely allied with his impetuous vigour, and always threatening to drag him down to the position of a partisan. His keen sense of beauty and his hearty manhood have saved him from becoming a dangerous fanatic, but in the *Water-Babies* enough of the narrowness remains to prevent us from ranking the author among the great humourists of literature. If we might venture to attribute characteristics to a class whose peculiar glory it is that each of its members is a law to himself, we should say that the humourists have been distinguished by wide-flowing sympathies, by excellent receptivity and passivity; but of the more contracted, energizing spirit, directed definitely to one object, they have shown little or nothing. Their great hearts have been, in the phrase of the Laureate "laughter stirred,"[2] and not only so, with laughter and play they have joined love, pity, infinite tenderness; but fiery indignation and vehement denunciation have not been theirs. Swift may seem to be an exception; we all remember the inscription on the monument in St. Patrick's Cathedral, he was gone *"ubi saeva indignatio ulterius lacerare nequit;"*[3] but it must be noted that he felt no partial rage, the depravity and the malignity of the Yahoos[4] admitted of no exception of person, much less of class; his universal hate is the reciprocal of universal love; had it been narrowed he would have been a powerful satirist, but we should hesitate to call him a great humourist. But about Mr. Kingsley there lingers some of the vehement partialities of youth. Every now and

---

1   Johann Friedrich Overbeck (1789-1869), a German painter.
2   From Tennyson's "Recollections of the Arabian Nights" (1830): "Thereon, his deep eye laughter-stirr'd/ With merriment of kingly pride."
3   The correct version is "Ubi saeva indignatio ulterius cor lacerare nequit" (savage indignation cannot lacerate his heart). Jonathan Swift wrote his own epitaph.
4   The Yahoos are vicious, dirty animals with human traits in Swift's *Gulliver's Travels* (1726) and are meant to represent the depravity of humankind.

then a littleness appears in the conduct of his fairy-tale; he indulges in small didactic digressions, which we could spare with much satisfaction, or with wonderful complacency he begins to measure oceans with a pint-pot measure. Now even an imperial pint is a small measure with which to gauge the Atlantic, and Mr. Kingsley's pints are of the smallest that can pass muster as reputed. There is something laughable in the gravity with which he weighs such a matter as the American war, and passes judgment on a transaction the very magnitude of which would deter men having a keen sense of the ludicrousness from giving an *ex cathedra* opinion upon it.

Apart from these occasional blemishes, Mr. Kingsley's book shows a good conception well carried out. Manifold as have been the modes which authors have adopted to give the world the benefit of their speculations on life and education, we do not remember that any one have before ventured on telling the history of a Water-Baby. Mr. Kingsley must have the credit of having revealed to us a new order of life. Neither Undine nor Lurline,[1] nor the Siren which tempted Goethe's Fisherman,[2] nor the strange beings in the Eastern tale[3] who walked about at the bottom of the sea and built palaces there and dwelt in them, are of the same kin as Tom and Ellie.

Tom and Ellie must rank by themselves; and it is probable that their existence would have remained undiscovered, had not mankind, about the middle of the 19th century, taken to sea anemones. But when Mr. Gosse[4] wrote books to describe the wonders which he saw on the coast of Devonshire and at Tenby, and Mr. Lewes[5] exchanged biography, metaphysics, novels, and

---

1 Mythic seductive creatures of the sea.
2 In Goethe's poem "The Fisherman," the Siren lures the fisherman into the sea with her song and he disappears.
3 In "The King of Persia and the Princess of the Sea" from the *Arabian Nights,* Queen Gulnare declares: "We can walk at the bottom of the sea with as much ease as you can upon land; and we can breathe in the water as you do in the air."
4 Philip Henry Gosse (1810-88), a popular author of books about birds and marine life, including *A Naturalist's Rambles on the Devonshire Coast* (1853) and *Tenby—A Seaside Holiday* (1856).
5 George Henry Lewes (1817-78), English author and critic. In addition to his poetry, plays, philosophical studies, and biography of Goethe, he wrote *Seaside Studies* (1858), *Physiology of Common Life* (1859), *Studies in Animal Life* (1862).

plays for sea-side studies, and another popular author published *Glaucus; or, The Wonders of the Shore,* and Germans wrote fat books on the sea, and insisted that Germany ought to be a naval Power and Kiel a German port, and Frenchmen wrote lively books and built La Gloire,[1] and every young lady had her aquarium, and maiden aunts carried about rare actinia[2] in jam-pots, to the fearful punishment of pilfering pages fond of sweets, Tom and Ellie could no longer remain in obscurity, and their delightful history was accordingly written. And if we should have never heard of Tom and Ellie but for the development of Marine Zoology, we may add that Master Tom's education would have been impossible had not Mr. Darwin published his book on the *Origin of Species.* Mr. Kingsley trips up the Darwinian theory, and asks us how we like its application, when, inverted. If an ascent in the order of life be possible, must not a degradation or movement downwards be also possible? If beasts can be turned into men, must not men be liable to be turned into beasts? Here, indeed, Mr. Kingsley might have quoted the authority of one of his great masters, Mr. Carlyle,[3] who long ago warned us of the fate of the dwellers by the Dead Sea who refused to listen to the preaching of Moses. They became apes, poor wretches, and having once had souls they lost them. Whether at the same time they lost the hippopotamus major from their brains, or what Mr. Darwin will say to the transformation, is luckily no business of ours. Professor Owen[4] and Professor Huxley[5] may fight it out in the Pump-room at Bath when the British Association meets there in the autumn; a ring shall be formed, and everything shall be on the square, which is perhaps somewhat of a bull, and the policemen shall be kept back, and all the lookers-on will be delighted.

Some of us who were born in the præ-scientific era may think it hard that we should have the Darwinian theory mixed up with

---

1   An iron-clad warship designed by Stanislas Dupuy de Lone and completed in 1860.

2   A genus of sea anemone common in rock pools.

3   This story is told in Thomas Carlyle's "Gospel of Dilettantism" in *Past and Present* (1843).

4   Richard Owen (1804-92), naturalist and England's foremost authority on animal anatomy.

5   Thomas Henry Huxley (1825-95), biologist and professor at the Royal College of Surgeons, an advocate of Darwin's theory of evolution; author of *Zoological Evidence as to Man's Place in Nature* (1863).

the Archaeopteryx[1] and the Crassicornis[2] in a fairy tale. We need not understand what they all are, it is true, but we should like to feel that we know something about the gentlemen before we were introduced to them, and it is possible that, if we were told before-hand what grand company we were going to meet, we should have an engagement and keep away. But Mr. Kingsley is too cunning to give us warning, and, after all, these members of the Upper Ten Thousand,[3] like many other grandees, are simple, quiet people. We do not meet with them till we have made the acquaintance of Tom, and Mr. Grimes, and Sir John Harthover, and Harthover Fell, and Vendale, and when we have got so far it is impossible to turn back. The opening chapters in which these are introduced are written in Mr. Kingsley's best style, and with genuine sentiment. The intense love and admiration which he has so often lavished over the combes and moors of Devon and West Somerset are kindled here at the contemplation of the dales and fells of the north country. What is the exact position of Vendale? Mr. Kingsley does not tell us, but we fancy it is not far from Chapel-le-Dale, which is itself near Ingleton, and where, accord-ing to another gentle humourist, was born Daniel, the son of Daniel Dove and Dinah his wife.[4] How beautiful the dales of West Yorkshire are can be fully known only by those who had tra-versed them on foot like Mr. Walter White,[5] but some glimmering of their loveliness may be gained from Mr. Kingsley's description of what Tom saw from Lewthwaite Crag [quotation omitted].

Mr. Kingsley is or was a canon of Middleham, and if there are any duties attached to that honourable office he must have been often led to the neighbourhood of Vendale; certainly the descrip-tion of its peculiar beauty is as accurate and hearty as it could have been had he known Vendale long and intimately, as he has known the Barb and the Lyn, and the Tor and the Torridge, and the other streams which flow from Exmoor and Dartmoor. Nor must we omit to mention for the use of would-be visitors to Vendale that there are two marks by which it may be infallibly recognized—first, there is a great black smudge all the way down

---

1 The fossil link between the birds and the dinosaur.
2 An anemone.
3 The upper class or aristocracy.
4 In *The Doctor* (1834), a Shandyesque novel by Robert Southey (1774-1843).
5 Librarian of the Royal Society, Walter White (1811-93) is the author of *A Month in Yorkshire* (1861).

Lewthwaite Crag, being the mark of poor Tom's descent, for, as the reader knows or ought to know, he was at that time of his life a dirty little sweep; and secondly, the dale is famous for the number of its black-beetles, "all, of course, owing to Tom's having blacked the original papa of them all, just as he was setting off to be married, with a sky-blue coat and scarlet leggings, as smart as a gardener's dog with a polyanthus in his mouth."

It is difficult to praise too highly the spirit and humour with which these early chapters of the *Water-Babies* are written, and when soft-hearted readers come to the mysterious transformation scene it is to be feared that they will be of the same mind as Sir John Harthover and do something as like crying as ever they have done in their lives. But their tears will be mixed with laughter when they are introduced to the famous Professor Ptthmllnsprts, who read a paper at the British Association at Melbourne, Australia, in the year 1999, which proved that nymphs, satyrs, fawns, inui, dwarfs, trolls, and so on through several lines of print, were nothing at all, and pure bosh and wind; and he had to get up very early in the morning to prove that, and to eat his breakfast overnight: and yet, strange to say, he left a chance of escape for pixies, at least Mr. Kingsley does not tell us he demolished them, so that his argument may be of no great value after all. Somewhat akin to the Professor, with a hard exterior but soft heart, is a very distinguished Lobster, with live barnacles on his claws, who threw out their casting-nets and swept the water, and always came in for their share of whatever the Lobster had for dinner, exactly like junior Lords of the Treasury making a House and cheering the Minister. But perhaps the best character of this kind is the old Lady Gairfowl, a lady of a very old house, which once held its own among the highest, but now so reduced that she was left the last of her race, an ancient and feeble lady, leading a solitary life at Allalonestone. She was dreadfully behind the age, poor old woman, and thought that every one should keep to their own station in life, instead of struggling, after the modern fashion to rise in the world; but withal, she was a kindly, weak-headed dame, very affable, in her old-fashioned, ceremonious way, to them who approached her with respect; for she was the last of the Gairfowl, and it behoved her to keep the honour of the house from degradation [quotation omitted].

With such excellent fooling as this, at times grave and subdued and at times boisterous and overflowing, are mixed theories of life and of education, theories good and bad, sayings sage and sayings simple; and we suppose it is idle to lament over the unequal character of the whole. In a book of this kind we must take what the author gives us; he is prattling out of a full heart, and if we do not like the discourse we must drop the *Water-Babies* and take up something else. We need not warn the reader who is at all acquainted with Mr. Kingsley's former books that he is of a somewhat precipitate turn, and that his reasonings occasionally appear inconsequent to slower-paced thinkers. He gives us guesses at truth, which may or may not prove sound. What is the value of the following statement upon which he insists in the *Water-Babies* with much energy? One of the deepest and wisest speeches, he says, which can come out of a human mouth is this— "It is so beautiful that it must be true,"[1] But, he adds, men will not accept it until they have subordinated Locke to Plato.[2] Mr. Kingsley does well in stoutly asserting this thesis, for it is the foundation of the theology of his school. To ground the scheme of Christian faith upon its beauty does, however, seem to some simple minds like balancing a pyramid upon its apex, and then sitting at rest upon its inverted base. One or two may be able to achieve the feat; but for the multitude equilibrium in such a position is only possible when it is accompanied by ceaseless and swift gyration. It is on this account that, with profound respect for Mr. Maurice,[3] we can scarcely avoid feeling some contempt for mere Mauricians. The criterion of moral beauty is painfully uncertain. The pious cannibal who eats his grandfather sees in the deed a touching reverence for human life, and an exquisite fulfillment of filial obligation. The body which has once been the home of a man may not, he thinks, suffer the indignity of being consigned to the cold, dead earth; no, it must be reabsorbed in a living frame, and who so fits as a grandson to carry out the idea— a grandson who thenceforth will truly work with his grandsire's

---

1 Kingsley's statement echoes the famous concluding lines in John Keats' "Ode on a Grecian Urn: "'Beauty is truth, truth beauty,—that is all/Ye know on earth, and all ye need to know.'"

2 John Locke (1632-1704), the English philosopher and founder of British empiricism, whose *Essay Concerning Human Understanding* (1690) aims to determine the limits of human understanding. Empiricists claim that sense experience is the ultimate source of all our concepts and knowledge, whereas Plato and rationalists argue that concepts can be shaped by reason that goes beyond the limits of sense experience.

3 Frederick Dennison Maurice (1805-72), an English clergyman, social reformer, and friend of Kingsley. Maurice's theology was both innovative and controversial.

spirit? He undertakes the duty; and should some missionary remonstrate, as haply he may, being fearful, perhaps, that some day he may coldly furnish forth the luncheon table, he will have the idea of the service expounded to him, and clinched with the proof that it is so beautiful that it must be true. The cannibal is, no doubt, rather a strong instance, but another philosopher may be adduced, between whom and Mr. Kingsley there are many curious points of resemblance, though on first impression they would appear utterly dissimilar. Jean Jacques Rousseau[1] seduced himself into the belief that his beautiful dreams must be true, but Experience had her revenge, and he who cared not to be taught by History had been confuted by History. Mr. Kingsley would probably repudiate nearly all Rousseau's conclusions, yet the educational theories of *Emile* are, in many respects, the same as those of the *Water-Babies*, and Jean Jacques adopted to the full the criterion which Mr. Kingsley so strongly approves—"It is so beautiful, it must be true." Jean Jacques, too, was capable of a joke. When some fond parent introduced his son to the philosopher, and added that he had been trained on the principles of *Emile*, "So much the worse for him and you" was the blunt rejoinder.

But theories apart, there is in the *Water-Babies* an abundance of wit, fun, good humour, geniality, élan, go; so we will suppress all querulous complaint and heartily recommend it to the reader's enjoyment.

4. *The Times* (12 December 1885): 4

"THE WATER-BABIES," ILLUSTRATED.

This new edition of Charles Kingsley's famous fairy-tale is likely to stand high in the favour of those who care for illustrated books, for it contains a hundred examples of the talent of one of the most inventive of our artists, Mr. Linley Sambourne. The wonder is that we have not had a fully illustrated edition of "The Water-Babies" before Sir Noel Paton's two charming plates in the original volume were an indication, and not more than an indication,

---

1   Rousseau (1712-78), a Swiss-French philosopher. In *Émile, or On Education* (1762) he proposes an educational theory based on the notion that people are born inherently good, but that they later become corrupted by the evils of society.

of what might be done. Every page of Kingsley's story contains situations in which a sympathetic artist would revel; for, whether the story is successful or not as an artistic whole, it is beyond all doubt rich in fanciful detail. Kingsley was not a man of science, but he had an extraordinary gift of observation and something of the true poetic fire. He loved "bird and man and beast"—especially bird and beast; and he knew enough of the strange creatures that dwell in the streams and the sea to make their life seem curiously real as he described it. Besides the human scenes of "The Water-Babies," the scenes of stream-life in Vendale, of river-life in the broad Northumbrian estuary, and of sea-life wherever Tom's later destiny carried him, are brimful of materials for an artist who, like Mr. Sambourne, is a naturalist as well.

Mr. Sambourne has been steadily making way in the public estimation ever since he began to draw for *Punch*, now several years ago. His talent is like that of no one else. As a political and social caricaturist he resembles neither Leech[1] nor Tenniel,[2] and he has nothing in common with the slighter though very admirable artists of past generations, such as "H.B."[3] and Gillray.[4] He combines the most curious power of grotesque invention with an equal power of seizing a likeness; and over and above these gifts he has those of a first-rate draughtsman. All this is aided by the knowledge of the habits and forms of living creatures of all sorts, especially of sea creatures; so that in his caricatures we often find ourselves transported from Westminster to "the deep's untrampled floor," or to the regions which nothing more human has ever visited than the dredging-tackle of the Challenger.[5] These idiosyncrasies were shown in a striking way in the remarkable diploma which Mr. Sambourne designed two years ago for the Fisheries Exhibition; a bit of quaint symbolical art of really high merit, and standing alone in its class in our time. It need not be said that in illustrating "The Water-Babies" Mr. Sambourne has found himself very much at home. Tom's adven-

---

1 John Leech (1817-64), cartoonist and illustrator; illustrated Dickens's *A Christmas Carol.*

2 John Tenniel (1820-1914), cartoonist and illustrator; illustrated Lewis Carroll's Alice books.

3 "H.B.," John Doyle (1797-1868), caricaturist and portrait painter, specialized in political satires.

4 James Gillray (1756-1815), political caricaturist.

5 *H.M.S. Challenger*, set out in 1872 for a four-year study of the ocean floor.

tures with the big brown trout or with the lobster, suit him perfectly; he is excellent with the group of eels that are starting for the sea, and the foolish sun-fish that has lost its way finds in him a portrait-painter equal to the representation of utter fatuity. His single human figures are capital too; such as Mr. Grimes imprisoned in the chimney, little Ellie, and, best of all, Professors Huxley and Owen examining a bottled water-baby. We could have wished that he had not ignored some of the delightful scenes which follow upon Tom's discovery of his water kindred; but perhaps Mr. Sambourne wished to avoid coming into direct competition with Sir Noel Paton. Altogether, the volume can be recommended as something more than a "Christmas book" of exceptional merit.

Bibliography

Editions of *The Water-Babies*

The Water-Babies. London and Cambridge: Macmillan, 1863.
First edition. Two illustrations by J. Noel Paton.
———. Boston: TOPH Burnham, 1864. First American edition.
Based upon the first British edition.
———. London: Macmillan, 1886. Illustrated by Linley Sam-
bourne, Macmillan's most popular edition.
———. New York: Dodd Mead, 1910. Illustrated by Jessie Willcox
Smith.
———. London: Constable, 1915. Illustrated by W. Heath Robin-
son.
———. Oxford: Oxford University Press, 1995. Edited with an
introduction and notes by Brian Alderson. Based upon the
first British edition.

Biographies and Letters

Chitty, Susan. *The Beast and the Monk: A Life of Charles
Kingsley*. New York: Mason/Charter, 1974.
Colloms, Brenda. *Charles Kingsley: the Lion of Eversley*. London:
Constable, 1975.
Kingsley, Frances, ed. *Charles Kingsley: His Letters and Memories
of his Life*. 2 vols. London: Macmillan, 1891.
Martin, Robert Bernard. *The Dust of Combat: A Life of Charles
Kingsley*. New York: W.W. Norton, 1960.
Thorp, Margaret Ferrand. *Charles Kingsley*. Princeton: Prince-
ton University Press, 1937.

Bibliography

Harris, Styron. *Charles Kingsley, A Reference Guide*. Boston:
G.K. Hall, 1981.

Studies of *The Water-Babies*

Alderson, Brian. "Introduction" to Charles Kingsley, *The Water-
Babies*. Oxford: Oxford University Press, 1995). ix-xxix.
Avery, Gillian (with the assistance of Angela Bull). *Nineteenth*

Century Children: Heroes and Heroines in English Children's Stories 1780-1900. London: Hodder and Stoughton, 1965.

Banerjee, Jacqueline. *Through the Northern Gate: Childhood and Growing Up in British Fiction, 1719-1901*. New York: Lang, 1996.

Beer, Gillian. *Darwin's Plots: Evolutionary Narrative in Darwin, George Eliot and Nineteenth-Century Fiction*. London: Routledge & Kegan Paul, 1983.

——. "Kingsley: 'pebbles on the shore'," *The Listener* 93 (17 April 1975): 506-7.

Carpenter, Humphrey. "Parson Lot Takes a Cold Bath: Charles Kingsley and *The Water-Babies*." *Secret Gardens: A Study of the Golden Age of Children's Literature*. Boston: Houghton Mifflin, 1985: 23-43.

Charques, R.D., Mrs. "Kingsley as Children's Writer." *Times Literary Supplement* 2576 (15 June 1951): I.

Chitty, Susan. *Charles Kingsley's Landscape*. Newton Abbot; North Pomfret, VT: David and Charles, 1976.

Coleman, Dorothy. "Rabelais and The Water-Babies." *Modern Language Review* 66.3 (July 1971): 511-21.

Cosslett, Tess. "Child's Place in Nature: Talking Animals in Victorian Children's Fiction" *Nineteenth-Century Contexts* 23.4 (2001): 475-95.

Cripps, Elizabeth A. "Lewis Carroll, and Charles and Henry Kingsley." *Jabberwocky: The Journal of the Lewis Carroll Society* 9.3 (Summer 1980): 59-66.

Cunningham, Valentine. "Soiled Fairy: The Water-Babies in its Time." *Essays in Criticism* 35.2 (April 1985): 121-48.

Darton, F.J. Harvey. *Children's Books in England: Five Centuries of Social Life*. 3rd ed. London: British Library, 1999: 252-55.

Duffy, Maureen. *The Erotic World of Faery*. London: Sphere Books, 1989.

Fasick, Laura. "The Failure of Fatherhood: Maleness and Its Discontents in Charles Kingsley." *Children's Literature Association Quarterly* 18.3 (Fall 1993): 106-11.

Hawley, John C., S.J. "The Water Babies as Catechetical Paradigm." *Children's Literature Association Quarterly* 14.1 (Spring 1989): 19-21.

Hodgson, Amanda. "Defining the Species: Apes, Savages and Humans in Scientific and Literary Writing of the 1860s." *Journal of Victorian Culture* 4.2 (Autumn 1999): 228-51.

Ison, Mary M. "Things Nobody Ever Heard Of: Jessie Willcox

Smith Draws the Water-Babies." *The Quarterly Journal of the Library of Congress* 39.2 (1982): 90-101.

Johnston, Arthur. "*The Water-Babies*: Kingsley's Debt to Darwin." 12 (Autumn 1959): 215-19.

Labbe, Jacqueline M. "The Godhead Regendered in Victorian Children's Literature." *Rereading Victorian Fiction*. Ed. Alice Jenkins and Juliet John. London: Macmillan, 2000: 96-114.

Leavis, Q.D. "*The Water Babies*." *Children's Literature in Education* 23 (Winter 1976): 155-63.

MacNeice, Louis. *Varieties of Parable*. Cambridge: Cambridge UP, 1965.

Makman, Lisa Hermine. "Child's Work is Child's Play: The Value of George MacDonald's Diamond." *Children's Literature Association Quarterly* 24.3 (Fall 1999): 119-29.

Manlove, C.N. "Charles Kingsley (1819-75) and *The Water-Babies*," *Modern Fantasy: Five Studies*. Cambridge: Cambridge UP, 1975. 13-54.

——. "Charles Kingsley: *The Water-Babies*." *Christian Fantasy: from 1200 to the Present*. Notre Dame: University of Notre Dame Press, 1992. 183-208.

——. "Charles Kingsley, H.G. Wells, and the Machine in Victorian Fiction," *Nineteenth-Century Literature* 48.2 (Sept. 1993): 212-39.

Muller, Charles H. "*The Water Babies*: Moral Lessons for Children." *UNISA English Studies* 24.1 (1986): 12-17.

Ostry, Elaine. "Magical Growth and Moral Lessons; or, How the Conduct Book Informed Victorian and Edwardian Children's Fantasy." *Lion and the Unicorn: A Critical Journal of Children's Literature* 27.1 (January 2003): 27-56.

Paget, Stephen. "*The Water-Babies*." *I Have Reason to Believe*. 1921. Freeport, New York: Books for Libraries Press, 1968. 102-16.

Paradis, James G. "Satire and Science in Victorian Culture." *Victorian Science in Context*. Ed. Bernard Lightman. Chicago: U of Chicago P, 1997: 143-75.

Prickett, Stephen. "Adults in Allegory Land: Kingsley and MacDonald," *Victorian Fantasy*. Bloomington: Indiana University Press, 1979. 150-97.

Rapple, Brendan. "The Motif of Water in Charles Kingsley's *The Water-Babies*." *University of Mississippi Studies in English* 11-12 (1993-95): 259-71.

Stevenson, Deborah. "Sentiment and Significance: The Impossibility of Recovery in the Children's Literature Canon or, The

Drowning of The Water Babies." *The Lion and the Unicorn* 21.1 (1997): 112-30.

Stolzenback, Mary M. "*The Water Babies*: An Appreciation." *Mythlore* 8.2 (1981): 20.

Tanner, Tony. "Mountains and Depths—An Approach to Nineteenth-century Dualism." *Review of English Literature* 3 (October 1962): 51-61.

Townsend, John Rowe. *Written for Children: An Outline of English-language Children's Literature.* 1965. New York: Lippincott, 1983. 94-100.

Uffelman, Larry. *Charles Kingsley.* Boston: Twayne, 1979.

Uffelman, Larry, and Patrick Scott. "Kingsley's Serial Novels, II: *The Water-Babies*." *Victorian Periodicals Review* 19.4 (Winter 1986): 122-31.

Wallace, Jo-Ann "De-Scribing The Water-Babies: 'The Child' in Post-Colonial Theory." *De-Scribing Empire: Post-colonialism and Textuality.* Ed. Chris Tiffin and Alan Lawson. London and New York: Routledge, 1994. 171-84.

Walsh, Susan A. "Darling Mothers, Devilish Queens: The Divided Woman in Victorian Fantasy." *The Victorian Newsletter* No. 72 (Fall 1987): 32-36.

Wood, Naomi. "A (Sea) Green Victorian: Charles Kingsley and the The Water-Babies." *The Lion and the Unicorn* 19.2 (1995): 233-52.

——. "(Em)Bracing Icy Mothers: Ideology, Identity, and Environment in Children's Fantasy." *Wild Things: Children's Culture and Ecocriticism.* Ed. Sidney I. Dobrin Kenneth B. Kidd. Detroit, MI: Wayne State UP, 2004. 198-214.

Film

The Water Babies (1978), an animated film directed by Lionel Jeffries. Writing credits: Charles Kingsley (novel) and Michael Robson. The story of a 12-year-old boy who discovers a complex underwater world where young children are held prisoner by an evil shark and an eel. Cast: James Mason as Mr. Grimes/Voice of Killer Shark; Bernard Cribbins as Masterman/Voice of Eel; Billie Whitelaw as Mrs. Doasyouwouldbe-doneby/Old Crone/Mrs. Tripp/Woman in Black/Water Babies Gate Keeper; Joan Greenwood as Lady Harriet; David Tomlinson as Sir John; Tommy Pender as Tom; Samantha Gates as Elly.